# ROYAL HIGHNESS

☼

*Thomas Mann*

# ROYAL HIGHNESS

*Translated from the German by A. CECIL CURTIS*

*With a new preface, translated by H. T. LOWE-PORTER*

Introduction by Alan Sica

## UNIVERSITY OF CALIFORNIA PRESS
Berkeley · Los Angeles

University of California Press
Berkeley and Los Angeles, California
Copyright 1939 by Alfred A. Knopf, Inc.
Copyright renewed 1967 by Frau Thomas Mann and
Fraulein Erika Mann
Translation copyright renewed 1967 by
Alfred A. Knopf, Inc.
First California Edition 1992
Introduction copyright © 1992 by Alan Sica
All rights reserved under International and
Pan-American Copyright Conventions. Published by
arrangement with Alfred A. Knopf, Inc. Originally published as
*Königliche Hoheit*; Copyright 1909 by S. Fischer Verlag,
Berlin.

Library of Congress Cataloging in Publication Data
Mann, Thomas, 1875-1955.
[Königliche Hoheit. English]
Royal highness / Thomas Mann ; translated from the German
by A. Cecil Curtis ; with a preface translated by H. T. Lowe-Porter ;
introduction by Alan Sica. — 1st California ed.
p. cm.
Translation of: Königliche Hoheit.
ISBN 0-520-07674-5. — ISBN 0-520-07673-7 (pbk.)
I. Title.
PT2625.A44K62 1992
833'.912—dc20                                    91-22886
CIP

The paper used in this publication meets the minimum requirements of
American National Standard for Information Sciences—Permanence of
Paper for Printed Library Materials, ANSI Z39.48–1984. ⊚
1   2   3   4   5   6   7   8   9

# INTRODUCTION

THIS beguiling, almost magical tale calls up a world of life and letters that was named *Gemeinschaft*—a community of people who know each other well—by the social theorist Ferdinand Tönnies in 1887. He contrasted this mode of life, for which he felt great affection, with the alienating, frozen, status-obsessed existence in the metropoles of his day. He named this bleak future for humanity *Gesellschaft*, or simply "society," and this stark distinction has remained the undisturbed foundation of social theory ever since. There is no better fictional path to understanding why this pair of terms explains—even over-explains—so much about twentieth-century life than *Royal Highness*. Even Balzac's *Lost Illusions*, one of so many realist novels that carries a bucolic naïf into the Moloch of urban life, to some sad and inevitable end, is less valuable than Mann's "fairytale." Here the splendid simplicity of a social condition that relies entirely on etiquette, demeanor, and speech staunchly tied to particular roles, highlights what social existence may have been like before urbanity swept it away. For this achievement alone, *Royal Highness* is worthwhile, simply for understanding how the nineteenth century became the twentieth, and what this era means now. But, as one would expect from Thomas Mann, there is much more to the book than an exhibition of brilliant social analysis.

Serious fiction today usually works best through satire, miniatures, phantasms, intrapsychic soliloquy—almost any form other than that which felt most natural to great novelists of the past, whose works college students are still urged to read without quite knowing why. The term "epic"—applied by Georg Lukács to this second of Mann's novels, when it appeared in 1909—now designates popular fiction of great length but little substance, the sort of consumer goods that mingle well with beach blankets and untroubled minds. That a novel setting out to capture an entire social order, and its transformation through a decisive act, could be simultaneously epic and aesthetically inspired reminds us how things have changed in literature and in the everyday since 1903, when Mann dreamed up "this little story of a prince." So he referred to it thirty years after it first met with a disappointed public. And with the First World War, soon after the tale saw print, social life as he described it in the tiny principality disappeared from European consciousness. Mann claimed that without *Royal Highness*, "neither *The Magic Mountain* nor *Joseph and His Brothers* could have been written"; actually, one might note that without the destruction of the social world Mann romanticized in the earlier book, the latter two would not have been necessary at all.

Mann wrote *Royal Highness* to celebrate his courtship and marriage, and the unaccustomed pleasures and trials of early domesticity. He composed the work between 1906 and 1909, having married its heroine, as it were, in February 1905. His wife, Katia, was a young woman of extraordinary familial connections, wealth, talent, beauty, and a sort of tomboy feistiness that Mann imported directly into his novel. She bore four children in the first five and a half years of marriage—beginning with a daughter only nine months and two days after the wedding—a feat which he thought "verges on the ridiculous," as if such events occurred without his artistic consent. But for all his grousing about the time he lost to fathering, time which he previously could have dedicated to his craft with the single-minded energy of bachelorhood, it was clear that he took pride in his new role and wished to commemorate it through a novel.

In a letter to Walter Opitz of December 1903, Mann explained his rationale for *Royal Highness*, while describing the problems of being a recognized author (at 28): "I mean to say that one leads a symbolic, representative existence, similar to that of a prince. And behold! In this pathos lies the seed of a curious situation, about which I am thinking of writing—a

novel of court life, a counterpart to 'Tonio Kröger,' which will
bear the title *Royal Highness*." In an elaborate extension of his
pet theme—alienation and marginality as the determining characteristics of the genuine artist in bourgeois society—he cre-
ated a prince whose deepest motivations for the life of royal
propriety paralleled Mann's own for the life of writing. Further-
more, he cast Katia as the barely accessible love-object, precisely imitating their actual courtship, and then caricatured
Heinrich Mann, the family's other novelist, as the older, more
cynical, remote, and intelligent sibling of the Prince. Finally,
he named the protagonist after his first son, Klaus Heinrich.
He even had the cheek to ask Katia for use of his pre-nuptial
love letters to her for inspiration while he wrote the novel.

Yet as is so often the case with art, the product dearest to
the creator's heart does not excite its intended audience as
much as other labors, those which speak less autobiographi-
cally perhaps and are therefore more easily interpreted to suit
diverse imaginations. Certainly *Magic Mountain* and *Doctor
Faustus* can be read for aesthetic, political, or psychological
meanings without number. This is perhaps less so with *Royal
Highness*. Yet its lesser complexity is not enough to explain
why, according to Richard Winston, "it was woefully misunderstood at the time of publication and has been largely neglected since." Perhaps the persistent irony, Mann's hallmark,
confused readers who expected to be charmed by a fantastic
tale that at first seems akin to the stories which gladden children's hearts. Others may have found the apparent appreciation
for monarchy repellent on political grounds, particularly given
the events of 1914—directly attributable to outsized royal egos.
It is indeed interesting, considering Mann's extraordinary political activity later in his career, that he wrote *Royal Highness*
without seeming to notice that nearby, in Russia, millions were
taking to the streets throughout 1905. There is no mention of
this in his letters or diaries. (Max Weber, by contrast, not so
far from Mann, became so fascinated with the revolution that
he learned Russian in six weeks in order to read press accounts

as events unfolded.) Yet the most common complaint at the time held that *Royal Highness* did not carry the sort of multigenerational sweep and weight that had brought masses of readers to *Buddenbrooks* nine years earlier. They wanted more of the same, something Mann never provided—a refusal that always marks inspired creativity rather than mere craftsmanship.

*Royal Highness* offers much to a sympathetic reader, especially one who values narrative vitality as much as the capacity to recreate a socio-political constellation that fed into twentieth-century European life. These are the moments before Germany was transmuted into patterns far removed from the Wilhelmine calm that Mann burlesqued. Mann sought the help of an expert, a Dr. Printz, in order to comprehend the workings of royal finance, and then wrote about it with the same attention to verisimilitude that marks *Doctor Faustus* (especially regarding music, thanks to Theodor Adorno). His concern for reality—even hyper-reality—manifested itself in precise knowledge, so that his novels' fantastic timbre was the result of his particular narrative alchemy, not of recourse to the simply grotesque or supernatural. As Lukács reminds us, Mann himself explained this technique crisply: "We describe the everyday, but the everyday becomes strange if it is cultivated on strange foundations." He clipped newspaper accounts of royal activities avidly, imitated exactly Wilhelm's 1905 wedding festivities in *Royal Highness*, and set out to teach his readers what the life of committed royalty—in a post-medieval epoch—was truly like. One involuntarily thinks of the present Prince Charles.

In developing and maintaining what Lukács calls a "composure ethic," Klaus Heinrich lives more a series of tableaux than a "life" proper. From the point of view of the vigorous, domineering bourgeoisie, it seems vapid, stylized, irrelevant, demeaning, and childish. Yet he accepts his older brother's charge, takes over his unwanted position, and spends years behaving in strict accordance with ritual. As his prospective father-in-law, Samuel Spoelman, puts it, with American-millionaire bluntness, "I see. Ceremonies, solemnities, food for spectators. . . . I wouldn't give a farthing for your calling." To which the Prince responds, "I understand entirely"—and he does! He chooses to live a "representative existence," as Mann called it in the letter, because he understands the significance of his role for social solidarity, especially in a kingdom without enough resources to thrive or enough power to exploit its neighbors. He does not very often enjoy his "calling," a term utterly out of fashion today, and on the verge of dissolution even then (as Weber explains in *The Protestant Ethic and the Spirit of Capitalism*). But what lawyers are today beginning to call "hedonic loss" is inconceivable to a character put together, through heritage and training, like Klaus Heinrich. Each day involves *Pflicht*—duty—and whatever small pleasures he can find in his round of official tasks will have to suffice. "How tiring life was, how strenuous," he thinks. His teacher, Ueberbein, sees his role as heroic: "I see in your existence the clearest, most express, and best-preserved form of the extraordinary in the world. . . . Reserve, etiquette, obligation, duty, demeanor, formality—has the man whose life is surrounded by these no right to despise others?" And here the fawning professor is speaking partly for Mann, who wrote of all this in an early letter:

> The artist is akin to the prince in that, like the latter, he leads a *representative* existence. What etiquette is to the prince, the lofty obligation to create form is to the artist. The artist, as I know him, is never the man who can "let himself be seen" freely and without more ado. He needs prudence in passion, idealization in self-depiction, or in short: art. That is his human weakness.
>
> Quoted by Richard Winston in his *Thomas Mann*.

But Klaus Heinrich, especially after espying Imma Spoelmann, sees his stagnant, prematurely aged "calling" for exactly what it is: "His young face looked slightly weary from the unreality, the loneliness, strictness, and difficulty of his life." When his teacher exclaims, "Representing is naturally something more and higher than simply Being, Klaus Heinrich—and that's why people call you Highness," he appreciates the encouragement, but over time begins to long for more than honorifics.

In short, he begins to mull over Spoelmann's denunciation of his "profession" and to see the virtue of instrumental rationality—the phrase social theorists of the time were beginning to use for putting aside traditional modes of behavior in favor of action that gains a new and pressing end. Though Mann nowhere states it in such crass terms, the story nevertheless confirms this strategy of princely activity, since in the end it is his father-in-law's money, that "bought [the debt] at par 350,000,000 new 3½ per cent. consols," that saves the principality.

Naturally, there is more to this novel than a recapitulation, in miniature, of that process which occurred throughout the West, termed by Weber "rationalization." There is Mann's ever-present symbolization of the aestheticized life—the Prince's—within the sharp confines of calculating mundanity. The love story, while hardly of the blood-boiling type more common to nineteenth-century realism—*Therese Raquin* comes to mind—holds its own charm, elegance, and credibility. Imma jolts the Prince out of his structured reverie, and he shows her the means to escape the brusque pursuit of learning she has used to protect herself from asking overmuch from life. Without tearing hair, threats of physical violence, eating disorders, or bouts of sexual athleticism, the love story proceeds on its civilized, heartfelt way—once again reminding the reader, these eighty-eight years after Mann conceived the story, that interpersonal intimacy was not always, at least among the genteel classes, what it has now become.

Another theorist of the time, Karl Mannheim, referred in the 1920s to "the democratization of culture," a trend which has even more thoroughly supplanted the aristocratic canons of propriety than Mann, Weber, or Mannheim could have foreseen. Yet they may well have applauded the direction culture, civility, and etiquette have taken. In one of Mann's most inspired passages, he describes the feelings of Klaus Heinrich as a small boy, seeing for the first time, and alone, one of his father's official reception rooms in the most formal of his castles:

Everything here was severe and empty show and a formal symmetry, self-sufficient, pointless, and uncomfortable— whose functions were obviously to create an atmosphere of awe and tension, not of freedom and ease, to inculcate an attitude of decorum and discreet self-obliteration towards an unnamed object. And it was cold in the silver hall.

From one point of view, any move taken to escape this chilly environment would be to the good. But, as in all things social, the other side presents itself as well: such forbidding surroundings—now reduced to the bureaucratic office of an appointed official—give some legitimacy to authority, and the satisfaction that comes from having been heard by the person from whom, in theory, one might expect wisdom and justice. It was to "represent" this beneficent side that Klaus Heinrich dedicated himself, before, that is, meeting his personal salvation, and that of his state's finances to boot, in the person of Imma. When he presents himself to his subjects, he does so through a form of "renunciation"—as the poet, Axel Martini, explains it to the prince—so that nothing of his private demands upon life are allowed to intrude on the workings of his public persona. As Mann put it:

The people had collected most thickly at the exit. . . . in order to watch him drive off. A way was kept free for him, a straight passage to the step of his landau, and he walked quickly down it, bowing continuously with his hand to his helmet—alone and formally separated from all those men who, in honouring him, were cheering their own archetype, their standard, and of whose lives, work, and ability, he was the splendid representative, though not participator.

# INTRODUCTION

What Mann called in his 1939 letter to Alfred Knopf "a wish for appeasement and reconciliation between two one-sided principles, the individual and the social, by dint of harmonizing them in the human" is precisely the theme that continues to give *Royal Highness* its intellectual weight and aesthetic success. We are at a point in Western history when the relations of subordination and superordination are completely undecided, and when, as one might expect, the question of love between men and women is also utterly confused. Reading this book reminds us of another purchase on the ancient human dilemmas, providing a quiet fictional refuge, away by many miles indeed, from our current din. It is like a cold drink from a spring after too many hours in an unforgiving sun.

*Alan Sica*
*Pennsylvania State University*

*Dear Alfred,*

The appearance of a new English edition of *Royal Highness* merits a new preface. It is no more than fitting that it should take the form of a letter to you, my American publisher, for it was your idea to revive this well-nigh forgotten little book. Moreover, I can thus seize the occasion to express publicly, once and for all, the gratitude I have so long and so deeply felt for all you have done for me and my work in the great country now beginning to be my home. I can bear witness to an author-publisher friendship long since interwoven with our more personal relations and decisive, I feel, for the effective reception of my works.

Our relation is, in fact, like that happy one — now, alas, dissolved by death — between myself and the great S. Fischer of Berlin. You, I know, admired his genius as a publisher, and chose him as your model when you founded your own house. Now you have taken his place, just as in the past few years my American public has replaced the German one snatched from me by evil and fatal political chance. It is an unnatural situation, yet a fact, that my books, all of them very German productions indeed, are today scarcely existent in their original form and language, and lead, in translation, an uprooted and necessarily somewhat foreshortened life. If anything could console me for this forced and futile situation — aside from my certain conviction that it cannot last — it is the cordial sympathy of the American educated public. That public stepped, as it were, into the breach; with a generosity and benevolence — strengthened and deepened by a highly intelligent literary critique — most happily and touchingly displayed in their reception of Mrs. Lowe-Porter's admirable translations of *Buddenbrooks*, *The Magic Mountain*, and the *Joseph* novels. And now, my dear Alfred, you would solicit their interest afresh, this time for *Royal Highness*.

It seems as though I were to be a three-novel man — the three I just named. But there is a fourth, of a smaller format, less imposing, less epic than the others — this little story of a prince. It was written in the blithe days of my youth; it is blithe in itself. Yet from the first its melancholy fate has been to be oddly overshadowed, almost, I might say, neglected. Sometimes I have really felt sorry for the creature. The same love, pains, and patience went to its shaping as to that of its more admired brothers; yet it remained an outsider. Things on which I spent much less time, long short stories like *Disorder and Early Sorrow* and *Mario and the Magician*, are much better known. Yet this little comedy in the form of a novel (always, since the hour it was conceived, bearing the ironic and symbolical title *Royal Highness*), was despite its conventional façade a parody; it had to do with moral and even political problems, and was far from being insensitive to the spirit of the times.

It came immediately after *Buddenbrooks*, which succeeded so happily with the great German reading public — and that was its misfortune. It was pronounced too light, both in itself

xiv

and by comparison; too light with reference to the German demand for weight and seriousness in a book; too light with reference to the author himself. It was a novel of high life, with a happy ending, almost suitable for a serial in a magazine; it told, in dignified journalese, the tale of a little princeling and how he became a benedict and a benefactor to his people. And it was a " come-down " after the humour and pessimism of the Buddenbrook saga. The author had not lived up to the justifiable expectations aroused by his first work. But what does the public — and not only the German public — expect of a writer who has won their favour? Nothing else than that he should keep on doing the same thing over and over. I have no doubt I should have best satisfied my German middle-class readers by writing more and more *Buddenbrookses* all the rest of my life. But that was just what I could not do; it did not satisfy my own demands on myself. To be ever eager for new things (*novarum rerum cupidus*), that, it always seemed to me, an artist was bound in honour to do. I was feeling after new things, I had been doing so in the stories I wrote after *Buddenbrooks;* in *Royal Highness* I was continuing along the same path. For this as I saw it was my problem as an artist: how to take the serious and weighty naturalism I had inherited from the nineteenth century and faithfully practised, and loosen and lighten, heighten and brighten it into a work of art which should be intellectual and symbolical, a transparency for ideas to shine through. In this sense *Royal Highness* was a step in advance, even though in actual scope and significance this single work could not compare with *Buddenbrooks.* The misunderstanding between author and reader is often due to the fact

xv

that the reader thinks of a book as an absolute, as a product standing by itself, and judges it accordingly; whereas the author regards it as a stage of progress, a pen trial, a connecting link, a preliminary canter, a means to an end. So whatever the intrinsic value of *Royal Highness,* it occupies in the life of its author its own proper and peculiar place; he is fain to hope that the pleasure it gives the reader may be enlarged by the author's testimony that without it neither *The Magic Mountain* nor *Joseph and His Brothers* could have been written.

In general, I confess, I think all criticism should have this biographical flavour, as a necessary human element. And criticism of *Royal Highness* can dispense with it even less than usual. The novel is the work of a young married man. The personal and human experiences of those early years entirely condition its treatment of that favourite theme of my youth, the theme of the artist as isolated and " different." It plays with the Tonio Kröger antithesis between art and life, and resolves it by harmonizing happiness and discipline. Its subject-matter lends itself to allusiveness: it analyses the life led by royalty as a formal, unreal existence, lifted above actualities; in a word, the existence of the artist. The resolution of the royal complex is brought about by a fairy-tale, comedy love-affair; it leads to marriage and to the solution of certain problems in political economy as well. But even so, it exhibits a rejection of empty and melancholy formalism in favour of life and companionship, which is not without symbolic meaning and shows some sensitiveness to coming events.

The novel dates from 1905, its atmosphere is the German Empire of that time, its narrative has certain attributes of the

Wilhelmine setting. The figure of Minister von Knobelsdorff, the man of the world with the cynical wrinkles round his eyes, is an attempt in little to portray the agile and airy Prince von Bülow. Then there is the famous shrunken arm. It is not used as a psychological motif, more as a moral symbol, a rather touching inhibition increasing the difficulties of a formal and heroic readiness for service, which, indeed, is more reminiscent of Andersen's Little Tin Soldier than of Wilhelm's baroque posturings. Any mention of the Reich would have lacked literary tact. Even to refer to Berlin would have jarred; it would have disturbed and broken the charmed circle of the little fairytale. But the monarchy was not only the atmosphere of the book; it was also, quite precisely, its subject, treated, if only allegorically, as a form of existence. And this was at the moment when the monarchy was at its height.

True, it took quite a while to disappear. Nobody, least of all the author of *Royal Highness*, dreamed of its approaching fall. And yet the dynastic idea is treated with an ironic sympathy which might suggest its ripeness for decay. Is literature a swan-song? No, rather it is a prophecy, though not in direct and explicit form. The artist's nature prevents him from being in the very least the servant and harbinger of new things, even when his words betray his unconscious intuition of the future. What happens is rather that the old and the new intersect in him; they play upon him and with him, and this play is his work, a dialectical product, almost always, of old and new, wherein his sympathy, yes, his love, is conservative and faces the old, and only the artist's sensitive responsiveness hints at the new. On its appearance thirty years ago *Royal Highness* was a portent, and the fact did not escape the knowing ones. It was a sign of that crisis of individualism which has since become a commonplace in the public consciousness; a sign of that surrender by the intellect of the individual point of view in favour of the communal, the social, the democratic, yes, the political, at the will of the times. But save in that respect, one might call the book a perfect orgy of individualism; the characters are a set of aristocratic monstrosities, assembled with the most loving care. It could not have been more complete or varied had the artist drawn his figures with the deliberate and defiant intention of glorifying the past — as indeed, in part, as opposed to the main plan of the book, he really had.

But the sympathy he felt for these various " special cases " is of a strange kind — it is hopeless, it inclines to satire, even to caricature. They are of every sort, these cases, down to the individualism of sheer insanity, as portrayed in the over-bred and unbalanced collie dog and the equally unbalanced Countess. I still enjoy the moralizing little jokes that come in here and there; as, for instance, that the Countess's aberrations are the result of " letting herself go " when she can no longer bear it to hold out against the " hard and stern " attitude of Klaus Heinrich. The book has a light-hearted attitude towards mental aberration: that, it seems to say, might happen to anyone! For a " high-life novel with a happy ending," it has a disconcerting way of referring to the border-line in whose seductive proximity all individualism dwells, being saved only by the steadfastness of the constant tin soldier from overstepping the boundary.

On the whole, the contradiction between sympathy and intention which dominates this odd little book is at bottom the expression of a wish for appeasement and reconciliation between two one-sided principles, the individual and the social, by dint of harmonizing them in the human. *Royal Highness,* written by the man of thirty, only continues what the same man at twenty began dreaming and writing of, in *Tonio Kröger,* with his ironic and sentimental formula about the " joys of the ordinary." It is also an essay in preparation for the dialectic orchestration of *The Magic Mountain,* that long-drawn-out dialogue between " life " and " sympathy with death " wherein the man of fifty gave shape to the eternal debate on man, his state and place in the universe, on a basis grown broader with the years. In the *Joseph* novels the sixty-year-old man has been striving, in three epic attacks, to garner the riches of the three elements of his own personal culture, German, European, and human. And now, looking back, he assures himself that even this humorous little interlude about the princeling and his bride is an organic part of his life task; yes, that in his present effort to lend aid by direct political writing, he is only doing in later life the same thing he began when he was young.

I felt it due, my dear Alfred, to your present enterprise and all your kindness to add to my gratitude for this new edition a few words of explanation to the reader on the more inward significance of this " new " work, which is today as old as I was when I wrote it. Let these few lines go with the little book on its way! It would be sad for you and for me were I to be alone in my gratitude for your undertaking.

*Thomas Mann*

*Noordwijk aan Zee, Holland*
*July 1939*

# PRELUDE

THE scene is the Albrechtstrasse, the main artery of the capital, which runs from Albrechtsplatz and the Old Schloss to the barracks of the Fusiliers of the Guard. The time is noon on an ordinary week-day; the season of the year does not matter. The weather is fair to moderate. It is not raining, but the sky is not clear; it is a uniform light grey, uninteresting and sombre, and the street lies in a dull and sober light which robs it of all mystery, all individuality. There is a moderate amount of traffic, without much noise and crowd, corresponding to the not over-busy character of the town. Tram-cars glide past, a cab or two rolls by, along the pavement stroll a few residents, colourless folk, passers-by, the public—"people."

Two officers, their hands in the slanting pockets of their grey great-coats, approach each other; a general and a lieutenant. The general is coming from the Schloss, the lieutenant from the direction of the barracks. The lieutenant is quite young, a mere stripling, little more than a child. He has narrow shoulders, dark hair, and the wide cheek-bones so common in this part of the world, blue rather tired-looking eyes, and a boyish face with a kind but reserved expression. The general has snow-white hair, is tall and broad-shouldered, altogether a commanding figure. His eyebrows look like cotton-wool, and his moustache hangs right down over his mouth and chin. He walks with slow deliberation, his sword rattles on the asphalt, his plume flutters in the wind, and at every step he takes the big red lapel of his coat flaps slowly up and down.

And so these two draw near each other. Can this rencontre lead to any complication? Impossible. Every

xxi

observer can foresee the course this meeting will naturally take. We have on one side and the other age and youth, authority and obedience, years of services and docile apprenticeship—a mighty hierarchical gulf, rules and prescriptions, separate the two. Natural organization, take thy course! And, instead, what happens? Instead, the following surprising, painful, delightful, and topsy-turvy scene occurs.

The general, noticing the young lieutenant's approach, alters his bearing in a surprising manner. He draws himself up, yet at the same time seems to get smaller. He tones down with a jerk, so to speak, the splendour of his appearance, stops the clatter of his sword, and, while his face assumes a cross and embarrassed expression, he obviously cannot make up his mind where to turn his eyes, and tries to conceal the fact by staring from under his cotton-wool eyebrows at the asphalt straight in front of him.

The young lieutenant too betrays to the careful observer some slight embarrassment, which however, strange to say, he seems to succeed, better than the grey-haired general, in cloaking with a certain grace and self-command. The tension of his mouth is relaxed into a smile at once modest and genial, and his eyes are directed with a quiet and self-possessed calm, seemingly without an effort, over the general's shoulder and beyond.

By now they have come within three paces of each other. And, instead of the prescribed salute, the young lieutenant throws his head slightly back, at the same time draws his right hand—only his right, mark you—out of his coat-pocket and makes with this same white-gloved right hand a little encouraging and condescending movement, just opening the fingers with palm upwards, nothing more. But the general, who has awaited this sign with his arms to his sides, raises his hand to his helmet, steps aside, bows, making a half-circle as if to leave the pavement free, and deferentially greets the lieutenant with reddening cheeks and honest modest eyes. Thereupon the lieutenant, his hand to his cap, answers the respectful greeting of his superior officer—answers it with a look of child-like friendliness; answers it—and goes on his way.

A miracle! A freak of fancy! He goes on his way. People look at him, but he looks at nobody, looks straight ahead through the crowd, with something of the air of a woman who knows that she is being looked at. People greet him; he returns the greeting, heartily and yet distantly. He seems not to walk very easily; it looks as if he were not much accustomed to the use of his legs, or as if the general attention he excites bothers him, so irregular and hesitating is his gait; indeed, at times he seems to limp. A policeman springs to attention, a smart woman, coming out of a shop, smiles and curtseys. People turn round to look at him, nudge each other, stare at him, and softly whisper his name. . . .

It is Klaus Heinrich, the younger brother of Albrecht II, and heir presumptive to the throne. There he goes, he is still in view. Known and yet a stranger, he moves among the crowd—people all around him, and yet as if alone. He goes on his lonely way and carries on his narrow shoulders the burden of his Highness!

# CONTENTS

# ROYAL HIGHNESS

# THE CONSTRICTION

ARTILLERY salvos were fired when the various new-fangled means of communication in the capital spread the news that the Grand Duchess Dorothea had given birth to a prince for the second time at Grimmburg. Seventy-two rounds resounded through the town and surrounding country, fired by the military in the walls of the "Citadel." Directly afterwards the fire brigade also, not to be outdone, fired with the town salute-guns; but in their firing there were long pauses between each round, which caused much merriment among the populace.

The Grimmburg looked down from the top of a woody hill on the picturesque little town of the same name, which mirrored its grey sloping roofs in the river which flowed past it. It could be reached from the capital in half an hour by a local railway which paid no dividends. There the castle stood, the proud creation of the Margrave Klaus Grimmbart, the founder of the reigning house in the dim mists of history, since then several times rejuvenated and repaired, fitted with the comforts of the changing times, always kept in a habitable state and held in peculiar honour as the ancestral seat of the ruling house, the cradle of the dynasty. For it was a rule and tradition of the house that all direct descendants of the Margrave, every child of the reigning couple, must be born there.

This tradition could not be ignored. The country had had sophisticated and unbelieving sovereigns, who had laughed at it, and yet had complied with it with a shrug of the shoulders. It was now much too late to break away from it

1

whether it was reasonable and enlightened or not: why, without any particular necessity, break with an honoured custom, which had managed somehow to perpetuate itself? The people were convinced that there was something in it. Twice in the course of fifteen generations had children of reigning sovereigns, owing to some chance or other, first seen the light in other schlosses: each had come to an unnatural and disgraceful end. But all the sovereigns of the land and their brothers and sisters, from Henry the Confessor and John the Headstrong, with their lovely and proud sisters, down to Albrecht, the father of the Grand Duke, and the Grand Duke himself, Johann Albrecht III, had been brought into the world in the castle; and there, six years before, Dorothea had given birth to her firstborn, the Heir Apparent.

The castle was also a retreat as dignified as it was peaceful. The coolness of its rooms, the shady charms of its surroundings, made it preferable as a summer residence to the stiff Hollerbrunn. The ascent from the town, up a rather badly paved street between shabby cottages and a scrubby wall, through massive gates to the ancient ruin at the entrance to the castle-yard, in the middle of which stood the statue of Klaus Grimmbart, the founder, was picturesque but tiring. But a noble park spread at the back of the castle hill, through which easy paths led up into the wooded and gently-swelling uplands, offering ideal opportunities for carriage drives and quiet strolls.

As for the inside of the castle, it had been last subjected at the beginning of the reign of Johann Albrecht III to a thorough clean-up and redecoration—at a cost which had evoked much comment. The furniture of the living-rooms had been completed and renewed in a style at once baronial and comfortable; the escutcheons in the "Hall of Justice" had been carefully restored to their original pattern. The gilding of the intricate patterns on the vaulted ceilings looked fresh and cheerful, all the rooms had been fitted with parquet, and both the larger and the smaller banqueting-halls had been

2

adorned with huge wall-paintings from the brush of Professor von Lindemann, a distinguished Academician, representing scenes from the history of the reigning House executed in a clear and smooth style which was far removed from and quite unaffected by the restless tendencies of modern schools. Nothing was wanting. As the old chimneys of the castle and its many-coloured stoves, reaching tier upon tier right up to the ceiling, were no longer fit to use, anthracite stoves had been installed in view of the possibility of the place being used as a residence during the winter.

But the day of the seventy-two salvos fell in the best time of the year, late spring, early summer, the beginning of June, soon after Whitsuntide. Johann Albrecht, who had been early informed by telegram that the labour had begun just before dawn, reached Grimmburg Station by the bankrupt local railway at eight o'clock, where he was greeted with congratulations by three or four dignitaries, the mayor, the judge, the rector, and the town physician. He at once drove to the castle. The Grand Duke was accompanied by Minister of State, Dr. Baron Knobelsdorff, and Adjutant-General of Infantry, Count Schmettern. Shortly afterwards two or three more ministers arrived at the royal residence, the Court Chaplin Dom Wislezenus, President of the High Consistory, one or two Court officials, and a still younger Adjutant, Captain von Lichterloh. Although the Grand Duke's Physician-in-Ordinary, Surgeon-General Dr. Eschrich, was attending the mother, Johann Albrecht had been seized with the whim of requiring the young local doctor, a Doctor Sammet, who was of Jewish extraction into the bargain, to accompany him to the castle. The unassuming, hard-working, and earnest man, who had as much as he could do and was not in the least expecting any such distinction, stammered "Quite delighted . . . quite delighted" several times over, thus provoking some amusement.

The Grand Duchess's bedroom was the "Bride-chamber,"

a five-cornered, brightly painted room on the first floor, through whose window a fine view could be obtained of woods, hills, and the windings of the river. It was decorated with a frieze of medallion-shaped portraits, likenesses of royal brides who had slept there in the olden days of the family history.

There lay Dorothea; a broad piece of webbing was tied round the foot of her bed, to which she clung like a child playing at horses, while convulsions shook her lovely frame. Doctor Gnadebusch, the midwife, a gentle and learned woman with small fine hands and brown eyes, which wore a look of mystery behind her round, thick spectacles, was supporting the Duchess, while she said:

"Steady, steady, your Royal Highness. . . . It will soon be over. It's quite easy. . . . Just once more . . . that's nothing. . . . Rest a bit: knees apart. . . . Keep your chin down. . . ."

A nurse, dressed like her in white linen, helped too, and moved lightly about with phials and bandages during the pauses. The Physician-in-Ordinary, a gloomy man with a greyish beard, whose left eyelid seemed to droop, superintended the birth. He wore his operating-coat over his surgeon-general's uniform. From time to time there peeped into the room, to ascertain the progress of the confinement, Dorothea's trusty Mistress of the Robes, Baroness von Schulenburg-Tressen, a corpulent and asthmatic woman of distinctly dragoon-like appearance, who nevertheless liked to display a generous expanse of neck and shoulders at the court balls. She kissed her mistress's hand and went back to an adjoining room, in which a couple of thin ladies-in-waiting were chatting with the Grand Duchess's Chamberlain-in-Waiting, a Count Windisch. Dr. Sammet, who had thrown his linen coat like a domino over his dress-coat, was waiting modestly and attentively by the washstand.

Johann Albrecht sat in a neighbouring room used as a study, which was separated from the "Bride-chamber" only

4

by a so-called powder closet and a passage-room. It was
called the library, in view of several manuscript folios, which
lay slanting in the massive book-shelves and contained
the history of the castle. The room was furnished as
a writing-room. Globes adorned the walls. The strong
wind from the hills blew through the open bow-window.
The Grand Duke had ordered tea, and the groom of the
chamber, Prahl, had himself brought the tray; but it was
standing forgotten on the leaf of the desk, and Johann
Albrecht was pacing the room from one corner to the other
in a restless, uncomfortable frame of mind. His top-boots
kept creaking as he walked. His aide-de-camp, von Lichterloh, listened to the noise, as he waited patiently in the
almost bare passage-room.

The Minister, the Adjutant-General, the Court Chaplain,
and the Court officials, nine or ten in all, were waiting in
the state-room on the ground floor. They wandered through
the larger and the smaller banqueting-halls, where trophies
of banners and weapons hung between Lindemann's pictures. They leaned against the slender pillars, which spread
into brightly coloured vaulting above their heads. They
stood before the narrow, ceiling-high windows, and looked
out through the leaded panes over river and town; they sat
on the stone benches which ran round the walls, or on seats
before the stoves, whose Gothic tops were supported by
ridiculous little stooping imps of stone. The bright sunlight made the gold lace on the uniforms, the orders on
the padded chests, the broad gold stripes on the trousers
of the dignitaries glisten.

The conversation flagged. Three-cornered hats and white-
gloved hands were constantly being raised to mouths which
opened convulsively. Nearly everybody had tears in his
eyes. Several had not had time to get any breakfast. Some
sought entertainment in a timid examination of the operating-
instruments and the round leather-cased chloroform jar,
which Surgeon-General Eschrich had left there in case of

5

emergency. After von Bühl zu Bühl, the Lord Marshal, a powerful man with mincing manners, brown toupée, gold-rimmed pince-nez, and long, yellow fingernails, had told several anecdotes in his quick, jerky way, he dropped into an armchair, in which he made use of his gift of being able to sleep with his eyes open—of losing consciousness of time and place while retaining a steady gaze and alert attitude, and in no way imperilling the dignity of the situation.

Dr. von Schröder, Minister of Finance and Agriculture, had had a conversation earlier in the day with the Minister of State, Dr. Baron Knobelsdorff, Minister of Home Affairs, Foreign Affairs, and the Grand Ducal Household. It was a spasmodic chat, which began with a discussion on art, went on to financial and economic questions, alluded, somewhat disapprovingly, to a High Court official, and did not leave even the most exalted personages out of account. It began with the •two men standing, with their hats in their hands behind their backs, in front of one of the pictures in the larger banqueting-hall, each of them thinking more than he said. The Finance Minister said: "And this? What's this? What's happening? Your Excellency is so well informed."

"Merely superficially. It is the investiture of two Grand princes of the blood by their uncle, the Emperor. As your Excellency can see, the two young men are kneeling and taking the oath with great solemnity on the Emperor's sword."

"Fine, extraordinarily fine! What colouring! Dazzling. What lovely golden hair the princes have! And the Emperor . . . exactly as he is described in the books! Yes, that Lindemann well deserves all the distinctions which have been given him."

"Absolutely. Those which have been given him; those he quite deserves."

Dr. von Schröder, a tall man with a white beard, a pair of thin gold spectacles on his white nose, a belly protruding slightly underneath his stomach, and a bull-neck, which lapped over the stiff collar of his coat, looked, without taking his eyes off the picture, somewhat doubtfully at it, under the influence of a diffidence which seized him from time to time during conversations with the baron. This Knobelsdorff, this favourite and exalted functionary, was so enigmatical. At times his remarks, his retorts, had an indefinable tinge of irony about them. He was a widely travelled man, he had been all over the world, he had so much general knowledge, and interests of such a strange and exotic kind. And yet he was a model of correctness. Herr von Schröder could not quite understand him. However much one agreed with him, it was impossible to feel that one really understood him. His opinions were full of a mysterious reserve, his judgments of a tolerance which left one wondering whether they implied approval or contempt.

But the most suspicious thing about him was his laugh, a laugh of the eyes in which the mouth took no part, a laugh which seemed to be produced by the wrinkles radiating from the corners of his eyes, or vice versa to have produced those same wrinkles in the course of years. Baron Knobelsdorff was younger than the Finance Minister; he was then in the prime of life, although his close-trimmed moustache and hair smoothly parted in the middle were already beginning to turn grey—for the rest a squat, short-necked man, obviously pinched by the collar of his heavily-laced court dress. He left Herr von Schröder to his perplexity for a minute, and then went on: "Only perhaps it might be to the interests of a prudent administration of the Privy Purse if the distinguished professor had rested content with stars and titles . . . to speak bluntly, what may all these delightful works of art have cost?"

Herr von Schröder recovered his animation. The desire, the hope of understanding the Baron, of getting on to intimate and confidential terms with him, excited him. "Just what I was thinking!" said he, turning round to resume his

7

walk through the galleries. "Your Excellency has taken the question out of my mouth. I wonder what this 'Investiture' cost, and all the rest of these wall-pictures. For the restoration of the castle six years ago cost a million altogether."

"At least that."

"A solid million! And that amount was audited and approved by Lord Marshal von Bühl zu Bühl, who is sitting yonder in a state of comfortable catalepsy—audited, approved, and disbursed by the Keeper of the Privy Purse, Count Trümmerhauff."

"Disbursed, or owing!"

"One of the two! . . . This total, I say, debited to a fund, a fund . . ."

"In a word, the fund of the Grand Ducal settled estates."

"Your Excellency knows as well as I what that means. No, it makes me run cold. . . . I swear I am neither a skinflint nor a hypochondriac, but it makes me run cold when I think of a man, with present conditions staring him in the face, coolly throwing a million away—on what? On a nothing, a pretty whim, on the beautification of the family schloss in which his babies have to be born. . . ."

Herr von Knobelsdorff laughed. "Yes, Heaven knows romance is a luxury, and a mighty expensive one too! Excellency, I agree with you—of course. But consider, after all the whole trouble in the Grand Ducal finances is due to this same romantic luxury. The root of the evil lies in the fact that the ruling dynasty are farmers; their capital consists in land and soil, their income in agricultural profits. At the present day. . . . They have not been able up to the present to make up their minds to turn into industrialists and financiers. They allow themselves with regrettable obstinacy to be swayed by certain obsolete and idealistic conceptions, such as, for instance, the conceptions of trust and dignity. The royal property is hampered by a trust entailed in fact. Advantageous alienations are barred. Mortgages, the raising of capital on credit for commercial

8

improvements, seem to them improper. The administration is seriously hindered in the free exploitation of business opportunities—by ideas of dignity. You'll forgive me, won't you? I'm telling you the absolute truth. People who pay so much attention to propriety as these of course cannot and will not keep pace with the freer and less hampered initiative of less obstinate and unpractical business people. Now then, what, in comparison with this negative luxury, does the positive million signify, which has been sacrificed to a pretty whim, to borrow your Excellency's expression? If it only stopped there! But we have the regular expenses of a fairly dignified Court to meet. There are the schlosses and their parks to keep up, Hollerbrunn, Monbrillant, Jägerpreis, aren't there? The Hermitage, Delphinenort, the Pheasantry, and the others. . . . I had forgotten Schloss Zegenhaus and the Haderstein ruins . . . not to mention the Old Schloss. . . . They are not well kept up, but they all cost money. . . . There are the Court Theatre, the Picture Gallery, the Library, to maintain. There are a hundred pensions to pay,—no legal compulsion to pay them, but motives of trust and dignity. And look at the princely way in which the Grand Duke behaved at the time of the last floods. . . . But I'm preaching you a regular sermon!"

"A sermon," said the Minister of Finance, "which your Excellency thought would shock me, while you really only confirmed my own view. Dear Baron"—here Herr von Schröder laid his hand on his heart,—"I am convinced that there is no longer room for any misunderstanding as to my opinion, my loyal opinion, between you and me. The King can do no wrong. . . . The sovereign is beyond the reach of reproaches. But here we have to do with a default . . . in both senses of the word! . . . a default which I have no hesitation in laying at the door of Count Trümmerhauff. His predecessors may be pardoned for having concealed from their sovereigns the true state of the Court finances; in those days nothing else was expected of them. But Count Trüm-

9

merhauff's attitude now is not pardonable. In his position as Keeper of the Privy Purse he ought to have felt it incumbent on him to put a brake on his Highness's thoughtlessness, to feel it incumbent on him now to open his Royal Highness's eyes relentlessly to the facts . . ."

Herr Knobelsdorff knitted his brows and laughed.

"Really?" said he. "So your Excellency is of the opinion that that is what the Count was appointed for! I can picture to myself the justifiable astonishment of his lordship, if you lay before him your view of the position. No, no . . . your Excellency need be under no delusion; that appointment was a quite deliberate expression of his wishes on the part of his Royal Highness, which the Count must be the first to respect. It expressed not only an 'I don't know,' but also an 'I won't know.' A man may be an exclusively decorative personality and yet be acute enough to grasp this. . . . Besides . . . honestly . . . we've all of us grasped it. And the only grain of comfort for all of us is this: that there isn't a prince alive to whom it would be more fatal to mention his debts than to his Royal Highness. Our Prince has a something about him which would stop any tactless remarks of that sort before they were spoken . . ."

"Quite true, quite true," said Herr von Schröder. He sighed and stroked thoughtfully the swansdown trimming of his hat. The two men were sitting, half turned towards each other, on a raised window seat in a roomy niche, past which a narrow stone corridor ran outside, a kind of gallery, through the pointed arches of which peeps of the town could be seen. Herr von Schröder went on:

"You answer me, Baron; one would think you were contradicting me, and yet your words show more incredulity and bitterness than my own."

Herr von Knobelsdorff said nothing, but made a vague gesture of assent.

"It may be so," said the Finance Minister, and nodded gloomily at his hat. "Your Excellency may be quite right.

10

Perhaps we are all blameworthy, we and our forefathers too. But it ought to have been stopped. For consider, Baron; ten years ago an opportunity offered itself of putting the finances of the Court on a sound footing, on a better footing anyhow, if you like. It was lost. We understand each other. The Grand Duke, attractive man that he is, had it then in his power to clear things up by a marriage which from a sound point of view might have been called dazzling. Instead of that . . . speaking not for myself, of course, but I shall never forget the disgust on everybody's faces when they mentioned the amount of the dowry. . ."

"The Grand Duchess," said Herr von Knobelsdorff, and the wrinkles at the corners of his eyes disappeared almost entirely, "is one of the handsomest women I have ever seen."

"That is an answer one would expect of your Excellency. It's an æsthetic answer, an answer which would have held quite as good if his Royal Highness's choice, like his brother Lambert's, had fallen on a member of the royal ballet."

"Oh, there was no danger of that. The Prince's taste is a fastidious one, as he has shown. He has always shown in his wants the antithesis to that want of taste which Prince Lambert has shown all his life. It was a long time before he made up his mind to marry. Everybody had given up all hope of a direct heir to the throne. They were resigned for better or worse to Prince Lambert, whose . . . unsuitability to be heir to the throne we need not discuss. Then, a few weeks after he had succeeded, Johann Albrecht met Princess Dorothea, cried, "This one or none!" and the Grand Duchy had its sovereign lady. Your Excellency mentioned the thoughtful looks which were exchanged when the figures of the dowry were published,—you did not mention the jubilation which at the same time prevailed. A poor princess, to be sure. But is beauty, such beauty, a power of happiness or not? Never shall I forget her entry! Her first smile, as it lighted on the gazing crowds, won their love. Your Excellency must allow me to profess once more my

11

belief in the idealism of the people. The people want to
see their best, their highest, their dream, what stands for
their soul, represented in their princes—not their money
bags. There are others to represent those. . . ."

"That's just what there are not; just what we have not
got."

"The more's the pity, then. The main point is, Dorothea
has presented us with an Heir Apparent."

"To whom may Heaven grant some idea of figures!"

"I agree."

At this point the conversation between the two Ministers
ceased. It was broken off by the announcement by aide-
de-camp von Lichterloh, of the happy issue of the confinement. The smaller banqueting-hall was soon filled with officials. One of the great carved doors was quickly thrown
open, and the aide-de-camp appeared in the hall. He had
a red face, blue soldier's eyes, a bristling flaxen moustache,
and silver lace on his collar. He looked somewhat excited,
like a man who had been released from deadly boredom
and was primed with good news. Conscious of the unusu-
alness of the occasion, he boldly ignored the rules of
decorum and etiquette. He saluted the company gaily,
and, spreading his elbows, raised the hilt of his sword
almost to his breast crying: "Beg leave to announce: a
prince!"

"Good!" said Adjutant-General Count Schmettern.

"Delightful, quite delightful, I call that perfectly delightful!" said Lord Marshal von Bühl zu Bühl in his jerky
way; he had recovered consciousness at once.

The President of the High Consistory, Dom Wislezenus—
a clean-shaven, well-built man, who, as a son of a general, and
thanks to his personal distinction, had attained to his high
dignity at a comparatively early age, and on whose black
silk gown hung the star of an Order—folded his white hands
on his breast, and said in a melodious voice, "God bless his
Grand Ducal Highness!"

"You forget, Captain," said Herr von Knobelsdorff, laughing, "that in making your announcement you are encroaching on my privileges and province. Until I have made the most searching investigations into the state of affairs, the question whether it is a prince or a princess remains undecided."

The others laughed, and Herr von Lichterloh replied: "As you wish, your Excellency! Then I have the honour to beg your Excellency to assume this most important charge. . . ."

This dialogue referred to the attributes of the Minister of State, as registrar of the Grand Ducal house, in which capacity he was required to satisfy himself with his own eyes of the sex of the princely offspring and to make an official declaration on the subject. Herr von Knobelsdorff complied with this formality in the so-called powder-closet in which the new-born babe was bathed. He stayed longer there, however, than he had intended to, as he was puzzled and arrested by a painful sight, which at first he mentioned to nobody except the midwife.

Doctor Gnadebusch showed him the child, and her eyes, gleaming mysteriously behind her thick spectacles, travelled between the Minister of State and the little copper-coloured creature, as it groped about with one—only one—little hand, as if she was saying: "Is it all right?"

It was all right. Herr von Knobelsdorff was satisfied, and the wise woman wrapped the child up again. But even then she continued to look down at the Prince and then up at the Baron, until she had drawn his eyes to the point to which she wished to attract them. The wrinkles at the corners of his eyes disappeared, he knit his brows, tried, compared, felt, examined for two or three minutes, and at last asked: "Has the Grand Duke yet seen it?"

"No, Excellency."

"When the Grand Duke sees it," said Herr von Knobelsdorff, "tell him that he will grow out of it."

13

And to the others on the ground-floor he reported—"A splendid prince!"

But ten or fifteen minutes after him the Grand Duke also made the disagreeable discovery,—that was unavoidable, and resulted for Surgeon-General Eschrich in a short, extremely unpleasant scene, but for the Grimmburg Doctor Sammet in an interview with the Grand Duke which raised him considerably in the latter's estimation and was useful to him in his subsequent career. What happened was briefly as follows:

After the birth Johann Albrecht had again retired to the library, and then returned to sit for some time at the bedside with his wife's hand in his. Thereupon he went into the "powder-closet," where the infant now lay in his high, richly gilded cradle, half covered with a blue silk curtain, and sat down in an armchair by the side of his little son. But while he sat and watched the sleeping infant it happened that he noticed what it was hoped that he would not notice yet. He drew the counterpane back, his face clouded over, and then he did exactly what Herr von Knobelsdorff had done before him, looked from Doctor Gnadebusch to the nurse and back again, both of whom said nothing, cast one glance at the half-open door into the bride-chamber, and stalked excitedly back into the library.

Here he at once rang the silver eagle-topped bell which stood on the writing-table, and said to Herr von Lichterloh, who came in, very curtly and coldly: "I require Herr Eschrich."

When the Grand Duke was angry with any member of his suite, he was wont to strip the culprit for the moment of all his titles and dignities, and to leave him nothing but his bare name.

The aide-de-camp again clapped his spurs and heels together and withdrew. Johann Albrecht strode once or twice in a rage up and down the room, and then, hearing Herr von Lichterloh bring the person he had summoned into the

14

ante-room, adopted an audience attitude at his writing-table.

As he stood there, his head turned imperiously in half-profile, his left hand planted on his hip, drawing back his satin-fronted frock coat from his white waistcoat, he exactly resembled his portrait by Professor von Lindemann, which hung beside the big looking-glass over the mantelpiece in the "Hall of the Twelve Months" in the Town Schloss, opposite the portrait of Dorothea, and of which countless engravings, photographs, and picture postcards had been published. The only difference was that Johann Albrecht in the portrait seemed to be of heroic stature, while he really was scarcely of medium height. His forehead was high where his hair had receded, and from under his grey eyebrows, his blue eyes looked out, with dark rings round them, giving them an expression of tired haughtiness. He had the broad, rather too high cheek-bones which were a characteristic of his people. His whiskers and the soft tuft on his chin were grey, his moustache almost white. From the distended nostrils of his small but well-arched nose, two unusually deep furrows ran down to his chin. The lemon-coloured ribbon of the Family Order always showed in the opening of his waistcoat. In his buttonhole the Grand Duke wore a carnation.

Surgeon-General Eschrich entered with a low bow. He had taken off his operating-coat. His eyelid drooped more heavily than usual over his eye. He looked apprehensive and uncomfortable.

The Grand Duke, his left hand on his hip, threw his head back, stretched out his right hand and waved it, palm upwards, several times up and down impatiently.

"I am awaiting an explanation, a justification, Surgeon-General," said he, with a voice trembling with irritation. "You will have the goodness to answer my questions. What is the matter with the child's arm?"

The Physician-in-Ordinary raised his hand a little—a feeble gesture of impotence and blamelessness. He said:

"An it please Your Royal Highness. . . . An unfortunate occurrence. Unfavourable circumstances during the pregnancy of her Royal Highness. . . ."

"That's all nonsense!" The Grand Duke was so much excited that he did not wish for any justification, in fact he would not allow one. "I would remind you, sir, that I am beside myself. Unfortunate occurrence! It was your business to take precautions against unfortunate occurrences. . . ."

The Surgeon-General stood with half-bowed head and, sinking his voice to a submissive tone, addressed the ground at his feet.

"I humbly beg to be allowed to remind you that I, at least, am not alone responsible. Privy Councillor Grasanger—an authority on gynæcology—examined her Royal Highness. But nobody can be held responsible in this case. . . ."

"Nobody . . . Really! I permit myself to make you responsible. . . . You are answerable to me. . . . You were in charge during the pregnancy, you superintended the confinement. I have relied on the knowledge to be expected from your rank, Surgeon-General, I have trusted to your experience. I am bitterly disappointed, bitterly disappointed. All that your skill can boast of is . . . that a crippled child has been born. . . ."

"Would your Royal Highness graciously weigh . . ."

"I have weighed. I have weighed and found wanting. Thank you!"

Surgeon-General Eschrich retired backwards, bowing. In the ante-room he shrugged his shoulders, while his cheeks glowed.

The Grand Duke again fell to pacing the library in his princely wrath, unreasonable, misinformed, and foolish in his loneliness. However, whether it was that he wished to humiliate the Physician-in-Ordinary still further, or that he regretted having robbed himself of any explanations—ten minutes later the unexpected happened, and the Grand Duke

16

sent Herr von Lichterloh to summon young Doctor Sammet
to the library.

The doctor, when he received the message, again said:
"Quite delighted . . . quite delighted, . . ." and at first
changed colour a little, then composed himself admirably.
It is true that he was not a complete master of the prescribed
etiquette, and bowed too soon, while he was still in the door,
so that the aide-de-camp could not close it behind him, and
had to ask him in a whisper to move forward; but afterwards
he stood in an easy and unconstrained attitude, and gave
reassuring answers, although he showed that he was naturally
rather slow of speech, beginning his sentences with hesitating
noises and frequently interspersing them with a "Yes," as if
to confirm what he was saying. He wore his dark yellow
hair cut *en brosse* and his moustache untrimmed. His chin
and checks were clean-shaved, and rather sore from it. He
carried his head a little on one side, and the gaze of his grey
eyes told of shrewdness and practical goodness. His nose,
which was too broad at the bottom, pointed to his origin. He
wore a black tie, and his shiny boots were of a country cut.
He kept his elbows close to his side, with one hand on his silver watch-chain. His whole appearance suggested candour
and professional skill; it inspired confidence.

The Grand Duke addressed him unusually graciously,
rather in the manner of a teacher who has been scolding
a naughty boy, and turns to another with a sudden assump-
tion of mildness.

"I have sent for you, doctor. . . . I want information from
you about this peculiarity in the body of the new-born prince.
. . . I assume that it has not escaped your notice. . . .
I am confronted with a riddle . . . an extremely painful
riddle. . . . In a word, I desire your opinion." And the
Grand Duke, changing his position, ended with a gracious
motion of the hand, which encouraged the doctor to speak.

Dr. Sammet looked at him silently and attentively, as if
waiting till the Grand Duke had completely regained his
17

princely composure. Then he said: "Yes; we have here to do with a case which is not of very common occurrence, but which is well known and familiar to us. Yes. It is actually a case of atrophy . . ."

"Excuse me . . . atrophy . . . ?"

"Forgive me, Royal Highness. I mean stunted growth. Yes."

"I see, stunted growth. Stunting. That's it. The left hand is stunted. But it's unheard of! I cannot understand it! Such a thing has never happened in my family! People talk nowadays about heredity."

Again the doctor looked silently and attentively at the lonely and domineering man, to whom the news had only just penetrated that people were talking lately about heredity. He answered simply: "Pardon me, Royal Highness, but in this case there can be no question of heredity."

"Really! You're quite sure!" said the Grand Duke rather mockingly. "That is one satisfaction. But will you be so kind as to tell me what there can be a question of, then."

"With pleasure, Royal Highness. The cause of the malformation is entirely a mechanical one. It has been caused through a mechanical constriction during the development of the embryo. We call such malformations constriction-formations, yes."

The Grand Duke listened with anxious disgust; he obviously feared the effect of each succeeding word on his sensitiveness. He kept his brows knit and his mouth open: the two furrows running down to his beard seemed deeper than ever. He said: "Constriction-formations, . . . but how in the world . . . I am quite sure every precaution must have been taken . . ."

"Constriction-formations," answered Dr. Sammet, "can occur in various ways. But we can say with comparative certainty that in our case . . . in this case it is the amnion which is to blame."

"I beg your pardon. . . . The amnion?"

"That is one of the fœtal membranes, Royal Highness. Yes. And in certain circumstances the removal of this membrane from the embryo may be retarded and proceed so slowly that threads and cords are left stretching from one to the other . . . amniotic threads as we call them, yes. These threads may be dangerous, for they can bind and knot themselves round the whole of a child's limb; they can entirely intercept, for instance, the life-ducts of a hand and even amputate it. Yes."

"Great heavens . . . amputate it. So we must be thankful that it has not come to an amputation of the hand?"

"That might have happened. Yes. But all that has happened is an unfastening, resulting in an atrophy."

"And that could not be discovered, foreseen, prevented?"

"No, Royal Highness. Absolutely not. It is quite certain that no blame whatever attaches to anybody. Such constrictions do their work in secret. We are powerless against them. Yes."

"And the malformation is incurable? The hand will remain stunted?"

Dr. Sammet hesitated; he looked kindly at the Grand Duke.

"It will never be quite normal, certainly not," he said cautiously. "But the stunted hand will grow a little larger than it is at present, oh yes, it assuredly will . . ."

"Will he be able to use it? For instance . . . to hold his reins or to make gestures, like any one else? . . ."

"Use it . . . a little. . . . Perhaps not much. And he's got his right hand, that's all right."

"Will it be very obvious?" asked the Grand Duke, and scanned Dr. Sammet's face earnestly. "Very noticeable? Will it detract much from his general appearance, think you?"

"Many people," answered Dr. Sammet evasively, "live and work under greater disadvantages. Yes."

The Grand Duke turned away, and walked once up and

down the room. Dr. Sammet deferentially made way for him, and withdrew towards the door. At last the Grand Duke resumed his position at the writing-table and said: "I have now heard what I wanted to know, doctor; I thank you for your report. You understand your business, no doubt about that. Why do you live in Grimmburg? Why do you not practise in the capital?"

"I am still young, Royal Highness, and before I devote myself to practising as a specialist in the capital I should like a few years of really varied practice, of general experience and research. A country town like Grimmburg affords the best opportunity of that. Yes."

"Very sound, very admirable of you. In what do you propose to specialise later on?"

"In the diseases of children, Royal Highness. I intend to be a children's doctor, yes."

"You are a Jew?" asked the Grand Duke, throwing back his head and screwing up his eyes.

"Yes, Royal Highness."

"Ah—will you answer me one more question? Have you ever found your origin to stand in your way, a drawback in your professional career? I ask as a ruler, who is especially concerned that the principle of 'equal chances for all' shall hold good unconditionally and privately, not only officially."

"Everybody in the Grand Duchy," answered Dr. Sammet, "has the right to work." But he did not stop there: moving his elbows like a pair of short wings, in an awkward, impassioned way, he made a few hesitating noises, and then added in a restrained but eager voice: "No principle of equalization, if I may be allowed to remark, will ever prevent the incidence in the life of the community of exceptional and abnormal men who are distinguished from the bourgeois by their nobleness or infamy. It is the duty of the individual not to concern himself as to the precise nature of the distinction between him and the common herd, but to see what is the essential in that distinction and to recognize that it imposes

20

on him an exceptional obligation towards society. A man is at an advantage, not at a disadvantage, compared with the regular and therefore complacent majority, if he has one motive more than they to extraordinary exertions. Yes, yes," repeated Dr. Sammet. The double affirmative was meant to confirm his answer.

"Good . . . not bad; very remarkable, anyhow," said the Grand Duke judicially. He found Dr. Sammet's words suggestive, though somewhat off the point. He dismissed the young man with the words: "Well, doctor, my time is limited. I thank you. This interview—apart from its painful occasion—has much reassured me. I have the pleasure of bestowing on you the Albrecht Cross of the Third Class with Crown. I shall remember you. Thank you."

This was what passed between the Grimmburg doctor and the Grand Duke. Shortly after Johann Albrecht left the castle and returned by special train to the capital, chiefly to show himself to the rejoicing populace, but also in order to give several audiences in the palace. It was arranged that he should return in the evening to the castle, and take up his residence there for the next few weeks.

All those present at the confinement at Grimmburg who did not belong to the Grand Duchess's suite were also accommodated in the special train of the bankrupt local railway, some of them travelling in the Sovereign's own saloon. But the Grand Duke drove from the castle to the station alone with von Knobelsdorff, the Minister of State, in an open landau, one of the brown Court carriages with the little golden crown on the door. The white feathers in the hats of the chasseurs in front fluttered in the summer breeze. Johann Albrecht was grave and silent on the journey; he seemed to be worried and morose. And although Herr von Knobelsdorff knew that the Grand Duke, even in private, disliked anybody addressing him unasked and uninvited, yet at last he made up his mind to break the silence.

"Your Royal Highness," he said deprecatingly, "seems to

take so much to heart the little anomaly which has been discovered in the Prince's body, . . . and yet one would think that on a day like this the reasons for joy and proud thankfulness so far outweigh . . ."

"My dear Knobelsdorff," replied Johann Albrecht, with some irritation and almost in tears, "you must forgive my ill-humour; you surely do not wish me to be in good spirits. I can see no reason for being so. The Grand Duchess is going on well—true enough, and the child is a boy—that's a blessing too. But he has come into the world with an atrophy, a constriction, caused by amniotic threads. Nobody is to blame, it is a misfortune; but misfortunes for which nobody is to blame are the most terrible of all misfortunes, and the sight of their Sovereign ought to awaken in his people other feelings than those of sympathy. The Heir Apparent is delicate, needs constant care. It was a miracle that he survived that attack of pleurisy two years ago, and it will be nothing less than a miracle if he lives to attain his majority. Now Heaven grants me a second son—he seems strong, but he comes into the world with only one hand. The other is stunted, useless, a deformity, he will have to hide it. What a drawback! What an impediment! He will have to brave it out before the world all his life. We must let it gradually leak out, so that it may not cause too much of a shock on his first appearance in public. No, I cannot yet get over it. A prince with one hand . . ."

" 'With one hand,' " said Herr von Knobelsdorff. "Did your Royal Highness use that expression twice deliberately?"

"Deliberately?"

"You did not, then? . . . For the Prince has two hands, yet as one is stunted, one might if one liked also describe him as a prince with one hand."

"What then?"

"And one must almost wish, not that your Royal Highness's second son, but that the heir to the throne were the victim of this small malformation."

"What do you mean by that?"

"Why, your Royal Highness will laugh at me; but I am thinking of the gipsy woman."

"The gipsy woman? Please go on, my dear Baron!"

"Of the gipsy woman—forgive me!—who a hundred years ago prophesied the birth of a Prince to your Royal Highness's house—a prince 'with one hand'—that is how tradition puts it—and attached to the birth of that prince a certain promise, couched in peculiar terms."

The Grand Duke turned on his seat and stared, without saying a word, at Herr von Knobelsdorff, at the outer corner of whose eyes the radiating wrinkles were playing. Then, "Mighty entertaining!" he said, and resumed his former attitude.

"Prophecies," continued Herr von Knobelsdorff, "generally come true to this extent, that circumstances arise which one can interpret, if one has a mind to, in their sense. And the broadness of the terms in which every proper prophecy is couched makes this all the more easy. 'With one hand'— that is regular oracle-style. What has actually happened is a moderate case of atrophy. But that much counts for a good deal, for what is there to prevent me, what is there to prevent the people, from assuming the whole by this partial fulfilment, and declaring that the conditional part of the prophecy has been fulfilled? The people will do so; if not at once, at any rate if the rest of the prophecy, the actual promise, is in any way realised, it will put two and two together, as it always has done, in its wish to see what is written turn out true. I don't see how it is going to come about— the Prince is a younger son, he will not come to the throne, the intentions of fate are obscure. But the one-handed prince is there—and so may he bestow on us as much as he can."

The Grand Duke did not answer, secretly thrilled by dreams of the future of his dynasty.

"Well, Knobelsdorff, I will not be angry with you. You want to comfort me, and you have not done it badly. But I must do what is expected of me. . . ."

23

The air resounded with the distant cheers of many voices. The people of Grimmburg were crowded in black masses behind the cordon at the station. Officials were standing apart in front, waiting for the carriages. There was the mayor, raising his top-hat, wiping his forehead with a crumpled handkerchief, and poring over a paper whose contents he was committing to memory. Johann Albrecht assumed the expression appropriate to listening to the smoothly worded address and to answering concisely and graciously: "Most excellent Mr. Mayor. . . ." The town was dressed with flags, and the bells were ringing.

In the capital all the bells were ringing. And in the evening there were illuminations; not by formal request of the authorities, but spontaneous—the whole city was a blaze of light.

## II

## THE COUNTRY

THE country measured eight thousand square kilometres, and numbered one million inhabitants.

A pretty, quiet, leisurely country. The tops of the trees in its forests rustled dreamily; its broad acres showed signs of honest care; its industries were undeveloped to the point of indigence.

It possessed some brick kilns, a few salt and silver-mines—that was almost all. A certain amount of tourist-traffic must also be mentioned, but he would be a bold man who described it as a flourishing industry. The alkali springs, which rose from the ground in the immediate neighbourhood of the capital and formed the centre of an attractive bathing-establishment, constituted the claims of the city to be considered a health resort. But while the baths at the end of the Middle Ages had been frequented by visitors from afar, they had later lost their repute, and been put in the shade by other baths and forgotten. The most valuable of the springs, that called the Ditlinde spring, which was exceptionally rich in lithium salts, had been opened up quite recently, in the reign of Johann Albrecht III, and as energetic business and advertising methods were not employed, its water had not yet succeeded in winning world-recognition. A hundred thousand bottles of it were sent away in the year—rather less than more. And but few strangers came to drink it on the spot. . . .

The Diet was the scene all the year round of speeches about the "barely" satisfactory results of the trade returns, by which was really meant the entirely unsatisfactory results, which nobody could dispute, that the local railways did not cover their expenses and the main lines did not pay any dividends—distressing but unalterable and inveterate facts, which the Minister for Trade in luminous but monotonous declarations explained by the peaceful commercial and industrial circumstances of the country, as well as by the inaccessibility of the home coal-deposits. Critics added something about defective organization of the State industrial administration. But the spirit of contradiction and negation was not strong in the Diet; the prevailing frame of mind among the representatives of the people was one of dull and true-hearted loyalty.

So the railway revenues did not by any means rank first among the public revenues of a private-investment nature; the forest revenues had ranked first for years in this land of woods and plough. The fall in them, their startling depreciation, however sufficient reasons there were for it, was a much more difficult matter to mend.

The people loved their woods. They were a fair and compact type, with searching blue eyes and broad, rather high cheek-bones, a sensible and honest, solid and backward stamp of men. They clung to their country's forest with all the strength of their nature; it lived in their bones, it was to the artists which it bred the source and home of their inspirations, and it was quite properly the object of popular gratitude, not only in regard to the gifts of soul and intellect of which it was the donor. The poor gathered their firewood in the forest; it gave to them freely, they had it for nothing. They went stooping and gathering all kinds of berries and mushrooms among its trunks, and earned a little something by doing so. That was not all. The people recognized that their forest had a very distinctly favourable influence on the weather and the healthy condition of the country; they were well aware that without the lovely woods in the neighbourhood of the capital the spa-garden outside would

26

not attract foreigners with money to spend; in short, this not over-industrious and up-to-date people could not help knowing that the forest stood for the most important asset, the most profitable heritage of the country.

And yet the forest had been sinned against, outraged for ages and ages. The Grand Ducal Department of Woods and Forests deserved all the reproaches that were laid against it. That Department had not political insight enough to see that the wood must be maintained and kept as inalienable common property, if it was to be useful not only to the present generation, but also to those to come; and that it would surely avenge itself if it were exploited recklessly and short-sightedly, without regard to the future, for the benefit of the present.

That was what happened, and was still happening. In the first place great stretches of the floor of the forest had been impoverished by reckless and excessive spoliation of its litter. Matters had repeatedly gone so far that not only the most recent carpet of needles and leaves, but the greatest part of the fall of years past had been removed and used in the fields partly as litter, partly as mould. There were many forests which had been completely stripped of mould; some had been crippled by the raking away of the litter: instances of this were to be found in the public woodlands as well as in the State woodlands.

If the woods had been put to these uses in order to tide over a sudden agricultural crisis, there would have been no reason to complain. But although there were not wanting those who declared that an agricultural system founded on the appropriation of wood-litter was inexpedient, indeed dangerous, the trade in litter went on without any particular reason, on purely fiscal grounds, so it was put—that is to say, on grounds which, examined closely, proved to be only one ground and object, namely, the making of money. For it was money which was wanted. But to get this money, ceaseless inroads were made on the capital, until

27

one fine day it was realised with dismay that an unsuspected depreciation in that capital had ensued.

The people were a peasant race, and thought that the way to be up-to-date was to display a perverted, artificial, and improper zeal and to employ reckless business methods. A characteristic instance was the dairy-farming . . . one word about that. Loud complaints were heard, principally in the official medical annual, that a deterioration was noticeable in the nourishment, and consequently in the development, of the country people. What was the reason? The owners of cows were bent on turning all the full-milk at their disposal into money. The spread of the dairy industry, the development and productiveness of the milk trade, tempted them to disregard the claims of their own establishments. A strength-giving milk diet became a rarity in the country, and in its stead recourse was had to unsubstantial skimmed milk, inferior substitutes, vegetable oils, and, unfortunately, alcoholic drinks as well. The critics talked about underfeeding, they even called it physical and moral debilitation of the population; they brought the facts to the notice of the Diet, and the Government promised to give the matter their earnest attention.

But it was only too clear that the Government was at bottom infected with the same perversity as the mistaken dairy-farmers. Timber continued to be cut to excess in the State forests; once cut it was gone, and meant a continual shrinkage of public property. The clearings might have been necessary occasionally, when the forests had been damaged in one way or another, but often enough they had been due simply to the fiscal reasons referred to: and instead of the proceeds of the clearings being used for the purchase of new tracts, instead of the cleared tracts being replanted as quickly as possible—instead, in a word, of the damage to the capital value of the State forests being balanced by an addition to their capital value, the quickly earned profits had been devoted to the payment of current expenses and

28

the redemption of bonds. Of course there could be no doubt that a reduction of the National Debt was only too desirable; but the critics expressed the opinion that that was not the time to devote extraordinary revenues to the building up of the sinking-fund.

Anybody who had no interest in mincing matters must have described the State finances as in a hopeless muddle. The country carried a debt of thirty million pounds—it struggled along under it with patience and devotion, but with secret groans. For the burden, much too heavy in itself, was made trebly heavy through a rise in the rate of interest and through conditions of repayment such as are usually imposed on a country whose credit is shaken, whose exchange is low, and which has already almost come to be reckoned as "interesting" in the world of financiers.

The succession of financial crises appeared to be never-ending. The list of failures seemed without beginning or end. And a maladministration, which was made no better by frequent changes in its personnel, regarded borrowing as the only cure for the creeping sickness in the State finances. Even the Chancellor of the Exchequer, von Schröder, whose probity and singleness of purpose were beyond all doubt, had been given a peerage by the Grand Duke, because he had succeeded in placing a loan at a high rate of interest in the most difficult circumstances. His heart was set on an improvement in the credit of the State: but as his resource was to contract new debts while he paid off the old, his policy proved to be no better than a well-meant but costly blind. For a simultaneous sale and purchase of bonds meant a higher purchase than selling price, involving the loss of thousands of pounds.

It seemed as if the country were incapable of producing a man of any adequate financial gifts. Improper practices and a policy of "hushing-up" were the fashion. The budget was so drawn up that it was impossible to distinguish between ordinary and extraordinary State require-
29

ments. Ordinary and extraordinary items were jumbled up together, and those responsible for the budgets deceived themselves, and everybody else, as to the real state of affairs, by appropriating loans, which were supposed to be raised for extraordinary purposes, to cover a deficit in the ordinary exchequer. . . . The holder of the finance portfolio at one time was actually an ex-court marshal.

Dr. Krippenreuther, who took the helm towards the end of Johann Albrecht III's reign, was the Minister who, convinced like Herr von Schröder of the necessity for a strenuous reduction in the debt, induced the Diet to consent to a final and extreme addition to the burden of taxation. But the country, naturally poor as it was, was on the verge of insolvency, and all Krippenreuther got was unpopularity. His policy really meant merely a transfer from one hand to the other, a transfer which itself involved a loss; for the increase in taxation laid a burden on the national economy which pressed more heavily and more directly than that which was removed by the sinking of the National Debt.

Where, then, were help and a remedy to be found? A miracle, so it seemed, was needed—and meanwhile the sternest economy. The people were pious and loyal, they loved their princes as themselves, they were permeated with the sublimity of the monarchical idea, they saw in it a reflexion of the Deity. But the economical pressure was too painful, too generally felt. The most ignorant could read in the thinned and crippled forests a tale of woe. The consequence was that repeated appeals had been made in the Diet for a curtailment of the Civil List, a cutting down of the appanages and Crown endowments.

The Civil List amounted to twenty-five thousand pounds, the revenues of the Crown demesnes to thirty-seven thousand pounds. That was all. And the Crown was in debt —to what extent was perhaps known to Count Trümmerhauff, the Keeper of the Grand Ducal Purse, a regular stickler, but a man of absolutely no business instincts. It

30

was not known to Johann Albrecht; at any rate he seemed not to know it, and therein followed the example of his forefathers, who had rarely deigned to give more than a passing thought to their debts.

The people's attitude of veneration was reflected in their princes' extraordinary sense of their own dignity, which had sometimes assumed fanciful and even extravagant forms, and had found its most obvious and most serious expression in every period in a tendency to extravagance and to a reckless ostentation as exaggerated as the dignity it represented. One Grimmburger had been christened "the luxurious" in so many words,—they had almost all deserved the nickname. So that the state of indebtedness of the House was an historical and hereditary state, reaching back to the times when all loans were a private concern of the Sovereign, and when John the Headstrong, wishing to raise a loan, pledged the liberty of the most prominent of his subjects to do so.

Those times were past; and Johann Albrecht III, a true-born Grimmburger in his instincts, was unfortunately no longer in a position to give free rein to his instincts. His fathers had played ducks and drakes with the family funds, which were reduced to nothing or little better than nothing. They had been spent on the building of country-seats with French names and marble colonnades, on parks with fountains, on splendid operas and all kinds of glittering shows. Figures were figures, and, much against the inclination of the Grand Duke, in fact without his consent, the Court was gradually cut down.

The Princess Catherine, the sister of the Grand Duke, was never spoken of in the capital without a touch of sympathy. She had been married to a member of a neighbouring ruling House, had been left a widow, and had come back to her brother's capital, where she lived with her red-headed children in what used to be the Heir Apparent's palace on the Albrechtstrasse, before whose gates a gigantic doorkeeper stood all day long in a pompous attitude with staff and shoulder-belt

31

complete, while life went on with peculiar moderation inside.

Prince Lambert, the Grand Duke's brother, did not come in for much attention. There was a coolness between him and his relations, who could not forgive him his *mésalliance,* and he hardly ever came to Court. He lived in his villa overlooking the public gardens with his wife, an ex-dancer from the Court Theatre who bore the title of Baroness von Rohrdorf, after one of the Prince's properties; and there he divided his time between sport and theatre-going, and struggling with his debts. He had dropped his dignities and lived just like a private citizen; and if he was generally supposed to have a struggle to make two ends meet, nobody gave him much sympathy for it.

But alterations had been made in the old castle itself— reductions of expenses, which were discussed in the city and the country, and discussed usually in an apprehensive and regretful sense, because the people at bottom wished to see themselves represented with due pride and magnificence. Several high posts at the Court had been amalgamated for economy's sake, and for years past Herr von Bühl zu Bühl had been Lord Marshal, Chief Master of the Ceremonies, and Marshal of the Household at once. There had been many discharges in the Board of Green Cloth and the servants' hall, among the pike-staffs, yeomen of the guard, and grooms, the master cooks and chief confectioners, the court and chamber lackeys. The establishment of the royal stable had been reduced to the barest minimum. . . . And what was the good of it all? The Grand Duke's contempt for money showed itself in sudden outbursts against the squeeze; and while the catering at the Court functions reached the extreme limits of permissible simplicity, while at the supper at the close of the Thursday concerts in the Marble Hall nothing but continual roast beef with sauce remoulade and ice-pudding were served on the red velvet coverings of the gilt-legged tables, while the daily fare at the Grand Duke's own candle-decked table was no better than that of an ordinary middle-class family, he defiantly threw away a whole year's income on the repair of the Grimmburg.

But meanwhile the rest of his seats were falling to pieces. Herr von Bühl simply had not the means at his disposal for their upkeep. And yet it was a pity in the case of many of them. Those which lay at some little distance from the capital, or right out in the country, those luxurious asylums cradled in natural beauties whose dainty names spoke of rest, solitude, content, pastime, and freedom from care, or recalled a flower or a jewel, served as holiday resorts for the citizens and strangers, and brought in a certain amount in entrance-money which sometimes—not always—was devoted to their upkeep. This was not the case, however, with those in the immediate neighbourhood of the capital. There was the little schloss in the Empire style, the Hermitage, standing silent and graceful on the edge of the northern suburbs, but long uninhabited and deserted in the middle of its over-grown park, which joined on to the public gardens, and looked out on its little, mud-stiff pond. There was Schloss Delphinenort which, only a quarter of an hour's walk from the other, in the northern part of the public gardens themselves, all of which had once belonged to the Crown, mirrored its untidiness in a huge square fountain-basin; both were in a sad state. That Delphinenort in particular—that noble structure in the early baroque style, with its stately entrance-colonnade, its high windows divided into little white-framed panes, its carved festoons, its Roman busts in the niches, its splendid approach-stairs, its general magnificence—should be abandoned to decay for ever, as it seemed, was the sorrow of all lovers of architectural beauty; and when one day, as the result of unforeseen, really strange circumstances, it was restored to honour and youth, among them at any rate the satisfaction was general. . . . For the rest, Delphinenort could be reached in fifteen or twenty minutes from the spa-garden, which lay a little to the north-west of the city, and was connected with its centre by a direct line of trams.

33

The only residences used by the Grand Ducal family were Schloss Hollerbrunn, the summer residence, an expanse of white buildings with Chinese roofs, on the farther side of the chain of hills which surrounded the capital, coolly and pleasantly situated on the river and famed for the elder-hedges in its park; farther, Schloss Jägerpreis, the ivy-covered hunting-box in the middle of the woods to westward; and lastly, the Town Castle itself, called the "Old" Castle, although no new one existed.

It was called thus, with no idea of comparison, simply because of its age, and the critics declared that its redecoration was more a matter of urgency than that of the Grimmburg. Even the inner rooms, which were in daily use by the family, were faded and cracked, not to mention the many uninhabited and unused rooms in the oldest parts of the many-styled building, which were all choked and flyblown. For some time past the public had been refused admission to them,—a measure which was obviously due to the shocking state of the castle. But people who could get a peep, the tradesmen and the staff, declared that there was stuffing peeping out of more than one stiff, imposing piece of furniture.

The castle and the Court Church together made up a grey, irregular, and commanding mass of turrets, galleries, and gateways, half fortress, half palace. Various epochs had contributed to its erection, and large parts of it were decaying, weather-beaten, spoilt, and ready to fall into pieces. To the west it dropped steeply down to the lower-lying city, and was connected with it by battered steps clamped together with rusty iron bars. But the huge main gate, guarded by lions couchant, and surmounted by the pious, haughty motto: "Turris fortissima nomen Domini," in almost illegible carving, faced the Albrechtsplatz. It had its sentries and sentry boxes; it was the scene of the changing of the guard, with drums and martial display; it was the playground of all the urchins of the town.

The Old Castle had three courtyards, in the corners of

which rose graceful stair-turrets and between whose paving stones an unnecessary amount of weeds was generally growing. But in the middle of one of the courtyards stood the rose-bush,—it had stood there for ages in a bed, although there was no other attempt at a garden to be seen. It was just like any other rose-bush; it had a porter to tend it, it stood there in snow, rain, and sunshine, and in due season it bore roses. These were exceptionally fine roses, nobly formed, with dark-red velvet petals, a pleasure to look at, and real masterpieces of nature. But those roses had one strange and dreadful peculiarity: they had no scent! Or rather, they had a scent, but for some unknown reason it was not the scent of roses, but of decay—a slight, but plainly perceptible scent of decay. Everybody knew it; it was in the guide-books, and strangers visited the courtyard to convince themselves of it with their own noses. There was also a popular idea that it was written somewhere that at some time or other, on a day of rejoicings and public felicity, the blossoms of the rose-bush would begin to give forth a natural and lovely odour.

After all, it was only to be expected that the popular imagination would be exercised by the wonderful rose-bush. It was exercised in precisely the same way by the "owl-chamber" in the Old Castle, which was used as a lumber room. Its position was such that it could not be ignored, not far from the "Gala Rooms," and the "Hall of the Knights," where the Court officers used to assemble on Court days, and thus in a comparatively modern part of the building. But there was certainly something uncanny about it, especially as from time to time noises and cries occurred there, which could not be heard outside the room and whose origin was unascertainable. People swore that it came from ghosts, and many asserted that it was especially noticeable when important and decisive events in the Grand Ducal family were impending,—a more or less gratuitous rumour, which deserved no more serious attention than other national products of an historical and dynastic frame of mind, as for instance a certain dark prophecy which had been handed down for hundreds of years and may be mentioned in this connexion. It came from an old gipsy-woman, and was to the effect that a prince "with one hand" would bring the greatest good fortune to the country. The old hag had said: "He will give to the country with one hand more than all the rest could give it with two." That is how the prophecy was recorded, and how it was quoted from time to time.

Round the Old Castle lay the capital, consisting of the Old Town and the New Town, with their public buildings, monuments, fountains, and parks, their streets and squares, named after princes, artists, deserving statesmen, and distinguished citizens, divided into two very unequal halves by the many-bridged river, which flowed in a great loop round the southern end of the public garden, and was lost in the surrounding hills. The city was a university town, it possessed an academy which was not in much request and whose curricula were unpractical and rather old-fashioned; the Professor of Mathematics, Privy Councillor Klinghammer, was the only one of any particular repute in the scientific world. The Court Theatre, though poorly endowed, maintained a decent level of performances. There was a little musical, literary, and artistic life; a certain number of foreigners came to the capital, wishing to share in its well-regulated life and such intellectual attractions as it offered, among them wealthy invalids who settled down in the villas round the spa-gardens and were held in honour by the State and the community as doughty payers of taxes.

And now you know what the town was like, what the country was like, and how matters stood.

# III

## HINNERKE THE SHOEMAKER

THE Grand Duke's second son made his first public appearance
on the occasion of his christening. This festivity aroused
the same interest in the country as always attached to happenings within the Royal Family circle. It took place after
weeks of discussion and research as to the manner of its
arrangement, was held in the Court Church by the President
of the High Consistory, Dom Wislezenus, with all the due
ceremonial, and in public, to the extent that the Lord Marshal's
office, by the Prince's orders, had issued invitations to it
to every class of society.

Herr von Bühl zu Bühl, a courtly ritualist of the greatest circumspection and accuracy, in his full-dress uniform
superintended, with the help of two masters of the ceremonies, the whole of the intricate proceedings: the gathering of the princely guests in the Gala Rooms, the solemn
procession in which they, attended by pages and squires,
walked up the staircase of Heinrich the Luxurious and through
a covered passage into the church, the entry of the spectators
from the highest to the lowest, the distribution of the seats,
the observance of due decorum during the religious service
itself, the order of precedence at the congratulations which
took place directly after the service was ended. . . . He
panted and puffed, smiled ingratiatingly, brandished his staff,
laughed in nervous bursts, and kept executing retreating
bows.

The Court Church was decorated with plants and draperies. In addition to the representatives of the nobility,
37

of the Court and country, and of the higher and lower Civil Service, tradesmen, country folk, and common artisans, in high good humour, filled the seats. But in a half-circle of red-velvet arm-chairs in front of the altar sat the relations of the infant, foreign princes as sponsors and the trusty representatives of such as had not come in person. The assemblage at the christening of the Heir Apparent six years before had not been more distinguished. For in view of Albrecht's delicacy, the advanced age of the Grand Duke, and the dearth of Grimmburg relations, the person of the second-born prince was at once recognized as an important guarantee for the future of the dynasty. Little Albrecht took no part in the ceremony; he was kept to his bed with an indisposition which Surgeon-General Eschrich declared to be of a nervous character.

Dom Wislezenus preached from a text of the Grand Duke's own choosing. The *Courier*, a gossiping city newspaper, had given a full account of how the Grand Duke had one day fetched with his very own hands the large metal-clasped family Bible out of the rarely visited library, had shut himself up with it in his study, searched in it for a whole hour, at last copied the text he had chosen on to a piece of paper with his pocket-pencil, signed it "Johann Albrecht," and sent it to the Court preacher. Dom Wislezenus treated it in a musical style, so as to speak, like a *leit motif*. He turned it inside and out, dressed it in different shapes and squeezed it dry; he announced it in a whisper, then with the whole power of his lungs; and whereas, delivered lightly and reflectively at the beginning of his discourse, it seemed a thin, almost unsubstantial subject; at the close, when he for the last time thundered it at the congregation, it appeared richly orchestrated, heavily scored, and pregnant with emotion. Then he passed on to the actual baptism, and carried it out at full length so that all could see it, with due stress on every detail.

This, then, was the day of the prince's first public appearance, and that he was the chief actor in the drama was clearly shown by the fact that he was the last to come on the stage, and that his entry was distinct from that of the rest of the company. Preceded by Herr von Bühl, he entered slowly, in the arms of the Mistress of the Robes, Baroness von Schulenburg-Tressen, and all eyes were fixed on him. He was asleep in his laces, his veils, and his white silk robe. One of his little hands happened to be hidden. His appearance evoked unusual delight and emotion. The cynosure and centre of attraction, he lay quietly there, bearing it all, as may be supposed, patiently and unassumingly. It was to his credit that he did not make any disturbance, did not clutch or struggle; but, doubtless from innate trustfulness, quietly resigned himself to the state which surrounded him, bore it patiently, and even at that early date sank his own emotions in it. . . .

The arms in which he reposed were frequently changed at fixed points in the ceremony. Baroness Schulenburg handed him with a curtsey to his aunt, Catherine, who, with a stern look on her face, was dressed in a newly remade lilac silk dress, and wore Crown jewels in her hair. She laid him, when the moment came, solemnly in his mother Dorothea's arms, who, in all her stately beauty, with a smile on her proud and lovely mouth, held him out a while to be blessed, and then passed him on. A cousin held him for a minute or two, a child of eleven or twelve years with fair hair, thin sticks of legs, cold bare arms, and a broad red silk sash which stuck out in a huge knot behind her white dress. Her peaked face was anxiously fixed on the Master of the Ceremonies. . . .

Once the Prince woke up, but the flickering flames of the altar-candles and a many-coloured shaft of sunlight dust blinded him, and made him close his eyes again. And as there were no thoughts, but only soft unsubstantial dreams in his head, as moreover he was feeling no pain at the moment, he at once fell asleep again.

39

He received a number of names while he slept; but the chief names were Klaus Heinrich.

And he slept on in his cot with its gilded cornice and blue silk curtains, while the royal family feasted in the Marble Hall, and the rest of the guests in the Hall of the Knights, in his honour.

The newspapers reported his first appearance; they described his looks and his dress, and emphasized his truly princely behaviour, couching the moving and inspiring account in words which had often done duty on similar occasions. After that, the public for a long time heard little of him, and he nothing of them.

He knew nothing as yet, understood nothing as yet, guessed nothing as to the difficulty, danger, and sternness of the life prescribed for him; nothing in his conduct suggested that he felt any contrast between himself and the great public. His little existence was an irresponsible, carefully supervised dream, played on a stage remote from the public stage; and this stage was peopled with countless tinted phantoms, both stationary and active, some emerging but transiently, some permanently at hand.

Of the permanent ones, the parents were far in the background, and not altogether distinguishable. They were his parents, that was certain, and they were exalted, and friendly too. When they approached there was a feeling as if everything else slipped away to each side, and left a respectable passage along which they advanced towards him to show him a moment's tenderness. The nearest and clearest things to him were two women with white caps and aprons, two beings who were obviously all goodness, purity, and loving-kindness, who tended his little body in every way, and were much distressed when he cried. . . . A close partner in his life, too, was Albrecht, his brother; but he was grave, distant, and much more advanced.

When Klaus Heinrich was two years old, another birth took place in the Grimmburg, and a princess came into the world. Thirty-six guns were allotted to her, because she was of the female sex, and she was given the name of Ditlinde at the font. She was Klaus Heinrich's sister, and it was a good thing for him that she appeared. She was at first surprisingly small and weak, but she soon grew like him, caught him up, and the two became inseparable. They shared each other's lives, each other's views, feelings, and ideas: they communicated to each other their impressions of the world outside them.

It was a world, they were impressions, calculated to produce a reflective frame of mind. In winter they lived in the old castle. In summer they lived in Hollerbrunn, the summer schloss, on the river, in the cool, in the scent of the violet hedges with white statues between them. On the way thither, or if at any other time father or mother took them with them in one of the brown carriages with the little golden crown on the door, all the passers-by stopped, cheered, and took their hats off; for father was Prince and Ruler of the country, consequently they themselves were Prince and Princess—undoubtedly in precisely the same sense as were the princes and princesses in the French stories which their Swiss governess told them. That was worth consideration, it was at any rate a peculiar occurrence. When other children heard the stories, they necessarily regarded the princes which figured in them from a great distance, and as solemn beings whose rank was a glorification of reality and with whom to concern themselves was undoubtedly a chastening of their thoughts, and an escape from the ordinary existence. But Klaus Heinrich and Ditlinde regarded the heroes of the stories as their own equals and fellows, they breathed the same air as them, they lived in a schloss like them, they stood on a fraternal footing with them, and were justified in identifying themselves with them. Was it their lot, then, to live always and continually on the height to which others only climbed when stories were being told to them? The Swiss governess, true to her general principles, would have
41

found it impossible to deny it, if the children had asked the question in so many words.

The Swiss governess was the widow of a Calvanistic minister and was in charge of both children, each of whom had two lady's maids as well. She was black and white throughout: her cap was white and her dress black, her face was white, with white warts on one cheek, and her smooth hair had a mixed black-and-white metallic sheen. She was very precise and easily put out. When things happened which, though quite without danger, could not be allowed, she clasped her white hands and turned her eyes up to heaven. But her quietest and severest mode of punishment for serious occasions was to "look sadly" at the children—implying that they had lost their self-respect. On a fixed day she began, on a hint from higher quarters, to address Klaus Heinrich and Ditlinde as "Grand Ducal Highness," and from that day she was more easily put out than before. . . .

But Albrecht was called "Royal Highness." Aunt Catherine's children were members of the family only on the distaff side, and so were of less importance. But Albrecht was Crown Prince and Heir Apparent, so that it was not at all unfitting that he should look so pale and distant and keep so much to his bed. He wore Austrian coats with flap pockets and cut long behind. His head had a big bump at the back and narrow temples, and he had a long face. While still quite young he had come through a serious illness, which, in the opinion of Surgeon-General Eschrich, was the reason for his heart having "shifted over to the right." However that might be, he had seen Death face to face, a fact which had probably intensified the shy dignity which was natural to him. He seemed to be extremely standoffish, cold from embarrassment, and proud from lack of graciousness. He lisped a little and then blushed at doing so, because he was always criticizing himself. His shoulder-blades were a little uneven. One of his eyes had some weakness or other, so that he used glasses for writing his exercises,

42

which helped to make him look old and wise. . . . Albrecht's tutor, Doctor Veit, a man with hanging mud-coloured moustaches, hollow cheeks, and wan eyes unnaturally far apart, was always at his left hand. Doctor Veit was always dressed in black, and carried a book dangling down his thigh, with his index-finger thrust between its leaves.

Klaus Heinrich felt that Albrecht did not care much for him, and he saw that it was not only because of his inferiority in years. He himself was tender-hearted and prone to tears, that was his nature. He cried, when anybody "looked sadly" at him, and when he knocked his forehead against a corner of the nursery table, so that it bled, he howled from sympathy with his forehead. But Albrecht had faced Death, yet never cried on any condition. He stuck his short, rounded underlip a little forward, and sucked it lightly against the upper one—that was all. He was most superior. The Swiss governess referred in so many words to him in matters of *comme il faut* as a model. He had never allowed himself to converse with the gorgeous creatures who belonged to the court, not exactly men and human beings, but lackeys—as Klaus Heinrich had sometimes done in unguarded moments. For Albrecht was not curious. The look in his eyes was that of a lonely boy, who had no wish to let the world intrude upon him. Klaus Heinrich, on the contrary, chatted with the lackeys from that same wish, and from an urgent though perhaps dangerous and improper desire to feel some contact with what lay outside the charmed circle. But the lackeys, young and old, at the doors, in the corridors and the passage-rooms, with their sand-coloured gaiters and brown coats, on the red-gold lace of which the same little crown as on the carriage doors was repeated again and again—they straightened their knees when Klaus Heinrich chatted to them, laid their great hands on the seams of the thick velvet breeches, bent a little forward towards him, so that the aiguillettes dangled from their shoulders, and returned various, highly proper answers, the

43

most important part of which was the address "Grand Ducal Highness," and smiled as they did so with an expression of cautious sympathy, which recalled the words of the old song, "The lad that is born to be king." Sometimes when he got the chance, Klaus Heinrich went on voyages of discovery in uninhabited parts of the schloss, with Ditlinde, his sister, when she was old enough.

At that time he was having lessons from Schulrat Dröge, Rector of the city schools, who was chosen to be his first tutor. Schulrat Dröge was a born pedagogue. His index-finger, with its folds of dry skin and gold stoneless signet-ring, followed the line of print when Klaus Heinrich read, waiting before going on to the next word until the preceding one had been read. He came in a frock-coat and white waistcoat, with the ribbon of some inferior order in his button-hole, and in broad shiny boots with brown upper-leathers. He wore a pointed grey beard, and bushy grey hair grew out of his big, broad ears. His brown hair was brushed up into points on his temples, and so precisely parted as to show clearly his yellow dry scalp, which was full of holes like canvas. But thin grey hair was visible under the strong brown hair behind and at the sides. He bowed slightly to the lackeys who opened the door for him to the big schoolroom at whose table Klaus Heinrich sat waiting for him. But to Klaus Heinrich he did not confine himself to a superficial bow as he entered the room, but made a pronounced and deliberate bow before he came up to him, and waited for his exalted pupil to offer him his hand. This Klaus Heinrich did; and the fact that he did so twice, not only when he greeted him, but also when he took his departure, just in the graceful and winning way in which he had seen his father give his hand to those who expected it, seemed to him far more important and essential than all the instruction which came between the two ceremonies.

After Schulrat Dröge had come and gone any number of times, Klaus Heinrich had imperceptibly gained a knowl-

edge of all sorts of practical things: to everybody's surprise
he was quite at home in every kind of reading, writing, and
arithmetic, and could reel off to order the names of the
towns in the Grand Duchy pretty well without an omission.
But, as has been said, this was not what was in his opinion
really necessary and essential for him. From time to time,
when he was inattentive at his lessons, the Schulrat rebuked
him with a reference to his exalted calling. "Your exalted
calling requires you . . ." he would say or: "You owe it
to your exalted calling. . . ." What was his calling, and how
was it exalted? Why did the lackeys smile as if to say,
"The lad that is born to be king," and why was his governess
so much put out when he let himself go a little in speech
or action? He looked round him, and at times, when he
looked steadily and long and forced himself to probe the
essence of the phenomena around him, a dim apprehension
arose in him of the "aloofness" of his position.

He was standing in one of the "gala rooms," the Silver
Hall, in which, as he knew, his father the Grand Duke received solemn deputations—he happened to have wandered
into it by himself and he took stock of his surroundings.

It was winter-time and cold, his little shoes were reflected
in the glass-clear yellow squares of the parquet which spread
like a sheet of ice before him. The ceiling, covered with
silvered arabesque-work, was so high that a long metal shaft
was necessary to allow the many-armed silver chandelier
with its forest of tall white candles to swing in the middle
of the great space. Below the ceiling came silver-framed
coats-of-arms in faded colours. The walls were edged with
silver, and hung with white silk with yellow spots, not to
mention a split here and there. A sort of monumental
baldachin, resting on two strong silver columns and decorated
in front with a silver garland, broken in two places, from
the top of which looked down a portrait of a deceased, pow-
dered ancestress draped in imitation ermine, formed the
chimney-piece. On each side of the fireplace were broad

45

silvered arm-chairs upholstered in torn white silk. On the side walls opposite each other towered enormous silver-framed mirrors, whose glass was covered with blind spots, and on each side of whose broad white marble ledges stood two candelabra which carried big white candles like the sconces on the walls all round, and like the four silver candlesticks which stood in the corners. Before the high windows to the right, looking over the Albrechtsplatz, whose outer ledges were covered with snow, white silk curtains, yellow spotted, with silver cords and trimmed with lace, fell in rich, and heavy folds to the floor. In the middle of the room, under the chandelier, a moderate-sized table, with a pedestal made like a knobby silver tree-stump and a top made of eight triangles of opaque mother-of-pearl, stood useless, as there were no chairs round it, and it could only serve, and be meant to serve, at the very best, as a support for your Highness, when the lackeys opened the doors and ushered in the solemn figures in Court dress who came to present their respects to you. . . .

Klaus Heinrich looked round the hall, and clearly saw that there was nothing here which reminded him of the realities which Schulrat Dröge, for all his bows, was always impressing upon him. Here all was Sunday and solemnity, just as in church, where also he would have felt the calls made on him by his tutor out of place. Everything here was severe and empty show and a formal symmetry, self-sufficient, pointless, and uncomfortable—whose functions were obviously to create an atmosphere of awe and tension, not of freedom and ease, to inculcate an attitude of decorum and discreet self-obliteration towards an unnamed object. And it was cold in the silver hall—cold as in the halls of the snow-king, where the children's hearts froze stiff.

Klaus Heinrich walked over the glassy floor and stood at the table in the middle. He laid his right hand lightly on the mother-of-pearl table, and placed the left hand on his hip, so far behind that it rested almost in the small of his

46

back, and was not visible from in front, for it was an ugly sight, brown and wrinkled, and had not kept pace with the right in its growth. He stood resting on one leg, with the other a little advanced, and kept his eyes fixed on the silver ornaments of the door. It was not the place nor the attitude for dreaming, and yet he dreamed.

He saw his father, and looked at him as he looked at the hall, to try to grasp his meaning. He saw the dull haughtiness of his blue eyes, the furrows which, proudly and morosely, ran from nostril down to his beard, and were often deepened or accentuated by weariness and boredom. . . . Nobody dared to address him or to go freely up to him and speak to him unasked—not even the children: it was forbidden, it was dangerous. He answered, it is true: but he answered distantly and coldly, a look of helplessness, of *gêne,* passed over his face, which Klaus Heinrich was quite able to understand.

Papa made a speech and sent his petitioners away; that is what always happened. He gave an audience at the beginning of the Court ball, and at the end of the dinner with which the winter began. He went with mamma through the rooms and halls, in which the members of the Court were gathered, went through the Marble Hall and the Gala Rooms, through the Picture Gallery, the Hall of the Knights, the Hall of the Twelve Months, the Audience Chamber, and the Ball-room—went not only in a fixed direction, but along a fixed path which bustling Herr von Bühl kept free for him, and addressed a few words to the assembled throng. Whoever was addressed by him bowed low, left a space of parquet between himself and papa, and answered soberly and with signs of gratification. Thereupon papa greeted them over the intervening space, from the stronghold of precise regulations which prescribed the others' movements and warranted his own attitude, greeted them smilingly and lightly and passed on. Smilingly and lightly. . . . Of course, of course, Klaus Heinrich quite understood it, the look of helplessness

47

which passed for one moment over papa's face when anybody was impetuous enough to address him unasked—understood it, and shared his feeling of *gêne!* It wounded something, some soft, virgin envelope of our existence which was so essential to it that we stood helpless when anybody roughly broke through it. And yet it was this same something which made our eyes so dull, and gave us those deep furrows of boredom. . . .

Klaus Heinrich stood and saw—he saw his mother and her beauty, which was famed and extolled far and wide. He saw her standing *en robe de ceremonie,* in front of her great candle-lighted glass, for sometimes, on solemn occasions, he was allowed to be present when the Court hairdresser and the bed-chamber women put the last touches to her toilette. Herr von Knobelsdorff also was present when mamma put on jewels from the Crown regalia, watched and noted down the stones which she decided to use. With all the wrinkles at the corners of his eyes showing, he would make mamma laugh with his droll remarks, so that her soft cheeks filled with lovely little dimples. But her laugh was full of art and grace, and she looked in the glass as she laughed, as if she were practising it.

People said that Slav blood flowed in her veins, and that it was that which gave the sweet radiance to her deep-blue eyes and the night of her raven hair. Klaus Heinrich was like her, so he heard people say, in that he too had steel-blue eyes with dark hair, while Albrecht and Ditlinde were fair, just as papa had been before his hair turned grey. But he was far from handsome, owing to the breadth of his cheek-bones, and especially to his left hand, which mamma was always reminding him to hide adroitly, in the side-pocket of his coat, behind his back, or under the breast of his jacket—especially when his affectionate impulses prompted him to throw both his arms round her. Her look was cold when she bade him mind his hand.

He saw her as she was in the picture in the Marble Hall:

48

in a short silk dress with lace flounces and long gloves, which showed only a glimpse of her ivory arm under her puffed sleeves, a diadem in the night of her hair, her stately form erect, a smile of cool perfection on her strangely hard lips—and behind her the metallic-blue wheel of a peacock's tail. Her face was soft, but its beauty made it stern, and it was easy to see that her heart too was stern and absorbed in her beauty. She slept far into the day when a ball or party was in prospect, and ate only yolks of eggs, so as not to overload herself. Then in the evening she was radiant as she walked on papa's arm along the prescribed path through the halls—grey-haired dignitaries blushed when they were addressed by her, and the *Courier* reported that it was not only because of her exalted rank that her Royal Highness had been the queen of the ball. Yes, people felt happier for the sight of her, whether it was at the Court or outside in the streets, or in the afternoon driving or riding in the park—and their cheeks kindled. Flowers and cheers met her, all hearts went out to her, and it was clear that the people in cheering her were cheering themselves, and that their glad cries meant that they were cheered and elevated by the sight of her. But Klaus Heinrich knew well that mamma had spent long, anxious hours on her beauty, that there was practice and method in her smiles and greetings, and that her own pulse beat never the quicker for anything or anyone.

Did she love anyone—himself, Klaus Heinrich, for instance, for all his likeness to her? Why, of course she did, when she had time to, even when she coldly reminded him of his hand. But it seemed as if she reserved any expression or sign of her tender feelings for occasions when lookers-on were present who were likely to be edified by them. Klaus Heinrich and Ditlinde did not often come into contact with their mother, chiefly because they, unlike Albrecht, the Heir Apparent, for some time past, did not have their meals at their parents' table, but apart with the Swiss

49

governess; and when they were summoned to mamma's boudoir, which happened once a week, the interview consisted in a few casual questions and polite answers—giving no scope for displays of feeling, while its whole drift seemed to be the proper way to sit in an arm-chair with a teacup full of milk.

But at the concerts which took place in the Marble Hall every other Thursday under the name of "The Grand Duchess's Thursdays," and were so arranged that the Court sat at little gilt-legged velvet-covered tables, while the leading tenor Schramm from the Court Theatre, accompanied by an orchestra, sang so lustily that the veins swelled on his bald temples—at the concerts Klaus Heinrich and Ditlinde, in their best clothes, were sometimes allowed in the Hall for one song and the succeeding pause, when mamma showed how fond she was of them, showed it to them and to everybody else in so heartfelt and expressive a way that nobody could have any doubt about it. She summoned them to the table at which she sat, and told them with a happy smile to sit beside her, laid their cheeks on her shoulders or bosom, looked at them with a soft, soulful look in her eyes and kissed them both on forehead and mouth. Then the ladies bent their heads and their eyelids quivered, while the men slowly nodded and bit their lips in order, in manly wise, to restrain their emotions. . . . Yes, it was beautiful, and the children felt they had their share in the effect, which was greater than anything Schramm the singer could procure with his most inspired notes, and nestled close to mamma. For Klaus Heinrich at last realized that it was in the nature of things, no business of ours, to have a simple feeling and to be made happy by it, but that it was our duty to make our tenderness visible to the Hall and to exhibit it, that the hearts of our guests might swell.

Occasionally the people outside in the town and park also were allowed to see that mamma loved us. For while Albrecht drove or rode—bad rider though he was—with the

Grand Duke early in the morning, Klaus Heinrich and Ditlinde had from time to time to take turns at accompanying mamma on her drives, which took place in the spring and autumn at the time of the afternoon promenade, with Baroness von Schulenburg-Tressen in attendance. Klaus Heinrich was a little excited and feverish before these drives, to which unfortunately no enjoyment, but on the contrary a great deal of trouble and effort attached. For, directly the open carriage came out through the Lions Gate on to the Albrechtsplatz, past the grenadiers at the "present," there were a lot of people collected, waiting for it—men, women, and children, who shouted and stared full of curiosity; and that meant pulling oneself together, sitting up erect, smiling, hiding the left hand, and saluting in such a way as to make the people happy. And so it went on right through the city and the fields. Other vehicles were obliged to keep away from ours; the police looked to that. But the foot-passengers stood on the kerb, the women curtseyed, the men took off their hats and looked with eyes full of devotion and importunate curiosity,—and this was the impression Klaus Heinrich got: that they all were there just to be there and to stare, while he was there to show himself and to be stared at; and his was far the harder part. He kept his left hand in his coat-pocket and smiled as mamma wished him to, while he felt that his cheeks were aglow. But the *Courier* reported that the rosy redness of our little duke's cheeks showed what a healthy boy he was.

Klaus Heinrich was thirteen years old when he stood at the solitary mother-of-pearl table in the middle of the cold silver hall, and tried to probe the reality of things around him. And as he scrutinized the various phenomena: the empty, torn pride of the room, aimless and uncomfortable, the symmetry of the white candles, which seemed to express awe and tension and discreet self-obliteration, the passing shadow on his father's face when anybody addressed him unasked, the cool and calculated beauty of his mother, whose

51

one object was admiration, the devoted and importunately curious gaze of the people outside—then a suspicion seized him, a vague and approximate conception of his situation. But simultaneously horror seized him, terror at such a destiny, a dread of his "exalted calling," so strong that he turned round and covered his eyes with both his hands—both, the little wrinkled left one too—and sank down at the lonely table and cried, cried from sympathy with himself and his heart—till they came, and wrung their hands and turned their eyes up to heaven and questioned him, and led him away. . . . He gave out that he had been frightened, and that was quite true.

He had known nothing, understood nothing, suspected nothing of the difficulty and sternness of the life prescribed for him; he had been merry and careless, and had given his guardians many a scare. But there was no resisting the impressions which soon came thronging upon him and forcing him to open his eyes to the real state of things. In the northern suburbs, not far from the spa-gardens, a new road had been opened: people told him that the City Council had decided to call it "Klaus Heinrich Strasse." Once when driving out with his mother and he called at a picture-dealer's, they wanted to buy something. The footman waited at the carriage door, the public gathered round, the picture-dealer bustled about—there was nothing new in all that. But Klaus Heinrich for the first time noticed his photograph in the shop window. It was hanging next those of artists and great men, men with lofty brows, with a look of the loneliness of fame in their eyes.

People were satisfied with him on the whole. He gained dignity with years, and self-possession under the pressure of his exalted calling. But the strange thing was that his longing increased at the same time: that roving inquisitiveness which Schulrat Dröge was not the man to satisfy, and which had impelled him to chat with the lackeys. He had given up doing that; it did not lead to anything. They smiled at him, confirming him by that very laugh in the suspicion that his world of the symmetrically marshalled candles presented an unconscious antithesis to the world outside, but they were no manner of help to him. He looked round about him on the expeditions, in the walks he took through the town gardens with Ditlinde and the Swiss governess, followed by a lackey. He felt that if they were all of one mind to stare at him, while he was all alone and made conspicuous just to be stared at, he also had no share in their being and doing. He realized that they presumably were not always as he saw them, when they stood and greeted him with deferential looks; that it must be his birth and upbringing which made their looks deferential, and that it was with them as with the children when they heard about fairy princes, and were thereby refined and elevated above their work-a-day selves. But he did not know what they looked like and were when they were not refined and elevated above their work-a-day selves—his "exalted calling" concealed this from him, and it was a dangerous and improper wish to allow his heart to be moved by things which his exaltedness concealed from him. And yet he wished it, he wished it from a jealousy and that roving inquisitiveness which sometimes drove him to undertake voyages of exploration into unknown regions of the old Schloss, with Ditlinde his sister, when the opportunity offered.

They called it "rummaging," and great was the charm of "rummaging"; for it was difficult to acquire familiarity with the ground-plan and structure of the old Schloss, and every time they penetrated far enough into the remoter parts they found rooms, closets, and empty halls which they had not yet trodden, or strange round-about ways to already-known rooms. But once when thus wandering about they had a rencontre, an adventure befell them, which made a great impression on Klaus Heinrich, though he did not show it, and opened his eyes.

The opportunity came. While the Swiss governness was

absent on leave to attend the evening service, they had drunk their milk from tea-cups with the Grand Duchess, accompanied by the two ladies-in-waiting, had been dismissed and directed to go back hand-in-hand to their ordinary occupations in the nursery, which lay not far off. It was thought that they needed nobody to go with them; Klaus Heinrich was old enough to take care of Ditlinde, of course. He was; and in the corridor he said: "Yes, Ditlinde, we will certainly go back to the nursery, but we need not go, you know, the shortest, dullest way. We'll rummage a bit first. If you go up one step and follow the corridor as far as where the arches begin, you'll find a hall with pillars behind them, and if you go out of one of the doors of the hall with pillars—clamber up the corkscrew staircase, you come to a room with a wooden roof; and there are lots of funny things lying about there. But I don't know what comes after the room, and that's what we've got to find out. So let's go."

"Yes, let's," said Ditlinde, "but not too far, Klaus Heinrich, and not where it's too dusty, for this dress shows everything.

She was wearing a dress of dark-red velvet, trimmed with satin of the same colour. She had at that time dimples in her elbows, and light golden hair, that curled round her ears like ram's horns. In after years she was pale and thin. She too had the broad, rather over-prominent cheekbones of her father and nation, but they were not accentuated, so that they did not spoil the lines of her face. But with Klaus Heinrich they were strong and emphatic, so that they seemed somewhat to encroach upon, to narrow and to lengthen his steel-coloured eyes. His dark hair was smoothly parted, cut in a careful rectangle on the temples, and brushed straight back from the forehead. He wore an open jacket with a waistcoat buttoning at the throat and a white turn-down collar. In his right hand he held Ditlinde's little hand, but his left arm hung down, with its

54

brown, wrinkled, and undeveloped hand, thin and short from the shoulder. He was glad that he could let it hang without bothering to conceal it; for there was nobody there to stare and to require to be elevated and inspired, and he himself might stare and examine to his heart's content.

So they went and rummaged as they liked. Quiet reigned in the corridors, and they saw hardly a lackey in the distance. They climbed up a staircase and followed the passage till they came to the arches, showing that they were in the part of the Schloss which dated from the time of John the Headstrong and Heinrich the Confessor, as Klaus Heinrich knew and explained. They came to the hall of the pillars, and Klaus Heinrich there whistled several notes close after each other, for the first were still sounding when the last came, and so a clear chord rang under the vaulted ceiling. They scrambled groping and often on hands and knees up the stone winding staircase which opened behind one of the heavy doors, and reached the room with the wooden ceiling, in which there were several strange objects. There were some broken muskets of clumsy size with thickly rusted locks, which had been too bad for the museum, and a discarded throne with torn red velvet cushions, short wide-splayed lion-legs, and cupids hovering over the chair-back, bearing a crown. Then there was a wicked-looking, dusty, cage-like, and horribly interesting thing, which intrigued them much and long. If they were not quite mistaken, it was a rat-trap, for they could see the iron spike to put the bacon on, and it was dreadful to think how the trap-door must fall down behind the great beast. . . . Yes, this took time, and when they stood up after examining the rat-trap their faces were hot, and their clothes stiff with rust and dust. Klaus Heinrich brushed them both down, but that did not do much good, for his hands were as filthy as his clothes. And suddenly they saw that dusk had begun to fall. They must return quickly, Ditlinde insisted anxiously on that; it was too late to go any farther.

"That's an awful pity," said Klaus Heinrich. "Who knows what else we mightn't have found, and when we shall get another chance of rummaging, Ditlinde!" But he followed his sister and they hurried back down the turret-stairs, crossed the hall of the pillars, and came out into the arcade, intending to hurry home hand-in-hand.

Thus they wandered on for a time; but Klaus Heinrich shook his head, for it seemed to him that this was not the way he had come. They went still farther; but several signs told them that they had mistaken their direction. This stone seat with the griffin-heads was not standing here before. That pointed window looked to the west over the low-lying quarter of the town and not over the inner courtyard with the rose-bush. They were going wrong, it was no use denying it; perhaps they had left the hall of the pillars by a wrong exit—anyhow they had absolutely lost their way.

They went back a little, but their disquietude would not allow them to go very far back, so they turned right about again, and decided to push on the way they had already come, and to trust to luck. Their way lay through a damp, stuffy atmosphere, and great undisturbed cobwebs stretched across the corners; they went with heavy hearts, and Ditlinde especially was full of repentance and on the brink of tears. People would notice her absence, would "look sadly" at her, perhaps even tell the Grand Duke; they would never find the way, would be forgotten and die of hunger. And where there was a rat-trap, Klaus Heinrich, there were also rats. . . . Klaus Heinrich comforted her. They only had to find the place where the armour and crossed standards hung; from that point he was quite sure of the direction. And suddenly —they had just passed a bend in the winding passage—suddenly something happened. It startled them dreadfully.

What they had heard was more than the echo of their own steps, they were other, strange steps, heavier than theirs; they came towards them now quickly, now hesitatingly, and were accompanied by a snorting and grumbling which made their

56

blood run cold. Ditlinde made as if to run away from fright: but Klaus Heinrich would not let go her hand, and they stood with starting eyes waiting for what was coming.

It was a man who was just visible in the half-darkness, and, calmly considered, his appearance was not horrifying. He was squat in figure, and dressed like a veteran soldier. He wore a frock-coat of old-fashioned cut, a woollen comforter round his neck and a medal on his breast. He held in one hand a curly top-hat and in the other the bone handle of his clumsily rolled-up umbrella, which he tapped on the flags in time with his steps. His thin grey hair was plastered up from one ear in wisps over his skull. He had bow-shaped black eyebrows, and a yellow-white beard, which grew like the Grand Duke's, heavy upper-lids, and watery blue eyes with pouches of withered skin under them; he had the usual high cheek-bones, and the furrows of his sun-burnt face were like crevasses. When he had come quite close he seemed to recognize the children, for he placed himself against the outer wall of the passage, at once fronted round and began to make a number of bows, consisting of several short forward jerks of his whole body from the feet upwards, while he imparted a look of honesty to his mouth and held his top-hat crown-downwards in front of him. Klaus Heinrich meant to pass him by with a nod, but was surprised into halting, for the veteran began to speak.

"I beg pardon!" he suddenly grunted; then went on in a more natural voice: "I earnestly beg your young Highnesses' pardon! But would your young Highnesses take it amiss if I addressed to them the request that they would very kindly acquaint me with the nearest way to the nearest exit? It need not actually be the Albrechtstor—not in the least necessary that it should be the Albrechtstor. But any exit from the Schloss, if I dare be so free as to address this inquiry to your young Highnesses. . . ."

Klaus Heinrich had laid his left hand on his hip, right behind, so that it lay almost in his back, and looked at the ground. The man had simply spoken to him, had engaged him directly and unavoidably in conversation; he thought of his father and knitted his brows. He pondered feverishly over the question how he ought to behave in this topsy-turvy and incorrect situation. Albrecht would have pursed up his mouth, sucked with his short, rounded under-lip lightly against the upper, and passed on in silence—so much was certain. But what was the use of rummaging if at the first serious adventure one intended to pass on in dignity and dudgeon? And the man was honest, and had nothing wicked about him: that Klaus Heinrich could see when he forced himself to raise his eyes. He simply said: "You come with us, that's the best way. I will willingly show you where you must turn off to get to an exit." And they went on.

"Thanks!" said the man. "Ever so many thanks for your kindness! Heaven knows I should never have thought that I should live to walk about the Old Schloss one day with your young Highnesses. But there it is, and after all my annoyance—for I have been annoyed, terribly annoyed, that's true and certain—after all my annoyance I have at any rate this honour and this satisfaction."

Klaus Heinrich longed to ask what might have been the reason for so much annoyance; but the veteran went straight on (and tapped his umbrella in regular time on the flags as he went). ". . . and I recognized your young Highnesses at once, although it is a bit dark here in the passage, for I have seen you many a time in the carriage, and was always delighted, for I myself have just such a couple of brats at home —I mean to say, mine are brats, mine are . . . and the boy is called Klaus Heinrich too."

"Just like me?" said Klaus Heinrich, overjoyed. . . . "What luck!"

"There's no luck about it," said the man, "considering he was named expressly after you, for he is a couple of months younger than you, and there are lots of children in the town and country who are called that, and all of them after you. No, one can hardly call it luck. . . ."

Klaus Heinrich concealed his hand and remained silent.

"Yes, recognized you at once," said the man. "And I thought, thank Heaven, thought I, that's what I call fortune in misfortune, and they'll help you out of the trap into which you have stuck your nose, you old blockhead, and you've good reason to laugh, thought I, for there's many a one has trudged about here and been guyed by those popinjays, and hasn't got out of it so well. . . ."

Popinjays? thought Klaus Heinrich . . . and guyed? He looked straight in front of him, he did not dare to ask. A fear, a hope struck him. . . . He said quite simply: "They . . . they guyed you?"

"Not half!" said the man. "I should think they did, the ogres, and no mistake! But I don't mind telling your young Highnesses, young though you are, but it'll do you good to hear it, that these people here are a set of wasters. A man comes and delivers his work as respectfully as possible Yes, bless my soul!" he cried suddenly, and tapped his forehead with his hat. "I haven't yet introduced myself to your young Highnesses and told you who I am, have I?—Hinnerke!" he said, "Master-cobbler Hinnerke, Royal warrant-holder, pensioner and medallist." And he pointed with the index-finger of his great, rough, yellow-spotted hand to the medal on his breast. "The fact is, that his Royal Highness, your father, has been graciously pleased to order a pair of boots from me, top-boots, riding-boots, with spurs, and made of the best quality patent-leather. They're my speciality, and I made them myself and took a lot of trouble about them, and they were ready to-day and ever so smart. 'You must go yourself,' says I to myself. . . . I have a boy who delivers, but I says to myself: 'You must go yourself, they are for the Grand Duke.' So I rig myself out and take my boots and go to the Schloss. 'All right,' say the lackeys down below,

59

and want to take them from me. 'No!' say I, for I don't trust them. It's my reputation gets me my orders and my warrant, let me tell your Highnesses, not because I tip the lackeys. But the fellows are spoilt by tips from the warrant-holders, and want to get something out of me for their trouble. 'No,' say I, for I'm not a one for bribing and underhand dealings, 'I'll deliver them myself, and if I can't give them to the Grand Duke himself, I'll give them to Valet Prahl.' They looked daggers, but they say: 'Then you must go up there!' And I go up there. There are some more of them up there, and they say 'All right!' and want to take charge of the boots, but I ask for Prahl and stick to it. They say: 'He's having his tea,' but I'm determined and say, 'Then I'll wait till he's finished.' And just as I say it, who comes by in his buckled shoes but Valet Prahl. And he sees me, and I give him the boots with a few modest words, and he says 'All right!' and actually adds: 'They're fine!' and nods and takes them off. Now I'm satisfied, for Prahl, he's safe, so off I go. 'Hi!' cries somebody. 'Mr. Hinnerke! You're going wrong!' 'Damn!' says I, and right about, and go off in the other direction. But that was the stupidest thing I could do, for they had sent me to Jericho, and that's just where I don't want to go. I walk on a bit and meet another one, and ask him the way to the Albrechtstor. But he spots at once what's up, and says: 'Go up the stairs, and then keep to the left and then down again, and you'll cut off a large corner!' And I believe he means it kindly and do what he says, and get more and more muddled and altogether lose my bearings. Then I see that it's not my fault, but the rogues', and it strikes me that I have heard that they often play that trick on Court tradesmen who don't tip them, and let them wander about till they sweat. And my fury makes me blind and stupid, and I get to places where there's not a living soul, and don't know where I am and get properly put about. And at last I meet your young Highnesses. Yes, that's how it is with me and my boots!" ended Shoemaker Hinnerke, and wiped his forehead with the back of his hand.

Klaus Heinrich squeezed Ditlinde's hand. His heart beat so loud that he absolutely forgot to hide his left hand. That was it. That was a touch of it, an outline! No doubt about it, that was the sort of thing his "exalted calling" shielded him from, the sort of thing people did when they were in the ordinary, work-a-day frame of mind. The lackeys. . . . He said nothing, words failed him.

"I see that your young Highnesses don't answer," said the shoemaker. And his honest voice was filled with emotion. "I oughtn't to have told you, because it isn't your business to get to know all the wickedness that goes on. But yet I don't know," he said, laid his head on one side and snapped his fingers, "that it can do any harm, that it can do you any harm for the future and later on. . . ."

"The lackeys . . ." said Klaus Heinrich, and took a plunge . . . "are they wicked? I can quite well fancy . . ."

"Wicked?" said the cobbler. "Good-for-nothings they are. That's the name for them. Do you know what they're good for? They keep the goods back when no tip's forthcoming, keep them back when the tradesman delivers them punctually at the time ordered, and only hand them over days late, so that the tradesman gets blamed, and is considered by the Grand Duke to have failed in his duty and he loses his orders. That's what they do without scruple, and the whole town knows it. . . ."

"That's most annoying!" said Klaus Heinrich. He listened, listened. He hardly realized how much shocked he was. "Do they do anything else?" he said. "I'm quite sure they must do other things of the same kind."

"You bet!" said the man, and laughed. "No, they don't miss a chance, let me tell your Highnesses, they have all sorts of dodges. There's the door-opening joke, for instance. . . . That's like this. Your father, our gracious Grand Duke,

61

grants an audience to somebody, let's suppose he's a new hand
and it's his first time at Court. And he comes in a frock
coat all sweat and shivers, for it is of course no trifle to stand
before his Royal Highness for the first time. And the lackeys
laugh at him, because they're quite at home here, and tow
him into the ante-room, and he doesn't know where he is,
and absolutely forgets to tip the lackeys. But then comes
his moment, and the adjutant says his name, and the lackeys
throw open the double-doors and let him into the room in
which the Grand Duke is waiting. Then the new hand stands
there and bows and says what he has to say, and the Grand
Duke graciously gives him his hand, and so he is dismissed
and walks backwards, and thinks the folding-doors are going
to open behind him, as he has been definitely promised. But
they don't open, I tell your Highnesses, for the lackeys have
got their knife into him, because they haven't been tipped,
and don't stir a finger for him outside there. But he daren't
turn round, absolutely daren't, because he daren't show the
Grand Duke his back, that would be grossly bad manners and
an insult to his Highness. And then he feels behind him for
the door-handle and can't find it, and gets the jumps and
scrabbles around on the door, and when at last by the mercy
of Providence he finds the knob it's an old-fashioned lock,
and he doesn't understand it and fiddles and dislocates his
arm and tires himself out and keeps bowing all the time in
his agitation, until at last his Highness graciously lets him
out with his own hand. Yes, that's the door-opening joke!
But that's nothing to what I'm going to tell your Highness. . . ."

They had been so deep in conversation that they had
scarcely noticed where they were going, had gone down the
stairs and reached the ground-floor, close to the Albrechtstor.
Eiermann, one of the Grand Duchess's grooms-of-the-chamber,
came towards them. He wore a violet coat and side-whiskers.
He had been sent out to look for their Grand Ducal Highnesses. He shook his head while still at a distance, in lively

concern, and pursed his mouth up like a funnel. But when he noticed Shoemaker Hinnerke walking with the children and tapping with his umbrella, all the muscles of his face relaxed and his jaw dropped.

There was scarcely time for thanks and farewells, Eiermann was in such a hurry to part the children from the shoemaker. And with many a gloomy prophecy he led their Grand Ducal Highnesses up to their room to the Swiss governess.

Eyes were turned to heaven, hands were wrung about their absence and the state of their clothes. The worst of all happened, they were "looked at sadly." But Klaus Heinrich confined his contrition to the bare minimum. He thought: "So the lackeys took money and let the tradesmen wander about the corridors if they did not get any, kept the goods back, that the tradesmen might get blamed, and did not open the folding-doors, so that the suitor had to scrabble. That's what happened in the Schloss, and what must it be outside? Outside among the people who stared at him so respectfully and so strangely, when he drove by with his hand to his hat . . . ? But how had the man dared to tell it him? Not one single time had he called him Grand Ducal Highness; he had forced himself on him and offended his birth and upbringing. And yet, why was it so extraordinarily pleasant to hear all that about the lackeys? Why did his heart beat with such rapt pleasure, when moved by some of the wild and bold things in which his Highness bore no part?"

## IV

## DOCTOR UEBERBEIN

KLAUS HEINRICH spent three of his boyhood's years in the company of boys of his own age of the Court and country nobility of the monarchy in an institution, a kind of aristocratic seminary, which von Knobelsdorff, the House Minister, had founded and set in order on his behalf in the "Pheasantry" hunting-schloss.

A Crown property for centuries past, Schloss "Pheasantry" gave its name to the first stopping-place of a State railway running north-west from the capital, and itself took it from a "tame" pheasant preserve, situated not far off among the meadows and woods, which had been the hobby of a former ruler. The Schloss, a one-storied box-like country house with a shingle roof topped by lightning conductors, stood with stables and coach-house on the skirts of extensive fir plantations. With a row of aged lime trees in front, it looked out over a broad expanse of meadowland fringed by a distant bluish circle of woods and intersected by paths, with many a bare patch of play-ground and hurdles for obstacle riding. Opposite the corner of the Schloss was a refreshment pavilion, a beer and coffee garden planted with high trees, which a prudent man called Stavenüter had rented and which was thronged on Sundays in summer by excursionists, especially bicyclists, from the capital. The pupils of the "Pheasantry" were only allowed to visit the pavilion in charge of a tutor.

There were five of them, not counting Klaus Heinrich: Trümmerhauff, Gumplach, Platow, Prenzlau, and Wehrzahn. They were called "the Pheasants" in the country round. They

64

had a landau from the Court stables which had seen its best days, a dog-cart, a sledge, and a few hacks, and when in winter some of the meadows were flooded and frozen over, they had an opportunity of skating. There was one cook, two chamber-maids, one coachman, and two lackeys at the "Pheasantry," one of whom could drive at a pinch.

Professor Kürtchen, a little suspicious and irritable bachelor with the airs of a comic actor and the manners of an old French chevalier, was head of the seminary. He wore a stubby grey moustache, a pair of gold spectacles in front of his restless brown eyes, and always out-of-doors a top hat on the back of his head. He stuck his belly out as he walked and held his little fists on each side of his stomach like a long-distance runner. He treated Klaus Heinrich with self-satisfied tact, but was full of suspicion of the noble arrogance of his other pupils and fired up like a tom-cat when he scented any signs of contempt for him as a commoner. He loved when out for a walk, if there were people close by, to stop and gather his pupils in a knot around him and explain something to them, drawing diagrams in the sand with his stick. He addressed Frau Amelung, the housekeeper, a captain's widow who smelt strongly of drugs, as "my lady" and showed thus that he knew what was what in the best circles.

Professor Kürtchen was helped by a yet younger assistant teacher with a doctor's degree—a good-humoured, energetic man, bumptious but enthusiastic, who influenced Klaus Heinrich's views and conscience perhaps more than was good for him. A gymnastic instructor called Zotte had also been appointed. The assistant teacher, it may be remarked in passing, was called Ueberbein, Raoul Ueberbein. The rest of the staff came every day by railway from the capital.

Klaus Heinrich remarked with appreciation that the demands made on him from the point of view of learning quickly abated. Schulrat Dröge's wrinkled fore-finger no longer paused on the lines, he had done his work; and during

65

the lessons as well as while correcting his written work Professor Kürtchen seized every opportunity of showing his tact.

One day, quite soon after the institution had started—it was after luncheon in the high-windowed dining-room—he summoned Klaus Heinrich into his study, and said in so many words: "It is contrary to the public interest that your Grand Ducal Highness, during our scientific studies together, should be compelled to answer questions which are at the moment unwelcome to you. On the other hand, it is desirable that your Grand Ducal Highness should continually announce your readiness to answer by holding up your hand. I beg your Grand Ducal Highness accordingly, for my own information, in the case of unwelcome questions, to stretch out your arm to its full length, but in the case of those an invitation to answer which would be agreeable to you, to raise it only half way and in a right angle."

As for Doctor Ueberbein, he filled the schoolroom with a noisy flow of words, whose cheerfulness disguised the teacher's object without losing sight of it altogether. He had come to no sort of understanding with Klaus Heinrich, but questioned him when it occurred to him to do so, in a free and friendly way without causing him any embarrassment. And Klaus Heinrich's by no means apropos answers seemed to enchant Doctor Ueberbein, to inspire him with warm enthusiasm. "Ha, ha," he would cry and throw his head back laughing. "Oh, Klaus Heinrich! Oh, scion of princes! Oh, your innocency! The crude problems of life have caught you unprepared! Now then, it is for me with my experience to put you straight." And he gave the answer himself, asked nobody else, when Klaus Heinrich had answered wrong. The mode of instruction of the other teachers bore the character of an unassuming lecture. And gymnastic-instructor Zotte had received orders from high quarters to conduct the physical exercises with every regard to Klaus Heinrich's left hand —so strictly that the attention of the Prince himself or of his companions should never be drawn unnecessarily to his little failing. So the exercises were limited to running games, and during the riding lessons, which Herr Zotte also gave, all feats of daring were rigorously excluded.

Klaus Heinrich's relations with his comrades were not what one might call intimate, they did not extend to actual familiarity. He stood for himself, was never one of them, by no means counted amongst their number. They were five and he was one; the Prince, the five, and the teachers, that was the establishment. Several things stood in the way of a free friendship. The five were there on Klaus Heinrich's account, they were ordered to associate with him; when during the lessons he answered wrong they were not asked to correct him, they had to adjust themselves to his capacity when riding or playing. They were too often reminded of the advantages they gained by being allowed to share his life. Some of them, the young von Gumplach, von Platow, and von Wehrzahn, sons of country squires of moderate means, were oppressed the whole time by the gratified pride their parents had shown when the invitation from the House Minister reached them, by the congratulations which had poured in from every side.

Count Prenzlau on the other hand, that thick-set, red-haired, freckled youth with the breathless way of speaking and the Christian name Bogumil, was a sprig of the richest and noblest family of landowners in the land, spoilt and self-conscious. He was well aware that his parents had not been able to refuse Baron von Knobelsdorff's invitation, but that it had not seemed to them by any means a blessing from the clouds, and that he, Count Bogumil, could have lived much better and more in accordance with his position on his father's property than at the "Pheasantry." He found the hacks bad, the landau shabby, and the dog-cart old-fashioned; he grumbled privately over the food.

Dagobert Count Trümmerhauff, a spare, greyhound-looking youth, who spoke in a whisper, was inseparable from him. They had a word among themselves which fully expressed their critical and aristocratic bent, and which they constantly

67

uttered in a biting tone of voice: "hog-wash." It was hog-wash to have loose collars buttoning on to one's shirt. It was hog-wash to play lawn-tennis in one's ordinary clothes.

But Klaus Heinrich felt himself unequal to using the word. He had not hitherto been aware that there were such things as shirts with collars sewed on to them and that people could possess so many changes of clothes at one time as Bogumil Prenzlau. He would have liked to say "hog-wash," but it occurred to him that he was wearing at that very time darned socks. He felt inelegant by the side of Prenzlau and coarse compared with Trümmerhauff. Trümmerhauf had the nobility of a wild beast. He had a long pointed nose with a sharp bridge and broad, quivering, thin-walled nostrils, blue veins on his delicate temples and small ears without lobes. He wore broad coloured cuffs fastened with gold links, and his hands were like those of a dainty woman, with filbert nails; a gold bracelet adorned one of his wrists. He half closed his eyes as he whispered. . . . No, it was obvious that Klaus Heinrich could not compete with Trümmerhauff in elegance. His right hand was rather broad, he had cheek bones like the men in the street, and he looked quite stumpy by Dagobert's side. It was quite possible that Albrecht might have been better qualified to join the "Pheasants" in their use of "hog-wash." Klaus Heinrich for his part was no aristocrat, absolutely none, unmistakable facts showed that. For consider his name, Klaus Heinrich, that's what the shoemaker's sons were called all over the place. Herr Stavenüter's children over the road too, who blew their noses with their fingers, bore the same names as himself, his parents, and his brother. But the lordlings were called Bogumil and Dagobert—Klaus Heinrich stood solitary and alone among the five.

However, he formed one friendship at the "Pheasantry," and it was with Doctor Ueberbein. The Usher Raoul Ueberbein was not a handsome man. He had a red beard and a greenish-white complexion with watery blue eyes, thin red hair, and unusually ugly, protruding, sharp-pointed ears.

But his hands were small and delicate. He wore white ties exclusively, which gave him rather a distinguished appearance, although his wardrobe was scanty. He wore a long great-coat out-of-doors, and when riding—for Dr. Ueberbein rode, and excellently well too—a worn-out frock-coat whose skirts he fastened up with safety-pins, tight buttoned breeches, and a high hat.

Where lay the attraction he exercised on Klaus Heinrich? That attraction was very composite. The "Pheasants" had not been long together before a report went about that the usher had dragged a child a long time ago, in circumstances of extreme peril, out of a swamp or bog, and was the possessor of a medal for saving life. That was one impression. Later other details of Doctor Ueberbein's life came to be known, and Klaus Heinrich too heard of them. It was said that his origin was obscure, that he had no father, his mother had been an actress who had paid some poor people to adopt him, and that he had once been starved, which accounted for the greenish tint of his complexion. These were things which did not bear being brought into the light or even being thought of, wild, remote things, to which, however, Doctor Ueberbein himself sometimes alluded—when, for instance, the lordlings, who could not forget his obscure origin, behaved impudently or unbecomingly towards him.

"Suck-a-thumbs and mammy's darlings!" he would say then in loud dudgeon. "I've knocked about long enough to deserve some respect from you young gentlemen!" This fact too, that Doctor Ueberbein had "knocked about," did not fail of effect on Klaus Heinrich. But the especial charm of the doctor's person lay in the directness of his attitude towards Klaus Heinrich, the tone in which he addressed him from the very beginning, and which distinguished him clearly from everybody else. There was nothing about him which reminded one of the stiff reticence of the lackeys, of the governess's pale horror, of Schulrat Dröge's professional bows, or of Professor Kürtchen's self-satisfied deference. There

69

was nothing about him to recall the strange, loyal, and yet impertinent way in which people outside stared at Klaus Heinrich.

During the first few days after the seminary assembled, he kept silence and confined himself to observation, but then he approached the Prince with a jovial and cheery frankness, a fresh fatherly camaraderie such as Klaus Heinrich had never before experienced. It disturbed him at first, he looked in terror at the doctor's green face; but his confusion found no echo in the doctor, and in no way discouraged him, it confirmed him in his hearty bumptious ingenuousness, and it was not long before Klaus Heinrich was warmed and won, for there was nothing vulgar, nothing degrading, not even anything designed and school-masterish in Doctor Ueberbein's methods—all they showed was the superiority of a man who had knocked about the world, and, at the same time, his tender and open respect for Klaus Heinrich's different birth and position; they showed affection and recognition, at the same time as the cheerful offer of a league between their two different kinds of existence. He called him "Highness" once or twice, then simply "Prince," then quite simply "Klaus Heinrich." And he stuck to the last.

When the "Pheasants" went out for a ride, these two rode at the head, the doctor on his stout piebald to the left of Klaus Heinrich on his docile chestnut—trotted when snow or leaves were falling, through springtime thaws or summer heat, along the edge of the woodlands across country, or through the villages, while Doctor Ueberbein related anecdotes of his life. Raoul Ueberbein sounds funny, doesn't it? The very reverse of *chic*. Yes, Ueberbein had been the name of his adoptive parents, a poor, oldish couple of the inferior bank-clerk class, and he had a quite legal right to it. But that he should be called Raoul had been the decision and mandate of his mother, when she handed over the sum agreed on, together with his fateful little person, to the others—a sentimental decision obviously, a decision prompted by piety.

At least it was quite possible that his legal and real father had been called Raoul, and it was to be hoped that his surname had been something which harmonized with it.

For the rest, it had been rather a wild undertaking on the part of his adoptive parents to adopt a child, for "Barmecide had been cook" in the Ueberbein establishment, and it was obvious that it had been only the most urgent necessity which had made them jump at the money. The boy had been given only the scantiest of school educations, but he had taken the liberty of showing what he was made of, had distinguished himself to some extent, and as he was keen to become a teacher, he had been granted out of a public fund the means of obtaining a college education. Well, he had finished his college course not without distinction, as indeed it was expected of him that he should, and he had then been appointed a teacher in a public elementary school, with a good salary, out of which he had managed to give occasional doles by way of gratitude to his honest adoptive parents, until they died almost simultaneously. And a happy release it was for them!

And so he had been left alone in the world, his very birth a misfortune, as poor as a sparrow and endowed by Providence with a green face and dog's ears by way of personal recommendations. Attractive qualifications, were they not? But such qualifications were really favourable ones—once for all, so they proved. A miserable boyhood, loneliness and exclusion from good fortune and all that good fortune brings, a never-ceasing, imperious call to be up and doing, no fear of getting fat and lazy, one's moral fibre was braced, one could never rest on one's oars, but must be always overhauling and passing others. Could anything be more stimulating, when the hard facts were brought home to one? What a handicap over others who "were not obliged to" to the same extent! People who could smoke cigars in the morning. . . .

At that time, by the bedside of one of his unwashed little pupils, in a room which did not smell exactly of spring blos-
71

soms, Raoul Ueberbein had made friends with a young man —some years older than he, but in a similar position and like him ill-fated by birth in so far as he was a Jew. Klaus Heinrich knew him—indeed, he might be said to have got to know him on a very intimate occasion. Sammet was his name, a doctor of medicine; he happened by chance to have been in the Grimmburg when Klaus Heinrich was born, and had set up a couple of years later in the capital as a children's doctor. Well, he had been a friend of Ueberbein's, still was one, and they had had many a good talk about fate and duty. What is more, they had both knocked about the world.

Ueberbein, for his part, looked back with sincere pleasure to the time when he had been an elementary teacher. His activities had not been entirely confined to the class-room, he had amused himself by showing also some personal and human concern for his charges' welfare, by visiting them at home, by sharing at times their not too idyllic family life, and in doing so he did not fail to bring away impressions of a most varied kind. In truth, if he had not already tasted the bitterness of the cup of life, he would have had plenty of opportunity then to do so. For the rest, he had not ceased to work by himself, had given private lessons to plump tradesmen's sons, and tightened his waist belt so as to save enough to buy books with—had spent the long, still, and free nights in study. And one day he had passed the State examination with exceptional distinction, had soon received his promotion, had been transferred to a grammar school. As a matter of fact, it had been a sore grief to him to leave his little charges, but so the fates willed. And then it had so happened that he had been chosen to be usher at the "Pheasantry," for all that his very birth had been a misfortune.

That was Doctor Ueberbein's story, and Klaus Heinrich, as he listened to it, was filled with friendly feelings. He shared his contempt for those who "weren't obliged to" and smoked cigars in the morning, he felt a fearful joy when Ueberbein

72

talked in his jolly blustering way about "knocking about," "impressions," and the bitterness of the cup of life, and he felt as if he had been personally an actor in the scenes as he followed his luckless and gallant career from his adoption up to his appointment as grammar-schoolmaster. He felt as if he were in some general sort of way qualified to take part in a conversation about fate and duty. His attitude of reserve relaxed, the experiences of his own fifteen years of life came crowding in upon him, he felt a longing himself to retail confidences, and he tried to tell Doctor Ueberbein all about himself.

But the funny thing was that Doctor Ueberbein himself checked him, opposed any such intention most decidedly. "No, no, Klaus Heinrich," he said; "full stop there! No confidences, if you please! Not but that I know that you have all sorts of things to tell me. . . . I need only watch you for half a day to see that, but you quite misunderstand me if you think I'm likely to encourage you to weep round my neck. In the first place, sooner or later you'd repent it. But in the second, the pleasures of a confidential intimacy are not for the likes of you. You see, there's no harm in my chattering. What am I? An usher. Not a common or garden one, in my own opinion, but still no better than such. Just a categorical unit. But you? What are you? That's harder to say. . . . Let's say a conception, a kind of ideal. A frame. An emblematical existence, Klaus Heinrich, and at the same time a formal existence. But formality and intimacy—haven't you yet learnt that the two are mutually exclusive? Absolutely exclusive. You have no right to intimate confidences, and if you attempted them you yourself would discover that they did not suit you, would find them inadequate and insipid. I must remind you of your duty, Klaus Heinrich."

Klaus Heinrich laughed and saluted with his crop, and on they rode.

On another occasion Doctor Ueberbein said casually:

"Popularity is a not very profound, but a grand and comprehensive kind of familiarity." And that was all he said on the subject.

Sometimes in summer, during the long intervals between the morning lessons, they would sit together in the empty pavilion, or stroll about the "Pheasants" playground, discussing various topics, and breaking off to drink lemonade provided by Herr Stavenüter. Herr Stavenüter beamed as he wiped the rough table and brought the lemonade with his own hands. The glass ball in the bottle-neck had to be pushed in. "Sound stuff!" said Herr Stavenüter. "The best that can be got. No muck, Grand Ducal Highness, and you, doctor, but just sweetened fruit-juice. I can honestly recommend it!"

Then he made his children sing in honour of the visit. There were three of them, two girls and a boy, and they could sing trios. They stood some way off with the green leaves of the chestnut trees for roof, and sang folk-songs while they blew their noses with their fingers. Once they sang a song beginning: "We are all but mortal men," and Doctor Ueberbein took advantage of the pauses to express his disapproval of this number on the programme. "A paltry song," he said, and leaned over towards Klaus Heinrich. "A really commonplace song, a lazy song, Klaus Heinrich; you must not let it appeal to you."

Later, when the children had stopped singing, he returned to the song and described it as "sloppy." "We are all but mortal men," he repeated. "God bless us, yes, no doubt we are. But on the other hand we ought perhaps to remember that it is those of us who count for most who may be the occasion for especially emphasizing this truth. . . . Look you," he said, leaning back and crossing one leg over the other, while he stroked his beard up from underneath his chin, "look you, Klaus Heinrich, a man who has my intellectual aspirations will not be able to help searching for and clinging to whatever is out of the ordinary in this drab world of ours, wherever and however it appears—he cannot help

74

being put out by such a slovenly song, by such a sheepish abjuration of the exceptional, of the lofty and of the miserable, and of that which is both at once. You may well say: 'That's talking for effect.' I'm only an usher, but there's something in my blood, Heaven knows what—I can't find any pleasure in emphasizing the fact that we are all ushers at bottom. I love the extraordinary in every form and in every sense. I love those who are conscious of the dignity of their exceptional station, the marked men, those one can see are not as other men, all those whom the people stare at open-mouthed—I hope they'll appreciate their destiny, and I do not wish them to make themselves comfortable with the slip-shod and luke-warm truth which we have just heard set to music for three voices. Why have I become your tutor, Klaus Heinrich? I am a gipsy, a hard-working one, maybe, but still a born gipsy. My predestination to the rôle of squire of princes is not particularly obvious. Why did I gladly obey the call when it came to me, in view of my energy, and although my very birth was a misfortune? Because, Klaus Heinrich, I see in your existence the clearest, most express, and best-preserved form of the extraordinary in the world. I have become your tutor that I might keep your destiny alive in you. Reserve, etiquette, obligation, duty, demeanour, formality—has the man whose life is surrounded by these no right to despise others? Ought he to allow himself to be reminded of humanity and good nature? No, come along, let's go, Klaus Heinrich, if you don't mind. They're tactless brats, these little Stavenüters." Klaus Heinrich laughed, he gave the children some of his pocket-money, and they went.

"Yes, yes," said Doctor Ueberbein in the course of an ordinary walk in the woods to Klaus Heinrich—they had drifted a little distance away from the five "Pheasants"— "nowadays the soul's thirst for veneration has to be satisfied with what it can get. Where will you find greatness? I only hope you may! But quite apart from all actual greatness and high-calling, there is always what I call Highness, select and sadly isolated forms of life, towards which an attitude of the tenderest sympathy should be adopted. For the rest, greatness is strong, it wears jack-boots, it has no need of the knight-services of the mind. But Highness is affecting—damme if it isn't the most affecting thing on earth."

Once or twice a year the "Pheasantry" journeyed to the capital to attend performances of classical operas and dramas in the Grand Ducal Court Theatre; Klaus Heinrich's birthday in particular was the signal for a visit to the theatre. He would then sit quietly in his carved arm-chair, leaning against the red plush ledge of the Court box, whose roof rested on the heads of two female figures with crossed hands and empty stern faces, and watched his colleagues, the princes, whose destinies were played out on the stage, while he stood the fire of the opera-glasses which from time to time, even during the play, were directed at him from the audience. Professor Kürtchen sat on his left hand and Doctor Ueberbein with the "Pheasants" in an adjoining box.

Once they heard the "Magic Flute," and on the way home to "Pheasantry" station, in the first-class carriage, Doctor Ueberbein made the whole collection of them laugh by imitating the way in which singers talk when their rôles oblige them to talk in prose. "He is a prince!" he said with pathos, and answered himself in a drawly, sing-song parsonical voice. "He is more than that, he is a man!" Even Professor Kürtchen was so much amused that he bleated.

But next day, in the course of a private lesson in Klaus Heinrich's study, with the round mahogany table, whitened ceiling, and Greek bust on the stove, Doctor Ueberbein repeated his parody, and said then: "Great heavens, that was something new in its time, it was a piece of news, a startling truth! There are paradoxes which have stood so long on their heads that one has to put them on their feet to make anything even moderately daring out of them. 'He is a man. He is more than that'—that is getting gradually bolder, pret-

76

tier, even truer. The converse is mere humanity, but I have no hearty love for humanity, I'm quite content to leave it out of account. One must, in a certain sense, be one of those of whom the people say: 'They are, after all, mortal men too'—or one is as deadly dull as an usher. I cannot honestly wish for the general comfortable obliteration of conflicts and gulfs, that's the way I am made, for better or worse, and the idea of the *principe uomo* is to me, to speak plainly, an abomination. I am not anxious that it should particularly appeal to you. . . . Look you, there have always been princes and exceptional persons who live their life of exception with a light heart, simply unconscious of their dignity or denying it outright, and capable of playing skittles with the townsfolk in their shirt-sleeves, without the slightest attempt at an inward qualm. But they are not very important, just as nothing is important which lacks mind. For mind, Klaus Heinrich, mind is the tutor which insists inexorably on dignity, indeed actually creates dignity, it is the arch-enemy and chief antagonist of all human good nature. 'More than that?' No! to be a representative, to stand for a number when one appears to be the exalted and refined expression of a multitude. Representing is naturally something more and higher than simply Being, Klaus Heinrich—and that's why people call you Highness."

So argued Doctor Ueberbein, in loud, hearty, and fluent terms, and what he said influenced Klaus Heinrich's mind and susceptibilities more, perhaps, than was desirable. The prince was then about fifteen years old, and therefore quite competent, if not properly to understand, yet to imbibe the essence of ideas of that sort. The main point was that Doctor Ueberbein's doctrines and apophthegms were so exceptionally supported by his personality.

When Schulrat Dröge, the man who used to bow to the lackeys, reminded Klaus Heinrich of his "exalted calling," that was nothing more than an exaggerated form of speech, devoid of inner meaning and calculated mainly to add em-

phasis to his professional claims. But when Doctor Ueberbein, whose very birth had been a misfortune, as he said,
and who had a green complexion because he had been half
starved; when this man who had dragged a child out of a
bog, who had received "impressions" and "knocked about"
in all sorts of ways; when he who not only did not bow to
the lackeys, but who bawled at them in strident tones when
the fancy took him, and who had called Klaus Heinrich himself straight out by his Christian names when he had known
him only three days, without asking leave to do so,—when he
with a paternal laugh declared that Klaus Heinrich's "path
lay among the heights of mankind" (a favourite expression
of his), the effect was a feeling of freedom and originality
which awoke an echo deep down in the prince's soul.

When Klaus Heinrich listened to the doctor's loud and jolly
anecdotes of his life, of the "bitterness of the cup of life,"
he felt as he used to when he went rummaging with Ditlinde
his sister, and that the man who could tell such anecdotes,
that this "rolling stone," as he called himself, did not, like
the others, adopt a reserved and deferential attitude towards
him, but, without prejudice to a free and cheerful homage,
treated him as a comrade in fate and destiny, warmed Klaus
Heinrich's heart to inexpressible gratitude and completed the
charm which bound him to the usher for ever. . . .

Shortly after his sixteenth birthday (Albrecht, the Heir
Apparent, was at the time in the South for his health) the
Prince was confirmed, together with the five "Pheasants," in
the Court Church. The *Courier* reported the fact without
making any sensation of it. Dom Wislezenus, the President
of the High Consistory, treated a Bible text in counterpoint,
this time to the choice of the Grand Duke, and Klaus Heinrich was on this occasion gazetted a Lieutenant, although he
had not the foggiest notion of things military. . . . His existence was becoming more and more barren of *expertise*.
The ceremonial of the confirmation also lacked incisive sig-

nificance, and the Prince returned immediately afterwards quietly back to the "Pheasantry" to continue his life amongst his tutors and schoolfellows without any alteration.

It was not till one year later that he left his old-fashioned homely schoolroom with the torso on the stove; the seminary was broken up, and while his five noble comrades were transferred to the Corps of Cadets, Klaus Heinrich again took up his abode in the Old Schloss, intending, in accordance with an agreement which Herr von Knobelsdorff had come to with the Grand Duke, to spend a year at the upper gymnasium classes in the capital. This was a well-calculated and popular step, which however did not make much difference from the point of view of *expertise*. Professor Kürtchen had gone back to his post at the public academy, he instructed Klaus Heinrich as before in several branches of knowledge, and showed even greater zeal than he had at the seminary, being determined to let everybody see how tactful he was. It also appeared that he had told the rest of the staff of the agreement reached with regard to the two ways in which the Prince should announce his feelings with regard to answering a question.

As to Doctor Ueberbein, who had also returned to the academy, he had not yet advanced so far in his unusual career as to teach the highest class. But at Klaus Heinrich's lively, even insistent request, preferred by him to the Grand Duke, not by word of mouth but by official channels, so to speak, through the benevolent Herr von Knobelsdorff, the usher was appointed tutor and superintendent of home studies, came daily to the Schloss, bawled at the lackeys, and had every opportunity of working on the Prince with his intellectual and enthusiastic talk. Perhaps it was partly the fault of this influence that Klaus Heinrich's relations with the young people with whom he shared the much-hacked school-benches continued even looser and more distant than his connexion

79

with the five at the "Pheasantry"; and if thus the popularity which this year was intended to secure was not attained, the intervals, which both in summer and in winter were spent by all the scholars in the roomy paved courtyard, offered opportunities for camaraderie.

But these intervals, intended to refresh the ordinary scholars, brought with them for Klaus Heinrich the first actual effort of the kind of which his life was to be full. He was naturally, at least during the first term, the cynosure of every eye in the play-ground—no easy matter for him, in view of the fact that here the surroundings deprived him of every external support and attribute of dignity, and he was obliged to play on the same pavement as those whose common idea was to stare at him. The little boys, full of childlike irresponsibility, hung about close to him and gaped, while the bigger ones hovered around with wide-open eyes and looked at him out of the corners of them or from under their eyelids. . . . The excitement dwindled in course of time, but even then— whether the fault was Klaus Heinrich's or the others'—even later the camaraderie somehow did not make much progress. One might see the prince, on the right of the head master or the usher-in-charge, followed and surrounded by the curious, strolling up and down the courtyard. One could see him, too, chatting with his schoolfellows.

What a charming sight it was! There he leaned, half-sitting on the slope of the glazed-brick wall, with his feet crossed, and his left hand thrust far behind on his hips, with the fifteen members of the first class in a half-circle round him. There were only fifteen this year, for the last promotions had been made with the object in view that the select should contain no elements which were unfitted by origin or personality to be for a year on Christian-name terms with Klaus Heinrich. For the use of Christian names was ordered. Klaus Heinrich conversed with one of them, who had advanced a little towards him out of the semicircle, and answered him

80

with little short bows. Both laughed, everybody laughed directly they began to talk to Klaus Heinrich. He asked him for instance: "Have you yet done your German essay for next Tuesday?"

"No, Prince Klaus Heinrich, not quite yet; I haven't yet done the last part."

"It's a difficult subject. I haven't any idea yet what to write."

"Oh, your Highness will. . . . You'll soon think of something!"

"No, it's difficult. . . . You got an alpha in arithmetic, didn't you?"

"Yes, Prince Klaus Heinrich, I was lucky."

"No, you deserved it. I shall never be able to make anything of it!"

Murmurs of amusement and gratification in the semicircle. Klaus Heinrich turned to another schoolfellow, and the first stepped quickly back. Everybody felt that the really important point was not the essay nor the arithmetic, but the conversation as an event and an undertaking, one's attitude and tone, the way one advanced or retired, the success with which one assumed a sympathetic, self-collected, and refined demeanour. Perhaps it was the consciousness of this which brought the smile to everybody's lips.

Sometimes, when he had the semicircle in front of him, Klaus Heinrich would say some such words as "Professor Nicolovius looks an owl."

Great then was the merriment among the others. Such a remark was the signal for general unbending, they kicked over the traces, "Ho, ho, ho!" 'd in chorus in their newly cracked voices, and one would declare Klaus Heinrich to be a "ripping chap." But Klaus Heinrich did not often say such things, he only said them when he saw the smile on the others' faces grow faint and wan, and signs of boredom or even of impatience showing themselves; he said them by way

81

of cheering them up, and at the extravagant laughter by which they were followed he wore a look half of curiosity, half of dismay.

It was not Anselm Schickedanz who called him a "ripping chap," and yet it was directly on his account that Klaus Heinrich had compared Professor Nicolovius to an owl. Anselm Schickedanz had laughed like the others at the joke, but not in quite the same approving way, but with an intonation which implied, "Gracious heavens!" He was a dark boy, with narrow hips, who enjoyed the reputation throughout the school of being a devil of a chap. The tone of the top class this year was admirable. The obligations which membership of Klaus Heinrich's class entailed had been impressed on every boy from various quarters, and Klaus Heinrich was not the boy to tempt them to forget these obligations. But that Anselm Schickedanz was a devil of a chap had often come to his ears, and Klaus Heinrich, when he looked at him, felt a kind of satisfaction in believing what he heard, although it was an obscure problem to him how he could have come by his reputation.

He made several inquiries privately, broached the subject apparently by chance, and tried to find out from one or other of his comrades something about Schickedanz's devilry. He discovered nothing definite. But the answers, whether disparaging or complimentary, filled him with the suspicion of a mad amiability, an unlawful glorious humanity, which was there for the eyes of all, save his own, to see—and this suspicion was almost a sorrow. Everybody said at once, with reference to Anselm Schickedanz, and in saying it dropped into the forbidden form of address: "Yes, Highness, you ought to see him when you are not there!"

Klaus Heinrich would never see him when he was not there, would never get near him, never get to know him. He stole peeps at him when he stood with the others in a semicircle before him, laughing and braced up like all the rest. Everybody braced himself up in Klaus Heinrich's presence, his very existence was accountable for that, as he well knew, and he would never see what Schickedanz was like, how he behaved when he let himself go. At the thought he felt a twinge of envy, a tiny spark of regret.

At this juncture something painful, in fact revolting, occurred, of which nothing came to the ears of the Grand Ducal couple, because Doctor Ueberbein kept his mouth closed and about which scarcely any rumour spread in the capital because everybody who had had a share or any responsibility in the matter, obviously from a kind of feeling of shame, preserved strict silence about it. I refer to the improprieties which occurred in connexion with Prince Klaus Heinrich's presence at that year's citizens' ball, and in which a Fräulein Unschlitt, daughter of the wealthy soap-boiler, was especially concerned.

The citizens' ball was a chronic fixture in the social life of the capital, an official and at the same time informal festivity, which was given by the city every winter in the "Townpark Hotel," a big, recently enlarged and renovated establishment in the southern suburbs, and provided the bourgeois circles with an opportunity of establishing friendly relations with the Court. It was known that Johann Albrecht III had never cultivated a taste for this civil and rather free-and-easy entertainment, at which he appeared in a black frock-coat in order to lead off the polonaise with the Lady Mayoress, and that he was wont to withdraw from it at the earliest possible moment. This only heightened the general satisfaction when his second son, although not yet bound to do so, already made his appearance at the ball that year— indeed, it became known that he did so at his own express request. It was said that the Prince had employed Excellency von Knobelsdorff to transmit his earnest wish to the Grand Duchess, who in her turn had contrived to obtain her husband's consent.

Outwardly the festivity pursued its wonted course. The

most distinguished guests, Princess Catherine, in a coloured silk dress and cap, accompanied by her red-haired children, Prince Lambert with his pretty wife, and last of all Johann Albrecht and Dorothea with Prince Klaus Heinrich, made their appearance in the "Townpark Hotel," greeted by city officials, with long-ribboned rosettes pinned on their coats. Several Ministers, aides-de-camp in mufti, numbers of men and women of the Court, the leaders of society, as well as landowners from the surrounding country, were present. In the big white hall the Grand Ducal pairs first received a string of presentations, and then, to the strains of the band which sat in the curved gallery up above, Johann Albrecht with the Lady Mayoress, Dorothea with the Lord Mayor, opened the ball by a procession round the room.

Then, while the polonaise gave place to a round dance, contentment spread, cheeks glowed, the heat of the throng kindled feelings of fondness, faintness, and foreboding among the dancers, the distinguished guests stood as distinguished guests are wont to stand on such occasions—apart and smiling graciously on the platform, at the top of the hall under the gallery. From time to time Johann Albrecht engaged a distinguished man, and Dorothea engaged his wife, in conversation. Those addressed stepped quickly and smartly forward and back, kept their distance half-bowing with their heads bent, nodded, shook their heads, laughed in this attitude at the questions and remarks addressed to them—answered eagerly on the spur of the moment, with sudden and anticipatory changes from hearty amusement to the deepest earnestness, with a passionateness which was doubtless unusual to them, and obviously in a state of tension. Curious guests, still panting from the dance, stood in a semicircle round and stared at these purposely trivial conversations with a peculiarly tense expression on their faces.

Klaus Heinrich was the object of much attention. Together with two red-headed cousins who were already in the army, but were wearing mufti that evening, he kept a little behind

84

his parents, resting on one leg, his left hand placed far back on his hip, his face turned with his right half-profile to the public. A reporter of the *Courier* who had been bidden to the ball made notes upon him in a corner. The Prince could be seen to greet with his white-gloved right hand his tutor, Doctor Ueberbein, who with his red beard and greenish tint came along the fence of spectators; he was seen even to advance some way into the hall to meet him.

The doctor, with big enamel studs in his shirt front, began by bowing when Klaus Heinrich stretched out his hand to him, but then at once spoke to him in his free and fatherly way. The Prince seemed to be rejecting a proposal, and laughed uneasily as he did so, but then a number of people distinctly heard Doctor Ueberbein say: "No—nonsense, Klaus Heinrich, what was the good of learning? Why did the Swiss governess teach you your steps in your tenderest years? I can't understand why you go to balls if you won't dance? One, two, three, we'll soon find you a partner!" And with a continual shower of witticisms he presented to the Prince four or five young maidens, whom he dropped on without ceremony and dragged forward. They ducked and shot up again, one after the other, in the trailing fluctuations of the Court curtsey, set their teeth and did their best. Klaus Heinrich stood with his heels together and murmured, "Delighted, quite delighted."

To one he went so far as to say: "It's a jolly ball, isn't it?"

"Yes, Grand Ducal Highness, we are having great fun," answered she in a high chirping voice. She was a tall, rather bony bourgeoise maiden, dressed in white muslin, with fair wavy hair dressed over a pad, and a pretty face, a gold chain round her bare neck, the collar-bones of which showed prominently, and big white hands in mittens. She added: "The quadrille is coming next. Will your Grand Ducal Highness dance it with me?"

"I don't know . . ." he said. "I really don't know . . ."

85

He looked round. The machinery of the ball was already falling into geometrical order. Lines were being drawn, squares were forming, couples came forward and called to *vis-à-vis*. The music had not yet started.

Klaus Heinrich asked his cousins. Yes, they were taking part in the lancers, they already had their lucky partners on their arms.

Klaus Heinrich was seen to go up behind his mother's red damask chair and whisper something excitedly to her, whereupon she turned her lovely neck and passed on the question to her husband, and the Grand Duke nodded. And then some laughter was caused by the youthful impetuosity with which the Prince ran down, so as not to miss the beginning of the square dance.

The reporter of the *Courier*, notebook in one hand and pencil in the other, peered with neck thrust forward over the hall out of his corner, so as to make sure whom the Prince was going to engage. It was the fair, tall girl, with the collar-bones and the big white hands, Fräulein Unschlitt, the soap-boiler's daughter. She was still standing where Klaus Heinrich had left her.

"Are you still there?" he said breathlessly. . . . "May I have the pleasure? Come along!"

The sets were complete. They wandered about for a while without finding a place. A man with a ribbon rosette hurried up, seized a pair of young people by the shoulders and induced them to leave their stand under the chandelier, that his Grand Ducal Highness might occupy it with Fräulein Unschlitt. The band had been hesitating, it now struck up, the prescribed compliments were exchanged, and Klaus Heinrich danced like the rest of the world.

The doors into the next room stood open. In one of them was a buffet with flower vases, punch bowls, and dishes of many-coloured cakes. The dance extended right into this room, two sets were dancing in it. In the other room some

86

white-covered tables were arrayed, which were still standing empty.

Klaus Heinrich stepped forwards and backwards, laughed to the others, stretched out his hand and grasped theirs, and then again seized his partner's big white hand, put his right arm round the maiden's muslin-clad waist and revolved with her on their particular patch, while he kept his left hand, which also wore a little white glove, on his hip. They laughed and talked as they danced. The Prince made mistakes, forgot himself, upset figures, and lost his place. "You must keep me straight!" he said in the confusion. "I'm upsetting everything! Nudge me in the ribs!" and the others gradually plucked up courage and set him right, ordered him laughingly hither and thither, even laid their hands on him and pushed him a little when necessary. The fair damsel with the collar-bones was particularly zealous in pushing him about.

The spirits of the dancers rose with every figure. Their movements became freer, their calls bolder, they began to stamp their feet and to prance as they advanced and retired, while they held each other's hands and balanced themselves with their arms. Klaus Heinrich too stamped, at first only by way of signal, but soon more loudly; and as far as the balancing with the arms was concerned, the fair maiden looked after that when they advanced together. Also every time she danced facing him she made an exaggerated scrape before him which much increased the merriment.

The refreshment room was full of chatter and babble, which attracted everybody's envious glances. Some one had left his set in the middle of the dance, purloined a sandwich from the buffet, and was now chewing away proudly as he swerved and stamped, to the amusement of the rest.

"What cheek!" said the fair maiden. "They don't stand on ceremony!" and the idea gave her no peace. Before you could look round, she was off, had dashed lightly and nimbly between the lines of dancers, had seized a sandwich from the buffet and was back in her place.

Klaus Heinrich was the one who applauded her most heartily. His left hand was a difficulty, and so he managed without it, while with his right he beat on the top of his head and doubled up with laughter. Then he became quieter and rather pale. He was struggling with himself. . . . The quadrille was nearing its end. What he meant to do he must do quickly. They had already got to the grand chain.

And as he was already almost too late, he did what he had been struggling with himself about. He broke away, ran swiftly through the dancers, with muttered apologies when he collided with anybody, reached the buffet, seized a sandwich, rushed back, and came sliding into his set; that was not all, he put the sandwich—it was an egg and sardine one—to the lips of his partner, the damsel with the big white hands; she curtseyed a little, bit into it, bit almost half off without using her hands, and throwing back his head he stuffed the rest into his mouth!

The high spirits of the set found a vent in the grand chain, which was just beginning. Right round the hall went the dancers, winding zig-zag in and out and stretching out their hands. Then it stopped, the tide turned, and once more the stream went round, laughing and chattering, with mistakes and entanglements and hurriedly rectified complications.

Klaus Heinrich pressed the hands he grasped without knowing to whom they belonged. He laughed and his chest heaved. His smoothly parted hair was ruffled, and a bit fell over his forehead, his shirt-front bulged a little out of his waistcoat, and in his face and sparkling eyes was that look of tender emotion which is sometimes the expression of happiness. He said several times during the chain, "What awful fun! What glorious fun!" He met his cousins, and to them too he said, "We have had such fun—in our set over there!"

Then came the clapping and au revoirs; the dance was over. Klaus Heinrich again stood facing the fair maiden

with the collar-bones, and when the music changed time he
once more put his arm round her tender waist, and away they
danced.

Klaus Heinrich did not steer well and often knocked into
other couples, because he kept his left hand planted on his
hip, but he brought his partner somehow or other to the entrance to the refreshment room, where they called a halt and
refreshed themselves with pineappleade which was handed to
them by the waiters. They sat just at the entrance on two
velvet stools, drank and chatted about the quadrille, the Citizens' Ball, and other social functions in which the fair
maiden had already taken part that winter. . . .

It was then that one of the suite, Major von Platow, the
Grand Duke's aide-de-camp, came up to Klaus Heinrich,
bowed and begged leave to annouce that their Royal Highnesses were now going. He had been charged . . . But
Klaus Heinrich gave him to understand that he wished to remain, in so emphatic a fashion that the aide-de-camp did not
like to insist upon his errand.

The Prince uttered exclamations of an almost rebellious
regret and was obviously bitterly grieved at the idea of going
home at once. "We are having such fun!" he said, stood
up and gripped the Major's arm gently. "Dear Major von
Platow, please do intercede for me! Talk to Excellency von
Knobelsdorff, do anything you like—but to go now, when
we are all having such fun together! I'm sure my cousins
are going to stay. . . ." The Major looked at the fair
maiden with the big white hands, who smiled at him; he too
smiled and promised to do his best. This little scene was
enacted while the Grand Duke and the Grand Duchess were
already taking leave of the city dignitaries at the entrance
into the town park. Immediately afterwards the dancing on
the first floor began again.

The ball was at its height. Everything official had gone,
and the king of revelry came into his own. The white-
covered tables in the adjoining rooms were occupied by fam-

ilies drinking punch and eating supper. Youth streamed to
and fro, sitting excitedly and impatiently on the edges of the
chairs to eat a mouthful, drink a glass, and again plunge
into the merry throng. On the ground-floor there was an
old-German beer-cellar, which was crowded with the more
sedate men. The big dancing-hall and the buffet-room were
by now monopolized by the dancers. The buffet-room was
filled with fifteen or sixteen young people, sons and daughters
of the city, among them Klaus Heinrich. It was a kind of
private ball in there. They danced to the music which floated
in from the main hall.

Doctor Ueberbein, the Prince's tutor, was seen there for a
minute or two, having a short talk with his pupil. He was
heard to mention, watch in hand, Herr von Knobelsdorff's
name, and to say that he was down in the beer-cellar and was
coming back to take the Prince away. Then he went. The
time was half-past ten. And while he sat below and conversed
with his friends over a tankard of beer, only for an hour or
perhaps an hour and a half, not more, those dreadful things,
that simply incredible scandal, happened in the buffet-room,
to which it fell to him to put a stop, though unfortunately
too late.

The punch provided was weak, it contained more soda-
water than champagne, and if the young people lost their
equilibrium it was more the intoxication of the dance than of
the wine. But in view of the Prince's character and the solid
bourgeois origin of the rest of the company, that was not
enough to explain what happened. Another, a peculiar intoxication, was a factor here on both sides. The peculiar thing
was that Klaus Heinrich was fully conscious of each separate
stage in this intoxication, and yet had not the power or the
will to shake it off.

He was happy. He felt on his cheeks the same glow burning as he saw in the faces of the others, and as his eyes, dazed
by a soft mist, travelled about the room, and rested admiringly
on one fair form after another, his look seemed to say:

"We!" His mouth too said it—said, for the pure joy of saying them, sentences in which a "We" occurred. "Shall *we* sit down? shall *we* have another turn? shall *we* have a drink? shall *we* make up two sets?" It was especially to the maiden with the collar-bones that Klaus Heinrich made remarks with a "We" in them. He had quite forgotten his left hand, it hung down, he felt so happy that it did not worry him and he never thought of hiding it. Many saw now for the first time what really was the matter with it, and looked curiously on with an unconscious grimace at the thin, short arm in the sleeve, the little, by now rather dirty white kid glove which covered the hand. But as Klaus Heinrich was so careless about it, the others plucked up courage, the result being that everybody took hold of the malformed hand quite unconcernedly in the round or square dances.

He did not keep it back. He felt himself borne along, nay rather whirled around by a feeling, a strong, wild feeling of contentment, that grew, gathered heat from itself, possessed itself of him more and more recklessly, overpowered him even more vehemently and breathlessly, seemed to lift him triumphantly from the floor. What was happening? It was difficult to say, difficult to be quite sure. The air was full of words, detached cries, not spoken but expressed on the dancers' faces, in their attitudes, in all they were doing and saying. "He must just once! Bring him along, bring him along . . . ! Caught, caught!" A young damsel with a turned-up nose, who asked him for a gallop when the "leap-year" dance came, said quite clearly without any obvious connexion, "Chucker up!" as she got ready to start off with him.

He saw pleasure in every eye, and saw that their pleasure lay in drawing him out, in having him amongst them. In his happiness, his dream, to be with them, amongst them, one of them, there obtruded itself from time to time a cold, uncomfortable feeling that he was deluding himself, that the warm, glorious "We" was deceiving him, that he did not really
91

blend in with them, that he was all the time the centre and object of the show, but in a different and more unsatisfactory way than before. They were his enemies to a certain extent, he saw it in the malice of their eyes. He heard as if at a distance, with a peculiar dismay, how the fair damsel with the big white hands called him simply by his names—and he felt that she did so in quite a different spirit to that of Doctor Ueberbein when he did the same. She had the right and the permission to do so, in a certain manner, but was nobody here then jealous for his dignity, if he himself was not? It seemed to him that they plucked at his coat, and sometimes in their excitement made wild, sneering remarks about him. A tall, fair young man with pince-nez, with whom he collided while dancing, said quite loud so that everybody could hear it: "Now then, clumsy!" And there was malice in the way in which the fair young maiden, her arm in his and a grin on her lips, whirled round with him till he was ready to drop with giddiness. While they whirled he gazed with swimming eyes at the collar-bones showing under the white, rather rough skin on her neck.

They fell; they had gone too hard at it and tumbled when they tried to stop revolving, and over them stumbled a second pair, not entirely by themselves, but rather at a push from the tall young man with pince-nez. There was a scrimmage on the floor, and Klaus Heinrich heard above him in the room the chorus which came back to him from the school-playground when he had ventured on a rather daring joke by way of amusing his fellows—a "Ho, ho, ho!" only it sounded more wicked and bolder here. . . .

When shortly after midnight, unfortunately a little behind time, Doctor Ueberbein appeared on the threshold of the buffet-room, this is what he saw: His young pupil was sitting alone on the green plush sofa by the left-hand wall, his clothes all disarranged and himself decorated in an extraordinary way. A quantity of flowers, which had previously adorned the buffet in two Chinese vases, were stuck in the opening of his waistcoat, between the studs of his shirtfront, even in his collar; round his neck lay the gold chain which belonged to the maiden with the collar-bones, and on his head the flat metal cover of a punch-bowl was balanced like a hat. He kept saying, "What are you doing? What are you doing . . . ?" while the dancers, hand-in-hand in a semi-circle, danced a round dance backwards and forwards in front of him with half-suppressed giggles, whispers, smirks, and ho, ho, ho's.

An unusual and unnatural flush mantled in Doctor Ueber-bein's face. "Stop it! Stop it!" he cried in his resonant voice, and, in the silence, consternation, and dismay which at once ensued, he walked with long strides up to the Prince, tore away the flowers in two or three grasps, threw the chain and the cover away, then bowed and said with a stern look, "May I beg your Grand Ducal Highness . . .

"I've been an ass, an ass!" he repeated when he got outside.

Klaus Heinrich left the Citizens' Ball in his company.

That was the painful event which happened during Klaus Heinrich's year at school. As I have said, none of the participators talked about it; even to the Prince, Doctor Ueber-bein did not mention the subject for years afterwards, and, as nobody crystallized the event in words, it remained incorporeal and promptly faded away, at least apparently, into oblivion.

The Citizens' Ball had taken place in January. Shrove Tuesday, with the Court Ball and the big Court in the Old Schloss, which wound up the social year—regulation festivities, to which Klaus Heinrich was not yet admitted—were past and over. Then came Easter, and with it the close of the school year. Klaus Heinrich's diploma examination, that edifying formality, in the course of which the question, "You agree, do you not, Grand Ducal Highness?" was constantly recurring on the lips of the Professor, and at which the

Prince acquitted himself admirably in his very conspicuous position. This was not a very important phase in his life. Klaus Heinrich continued to live in the capital, but after Whitsuntide his eighteenth birthday drew near, and with it a complex of festivities which marked a serious turning-point in his life, and which taxed him severely for days together.

He had attained his majority, had been pronounced to be of age. For the first time again since his baptism, he was the centre of attention and chief actor in a great ceremony, but while he had then quietly, irresponsibly, and patiently resigned himself to the formalities which surrounded and protected him, it was incumbent on him on this day, in the midst of binding prescriptions and stern regulations, hemmed in by the drapery of weighty precedent, to inspire the spectators and to please them by maintaining an attitude of dignity and good-breeding, and at the same time to appear light-hearted.

It may be added that I use the word "drapery" not only as a figure of speech. The Prince wore a crimson mantle on this occasion, a sumptuous and theatrical article of raiment, which his father and grandfather before him had worn at their coming-of-age, and which notwithstanding days of airing, still smelt of camphor. The crimson mantle had originally belonged to the robes of the Knights of the Grimmburg Griffin, but was now nothing more than a ceremonial garb for the use of princes attaining their majority. Albrecht, the Heir Apparent, had never worn the family one. As his birthday fell in the winter, he always spent it in the South, in a place with a warm and dry climate, whither he was thinking of returning this autumn too, and as at the time of his eighteenth birthday his health had not permitted him to travel home, it had been decided to declare him officially of age in his absence, and to dispense with the Court ceremony.

As to Klaus Heinrich, there was only one opinion, especially among the representatives of the public, that the mantle

94

suited him admirably, and he himself, notwithstanding the way in which it hampered his movements, found it a blessing, as it made it easy for him to hide his left hand. Between the canopied bed and the bellying chest of drawers in his bedroom, that was situated on the second floor looking out on the yard with the rose-bush, he made himself ready for the show, carefully and precisely, with the help of his valet, Neumann, a quiet and precise man who had been recently attached to him as keeper of his wardrobe and personal servant.

Neumann was an ex-barber, and was filled, especially in the direction of his original calling, with that passionate con-scientiousness, that insatiable knowledge of the ideal, which gives rise to the highest skill. He did not shave like any ordinary shaver, he was not content to leave no stubble behind, he shaved in such a way that every shadow of a beard, every recollection of one, was removed, and without hurting the skin he managed to restore to it all its softness and smoothness. He cut Klaus Heinrich's hair exactly square above the ears, and arranged it with all the assiduity required, in his opinion, by this preparation for the Prince's ceremonial appearance. He managed that the parting should come over the left eye and run slanting back over the crown of the head, so that no tufts or wisps should stick up on it; he brushed the hair on the right side up from the forehead into a prim crest on which no hat or helmet could make an impression. Then Klaus Heinrich, with his help, squeezed himself carefully into his uniform of lieutenant in the Grenadier Guards, whose high-braided collar and tight fit favoured a dignified bearing, put on the lemon-coloured silk band and the flat gold chain of the House Order, and went down to the picture gallery where the members of the family and the foreign relations of the Grand Ducal pair were waiting. The Court was waiting in the adjoining Hall of the Knights, and it was there that Johann Albrecht himself invested his son with the crimson mantle.

95

## ROYAL HIGHNESS

Herr von Bühl zu Bühl had marshalled a procession, the ceremonial procession from the Hall of the Knights to the Throne-room. It had cost him no little worry. The composition of the Court made it difficult to contrive an impressive arrangement, and Herr von Bühl especially lamented the lack of upper Court officials, which on such occasions made itself most severely felt. The Royal Mews had recently been put under Herr von Bühl, and he felt himself quite up to his various functions, but he asked everybody how he could be expected to make a good impression, when the most important posts were filled simply by the master of the Buckhounds, von Stieglitz, and the director of the Grand Ducal Theatre, a gouty general.

While he, in his capacity as Lord Marshal, Chief Master of the Ceremonies, and House Marshal, in his embroidered clothes and brown toupée, covered with orders and with his golden pince-nez on his nose, came waddling and planting his long staff in front of him behind the cadets, who, dressed as pages, and their hair parted over the left eye, opened the procession, he pondered deeply over what came behind him. A few chamberlains—not many, for some were wanted for the end of the procession—their plumed hats under their arms and the Key on their coat-tails, followed close at his heels, in silk stockings. Next came Herr von Stieglitz, and the limping theatre-director in front of Klaus Heinrich, who, in his mantle between the exalted couple, and followed by his brother and sister, Albrecht and Ditlinde, formed the actual nucleus of the procession.

Behind their Highnesses came von Knobelsdorff, the House Minister and President of Council, his eye-wrinkles all at work; a little knot of aides-de-camp and palace ladies came next: General Count Schmettern and Major von Platow, a Count Trümmerhauff, cousin of the Keeper of the Privy Purse, as military aide-de-camp of the Heir Apparent, and the Grand Duchess's women led by the short-winded Baroness von Schulenburg-Tressen. Then followed, attended and fol-

96

lowed by aides-de-camp, chamberlains, and Court ladies, Princess Catherine, with her red-haired progeny, Prince Lambert with his lovely wife, and the foreign relations or their representatives. Pages brought up the rear.

Thus they went at a measured pace from the Hall of the Knights through the Gala Halls, the Hall of the Twelve Months, and the Marble Hall into the Throne-room. Lackeys, with red-gold aiguillettes on their brown coats, stood theatrically in couples at the open double doors. Through the broad windows the June morning sun streamed gaily and recklessly in.

Klaus Heinrich looked round him as he processed between his parents through the dreary arabesques, the dilapidated decorations of the show-rooms, now not favoured by kindly artificial light. The bright daylight cheerfully and soberly showed up their decay. From the big lustres with their stiff-bound stems, stripped of their coverings in honour of the day, rose thick forests of flameless candles, but everywhere there were prisms missing, crystal festoons torn, so that they gave a canker-bit and toothless impression. The silk damask upholstery of the State furniture, which was arranged stiffly and monotonously round the walls, was threadbare, the gilt of the frames chipped off, big blind patches marred the surfaces of the tall candle-decked mirrors, and daylight shone through the moth-holes in the faded and discoloured curtains. The gold and silver borders of the tapestry hangings had torn away in several places, and were hanging disconsolately from the walls. Even in the Silver Hall of the Gala Rooms, where the Grand Duke was wont to receive solemn deputations, and in the centre of which stood a mother-of-pearl table with stumpy silver feet, a piece of the silver work had fallen from the ceiling leaving a gaping patch of white plaster.

But why was it that it somehow seemed as if these rooms defied the sober, mocking daylight, and proudly answered its challenge? Klaus Heinrich looked sideways at his fa-

ther. . . . The condition of the rooms did not seem to worry
him. Never of more than medium height, the Grand Duke
had become almost small in the course of years, but he
strode majestically on with head thrown back, the lemon-
coloured ribbon of the Order over his general's uniform,
which he had donned to-day, though he had no military
leanings. From under his high and bald forehead and grey
eyebrows, his blue eyes, with dull rings round them, were
fixed with weary dignity on the distance, and from his pointed
white moustaches the two deep furrows ran down his yellow-
ish skin to his beard, imparting to his face a look of contempt.
No, the bright daylight could not do any harm to the rooms;
the dilapidations did not in the least impair their dignity,
they rather increased it. They stood in their discomfort,
their theatrical symmetry, their strange musty play-house
or church atmosphere, cold and indifferent to the merry and
sun-bathed world outside—stern background of a pompous
cult, at which Klaus Heinrich this day for the first time
officiated.

The procession passed through the pairs of lackeys, who,
with an expression of relentlessness, pressed their lips together
and closed their eyes, into the white and gold expanse of
the Throne-room. A wave of acts of homage, scrapings,
bows, curtseys and salutes, swept through the hall as the
procession passed in front of the assembled guests. There
were diplomats with their wives, nobility of the Court and
the country, the corps of officers of the capital, the Ministers,
amongst whom could be descried the affected, confident face
of the new Finance Minister, Dr. Krippenreuther, the Knights
of the Great Order of the Grimmburg Griffin, the Presidents
of the Diet, dignitaries of all kinds. High up in the little
box above the big looking-glass by the entrance door could
be descried the press representatives peering over each other's
shoulders and busily writing in their notebooks. . . . In front
of the throne-baldachin, itself a torn velvet arrangement,
crowned with ostrich feathers and framed with gold fillets

which would have been all the better for a touch-up, the procession divided as in a polonaise, and went through carefully prescribed evolutions.

The pages and chamberlains fell aside to right and left. Herr von Bühl, his face turned to the throne and his staff uplifted, stepped backwards and stood still in the middle of the hall. The Grand Ducal pair and their children walked up the rounded, red-carpeted steps to the capacious gilded chairs which stood at the top. The remaining members of the House, with the foreign princes, ranged themselves on both sides of the throne; behind them stood the suite, the maids of honour and the grooms of the chambers, and the pages stood on the steps. At a gesture from Johann Albrecht, Herr von Knobelsdorff, who had previously taken up his stand over against the throne, advanced straight to the velvet-covered table, which stood by the side of the steps, and began at once to read from various documents the official formalities.

Klaus Heinrich was declared to be of age and fit and entitled to wear the crown, should necessity require it—every eye was turned on him at this place, and at his Royal Highness Albrecht, his elder brother, who stood close to him. The Heir Apparent was wearing the uniform of a captain in the Hussar regiment which was called by his name. From his silver-laced collar stretched an unmilitary width of civil stand-up collar, and on it rested his fine, shrewd, and delicate head, with its long skull and narrow temples, the straw-coloured moustache on the upper lip, and the blue, lonely-looking eyes which had seen death. He looked not in the least like a cavalry officer, yet so slender and unapproachably aristocratic that Klaus Heinrich, with his national cheek-bones, looked almost coarse beside him. The Heir Apparent pursed up his lips when everybody looked at him, protruded his short rounded underlip, and sucked it lightly against the upper one.

Several of the country's orders were bestowed on the Prince who had just come of age, including the Albrecht Cross and

99

the Great Order of the Grimmburg Griffin, not to mention that he was confirmed in the House Order whose insignia he had possessed since his tenth birthday. Afterwards came the congratulations in the form of a processional Court, led by the fawning Herr von Bühl, after which the gala-breakfast began in the Marble Hall and in the hall of the Twelve Months.

The foreign princes were entertained for the next few days. A garden-party was given in Hollerbrunn, with fireworks and dancing for the young people of the Court in the park. Festive excursions with pages in attendance were made through the sunny country-side to Monbrillant, Jägerpreis, and Haderstein Ruins, and the people, that inferior order of creation with the searching eyes and the high cheek-bones, stood on the kerb and cheered themselves and their representatives. In the capital Klaus Heinrich's photograph hung in the windows of the art-dealers, and the *Courier* actually published a printed likeness of him, a popular and strangely idealized representation, showing the Prince in the crimson mantle. But then came yet another great day—Klaus Heinrich's formal entry into the Army, into the regiment of Grenadier Guards.

This is what happened. The regiment to which fell the honour of having Klaus Heinrich as one of its officers was drawn up on the Albrechtsplatz in open square. Many a plume waved in the middle. The princes of the House and the generals were all present. The public, a black mass against the gay background, crowded behind the barriers. Cameras were levelled in several places at the scene of action. The Grand Duchess, with the princesses and their ladies, watched the show from the windows of the Old Schloss.

First of all, Klaus Heinrich, dressed as a lieutenant, reported himself formally to the Grand Duke. He advanced sternly, without the shadow of a smile, towards his father, clapped his heels together and humbly acquainted him with his presence. The Grand Duke thanked him briefly, also without a smile, and then in his turn, followed by his aides-de-camp, advanced in his dress uniform and plumed hat into the square. Klaus Heinrich stood before the lowered colours, an embroidered, golden, and half-tattered piece of silk cloth, and took the oath. The Grand Duke made a speech in detached sentences and the sharp voice of command which he reserved for such occasions, in which he called his son "Your Grand Ducal Highness" and publicly clasped the Prince's hand. The Colonel of the Grenadier Guards, with crimson cheeks, led a cheer for the Grand Duke in which the guests, the regiment, and the public joined. A march past followed, and the whole ended with a military luncheon in the castle.

This picturesque ceremony in the Albrechtsplatz was without practical significance; its effect began and ended there. Klaus Heinrich never dreamed of going into garrison, but went the very same day with his parents and brother and sister to Hollerbrunn, to pass the summer there in the cool old French rooms on the river, between the wall-like hedges of the park, and then, in the autumn, to go up to the university. For so it was ordained in the programme of his life; in the autumn he went up to the university for a year, not that of the capital, but the second one of the country, accompanied by Doctor Ueberbein, his tutor.

The appointment of this young savant as mentor was once more attributable to an express, ardent wish of the Prince, and indeed, as far as the choice of tutor and older companions was concerned, whom Klaus Heinrich was to have at his side during this year of student freedom, it was considered necessary to give a reasonable amount of consideration to his expressed wishes. Yet there was much to be said against this choice; it was unpopular, or at least criticized aloud or in whispers in many quarters.

Raoul Ueberbein was not loved in the capital. Due respect was paid to his medal for life-saving and to all his feverish energy, but the man was no genial fellow-citizen, no jolly comrade, no blameless official. The most charitable saw in him an oddity with a determined and uncomfortably reckless dis-

101

position, who recognized no Sunday, no holiday, no relaxation, and did not understand being a man amongst men after work was done. This natural son of an adventuress had worked his way up from the depths of society, from an obscure and prospectless youth without means, by dint of sheer strength of will, to being, first school teacher, then academic professor, then university lecturer, had lived to see his appointment—had "engineered" it, as many said—to the "Pheasantry" as teacher of a Grand Ducal Prince, and yet he knew no rest, no contentment, no comfortable enjoyment of life. . . . But life, as every decent man, thinking of Doctor Ueberbein, truly observed, life does not consist only of profession and performance, it has its purely human claims and duties, the neglect of which is a greater sin than the display of some measure of joviality towards oneself and one's fellows in the sphere of one's work, and only that personality can be considered a harmonious one which succeeds in giving its due to each part, profession and human feelings, life and performance.

Ueberbein's lack of any sense of camaraderie was bound to tell against him. He avoided all social intercourse with his colleagues, and his circle of friends was confined to the person of one man of another scientific sphere, a surgeon and children's specialist with the unsympathetic name of Sammet, a very popular surgeon to boot, who shared certain characteristics with Ueberbein. But it was only very rarely—and then only as a sort of favour—that he turned up at the club where the teachers gathered after the day's work and worry, for a glass of beer, a rubber, or a free exchange of views on public and personal questions—but he passed his evenings, and, as his landlady reported, also a great part of the night, working at science in his study, while his complexion grew greener and greener, and his eyes showed more and more clearly signs of overstrain.

The authorities had been moved, shortly after his return from the "Pheasantry," to promote him to head master. Where was he going to stop? At Director? High-school

102

Professor? Minister for Education? Everybody agreed that his immoderate and restless energy concealed imprudence and defiance of public opinion—or rather did not conceal them. His demeanour, his loud, blustering mode of speaking annoyed, irritated, and exasperated people. His tone towards members of the teaching profession who were older and in higher positions than himself was not what it should be. He treated everybody, from the Director down to the humblest usher, in a fatherly way, and his habit of talking of himself as of a man who had "knocked about," of gassing about "Fate and Duty," and thereby displaying his benevolent contempt for all those who "weren't obliged to" and "smoked cigars in the morning," showed conceit pure and simple. His pupils adored him; he achieved remarkable results with them, that was agreed. But on the whole the Doctor had many enemies in the town, more than he ever guessed, and the misgiving that his influence on the Prince might be an undesirable one was put into words in at least one portion of the daily press. . . .

Anyhow Ueberbein obtained leave from the Latin school, and went first of all alone, in the capacity of billeter, on a visit to the famous student town, within whose walls Klaus Heinrich was destined to pass the year of his apprenticeship, and on his return he was received in audience by Excellency von Knobelsdorff, the Minister of the Grand Ducal House, to receive the usual instructions. Their tenour was that almost the most important object of this year was to establish traditions of comradeship on the common ground of academic freedom between the Prince and the student corps, especially in the interests of the dynasty—the regulation phrases, which Herr von Knobelsdorff rattled off almost casually, and which Doctor Ueberbein listened to with a silent bow, while he drew his mouth, and with it his red beard, a little to one side. Then followed Klaus Heinrich's departure with his mentor, a dog-cart and a servant or two, for the university.

A glorious year, full of the charm of artistic freedom, in the public eye and in the mirror of public report—yet with-
103

out technical importance of any kind. Misgivings which had been felt in some quarters that Doctor Ueberbein, through mistaking and misunderstanding the position, might worry the Prince with excessive demands in the direction of objective science, proved unfounded. On the contrary, it was obvious that the doctor quite realized the difference between his own earnest, and his pupil's exalted, sphere of existence. On the other hand (whether it was the mentor's or the Prince's own fault does not matter) the freedom and the unconstrained camaraderie, like the instruction, were interpreted in a very relative and symbolical sense so that neither the one nor the other, neither the knowledge nor the freedom, could be said to be the essence and peculiarity of the year. Its essence and peculiarity were rather, as it appeared, the year in itself, as the embodiment of custom and impressive ceremoniousness, to which Klaus Heinrich deferred, just as he had deferred to the theatrical rites on his last birthday—only now not with a purple cloak, but occasionally wearing a coloured student's cap, the so-called "Stürmer," in which he was portrayed in a photograph issued at once by the *Courier* to its readers.

As to his studies, his matriculation was not marked by any particular festivities, though some reference was made to the honour which Klaus Heinrich's admission bestowed on the university, and the lectures he attended began with the address: "Grand Ducal Highness!" He drove in his dogcart with a groom from the pretty green-clad villa, which the Marshal of his father's household had leased for him in a select and not too expensive square, amid the remarks and greetings of the passers-by, to the lectures, and there he sat with the consciousness that the whole thing was unessential and unnecessary for his exalted calling, yet with a show of courteous attention.

Charming anecdotes of the signs the Prince gave of interest in the lectures went about and had their due effect. Towards the end of one course on Nature Study (for Klaus Heinrich at-

104

tended these courses also "for general information") the Professor, by way of illustration, had filled a metal shell with water and announced that the water, when frozen, would burst the shell by expansion; he promised to show the class the pieces next lecture. Now he had not kept his word on this point at the next lecture, probably out of forgetfulness: the broken shell had not been forthcoming—Klaus Heinrich had therefore inquired as to the result of the experiment. He had joined in asking questions of the professor at the end of the lecture, just like any ordinary student, and had modestly asked him: "Has the bomb burst?"—whereupon the Professor, full of embarrassment at first, had then expressed his thanks with glad surprise, and indeed emotion, for the kind interest the Prince had expressed in his lectures.

Klaus Heinrich was honorary member of a student's club —only honorary, because he was not allowed to fight duels —and once or twice attended their wines, his Stürmer on his head. But since his guardians were well aware that the results the influence of strong drink had on his highly strung and delicate temperament were absolutely irreconcilable with his exalted calling, he did not dare to drink seriously, and his comrades were obliged on this point too to bear his Highness in mind. Their rude customs were judiciously limited to a casual one or two, the general tone was as exemplary as it used to be in the upper form at school, the songs they sang were old ones of real poetry, and the meetings were, as a whole, gala and parade nights, refined editions of the ordinary ones. The use of Christian names was the bond of union between Klaus Heinrich and his corps brothers, as the expression and basis of spontaneous comradeship. But it was generally observed that this use sounded false and artificial, however great the efforts to make it otherwise, and that the students were always falling back unintentionally into the form of address which took due notice of the Prince's Highness.

Such was the effect of his presence, of his friendly, alert, and always uncompromising attitude which sometimes produced strange, even comical phenomena in the demeanour of the persons with whom the Prince came into contact. One evening, at a soirée which one of his professors gave, he engaged a guest in conversation—a fat man of some age, a King's Counsel by his title, who, despite his social importance, enjoyed the reputation of a great roué and a regular old sinner. The conversation, whose subject is a matter of no consequence and indeed would be difficult to specify, lasted for a considerable time because no opportunity of breaking it off presented itself. And suddenly, in the middle of his talk with the Prince, the barrister whistled—whistled with his thick lips one of those pointless sequences of notes which one utters when one is embarrassed and wants to appear at one's ease, and then tried to cover his comic breach of manners by clearing his throat and coughing. Klaus Heinrich was accustomed to experiences of that kind, and tactfully passed on.

If at any time he wanted to make a purchase himself and went into a shop, his entrance caused a kind of panic. He would ask for what he wanted, a button perhaps, but the girl would not understand him, would look dazed, and unable to fix her attention on the button, but obviously absorbed by something else—something outside and above her duties as a shop-assistant—she would drop a few things, turn the boxes upside down in obvious helplessness, and it was all Klaus Heinrich could do to restore her composure by his friendly manner.

Such, as I have said, was the effect of his attitude, and in the city it was often described as arrogance and blameworthy contempt for fellow-creatures—others roundly denied the arrogance, and Doctor Ueberbein, when the subject was broached to him at a social gathering, would put the question, whether "every inducement to contempt for his fellow-creatures being readily conceded," any such contempt really was

106

possible in a case like the present of complete detachment from all the activities of ordinary men. Indeed, any remark of that kind he met in his unanswerable blustering way by the assertion that the Prince not only did not despise his fellow-creatures, but respected even the most worthless of them, only considered them all the more sound, serious, and good for the way in which the poor over-taxed and over-strained man in the street earned his living by the sweat of his brow. . . .

The society of the university town had no time to reach a definite verdict on the question. The year of student life was over before one could turn round, and Klaus Heinrich returned, as prescribed by the programme of his life, to his father's palace, there, despite his left arm, to pass a full year in serious military service. He was attached to the Dragoons of the Guard for six months, and directed the taking up of intervals of eight paces for lance-exercises as well as the forming of squares, as if he were a serious soldier; then changed his weapon and transferred to the Grenadier Guards, so as to get an insight into infantry work also. It fell to him to march to the Schloss and change the Guard —an evolution which attracted large crowds. He came swiftly out of the Guard-room, his star on his breast, placed himself with drawn sword on the flank of the company and gave not quite correct orders, which, however, did not matter, as his stout soldiers executed the right movements all the same.

On guest-nights, too, at head-quarters, he sat on the colonel's right hand, and by his presence prevented the officers from unhooking their uniform collars and playing cards after dinner. After this, being now twenty years old, he started on an "educational tour"—no longer in the company of Doctor Ueberbein, but in that of a military attendant and courier, Captain von Braunbart-Schellendorf of the Guards, a fair-haired officer who was destined to be Klaus Heinrich's
107

aide-de-camp, and to whom the tour gave an opportunity of establishing himself on a footing of intimacy and influence with him.

Klaus Heinrich did not see much in his educational tour, which took him far afield, and was keenly followed by the *Courier*. He visited the courts, introduced himself to the sovereigns, attended gala dinners with Captain von Braunbart, and on his departure received one of the country's superior Orders. He took a look at such sights as Captain von Braunbart (who also received several Orders) chose for him, and the *Courier* reported from time to time that the Prince had expressed his admiration of a picture, a museum, or a building to the director or curator who happened to be his cicerone. He travelled apart, protected and supported by the chivalrous precautions of Captain von Braunbart, who kept the purse, and to whose devoted zeal was due the fact that not one of Klaus Heinrich's trunks was missing at the end of the journey.

A couple of words, no more, may be devoted to an interlude, which had for scene a big city in a neighbouring kingdom, and was brought about by Captain von Braunbart with all due circumspection. The Captain had a friend in this city, a bachelor nobleman and a cavalry captain, who was on terms of intimacy with a young lady member of the theatrical world, an accommodating and at the same time trustworthy young person. In pursuance of an agreement by letter between Captain von Braunbart and his friend, Klaus Heinrich was thrown in contact with the damsel at her home—suitably arranged for the purpose—and the acquaintance allowed to develop *à deux*. Thus an expressly foreseen item in the educational tour was conscientiously realized, without Klaus Heinrich being involved in more than a casual acquaintance. The damsel received a memento for her services, and Captain von Braunbart's friend a decoration. So the incident closed.

Klaus Heinrich also visited the fair Southern lands, incognito, under a romantic-sounding title. There he would sit, alone, perhaps for a quarter of an hour, dressed in a suit of irreproachable cut, among other foreigners on a white restaurant terrace looking over a dark-blue sea, and it might happen that somebody at another table would notice him, and try, in the manner of tourists, to engage him in conversation. What could he be, that quiet and self-possessed-looking young man? People ran over the various spheres of life, tried to fit him into the merchant, the military, the student class. But they never felt that they had got it quite right—they felt his Highness, but nobody guessed it.

# V

## ALBRECHT II

GRAND DUKE JOHANN ALBRECHT died of a terrible illness, which had something naked and abstract about it, and to which no other name but just that of death could be given. It seemed as if death, sure of its prey, in this case disdained any mask or gloss, and came on the scene as its very self, as dissolution by and for itself. What actually happened was a decomposition of the blood, caused by internal hæmorrhages; and an exploratory operation, whch was conducted by the Director of the University Hospital, a famous surgeon, could not arrest the corroding progress of the gangrene. The end soon came, all the sooner that Johann Albrecht made little resistance to the approach of death. He showed signs of an unutterable weariness, and often remarked to his attendants, as well as to the surgeons attending him, that he was "dead sick of the whole thing"—meaning, of course, his princely existence, his exalted life in the glare of publicity. His cheek-furrows, those two lines of arrogance and boredom, resolved in his last days into an exaggerated, grotesque grimace, and continued thus until death smoothed them out.

The Grand Duke's illness fell in the winter. Albrecht, the Heir Apparent, called away from his warm dry resort, arrived in snowy wet weather, which was as bad for his health as it could be. His brother, Klaus Heinrich, interrupted his educational tour, which was anyhow nearing its close, and returned with Captain von Braunbart-Schellendorf in all haste from the fair land of the South to the capital. Besides the two prince-sons, the Grand Duchess Dorothea, the Princesses Catherine and Ditlinde, Prince Lambert without his lovely wife—the surgeons in attendance and Prahl the valet-de-chambre waited at the bedside, while the Court officials and Ministers on duty were collected in the adjoining room. If credence might be given to the assertions of the servants, the ghostly noise in the "Owl Chamber" had been exceptionally loud in the last weeks and days. According to them it was a rattling and a shaking noise, which recurred periodically, and whose meaning could not be distinguished outside the room.

Johann Albrecht's last act of Highness consisted in giving with his own hand to the professor, who had performed the useless operation with the greatest skill, his patent of nomination to the Privy Council. He was terribly exhausted, "sick of the whole thing," and his consciousness even in his more lucid moments was not at all clear; but he carried out the act with scrupulous care and made a ceremony of it. He had himself propped up, made a few alterations, shading his eyes with his wax-coloured hands, in the chance disposition of those present, ordered his sons to place themselves on both sides of his canopied bed—and while his soul was already tugging at her moorings, and floating here and there on unknown currents, he composed his features with mechanical skill into his smile of graciousness for the handing of the diploma to the Professor, who had left the room for a short time.

Quite towards the end, when the dissolution had already attacked the brain, the Grand Duke made one wish clear, which, though scarcely understood, was hastily complied with, although its fulfilment could not do the slightest good to the Grand Duke. Certain words, apparently disconnected, kept recurring in the murmurings of the sick man. He named several stuffs, silk, satin, and brocade, mentioned Prince Klaus Heinrich, used a technical expression in medicine, and said something about an Order, the Albrecht Cross of the Third Class with Crown. Between whiles one caught quite ordinary remarks, which apparently referred to the dying man's princely calling, and sounded like "extraordinary obligation" and

111

"comfortable majority"; then the descriptions of the stuffs began again, to which was appended in a louder voice the word "Sammet." [1]  At last it was realized that the Grand Duke wanted Doctor Sammet to be called in, the doctor who had happened to be present at the Grimmburg at the time of Klaus Heinrich's birth, twenty years before, and had, for a long time now, been practising in the capital.

The doctor was really a children's doctor, but he was summoned and came: already nearly grey on the temples, with a drooping moustache, surmounted by a nose which was rather too flat at the bottom, clean-shaven otherwise and with cheeks rather sore from shaving.  With head on one side, his hand on his watch-chain, and elbows close to his sides, he examined the situation, and began at once to busy himself in a practical, gentle way about his exalted patient, whereat the latter expressed his satisfaction in no uncertain fashion.  Thus it was that it fell to Doctor Sammet to administer the last injections to the Grand Duke, with his supporting hand to ease the final spasms, and to be, more than any of the other doctors, his helper in death—a distinction which indeed provoked some secret irritation amongst the others, but on the other hand resulted in the doctor's appointment shortly afterwards to the vacancy in the important post of Director and Chief Physician of the "Dorothea," a Children's Hospital, in which capacity he was destined later to play some part in certain developments.

So died Johann Albrecht the Third, uttering his last sigh on a winter's night.  The old castle was brightly illuminated while he was passing away.  The stern furrows of boredom were smoothed out in his face, and, relieved of any exertion on his own part, he was subjected to formalities which surrounded him for the last time, carried him along, and made his wax-like shell just once more the focus and object of theatrical rites. . . . Herr von Bühl zu Bühl showed his usual energy in organizing the funeral, which was attended by many

[1] *I.e.,* velvet.

princely guests. The gloomy ceremonies, the different exposures and identifications, corpse-parades, blessings, and memorial services at the catafalque took days to complete, and Johann Albrecht's corpse was for eight hours exposed to public view, surrounded by a guard of honour consisting of two colonels, two first lieutenants, two cavalry sergeants, two infantry sergeants, two corporals, and two chamberlains.

Then at last came the moment when the zinc shell was brought by eight lackeys from the altar recess of the Court Church, where it had been on show between crape-covered candelabra and six-foot candles, to the entry-hall, placed by eight foresters in the mahogany coffin, carried by eight Grenadier Guardsmen to the six-horsed and black-draped hearse, which set off for the mausoleum amidst cannon salvos and the tolling of bells. The flags hung heavy with rain from the middle of their poles. Although it was early morning, the gas-lamps were burning in the streets along which the funeral was to pass. Johann Albrecht's bust was displayed amongst mourning decorations in the shop-windows, and postcards with the portrait of the deceased ruler, which were everywhere for sale, were in great demand. Behind the rows of troops, the gymnastic clubs, and veteran associations which kept the road, stood the people on tiptoe in the snow-brash and gazed with bowed heads at the slowly passing coffin, preceded by the wreath-bearing lackeys, the Court officials, the bearers of the insignia and Dom Wislezenus, the Court preacher, and covered with a silver-worked pall, whose corners were held by Lord Marshal von Bühl, Master of the Royal Hunt von Stieglitz, Adjutant-General Count Schmettern, and Minister of the Household von Knobelsdorff.

By the side of his brother Klaus Heinrich, immediately behind the charger which was led in rear of the hearse, and at the head of the other mourners, walked Grand Duke Albrecht II. His clothes, the tall stiff plume in the front of his busby, the long boots under his gaudy, ample Hussar's pelisse, with the crape band, did not become him. He walked as if embarrassed by the eyes of the crowd, and his shoulder-blades, naturally rather crooked, were twisted in an awkward nervous way as he walked. Repugnance at having to be chief actor in this funeral pomp was clearly written on his pale face. He did not raise his eyes as he walked, and he sucked his short rounded lower lip against the upper. . . .

His demeanour remained the same during the Curialia accompanying his accession, which were so arranged as to spare him as much as possible. The Grand Duke signed the oath in the Silver Hall of the Gala Rooms before the assembled Ministers, and read aloud in the Throne-room, standing in front of the rounded chair under the baldachin, the Speech from the Throne, which Herr von Knobelsdorff had drawn up. The economic condition of the country was touched upon in it with earnestness and delicacy, while appreciative mention was made of the unanimity which despite all troubles existed between the princes and the country—at which place a prominent functionary, who was apparently discontented about promotion, was said to have whispered to his neighbour that the unanimity consisted in the Prince being as deeply in debt as the country —a caustic remark which was much repeated, and ended by getting into hostile newspapers. . . . To end up, the President of the Landtag called for a cheer for the Grand Duke, a service was held in the Court Chapel, and that was all.

Further, Albrecht signed an edict, by virtue of which a number of sentences of fines and imprisonment, which had been imposed for the less serious misdemeanours, chiefly infringement of the forest laws, were remitted. The solemn procession through the city and the acclamation in the Town Hall were omitted altogether, as the Grand Duke felt too tired for them. Having been a captain hitherto, he was promoted on the occasion of his accession at once to the colonelcy *à la suite* of his Hussar regiment, but scarcely ever put the uniform on, and kept as far away as possible from his sphere as a soldier. He made no change whatever in his staff, perhaps out of respect to his father's memory, either among the Court appointments or in the Ministry.

The public saw him but rarely. His proud and bashful disinclination to show himself, to put himself forward, to allow others to acclaim him, was so clearly shown from the very beginning as to shock public opinion. He never appeared in the large box at the Court Theatre. He never took part in the park parade. When in residence at the Old Schloss, he had himself driven in a closed carriage to a remote and empty part of the suburbs, where he got out to take a little exercise; and in the summer at Hollerbrunn he only left the hedged walks of the parks on exceptional occasions.

Did the people catch a glimpse of him—at the Albrechtstor it might be, when wrapped in his heavy fur coat, which his father had worn before him, and on whose thick collar his delicate head now rested, he stepped into his carriage—timid glances were levelled at him, and the cheering was faint and hesitating. For the lower classes felt that with a prince like this there could be no question of cheering him and thereby cheering themselves at the same time. They looked at him, and did not recognize themselves in him; his refined superiority made it clear that they were of different clay from his. And they were not accustomed to that. Was there not a commissionaire posted in the Albrechtsplatz that very day, who with his high cheek-bones and grey whiskers looked a coarse and homely replica of the late Grand Duke? And did one not similarly meet with Prince Klaus Heinrich's features in the lower classes?

It was not so with his brother. The people could not see in him an idealized version of themselves, whom it could make them happy to cheer—as it meant cheering themselves too! the Grand Duke's Highness—his undoubted Highness!—was a nobility of the usual kind, undomestic, and without the stamp of the graciousness which inspires confidence. He too knew that; and the consciousness of his Highness, together

115

with that of his want of popular graciousness, were quite enough to account for his shyness and haughtiness. He began already to delegate as far as possible his duties to Prince Klaus Heinrich. He sent him to open the new spring at Immenstadt and to the historical town-pageant at Butterburg. Indeed, his contempt for any exhibition of his princely person went so far that Herr von Knobelsdorff had the greatest difficulty in persuading him to receive the Presidents of the two Chambers in the Throne-room himself, and not, "for reasons of health," as he was minded, to give place to his brother on this solemn occasion.

Albrecht II lived a lonely life in the Old Schloss; that was unavoidable in the nature of things. In the first place, Prince Klaus Heinrich, since Johann Albrecht's death, kept a Court of his own. That was demanded by etiquette, and he had been given the "Hermitage" as a residence, that Empire Schloss on the fringe of the northern suburbs, which, reposeful and charming, but long uninhabited and neglected, in the middle of its overgrown park next the Town Gardens, looked down on its little mud-thick pond. Some time ago, when Albrecht came of age, the "Hermitage" had been freshened up and for form's sake destined to be the Heir Apparent's palace; but as Albrecht had always come in summer straight from his warm, dry foreign resort to Hollerbrunn, he had never used his palace. . . .

Klaus Heinrich lived there without unnecessary expense, with one major-domo, who superintended the household, a Baron von Schulenburg-Tressen, nephew of the Mistress of the Robes. Besides his valet, Neumann, he had two other lackeys for his daily needs; he borrowed the game-keeper when necessary for ceremonial shoots, from the Grand Duke's Court. One coachman and a couple of grooms in red waistcoats looked after the carriages and horses, which consisted of one pony-cart, one brougham, one dog-cart, two riding and two carriage horses. One gardener, helped by two boys, looked after the park and the garden; and one cook with her kitchen-maid,

116

as well as two chambermaids, made up the female staff of the "Hermitage."

It was Court Marshal von Schulenburg's business to keep his young master's establishment going on the apanage which the Landtag, after Albrecht's accession, had voted the Grand Duke's brother after a serious debate. It amounted to two thousand five hundred pounds. For the sum of four thousand pounds, which had been the original demand, had never had any prospect of recommending itself to the Landtag, and so a wise and magnanimous act of self-denial had been credited to Klaus Heinrich, which had made an excellent impression in the country. Every winter Herr von Schulenburg sold the ice from the pond. He had the hay in the park mowed twice every summer and sold. After the harvests the surface of the fields looked almost like English turf.

Further, Dorothea, the Dowager Grand Duchess, no longer lived in the Old Schloss, and the causes of her retirement were both sad and uncomfortable. For she too, the Princess whom the much-travelled Herr von Knobelsdorff had described more than once as one of the most beautiful women he had ever seen, the Princess whose radiant smiles had evoked joy, enthusiasm, and cheers whenever she had shown herself to the longing gaze of the toil-worn masses, she too had had to pay her tribute to time. Dorothea had aged, her calm perfection, the admiration and joy of everybody, had during recent years withered so fast and steadily that the woman in her had been unable to keep pace with the transformation. Nothing, no art, no measures, even the painful and repulsive ones, with which she tried to stave off decay, had availed to prevent the sweet brightness of her deep blue eyes from fading, rings of loose yellow skin from forming under them, the wonderful little dimples in her cheeks from turning into furrows, and her proud and hard mouth from looking drawn and bitter.

But since her heart had been hard as her beauty, and had been absorbed in that beauty, since her beauty had been her very soul and she had had no wish, no love, beyond the effect

117

of that beauty on the hearts of others, while her own heart never beat the faster for anything or anyone, she was now disconsolate and lost, could not accommodate herself to the change and rebelled against it. Surgeon-General Eschrich said something about mental disturbance resulting from an unusually quick climacteric, and his opinion was undoubtedly correct in a sense. The sad truth at any rate was that Dorothea during the last years of her husband's life had already shown signs of profound mental disturbance and trouble.

She became light-shy, gave orders that at the Thursday concerts in the Marble Hall all the lights should be shaded red, and flew into a passion because she could not have the same thing done at all other festivities, the Court Ball, the Private Ball, the Dinner Party, and the Great Court, as the kind of twilight feeling in the Marble Hall had been enough by itself to call forth many cutting remarks. She spent whole days before her looking-glasses, and it was noticed that she fondled with her hands those which for some reason or other reflected her image in a more favourable light. Then again she had all the looking-glasses removed from her rooms, and those fixed in the wall draped, went to bed and prayed for death.

One day Baroness von Schulenburg found her quite distracted and feverish with weeping in the Hall of the Twelve Months before the big portrait which represented her at the height of her beauty. . . . At the same time a diseased misanthropy began to take possession of her, and both Court and people were distressed to notice how the bearing of this erstwhile goddess began to lose its assurance, her deportment became strangely awkward, and a pitiful look came into her eyes.

At last she shut herself up altogether, and, at the last Court Ball he attended, Johann Albrecht had escorted his sister Catherine instead of his "indisposed Consort." His death was from one point of view a release for Dorothea, as it relieved her from all her duties as a sovereign. She chose as dower-house Schloss Segenhaus, a monastic-looking old hunting-seat, which lay in a solemn park about one and a half hour's drive from the capital, and had been decorated by some pious old sportsman with religious and sporting emblems curiously intermixed. There she lived, eclipsed and odd, and excursionists could often watch her from afar, walking in the park with Baroness von Schulenburg-Tressen, and bowing graciously to the trees on each side of the path.

Lastly, Princess Ditlande had married at the age of twenty, one year after her father's death. She bestowed her hand on a prince of a mediatised house, Prince Philipp zu Ried-Hohenried, a no longer young, but well-preserved, cultured little man of advanced views, who paid her flattering attentions for some considerable time, did all his courting at first-hand, and offered the Princess his heart and hand in an honest bourgeois way at a charity function.

It would be wrong to say that this alliance evoked wild enthusiasm in the country. It was received with indifference; it disappointed. It is true, more ambitious hopes had been secretly entertained for Johann Albrecht's daughter, and all the critics could say was that the marriage could not be called a *mésalliance* in so many words. It was a fact that Ditlinde, in giving her hand to the Prince—which she did of her own free will, and quite uninfluenced by others—had undoubtedly descended out of her sphere of Highness into a more free and human atmosphere. Her noble spouse was not only a lover and collector of oil paintings, but also a business man and tradesman on a large scale.

The dynasty had ceased to exercise any sovereign right hundreds of years ago, but Philipp was the first of his house to make up his mind to exploit his private means in a natural way. After spending his youth in travelling, he had looked around for a sphere of activity which would keep him busy and contented, and at the same time (a matter of necessity) would increase his income. So he launched out into various enterprises, started farms, a brewery, a sugar factory, several saw-mills on his property, and began to exploit his extensive

119

peat deposits in a methodical way. As he brought expert knowledge and sound business instincts to all his enterprises, they soon began to pay, and returned profits which, if their origin was not very princely, at any rate provided him with the means of leading a princely existence which he would otherwise not have had.

On the other hand the critics might have been asked what sort of a match they could expect for their Princess, if they viewed the matter soberly. Ditlinde, who brought her husband scarcely anything except an inexhaustible store of linen, including dozens of out-of-date and useless articles such as night-caps and neckerchiefs, which however by hallowed tradition formed part of her trousseau—she by this marriage acquired a measure of riches and comfort such as she had never been accustomed to at home: and no sacrifice of her affections was necessary to pay for them. She took the step into private life with obvious contentment and determination, and retained, of the trappings of Highness, nothing but her title. She remained on friendly terms with her ladies-in-waiting, but divested her relations with them of everything which suggested service, and avoided giving her household the character of a Court.

That might evoke surprise, especially in a Grimmburg and in Ditlinde in particular, but there was no doubt that it was her own choice. The couple spent the summer on the princely estates, the winter in the capital in the stately palace in the Albrechtstrasse, which Philipp zu Ried had inherited; and it was here, not in the Old Schloss, that the Grand Ducal family —Klaus Heinrich and Ditlinde, occasionally Albrecht as well— met now and again for a confidential talk.

So it happened that one day at the beginning of autumn, not quite two years after the death of Johann Albrecht, the *Courier,* well-informed as usual, published in its evening edition the news that this afternoon his Royal Highness the Grand Duke and his Grand Ducal Highness Prince Klaus Heinrich had been to tea with her Grand Ducal Highness the

120

Princess zu Ried-Hohenried. That was all. But on that afternoon several topics of importance for the future were discussed between the brothers and sister.

Klaus Heinrich left the Hermitage shortly before five
o'clock. As the weather was sunny, he had ordered the dog-
cart, and the open brown-varnished vehicle, clean and shining,
if not over-new or smart to look at, came slowly up the broad
drive of the Schloss, at a quarter to five, from the stables,
which with their asphalt yard lay in the right wing of the
home farm. The home farm, yellow-painted, old-fashioned
buildings of one story, made one long line with, though at
some distance from, the plain white mansion, the front of
which, adorned with laurels at regular intervals, faced the
muddy pond and the public part of the park.

For the front portion of the estate, that which marched
with the town gardens, was open to pedestrians and light
traffic, and all that was enclosed was the gently rising flower-
garden, at the top of which lay the Schloss and the very unkempt park behind, which was divided by hedges and fences
from the rubbish-encumbered waste ground at the edge of the
town suburbs. So the cart came up the drive between the
pond and the home farm, turned through the high garden
gates, adorned with lamps which had once been gilt, passed
on up the drive and waited in front of the stiff little laurel-
planted terrace which led to the garden-room.

Klaus Heinrich came out a few minutes before five. He
wore as usual the tight-fitting uniform of a lieutenant of the
Grenadier Guards, and his sword-hilt hung on his arm. Neumann, in a violet coat whose arms were too short, ran in front
of him down the steps and with his red barber's hands packed
his master's folded grey over-coat into the cart. Then, while
the coachman, his hand to his cockaded hat, inclined a little
sideways on the box, the valet arranged the light carriage rug
over Klaus Heinrich's knees and stepped back with a silent
bow. The horses started off.

Outside the garden gates a few promenaders had collected.
121

They greeted Klaus Heinrich, smiling with knitted brows and hats lifted, and Klaus Heinrich thanked them by raising his white-gloved right hand to the peak of his cap and making a succession of lively nods.

They skirted a piece of waste ground along a birch avenue, whose leaves were already turning, and then drove through the suburb, between poverty-stricken houses, over unpaved streets, where the ragged children left their hoops and tops for a moment to gaze at the carriage with curious eyes. Some cried, Hurrah! and ran for a while by the side of the carriage, with heads turned towards Klaus Heinrich. The carriage might have taken the road by the Spa-gardens; but that through the suburb was shorter, and time pressed. Ditlinde was particular on points of regularity, and easily put out if anybody disturbed her household arrangements by unpunctuality.

Yonder was the Dorothea Children's Hospital of which Doctor Sammet, Ueberbein's friend, was the Director; Klaus Heinrich drove by it. And then the carriage left the squalid neighbourhood and reached the Gartenstrasse, a stately tree-planted avenue, in which lay the houses and villas of wealthy citizens, and along which ran the tram-line from the Spa Gardens to the centre of the city. The traffic here was fairly heavy, and Klaus Heinrich was kept busy answering the greetings which met him. Civilians took off their hats and looked from under their eyebrows at him, officers on horse and on foot saluted, policemen front-turned, and Klaus Heinrich in his corner raised his hand to the peak of his cap and thanked on both sides with the well-trained bow and smile which were calculated to confirm the people in their feeling of participation in his splendid personality. . . . His way of sitting in his carriage was quite peculiar—he did not lean back indolently and comfortably in the cushions, but he took just as active a part in the motions of the carriage when driving as in those of his horse when riding; with hands crossed on his sword hilt and one foot a little advanced, he as it were "took" the

122

unevennesses of the ground, and accommodated himself to the motion of the badly hung carriage.

The carriage crossed the Albrechtsplatz, left the Old Schloss, with the two sentries presenting arms, to the right, followed the Albrechtstrasse in the direction of the barracks of the Grenadier Guards and rolled to the left into the courtyard of the palace of the Princess of Ried. It was a building of regular proportions in the pedantic style, with a soaring gable over the main door, festooned *œils-de-bœuf* in the mezzanine story, high French windows in the first story, and an elegant *cour d'honneur*, which was formed by the two one-storied wings and was separated from the street by a circular railing, on whose pillars stone babies played. But the internal arrangements of the Schloss were, in contradistinction to the historical style of its exterior, conceived throughout in an up-to-date and comfortable bourgeois taste.

Ditlinde received her brother in a large drawing-room on the first floor with several curved sofas in pale green silk; the back part of the room was separated from the front by slender pillars, and filled with palms, plants in metal bowls, and tables covered with brilliant flowers.

"Good afternoon, Klaus Heinrich," said the Princess. She was delicate and thin, and the only luxuriant thing about her was her fair hair, which used to lie like ram's horns round her ears and now was dressed in thick plaits above her face with its high Grimmburg cheek-bones. She wore an indoor dress of soft blue-grey stuff with a white lace collar, cut in a point like a breast-plate and fastened at the waist with an old-fashioned oval brooch. Blue veins and shadows showed here and there through the delicate skin of her face, in the temples, the forehead, at the corners of her soft and calm blue eyes. Signs of approaching maternity were beginning to show themselves.

"Good afternoon, Ditlinde, you and your flowers!" answered Klaus Heinrich, as, clapping his heels together, he bent over her little, white, rather over-broad hand. "How they do smell! And the garden's full of them, I see."

123

"Yes," she said, "I love flowers. I have always longed to be able to live among quantities of flowers, living, smelling flowers, which I could watch growing—it was a kind of secret wish of mine, Klaus Heinrich, and I might almost say that I married for flowers, for in the Old Schloss, as you know, there were no flowers. . . . The Old Schloss and flowers! We should have had to rummage a lot to find them, I'm sure. Rat-traps and such things, plenty of them. And really, when one comes to think, the whole thing was like a disused rat-trap, so dusty and horrid . . . ugh! . . ."

"But the rose-bush, Ditlinde."

"Yes, my goodness—one rose-bush. And that's in the guide-books, because its roses smell of decay. And the books say that it will one day smell quite natural and nice, just like any other rose. But I can't believe it."

"You will soon," he said, and looked at her laughingly, "have something better than your flowers to tend, little Ditlinde."

"Yes," she said and blushed lightly and quickly, "yes, Klaus Heinrich, I can hardly believe it. And yet it will be so, if God pleases. But come over here. We'll have a chat together once more. . . ."

The room, on whose threshold they had been talking, was small in comparison with its height, with a grey-blue carpet, and furnished with cheery-looking silver-grey furniture, the chairs of which were upholstered in blue silk. A milk-white china chandelier hung from the white-festooned centre of the ceiling, and the walls were adorned with oil paintings of various sizes, acquisitions of Prince Philipp's, light studies in the new style, representing white goats in the sun, poultry in the sun, sun-bathed meadows and peasants with blinking, sun-sprinkled faces.

The spindle-legged secretaire in the white-curtained window was covered with a hundred carefully arranged articles, knick-knacks, writing materials, and several dainty note-blocks— for the Princess was accustomed to make careful and comprehensive notes about all her duties and plans. In front of the inkstand a housekeeper's book, in which Ditlinde had apparently just been working, lay open, and by the table there hung on the wall a little silk-trimmed block-calendar, under the printed date of which could be seen the pencil note: "5 o'clock: my brothers." Between the sofa and a semicircle of chairs over against the white swing doors into the reception room stood an oval table with a damask cloth and blue-silk border; the flowered tea-service, a jam-pot, long dishes of sweet cakes, and tiny pieces of bread and butter were arranged in ordered disorder on it, and to one side steamed the silver tea-kettle over its spirit-flame on a glass table. But there were flowers everywhere—flowers in the vases on the writing-table, on the tea-table, on the glass table, on the china cabinet, on the table next the white sofa, and a flower-table full of flower-pots stood in the window.

This room, situated at the side and in a corner of the suite of reception rooms, was Ditlinde's cabinet, her boudoir, the room in which she used to entertain quite intimate friends and to make tea with her own hands. Klaus Heinrich watched her as she washed out the tea-pot with hot water and put the tea in with a silver spoon.

"And Albrecht . . . is he coming?" he asked with an involuntarily restrained voice.

"I hope so," she said, bending attentively over the crystal tea-caddy, as if to avoid spilling any tea (and he too avoided looking at her). "I have of course asked him, Klaus Heinrich, but you know he cannot bind himself. It depends on his health whether he comes. I'm making our tea at once, for Albrecht will drink his milk. . . . Possibly too Jettchen may look in for a bit to-day. You will enjoy seeing her again. She's so lively, and has always got such a lot to tell us."

"Jettchen" meant Fräulein von Isenschnibbe, the Princess's friend and confidant. They had been on Christian-name terms since they were children.

"In armour, too, as usual?" said Ditlinde, placing the filled

125

tea-pot on its stand and examining her brother. "In uniform as usual, Klaus Heinrich?"

He stood with heels together and rubbed his left hand, which was cold, on his chest with his right.

"Yes, Ditlinde, I like it, I'd rather. It fits so tight, you see, and it braces me up. Besides, it is cheaper, for a proper civil wardrobe runs into a terrible lot of money, I believe, and Schulenburg is always going on about how dear things are, without that. So I manage with two or three coats, and yet can show myself in my rich relations' houses."

"Rich relations!" laughed Ditlinde. "Still some way off that, Klaus Heinrich!"

They sat down at the tea-table, Ditlinde on a sofa, Klaus Heinrich on a chair opposite the window.

"Rich relations!" she repeated, and the subject obviously excited her. "No, far from it; how can we expect to be rich, where cash is so short and everything is sunk in various enterprises, Klaus Heinrich? And they are young and in the making, they're all in the development stage, as dear Philipp says, and won't bear full fruit till others have succeeded us. But things are improving, that much is true, and I keep the household straight. . . ."

"Yes, Ditlinde, you do keep it straight and no mistake!"

"Keep it straight, and write everything down and look after the servants, and after all the payments which one's duty to the world demands have been made, there is a nice little sum to put by every year for the children. And dear Philipp. . . . He sends his greetings, Klaus Heinrich—I forgot, he's very sorry not to be able to be here to-day. . . . We've only just got back from Hohenried, and there he is already under way, at his office, on his properties—he's small and delicate naturally, but when his peat or his saw-mills are in question he gets red cheeks, and he says himself that he has been much better since he has had so much to do."

"Does he say so?" asked Klaus Heinrich, and a sad look came into his eyes, as he looked straight beyond the flower-

table at the bright window. . . . "Yes, I can quite believe
that it must be very stimulating to be so really splendidly
busy. In my park too the meadows have been mowed a second
time this year already, and I love seeing the hay built up in
steep heaps with a stick through the middle of each, looking
for all the world like a camp of little Indians' huts, and then
Schulenburg intends to sell it. But of course that cannot be
compared . . ."

"Oh, you!" said Ditlinde, and drew her chin in. "With
you it's quite different, Klaus Heinrich! The next to the
throne! You are called to other things, I imagine. My goodness, yes! You enjoy your popularity with the people. . . ."

They were silent for a while. Then he said:

"And you, Ditlinde, if I'm not mistaken you're as happy
as, even happier than, before. I don't say that you have
got red cheeks, like Philipp from his peat; you always were
a bit transparent, and you are still. But you look flourishing.
I haven't yet asked, since you married, but I think there's nothing to worry about in connexion with you."

She sat in an easy position, with her arm lightly folded
across her lap.

"Yes," she said, "I'm all right, Klaus Heinrich, your eyes
don't deceive you, and it would be ungrateful of me not to
acknowledge my good fortune. You see, I know quite well
that many people in the country are disappointed by my
marriage and say that I have ruined myself, and demeaned
myself, and so on. And such people are not far to seek, for
brother Albrecht, as you know as well as I do, in his heart
despises my dear Philipp and me into the bargain, and can't
abide him, and calls him privately a tradesman and shop-
keeper. But that doesn't bother me, for I meant it when I
accepted Philipp's hand—seized it, I would say, if it didn't
sound so wild—accepted it because it was warm and honest,
and offered to take me away from the Old Schloss. For when
I look back and think of the Old Schloss and life in it as I
should have gone on living if it had not been for dear Philipp,

127

I shudder, Klaus Heinrich, and I feel that I could not have borne it and should have become strange and queer like poor mamma. I am a bit delicate naturally, as you know, I should have simply gone under in so much desolation and sadness, and when dear Philipp came, I thought: now's your chance. And when people say that I am a bad Princess, because I have in a way abdicated, and fled here where it is rather warmer and more friendly, and when they say that I lack dignity or consciousness of Highness, or whatever they call it, they are stupid and ignorant, Klaus Heinrich, because I have too much, I have on the contrary too much of it, that's a fact, otherwise the Old Schloss would not have had such an effect upon me, and Albrecht ought to see that, for he too, in his way, has too much of it—all we Grimmburgers have too much of it, and that's why it sometimes looks as if we had too little of it. And sometimes, when Philipp is under way, as he is now, and I sit here among my flowers and Philipp's pictures with all their sun—it's lucky that it's painted sun, for bless me! otherwise we should have to get sun-blinds—and everything is tidy and clean, and I think of the blessing, as you call it, in store for me, then I seem to myself like the little mermaid in the fairy-tale which the Swiss governess read to us, if you remember—who married a mortal and got legs instead of her fish's tail. . . . I don't know if you understand me. . . ."

"Oh yes, Ditlinde, of course, I understand you perfectly. And I am really glad that everything has turned out so well and happily for you. For it is dangerous, I may tell you, in my experience it is difficult for us to be suitably happy. It's so easy to go wrong and be misunderstood, for the nuisance is that nobody protects our dignity for us if we don't do it ourselves, and then blame and scandal so readily follow. . . . But which is the right way? You have found it. They have quite recently announced my engagement with Cousin Griseldis in the newspapers. That was a *ballon d'essai*, as they call it, and they think it was a very happy one. But Griseldis is a silly girl, and half-dead with anæmia, and never says anything but 'yes,' so far as I know. I've never given her a thought, nor has Knobelsdorff, thank goodness. The news was at once announced to be unfounded. . . . Here comes Albrecht!" he said, and stood up.

A cough was heard outside. A footman in olive-green livery threw open the swing doors with a quick, firm, and noiseless movement of both arms, and announced in a subdued voice: "His Royal Highness the Grand Duke."

Then he stepped aside with a bow. Albrecht advanced through the room.

He had traversed the hundred yards from the Old Schloss hither in a closed carriage, with his huntsman on the box. He was in mufti, as almost always, wore a buttoned-up frock-coat with little satin lapels, and patent leather boots on his small feet. Since his accession he had grown an imperial. His short fair hair was brushed back on each of his narrow, sunk temples. His gait was an awkward and yet indescribably distinguished strut, which gave his shoulder-blades a peculiar twist. He carried his head well back and stuck his short round underlip out, sucking gently with it against the upper one.

The Princess went to the threshold to meet him. He disliked hand-kissing, so he simply held out his hand with a soft almost whispered greeting—his thin, cold hand which looked so sensitive and which he stretched out from his chest while keeping his forearm close to his body. Then he greeted his brother Klaus Heinrich in the same way, who had waited for him standing with heels close together in front of his chair—and said nothing further.

Ditlinde talked. "It's very nice of you to come, Albrecht. So you're feeling well? You look splendid. Philipp wishes me to tell you how sorry he is to have to be out this afternoon. Sit down, won't you, anywhere you like—here, for instance, opposite me. That chair's a pretty comfortable one, you sat in it last time. I've made tea for us in the meantime. You'll have your milk directly. . . ."

"Thanks," he said quietly. "I must beg pardon . . . I'm late. You know, the shorter the road . . . And then I have to lie down in the afternoon. . . . There's no one else coming?"

"No one else, Albrecht. At the most, Jettchen Isenschnibbe may look in for a bit, if you don't object. . . ."

"Oh?"

"But I can just as well say 'Not at home.' "

"Oh no, pray don't."

Hot milk was brought. Albrecht clasped the tall, thick, studded glass in both hands.

"Ah, something warm," he said. "How cold it is already in these parts! And I've been frozen the whole summer in Hollerbrunn. Haven't you started fires yet? I have. But then again the smell of the stoves upsets me. All stoves smell. Von Bühl promises me central heating for the Old Schloss every autumn. But it seems not to be feasible."

"Poor Albrecht," said Ditlinde, "at this time of year you used to be already in the South, so long as father was alive. You must long for it."

"Your sympathy does you credit, dear Ditlinde," answered he, still in a low and slightly lisping voice. "But we must show that I am on the spot. I must rule the country, as you know, that's what I'm here for. To-day I have been graciously pleased to allow some worthy citizen—I'm sorry I can't remember his name—to accept and wear a foreign order. Further, I have had a telegram sent to the annual meeting of the Horticultural Society, in which I assumed the honorary Presidency of the Society and pledged my word to further its efforts in every way—without really knowing what furthering I could do beyond sending the telegram, for the members are quite well able to take care of themselves. Further, I have deigned to confirm the choice of a certain worthy fellow to be mayor of my fair city of Siebenberge—in connection with which I should like to know whether this my subject will be a

130

better mayor for my confirmation than he would have been
without it. . . ."

"Well, well, Albrecht, those are trifles!" said Ditlinde.
"I'm convinced that you've had more serious business to
do. . . ."

"Oh, of course. I've had a talk with my Minister of
Finance and Agriculture. It was time I did. Doctor Krippenreuther would have been bitterly disappointed with me if I
had not summoned him once more. He went ahead in sum-
mary fashion and laid before me a conspectus of several
mutually related topics at once—the harvest, the new principles
for the drawing up of the budget, the reform of taxation, on
which he is busy. The harvest has been a bad one, it seems.
The peasants have been hit by blight and bad weather; not
only they, but Krippenreuther too, are much concerned about
it, because the tax-paying resources of the land, he says, have
once more suffered contraction. Besides, there have unfortunately been disasters in more than one of the silver-mines.
The gear is at a standstill, says Krippenreuther, it is damaged
and will cost a lot of money to repair. I listened to the whole
recital with an appropriate expression on my face, and did
what I could to express my grief for such a series of misfortunes. Next, I was consulted as to whether the cost of
the necessary new buildings for the Treasury and for the
Woods and Customs and Inland Revenue Offices ought to be
debited to the ordinary or the extraordinary estimates; I
learnt a lot about sliding scales, and income tax, and tax
on tourist traffic, and the removal of burdens from oppressed
agriculture and the imposition of burdens on the towns; and
on the whole I got the impression that Krippenreuther was
well up in his subject. I, of course, know practically nothing
about it—which Krippenreuther knows and approves; so I
just said 'yes, yes,' and 'of course,' and 'many thanks,' and let
him run on."

"You speak so bitterly, Albrecht."

131

"No; I'll just tell you what struck me while Krippenreuther was holding forth to me to-day. There's a man living in this town, a man with small private means and a warty nose. Every child knows him and shouts 'Hi!' when he sees him; he is called 'the Hatter,' for he is not quite all there; his surname he has lost long ago. He is always on the spot when there is anything going on, although his half-wittedness keeps him from playing any serious part in anything; he wears a rose in his buttonhole, and carries his hat about on the end of his walking-stick. Twice a day, about the time when a train starts, he goes to the station, taps the wheels, examines the luggage, and fusses about. Then when the guard blows his whistle, 'the Hatter' waves to the engine-driver, and the train starts. But 'the Hatter' deludes himself into thinking that his waving sends the train off. That's like me. I wave, and the train starts. But it would start without me, and my waving makes no difference, it's mere silly show. I'm sick of it. . . ."

The brother and sister were silent. Ditlinde looked at her lap in an embarrassed way, and Klaus Heinrich gazed, as he tugged at his little bow-shaped moustache, between her and the Grand Duke at the bright window.

"I can quite follow you, Albrecht," said he after a while, "though it is rather cruel of you to compare yourself and us with 'the Hatter.' You see, I too understand nothing about sliding scales and taxation of tourist traffic and peat-cutting, and there is such a lot about which I know nothing—everything which is covered by the expression 'the misery in the world'—hunger and want, and the struggle for existence, as it is called, and war and hospital horrors, and all that. I have seen and studied not one of these, except death itself, when father died, and that too was not death as it can be, but rather it was edifying, and the whole Schloss was illuminated. And at times I feel ashamed of myself because I have not knocked about the world. But then I tell myself that mine is not a comfortable life, not at all comfortable, although I

132

'wander on the heights of mankind,' as people express it, or perhaps just because I do, and that I perhaps in my own way know more about the strenuousness of life, its 'tight-lipped countenance,' if you will allow me the expression, than many a one who knows all about the sliding scales or any other single department of life. And the upshot of that is, Albrecht, that my life is not a comfortable one—that's the upshot of everything—if you will allow me this retort, and that is how we justify ourselves. And if people cry 'Hi!' when they see me, they must know why they do so, and my life must have some *raison d'être*, although I am prevented from playing any serious part in anything, as you so admirably express it. And you're quite justified too. You wave to order, because the people wish you to wave, and if you do not really control their wishes and aspirations, yet you express them and give them substance, and may be that's no slight matter."

Albrecht sat upright at the table. He held his thin, strangely sensitive-looking hands crossed on the table-edge in front of the tall, half-empty glass of milk, and his eyelids dropped, and he sucked his underlip against his upper. He answered quietly: "I'm not surprised that so popular a prince as you should be contented with his lot. I for my part decline to express somebody else in my own person—I decline to, say, and you may think it's a case of sour grapes as much as you like. The truth is that I care for the 'Hi!' of the people just as little as any living soul possibly could care. I say soul, not body. The flesh is weak—there's something in one which expands at applause and contracts at cold silence. But my reason rises superior to all considerations of popularity or unpopularity. If I *did* succeed in being a true national representative, I know what that would amount to. A misconception of my personality. Besides, a few hand-claps from people one does not know are not worth a shrug of the shoulders. Others—you—may be inspired by the feeling of the people behind you. You must forgive me for being too matter-of-fact to feel any such mysterious feeling

133

of happiness—and too keen on cleanliness also, if you will allow me to put it thus. That kind of happiness stinks, to my thinking. Anyhow, I'm a stranger to the people. I give them nothing—what can they give me? With you . . . oh, that's quite different. Hundreds of thousands, who are like you, are grateful to you because they can recognize themselves in you. You may laugh if you like. The chief danger you run is that you submerge yourself in your popularity too readily; and yet after all you feel no apprehensions, although you are aware at this very moment . . ."

"No, Albrecht, I don't think so. I don't think I run any such danger."

"Then we shall understand each other all the better. I have no penchant for strong expressions as a rule. But popularity is hog-wash."

"It's funny, Albrecht. Funny that you should use that word. The 'Pheasants' were always using it—my schoolmates, the young sprigs, you know, at the 'Pheasantry.' I know what you are. You're an aristocrat, that's what's the matter."

"Do you think so? You're wrong. I'm no aristocrat, I'm the opposite, by taste and reason. You must allow that I do not despise the 'Hi's' of the crowd from arrogance, but from a propensity to humanity and goodness. Human Highness is a pitiable thing, and I'm convinced that mankind ought to see that everyone behaves like a man, and a good man, to his neighbour and does not humiliate him or cause him shame. A man must have a thick skin to be able to carry off all the flummery of Highness without any feeling of shame. I am naturally rather sensitive, I cannot cope with the absurdity of my situation. Every lackey who plants himself at the door, and expects me to pass him without noticing, without heeding him more than the door posts, fills me with embarrassment, that's the way I feel towards the people. . . ."

"Yes, Albrecht, quite true. It's often by no means easy to keep one's countenance when one passes by a fellow like that.

The lackeys! If one only did not know what frauds they are! One hears fine stories about them. . . ."

"What stories?"

"Oh, one keeps one's ears open. . . ."

"Come, come!" said Ditlinde. "Don't let's worry about that. Here you are talking about ordinary things, and I had two topics noted down which I thought we might discuss this afternoon. . . . Would you be so kind, Klaus Heinrich, as to reach me that notebook there in blue leather on the writing-table? Many thanks. I note down in this everything I have to remember, both household matters and other things. What a blessing it is to be able to see everything down in black and white! My head is terribly weak, it can't remember things, and if I weren't tidy and didn't jot everything down, I should be done for. First of all, Albrecht, before I forget it, I wanted to remind you that you must escort Aunt Catherine at the first Court on November 1st—you can't get out of it. I withdraw; the honour fell to me at the last Court Ball, and Aunt Catherine was terribly put out. . . . Do you consent? Good, then I cross out item 1. Secondly, Klaus Heinrich, I wanted to ask you to make a short appearance at the Orphan Children's Bazaar on the 15th in the Town Hall. I am patroness, and I take my duties seriously, as you see. You needn't buy anything—a pocket comb. . . . In short, all you need do is to show yourself for ten minutes. It's for the orphans. . . . Will you come? You see, now I can cross another off. Thirdly . . ."

But the Princess was interrupted. Fräulein von Isenschnibbe, the Court lady, was announced and tripped in at once through the big drawing-room, her feather boa waving in the draught, and the brim of her huge feather hat flapping up and down. The smell of the fresh air from outside seemed to cling to her clothes. She was small, very fair, with a pointed nose, and so short-sighted that she could not see the stars. On clear evenings she would stand on her balcony

135

and gaze at the starry heavens through opera-glasses, and rave about them. She wore two strong pairs of glasses, one behind the other, and screwed up her eyes and stuck her head forward as she curtseyed.

"Heavens, Grand Ducal Highness," she said, "I didn't know; I'm disturbing you, I'm intruding. I most humbly beg pardon!"

The brothers had risen, and the visitor, as she curtseyed to them, was filled with confusion. As Albrecht extended his hand from his chest, keeping his forearm close to his body, her arm was stretched out almost perpendicularly, when the curtsey which she made him had reached its lowest point.

"Dear Jettchen," said Ditlinde, "what nonsense! You are expected and welcome, and my brothers know that we call each other by our Christian names, so none of that Grand Ducal Highness, if you please. We are not in the Old Schloss. Sit down and make yourself comfortable. Will you have some tea? It's still hot, and here are some candied fruits, I know you like them."

"Yes, a thousand thanks, Ditlinde, I adore them!" And Fräulein von Isenschnibbe took a chair on the narrow side of the tea-table opposite Klaus Heinrich, with her back to the window, drew a glove off and began peering forward, to lay sweetmeats on her plate with the silver tongs. Her little bosom heaved quickly and nervously with pleasurable excitement.

"I've got some news," she said, unable any longer to contain herself. "News. . . . More than any reticule will hold! That is to say it is really only one piece of news, only one— but it's so weighty that it counts for dozens, and it is quite certain, I have it on the best authority—you know that I am reliable, Ditlinde; this very evening it will be in the *Courier* and to-morrow the whole town will be talking about it."

"Yes, Jettchen," said the Princess, "it must be confessed you never come with empty hands; but now we're excited, do tell us your news."

136

"Very well. Let me get my breath. Do you know, Ditlinde, does your Royal Highness know, does your Grand Ducal Highness know who's coming, who is coming to the spa, who is coming for six or eight weeks to the Spa Hotel to drink the waters?"

"No," said Ditlinde, "but do you know, dear Jettchen?"

"Spoelmann," said Fräulein von Isenschnibbe. "Spoelmann," she said, leaned back and made as if to draw with her fingers on the table-edge, but checked the movement of her hand just over the blue silk border.

The brothers and sister looked doubtfully at each other.

"Spoelmann?" asked Ditlinde. . . . "Think a moment, Jettchen, the real Spoelmann?"

"The real one!" Her voice cracked with suppressed jubilation. "The real one, Ditlinde! For there's only one, or rather only one whom everybody knows, and he it is whom they are expecting at the Spa Hotel—the great Spoelmann, the giant Spoelmann, the colossus Samuel N. Spoelmann from America!"

"But, child, what's bringing him here?"

"Really, forgive me for saying so, Ditlinde, but what a question! His yacht or some big steamer is bringing him over the sea of course, he's on his holidays making a tour of Europe and has expressed his intention of drinking the Spa waters."

"But is he ill, then?"

"Of course, Ditlinde; all people of his kind are ill, that's part of the business."

"Strange," said Klaus Heinrich.

"Yes, Grand Ducal Highness, it is remarkable. His kind of existence must bring that with it. For there's no doubt it's a trying existence, and not at all a comfortable one, and must wear the body out quicker than an ordinary man's life would. Most suffer in the stomach, but Spoelmann suffers from stone as everybody knows."

"Stone, does he?"

"Of course, Ditlinde, you must have heard it and forgotten it. He has stone in the kidneys, if you will forgive me the horrid expression—a serious, trying illness, and I'm sure he can't get the slightest pleasure from his frantic wealth."

"But how in the world has he pitched upon our waters?"

"Why, Ditlinde, that's simple. The waters are good, they're excellent; especially the Ditlinde spring, with its lithium or whatever they call it, is admirable against gout and stone, and only waiting to be properly known and valued throughout the world. But a man like Spoelmann, you can imagine, a man like that is above names and trade-puffs, and follows his own kind. And so he has discovered our waters—or his physician has recommended them to him, it may be that, and bought it in the bottle, and it has done him good, and now he may think that it must do him still more good if he drinks it on the spot."

They all kept silence.

"Great heavens, Albrecht," said Ditlinde at last, "whatever one thinks of Spoelmann and his kind—and I'm not going to commit myself to an opinion, of that you may be sure— but don't you think that the man's visit to the Spa may be very useful?"

The Grand Duke turned his head with his stiff and refined smile.

"Ask Fräulein von Isenschnibbe," he answered. "She has doubtless already considered the question from that point of view."

"If your Royal Highness asks me . . . enormously useful! Immeasurably, incalculably useful—that's obvious! The directors are in the seventh heaven, they're getting ready to decorate and illuminate the Spa Hotel! What a recommendation, what an attraction for strangers! Will your Royal Highness just consider—the man is a curiosity! Your Grand Ducal Highness spoke just now of 'his kind'—but there are none of 'his kind'—at most, only a couple. He's a Leviathan, a Crœsus! People will come from miles away to

138

see a being who has about half a million a day to spend!"

"Gracious!" said Ditlinde, taken aback. "And there's dear Philipp worrying about his peat beds."

"The first scene," the Fräulein went on, "begins with two Americans hanging about the Exchange for the last couple of days. Who are they? They are said to be journalists, reporters, for two big New York papers. They have preceded the Leviathan, and are telegraphing to their papers preliminary descriptions of the scenery. When he has got here they will telegraph every step he takes—just as the *Courier* and the *Advertiser* report about your Royal Highness. . . ."

Albrecht bowed his thanks with eyes downcast and underlip protuded.

"He has appropriated the Prince's suite in the Spa Hotel," said Jettchen, as provisional lodgings."

"For himself alone?" asked Ditlinde.

"Oh no, Ditlinde, do you suppose he'd be coming alone? There isn't any precise information about his suite and staff, but it's quite certain that his daughter and his physician-in-ordinary are coming with him."

"It annoys me, Jettchen, to hear you talking about a 'physician-in-ordinary' and the journalists, too, and the Prince's suite to boot. He's not a king, after all."

"A railway king, so far as I know," remarked Albrecht quietly with eyes downcast.

"Not only, nor even particularly, a railway king, Royal Highness, according to what I hear. Over in America they have those great business concerns called Trusts, as your Royal Highness knows—the Steel Trust for instance, the Sugar Trust, the Petroleum Trust, the Coal, Meat, and Tobacco Trusts, and goodness knows how many more, and Samuel N. Spoelmann has a finger in nearly all these trusts, and is chief shareholder in them, and managing director—that's what I believe they call them—so his business must be what is called over here a 'Mixed Goods Business.' "

139

"A nice sort of business," said Ditlinde, "it must be a nice sort of business! For you can't persuade me, dear Jettchen, that honest work can make a man into a Leviathan and a Crœsus. I am convinced that his riches are steeped in the blood of widows and orphans. What do you think, Albrecht?"

"I hope so, Ditlinde, I hope so, for your own and your husband's comfort."

"May be so," explained Jettchen, "yet Spoelmann—our Samuel N. Spoelmann—is hardly responsible for it, for he is really nothing but an heir, and may quite well not have had any particular taste for his business. It was his father who really made the pile, I've read all about it, and may say that I really know the general facts. His father was a German —simply an adventurer who crossed the seas and became gold-digger. And he was lucky and made a little money through gold-finds—or rather quite a decent amount of money —and began to speculate in petroleum and steel and railways, and then in every sort of thing, and kept growing richer and richer, and when he died everything was already in full swing, and his son Samuel, who inherited the Crœsus' firm, really had nothing to do but to collect the princely dividends and keep growing richer and richer till he beat all records. That's the way things have gone."

"And he has a daughter, has he, Jettchen? What's she like?"

"Yes, Ditlinde, his wife is dead, but he has a daughter, Miss Spoelmann, and he's bringing her with him. She's a wonderful girl from all I've read about her. He himself is a bit of a mixture, for his father married a wife from the South—creole blood, the daughter of a German father and native mother. But Samuel in his turn married a German-American of half-English blood, and their daughter is now Miss Spoelmann."

"Gracious, Jettchen, she's a creature of many colours!"

"You may well say so, Ditlinde, and she's clever, so I've

140

heard; she studies like a man—algebra, and puzzling things
of that sort."

"Hm, that too doesn't attract me much."

"But now comes the cream of the business, Ditlinde, for
Miss Spoelmann has a lady-companion, and that lady-
companion is a countess, a real genuine countess, who dances
attendance on her."

"Gracious!" said Ditlinde, "she ought to be ashamed of
herself. No, Jettchen, my mind is made up. I'm not going
to bother myself about Spoelmann. I'm going to let him
drink his waters and go, with his countess and his algebraical
daughter, and am not going so much as to turn my head to
look at him. He and his riches make no impression on me.
What do you think, Klaus Heinrich?"

Klaus Heinrich looked past Jettchen's head at the bright
window.

"Impression?" he said. . . . "No, riches make no impression on me, I think—I mean, riches in the ordinary way.
But it seems to me that it depends . . . It depends, I think,
on the standard. We too have one or two rich people in the
town here—Soap-boiler Unschlitt must be a millionaire. . . .
I often see him in his carriage. He's dreadfully fat and common. But when a man is quite ill and lonely from mere
riches . . . Maybe . . ."

"An uncomfortable sort of man anyhow," said Ditlinde,
and the subject of the Spoelmanns gradually dropped.
The conversation turned on family matters, the "Hohenried" property, and the approaching season. Shortly before seven o'clock the Grand Duke sent for his carriage.
Prince Klaus Heinrich was going too, so they all got up
and said good-bye. But while the brothers were being
helped into their coats in the hall, Albrecht said: "I should
be obliged, Klaus Heinrich, if you would send your coachman home and would give me the pleasure of your company
for a quarter of an hour longer. I've got a matter of some
141

importance to discuss with you—I might come with you to the Hermitage, but I can't bear the evening air."

Klaus Heinrich clapped his heels together as he answered: "No, Albrecht, you mustn't think of it! I'll drive to the Schloss with you if you like. I am of course at your disposal."

This was the prelude to a remarkable conversation between the young princes, the upshot of which was published a few days later in the *Advertiser* and received with general approval.

The Prince accompanied the Grand Duke to the Schloss, through the Albrechtstor, up broad stone steps, through corridors where naked gas lamps were burning, and silent anterooms, between lackeys into Albrecht's "closet," where old Prahl had lighted the two bronze oil-lamps on the mantelpiece. Albrecht had taken over his father's work-room—it had always been the work-room of the reigning sovereigns, and lay on the first floor between an aide-de-camp's room and the dining-room in daily use facing the Albrechtsplatz, which the princes had always overlooked and watched from their writing-table. It was an exceptionally unhomely and repellent room, small, with cracked ceiling-paintings, red silk and gold-bordered carpet, and three windows reaching to the ground, through which the draught blew keenly and before which the claret-coloured curtains with their elaborate fringes were drawn. It had a false chimney-piece in French Empire taste, in front of which a semicircle of little modern quilted plush chairs without arms were arranged, and a hideously decorated white stove, which gave out a great heat. Two big quilted sofas stood opposite each other by the walls, and in front of one stood a square book-table with a red plush cover. Between the windows two narrow gold-framed mirrors with marble ledges reached up to the ceiling, the right hand one of which bore a fairly cheerful alabaster group, the other a water bottle and medicine glasses. The writing-desk, an old piece made of rose-wood with a roll-top and metal clasps, stood clear in the middle of the room on the red carpet. An

142

antique stared down with its dead eyes from a pedestal in one corner of the room.

"What I have to suggest to you," said Albrecht—he was standing at the writing-table, unconsciously toying with a paper-knife, a silly thing like a cavalry-sabre with a grotesque handle, "is directly connected with our conversation this afternoon. I may begin by saying that I discussed the matter thoroughly with Knobelsdorff this summer at Hollerbrunn. He agrees, and if you do too, as I don't doubt you will, I can carry out my intention at once."

"Please let's hear it, Albrecht," said Klaus Heinrich, who was standing at attention in a military attitude by the sofa table.

"My health," continued the Grand Duke, "has been getting worse and worse lately."

"I'm very sorry, Albrecht—Hollerbrunn didn't agree with you, then?"

"Thanks, no, I'm in a bad way, and my health is showing itself increasingly unequal to the demands made upon it. When I say 'demands,' I mean chiefly the duties of a ceremonial and representative nature which are inseparable from my position—and that's the bond of connexion with the conversation we had just now at Ditlinde's. The performance of these duties may be a happiness when a contact with the people, a relationship, a beating of hearts in unison exists. To me it is a torture, and the falseness of my rôle wearies me to such a degree that I must consider what measures I can take to counteract it. In this—so far as the bodily part of me is concerned—I am at one with my doctors, who entirely agree with my proposal—so listen to me. I'm unmarried. I have no idea, I can assure you, of ever marrying; I shall have no children. You are heir to the throne by right of birth, you are still more so in the consciousness of the people, who love you. . . ."

"There you are, Albrecht, always talking about my being beloved. I simply don't believe it. At a distance, perhaps
143

—that's the way with us. It's always at a distance that we are beloved."

"You're too modest. Wait a bit. You've already been kind enough to relieve me of some of my representative duties now and then. I should like you to relieve me of all of them absolutely, for always."

"You're not thinking of abdicating, Albrecht?" asked Klaus Heinrich, aghast.

"I daren't think of it. Believe me, I gladly would, but I shouldn't be allowed to. What I'm thinking of is not a regency, but only a substitution—perhaps you have some recollection of the distinction in public law from your student's days—a permanent and officially established substitution in all representative functions, warranted by the need of indulgence required by my state of health. What is your opinion?"

"I'm at your orders, Albrecht. But I'm not quite clear yet. How far does the substitution extend?"

"Oh, as far as possible. I should like it to extend to all occasions on which a personal appearance in public is expected of me. Knobelsdorff stipulates that I should only devolve the opening and closure of Parliament on you when I'm bedridden, only now and again. Let's grant that. But otherwise you would be my substitute on all ceremonial occasions, on journeys, visits to cities, opening of public festivities, opening of the Citizens' Ball. . . ."

"That too?"

"Why not? We have also the weekly free audiences here —a sensible custom without a doubt, but it tires me out. You would hold the audiences in my place. I needn't go on. Do you accept my proposal?"

"I am at your orders."

"Then listen to me while I finish. For every occasion on which you act as my representative, I lend you my aides-de-camp. It is further necessary that your military promotion should be hastened—are you first lieutenant? You'll be made a captain or a major straight away *à la suite* of your regiment

144

—I'll see to that; but in the third place, I wish duly to emphasize our arrangement, to make your position at my side properly clear, by lending you the title of 'Royal Highness.' There were some formalities to attend to. Knobelsdorff has already seen to them. I'm going to express my intentions in the form of two missives to you and to my Minister of State. Knobelsdorff has already drafted them. Do you accept?"

"What am I to say, Albrecht? You are father's eldest son, and I've always looked up to you because I've always felt and known that you are the superior and higher of us two and that I am only a plebeian compared with you. But if you think me worthy to stand at your side and to bear your title and to represent you before the people, although I don't think myself anything like so presentable, and have this deformity here, with my left hand, which I've always got to keep covered—then I thank you and put myself at your orders."

"Then I'll ask you to leave me now, please; I want to rest."

They advanced towards each other, the one from the writing-table, the other from the book-table, over the carpet into the middle of the room. The Grand Duke extended his hand to his brother—his thin, cold hand which he stretched out from his chest without moving his forearm away from his body. Klaus Heinrich clapped his heels together and bowed as he took the hand, and Albrecht nodded his narrow head with its fair beard as a token of dismissal, while he sucked his short, rounded lower lip against the upper. Klaus Heinrich went back to the Schloss "Hermitage."

Both the *Advertiser* and the *Courier* published eight days later the two missives, which contained decisions of the highest importance, the one addressed to "My dear Minister of State, Baron von Knobelsdorff," and the other beginning with "Most Serene Highness and well-beloved brother," and signed "Your Royal Highness's most devoted brother Albrecht."

# VI

## THE LOFTY CALLING

HERE follows a description of Klaus Heinrich's mode of life and profession and their peculiarities.

On a typical occasion he stepped out of his carriage, walked with cloak thrown back down a short passage through cheering crowds over a pavement which was covered with red carpet, through a laurel-decked house-door, over which an awning had been erected, up a staircase flanked by pairs of candle-bearing footmen. . . . He was on his way to a festival dinner, covered to his hips with orders, the fringed epaulettes of a major on his narrow shoulders, and was followed by his suite along the Gothic corridor of the town hall. Two servants hurried in front of him and quickly opened an old window which rattled in its lead fastenings; for down below in the market-place stood the people, wedged together head to head, an oblique tract of upturned faces, dimly illuminated by smoky torchlight. They cheered and sang, and he stood at the open window and bowed, displayed himself to the general enthusiasm for a while and nodded his thanks.

There was nothing really everyday, nor was there anything really actual, about his life; it consisted of a succession of moments of enthusiasm. Wherever he went there was holiday, there the people were transfigured and glorified, there the grey work-a-day world cleared up and became poetry. The starveling became a sleek man, the hovel a homely cottage, dirty gutter-children changed into chaste little maidens and boys in Sunday clothes, their hair plastered with water, a poem on their lips, and the perspiring citizen in frock-coat and top-hat was moved to emotion by the consciousness of his own worth.

But not only he, Klaus Heinrich, saw the world in this light, but it saw itself too, as long as his presence lasted. A strange unreality and speciousness prevailed in places where he exercised his calling; a symmetrical, transitory window-dressing, an artificial and inspiring disguising of the reality by pasteboard and gilded wood, by garlands, lamps, draperies, and bunting, was conjured up for one fair hour, and he himself stood in the centre of the show on a carpet, which covered the bare ground, between masts painted in two colours, round which garlands twined—stood with heels together in the odour of varnish and fir-branches, and smiled with his left hand planted on his hip.

He laid the foundation stone of a new town hall. The citizens had, after juggling with the figures, got together the necessary sum, and a learned architect from the captital had been entrusted with the building. But Klaus Heinrich undertook the laying of the foundation stone. Amid the cheers of the population he drove up to the noble pavilion which had been built on the site, stepped lightly and collectedly out of the open carriage on to the ground, which had been rolled and sprinkled with yellow sand, and walked all alone towards the official personages in frock-coats and white ties who were waiting for him at the entrance. He asked for the architect to be presented to him, and, in full view of the public and with the officials standing with fixed smiles round him, he conducted a conversation with him for five full minutes, a conversation of weighty commonplaces about the advantages of the different styles of architecture, after which he made a decided movement, which he had meditated to himself beforehand during the conversation, and allowed himself to be conducted over the carpet and plank steps to his seat on the edge of the middle platform.

There, in his chain and stars, one foot advanced, his white-gloved hands crossed on his sword hilt, his helmet on the

147

ground beside him, visible to the holiday crowd on every side, he sat and listened with calm demeanour to the Lord Mayor's speech. Thereupon, when they came to the request, he rose, walked, without noticeable precaution and without looking at his feet, down the steps to where the foundation stone lay, and with a little hammer gave three slow taps to the block of sandstone, at the same time repeating in the deep hush, with his rather sharp voice, a sentence which Herr von Knobelsdorff had previously impressed upon him. School children sang in shrill chorus, and Klaus Heinrich drove away.

On the anniversary of the War of Independence he marched in front of the veterans. A grey-haired officer shouted in a voice which seemed hoarse with the smoke of gunpowder: "Halt! Off hats! Eyes right!" And they stood, with medals and crosses on their coats, the rough beavers in their hands, and looked up at him with blood-shot eyes like those of a hound as he walked by with a friendly look, and paused by one or two to ask where they had served, where they had been under fire. . . . He attended the gymnastic display, graced the sports with his presence, and had the victors presented to him for a short conversation. The lithe athletic youths stood awkwardly before him, just after they had done the most astonishing feats, and Klaus Heinrich quickly strung together a few technical remarks, which he remembered from Herr Zotte, and which he uttered with great fluency, the while he hid his left hand.

He attended the Five Houses' Fishing festival, he was present in his red-covered seat of honour at the Grimmburg horse-races and distributed the prizes. He accepted, too, the honorary Presidency and Patronage of the Associated Rifle Competition; he attended the prize-meeting of the privileged Grand Ducal Rifle Club. He "responded cordially to the toast of welcome," in the words of the *Courier*, by holding the silver cup for one moment to his lips, and then with heels clapped together, raising it towards the marksmen. Thereupon he fired several shots at the target of honour, concerning which there was nothing said in the reports as to where they hit; next ploughed through one and the same dialogue with three successive men, about the advantages of rifle-firing, which in the *Courier* was described as a "general conversation," and at last took leave with a hearty "Good luck!" which evoked indescribable enthusiasm. This formula had been whispered to him at the last moment by Adjutant-General von Hühnemann, who had made inquiries on the subject; for of course it would have had a bad effect, would have shattered the fair illusion of technical knowledge and serious enthusiasm, if Klaus Heinrich had wished the marksmen "Excelsior" and the Alpine Club "Bull's-eyes every time!"

As a general rule he needed in the exercise of his calling a certain amount of technical knowledge, which he acquired for each succeeding occasion, with a view to applying it at the right moment and in suitable form. It consisted preponderatingly of the technical terms current in the different departments of human activity as well as of historical dates, and before setting out on an official expedition Klaus Heinrich used to work up the necessary information at home in the Hermitage with the help of pamphlets and oral instructions. When he in the name of the Grand Duke, "my most gracious brother," unveiled the statue of Johann Albrecht at Knüppelsdorf, he delivered on the scene of festivities, directly after a performance by the massed choirs of the "Wreath of Harmony," a speech in which everything he had noted down about Knüppelsdorf was dragged in, and which produced the delightful impression everywhere that he had busied himself all his life with nothing so much as the historical vicissitudes of that hub of civilization.

In the first place, Knüppelsdorf was a city, and Klaus Heinrich alluded to that three times, to the pride of the inhabitants. He went on to say that the city of Knüppelsdorf, as her historical past witnessed, had been connected by bonds of loyalty to the House of Grimmburg for several centuries. As long ago as the fourteenth century, he said, Langrave Heinrich XV,

149

the Rutensteiner, had signalled out Knüppelsdorf for special favour. He, the Rutensteiner, had lived in the Schloss built on the neighbouring Rutensteine, whose girdle of proud towers and strong walls had sent its greeting to the country for miles round.

Then he reminded his hearers how through inheritance and marriage Knüppelsdorf had at last come into the branch of the family to which his brother and he himself belonged. Heavy storms had in the course of years burst over Knüppelsdorf. Years of war, conflagration, and pestilence had visited it, yet it had always risen again and had always remained loyal to the house of its hereditary princes. And this characteristic the Knüppelsdorf of to-day proved that it possessed by raising a memorial to his, Klaus Heinrich's, beloved father, and it would be with unusual pleasure that he would report to his gracious brother the dazzling and hearty reception which he, as his representative, had here experienced. . . . The veil fell, the massed choirs of the "Wreath of Harmony" again did their best. And Klaus Heinrich stood smiling, under his theatrical tent, with a feeling of having exhausted his store of knowledge, happy in the certainty that nobody dare question him further. For he couldn't have said one blessed word more about Knüppelsdorf!

How tiring his life was, how strenuous! Sometimes he felt as if he had constantly to keep upright, at a great strain to his elasticity, something which it was quite impossible, or possible only in favourable conditions, to keep upright. Sometimes his calling seemed to him a wretched and paltry one, although he liked it and gladly undertook every expedition required of him in his representative capacity.

He travelled miles to an agricultural exhibition, travelled in a badly hung cart from Schloss "Hermitage" to the station, where the Premier, the Chief of Police, and the directors of the railway company awaited him at the saloon carriage. He travelled for an hour and a half, the while carrying on, not without difficulty, a conversation with the Grand Ducal adjutants, who had been attached to him, and the Agricultural Commissioner, Assistant Secretary Heckepfeng, a severe and respectful man who also accompanied him. Then he reached the station of the city which had organized the agricultural exhibition. The Mayor, with a chain over his shoulders, was awaiting him at the head of six or seven other official persons. The station was decorated with a quantity of fir-branches and festoons. In the back-ground stood the plaster busts of Albrecht and Klaus Heinrich in a frame of greenery. The public behind the barriers gave three cheers, and the bells pealed.

The Mayor read an address of welcome to Klaus Heinrich. He thanked him, he said, brandishing his top-hat in his hand, he thanked him on behalf of the city for all the favour which Klaus Heinrich's brother and he himself showed them, and heartily wished him a long and blessed reign. He also begged the Prince twice over graciously to crown the work which had prospered so famously under his patronage, and to open the agricultural exhibition.

This Mayor bore the title of Agricultural Councillor, a fact of which Klaus Heinrich had been apprised, and on account of which he addressed him thus three times in his answer. He said that he was delighted that the work of the agricultural exhibition had prospered so famously under his patronage. (As a matter of fact he had forgotten that he was patron of this exhibition.) He had come to put the finishing touch that day to the great work, by opening the exhibition. Then he inquired as to four things: as to the economical circumstances of the city, the increase in the population in recent years, as to the labour-market (although he had no very clear idea what the labour-market was), and as to the price of victuals. When he heard that the price of victuals was high. he "viewed the matter in a serious light," and that of course was all he could do. Nobody expected anything more of him, and it came as a comfort to everybody that he had viewed the high prices in a serious light.

151

Then the Mayor presented the city dignitaries to him: the higher District Judge, a noble landed proprietor from the neighbourhood, the rector, the two doctors, and a forwarding agent, and Klaus Heinrich addressed a question to each, thinking over, while the answer came, what he should say to the next. The local veterinary surgeon and the local inspector of stock-breeding were also present. Finally they climbed into carriages, and drove, amid the cheers of the inhabitants, between fences of school-children, firemen, the patriotic societies, through the gaily decked city to the exhibition ground—not without being stopped once more at the gate by white-robed maidens with wreaths on their heads, one of whom, the Mayor's daughter, handed to the prince in his carriage a bouquet with white satin streamers, and in lasting memory of the moment received one of those pretty and valuable gew-gaws which Klaus Heinrich took with him on his journeys, a breast-pin embedded, for a reason she could not guess, in *velvet* (sammet), which figured in the *Courier* as a jewel mounted in gold.

Tents, pavilions, and stands had been erected on the ground. Gaudy pennons fluttered on long rows of poles strung together with festoons. On a wooden platform hung with bunting, between drapings, festoons, and parti-coloured flagstaffs, Klaus Heinrich read the short opening speech. And then began the tour of inspection.

There were cattle tethered to low crossbars, prize beasts of the best blood with smooth round particoloured bodies and numbered shields on their broad foreheads. There were horses stamping and snuffing, heavy farm-horses with Roman noses and bushes of hair round their pasterns, as well as slender, restless saddle horses. There were naked short-legged pigs, and a large selection of both ordinary and prize pigs. With dangling bellies they grubbed up the ground with their snouts, while great blocks of woolly sheep filled the air with a confused chorus of bass and treble. There were earsplitting exhibits of poultry, cocks and hens of every kind, from the big Brahmaputra to the copper-coloured bantam; ducks and pigeons of all sorts, eggs and fodder, both fresh and artificially preserved. There were exhibits of agricultural produce, grain of all sorts, beets and clover, potatoes, peas, and flax; vegetables, too, both fresh and dried; raw and preserved fruit; berries, marmalade, and syrups.

Lastly there were exhibits of agricultural implements and machines, displayed by several technical firms, provided with everything of service to agriculture, from the hand-plough to the great black-funnelled motors, looking like elephants in their stall, from the simplest and most intelligible objects to those which consisted of a maze of wheels, chains, rods, cylinders, arms, and teeth—a world, an entire overpowering world of ingenious utility.

Klaus Heinrich looked at everything; he walked, with his sword-hilt on his forearm, down the rows of animals, cages, sacks, tubs, glasses, and implements. The dignitary at his side pointed with his white-gloved hand to this and that, venturing on a remark from time to time, and Klaus Heinrich acted up to his calling. He expressed in words his appreciation of all he saw, stopped from time to time and engaged the exhibitors of the animals in conversation, inquired in an affable way into their circumstances, and put questions to the country people whose answers entailed a scratching behind their ears. And as he walked he bowed his thanks on both sides for the homage of the population which lined his path.

The people had collected most thickly at the exit, where the carriages were waiting, in order to watch him drive off. A way was kept free for him, a straight passage to the step of his landau, and he walked quickly down it, bowing continuously with his hand to his helmet—alone and formally separated from all those men who, in honouring him, were cheering their own archetype, their standard, and of whose lives, work, and ability he was the splendid representative, though not participator.

With a light and free step he mounted the carriage, settled
153

himself artistically so that he at once assumed a perfectly graceful and self-possessed pose, and drove, saluting as he went, to
the clubhouse, where luncheon was prepared. During luncheon—indeed, directly after the second course—the District
Judge proposed the health of the Grand Duke and the Prince,
whereupon Klaus Heinrich at once rose to drink to the welfare of the county, and city. After the luncheon, however, he
retired to the room which the Mayor had put at his disposal
in his official residence and lay down on the bed for an hour,
for the exercise of his calling exhausted him in a strange
degree, and that afternoon he was due not only to visit in that
city the church, the school, and various factories, especially
Behnke Brothers' cheese factory, and to express high satisfaction with everything, but also to extend his journey and visit
a scene of disaster, a burnt-out village, in order to express
to the villagers his brother's and his own sympathy, and to
cheer the afflicted by his exalted presence.

When he got back to the "Hermitage," to his soberly furnished Empire room, he read the newspaper accounts of his
expeditions. Then Privy Councillor Schustermann of the
Press Bureau, which was under the Home Secretary, appeared
in the "Hermitage," and brought the extracts from the papers,
cleanly pasted on white sheets, dated and labelled with the
name of the paper. And Klaus Heinrich read about the impression he had produced, read about his personal graciousness and Highness, read that he had acquitted himself nobly
and taken the hearts of young and old by storm—that he had
raised the minds of the people out of the ruck of everyday
and filled them with gladness and affection.

And then he gave free audiences in the Old Schloss, as it
had been arranged.

The custom of free audiences had been introduced by a
well-meaning ancestor of Albrecht II, and the people clung to
it. Once every week Albrecht, or Klaus in his place, was
accessible to everybody. Whether the petitioner was a man
of rank or not, whether the subject of his petitions were of

154

a public or personal nature—he had only to give in his name to Herr von Bühl, or even the aide-de-camp on duty, and he was given an opportunity of bringing his matter to notice in the highest quarters.

Indeed an admirable custom! For it meant that the petitioner did not have to go round by way of a written application, with the dismal prospect of his petition disappearing for ever into a pigeon-hole, but had the happy assurance that his application would go straight to the most exalted quarters. It must be admitted that the most exalted quarters—Klaus Heinrich at this time—naturally were not in a position to go into the matter, to scrutinize it seriously and to come to a decision upon it, but that they handed the matter on to the pigeon-holes, in which it "disappeared." But the custom was none the less helpful, though not in the sense of matter-of-fact utility. The citizen, the petitioner, came to Herr von Bühl with the request to be received, and a day and hour were fixed for him. With glad embarrassment he saw the day draw near, worked up in his own mind the sentences in which he intended to explain his business, had his frock-coat and his hat ironed, put on his best shirt, and generally made himself ready.

But in reality these solemn interviews were well calculated to turn the petitioner's thoughts away from the gross material end in view, and to make the reception itself seem to him the main point, the essential object of his excited anticipation. The hour came, and the citizen took, what he never otherwise took, a cab, in order not to dirty his clean boots. He drove between the lions at the Albrechtstor, and the sentries as well as the stalwart doorkeeper gave him free passage. He landed in the courtyard at the colonnade in front of the weather-beaten entrance, and was at once admitted by a lackey in a brown coat and sand-coloured gaiters to an ante-room on the ground floor to the left, in one corner of which was a stand of colours, and where a number of other supplicants, talking in low whispers, waited in a state of thoughtful tension for

155

their reception. The aide-de-camp, holding a list of those with appointments, went backwards and forwards and took the next on the list to one side, to instruct him in a low voice how to behave.

In a neighbouring room, called the "Free Audience Room," Klaus Heinrich, in his tunic with silver collar and several stars, stood at a round table with three golden legs, and received. Major von Platow gave him some superficial information about the identity of each petitioner, called the man in, and came back in the pauses, to prompt the Prince in a few words about the next comer. And the citizen walked in; with the blood in his head and perspiring slightly he stood before Klaus Heinrich. It had been impressed on him that he was not to go too near his Royal Highness, but must keep at a certain distance, that he must not speak without being spoken to, and even then must not gabble off all he had to say, but answer concisely, so as to leave the Prince material for his questions; that he must at the conclusion withdraw backwards and without showing the Prince his backside. The result was that the citizen's whole attention was centred on not breaking any of the rules given him, but for his part contributing to the smooth and harmonious progress of the interview.

Klaus Heinrich questioned him in the same way as he was wont to question the veterans, the marksmen, the gymnasts, the countrymen, and the victims of the fire, smiling, and with his left hand planted well back on his hip; and the citizen too smiled involuntarily—and was imbued with a feeling as if that smile lifted him far above the troubles which had held him prisoner. That common man, whose spirit otherwise cleaved to the dust, who gave a thought to nothing, not even to everyday politeness, beyond what was purely utilitarian, and had come here too with a definite object in view—he felt in his heart that there was something higher than business and his business in particular, and he left the Schloss elevated, purified,

156

with eyes dim with emotion and the smile still on his flushed face.

That was the way in which Klaus Heinrich gave free audiences, that the way in which he exercised his exalted calling. He lived at the "Hermitage" in his little refuge, the Empire room, which was furnished so stiffly and meagrely, with cool indifference to comfort and intimacy. Faded silk covered the walls above the white wainscot, glass chandeliers hung from the ugly ceiling, straight-lined sofas, mostly without tables, and thin-legged stands supporting marble clocks, stood along the walls, pairs of white-lacquered chairs, with oval backs and thin silk upholstery, flanked the white-lacquered folding-doors, and in the corner stood white-lacquered loo-tables, bearing vase-like candelabra. That was how Klaus Heinrich's room looked, and its master harmonized well with it.

He lived a detached and quiet life, feeling no enthusiasm or zeal for questions on which the public differed. As representative of his brother, he opened Parliament, but he took no personal part in its proceedings and avoided the yeas and nays of party divisions—with the disinterestedness and want of convictions proper to one whose position was above all parties. Everybody recognized that his station imposed reserve upon him, but many were of opinion that want of interest was rather repellently and insultingly visible in his whole bearing. Many who came in contact with him described him as "cold"; and when Doctor Ueberbein loudly refuted this "coldness," people wondered whether the one-sided and morose man was qualified to form an opinion on the point. Of course there were occasions when Klaus Heinrich's glance met looks which refused to recognize him—bold, scornful, invidious looks, which showed contempt for and ignorance of all his actions and exertions. But even in the well-disposed, loyal people, who showed themselves ready to esteem and honour his life, he remarked at times after a short while a

157

certain exhaustion, indeed irritation, as if they could no longer breathe in the atmosphere of his existence; and that worried Klaus Heinrich, though he did not know how he could prevent it.

He had no place in the everyday world; a greeting from him, a gracious word, a winning and yet dignified wave of the hand, were all weighty and decisive incidents. Once he was returning in cap and greatcoat from a ride, was riding slowly on his brown horse Florian, down the birch avenue which skirted the waste-land and led to the park and the "Hermitage," and in front of him there walked a shabbily dressed young man with a fur cap and a ridiculous tuft of hair on his neck, sleeves and trousers that were too short for him, and unusually large feet which he turned inwards as he walked. He looked like the student of a technical institute or something of that sort, for he carried a drawing-board under his arm, on which was pinned a big drawing, a symmetrical maze of lines in red and black ink, a projection or something of the sort. Klaus Heinrich held his horse back behind the young man for a good while, and examined the red and black projection on the drawing-board. Sometimes he thought how nice it must be to have a proper surname, to be called Doctor Smith, and to have a serious calling.

He played his part at Court functions, the big and small balls, the dinner, the concerts, and the Great Court. He joined in autumn in the Court's shoots with his red-haired cousins and his suite, for custom's sake and although his left arm made shooting difficult for him. He was often seen in the evening in the Court Theatre, in his red-ledged proscenium-box between the two female sculptures with the crossed hands and the stern, empty faces. For the theatre attracted him, he loved it, loved to look at the players, to watch how they behaved, walked off and on, and went through with their parts. As a rule he thought them bad, rough in the means they employed to please, and unpractised in the more subtle dissembling of the natural and artless. For the rest, he was

158

disposed to prefer humble and popular scenes to the exalted and ceremonious.

A soubrette called Mizzi Meyer was engaged at the "Vaudeville" theatre in the capital, who in the newspapers and on the lips of the public was never called anything but "our" Meyer, because of her boundless popularity with high and low. She was not beautiful, hardly pretty, her voice was a screech, and, strictly speaking, she could lay claim to no special gifts. And yet she had only to come on to the stage to evoke storms of approbation, applause, and encouragement. For this fair and compact person with her blue eyes, her broad, high cheek-bones, her healthy, jolly, even a little uproarious manner, was flesh of the people's flesh, and blood of their blood. So long as she, dressed up, painted, and lighted up from every side, faced the crowd from the boards, she was in very deed the glorification of the people itself—indeed, the people clapped itself when it clapped her, and in that alone lay Mizzi Meyer's power over men's souls. Klaus Heinrich was very fond of going with Herr von Braunbart-Schellendorf to the "Vaudeville" when Mizzi Meyer was playing, and joined heartily in the applause.

One day he had a rencontre which on the one hand gave him food for thought, on the other disillusioned him. It was with Martini, Axel Martini, the compiler of the two books of poetry which had been so much praised by the experts, "Evoë!" and "The Holy Life." The meeting came about in the following way.

In the capital lived a wealthy old man, a Privy Councillor, who, since his retirement from the State Service, had devoted his life to the advancement of the fine arts, especially poetry. He was founder of what was known as the "May-combat"—a poetical tournament which recurred every year in springtime, to which the Privy Councillor invited poets and poetesses by circulars and posters. Prizes were offered for the tenderest love-song, the most fervent religious poem, the most ardent

159

patriotic song, for the happiest lyrical effusions in praise of music, the forest, the spring, the joy of life—and these prizes consisted of sums of money, supplemented by judicious and valuable souvenirs, such as golden pens, golden breast-pins in the form of lyres or flowers, and more of the same kind. The city authorities also had founded a prize, and the Grand Duke gave a silver cup as a reward for the most absolutely admirable of all poems sent in. The founder of the "May-combat" himself, who was responsible for the first look-through the always numerous entries, shared with two University Professors and the editors of the literary supplements of the *Courier* and the *People* the duties of prize-judges. The prize-winners and the highly commended entries were printed and published regularly in the form of an annual at the expense of the Privy Councillor.

Now Axel Martini had taken part in the "May-combat" this year, and had come off victorious. The poem which he had sent in, an inspired hymn of praise to the joy of life, or rather a highly tempestuous outbreak of the joy of life itself, a ravishing hymn to the beauty and awfulness of life, was conceived in the style of both his books and had given rise to discord in the Board of Judges. The Privy Councillor himself and the Professor of Philology had been for dismissing it with a notice of commendation; for they considered it exaggerated in expression, coarse in its passion, and in places frankly repulsive. But the Professor of Literary History together with the editors had out-voted them, not only in view of the fact that Martini's contribution represented the best poem to the joy of life, but also in consideration of its undeniable pre-eminence, and in the end their two opponents too had not been able to resist the appeal of its foaming and stunning flow of words.

So Axel Martini had been awarded fifteen pounds, a gold breast-pin in the form of a lyre, and the Grand Duke's silver cup as well, and his poem had been printed first in the annual, surrounded with an artistic frame from the hand of Professor

160

von Lindemann. What was more, the custom was for the victor (or victrix) in the "May-combat" to be received in audience by the Grand Duke; and as Albrecht was unwell, this task fell to his brother.

Klaus Heinrich was a little afraid of Herr Martini.

"Oh dear, Doctor Ueberbein," he said when he met his tutor one day, "what subject am I to tackle him on? He's sure to be a wild, brazen-faced fellow."

But Doctor Ueberbein answered: "Anything; but, Klaus Heinrich, you need not worry! He's a very decent fellow. I know him, I'm rather in with his set. You'll get on splendidly with him."

So Klaus Heinrich received the poet of the "Joy of Life," received him at the "Hermitage," so as to give the business as private a character as possible. "In the yellow room, Braunbart if you please," he said, "that's the most presentable one for occasions like this." There were three handsome chairs in this room, which indeed were the only valuable pieces of furniture in the Schloss, heavy Empire arm-chairs of mahogany, with spiral arms and yellow upholstery on which blue-green lyres were embroidered. Klaus Heinrich on this occasion did not dispose himself ready for an audience, but waited in some anxiety near by, until Axel Martini on his side had waited for seven or eight minutes in the yellow room. Then he walked in hastily, almost hurriedly, and advanced towards the poet, who made a low bow.

"I am very much pleased to make your acquaintance," he said, "dear sir . . . dear Doctor, I believe?"

"No, Royal Highness," answered Axel Martini in an asthmatic voice, "not doctor, I've no title."

"Oh, forgive me . . . I assumed . . . Let's sit down, dear Herr Martini. I am, as I have said, delighted to be able to congratulate you on your great success. . . ."

Herr Martini drew down the corners of his mouth. He sat down on the edge of one of the mahogany arm-chairs, at the uncovered table, round whose edge ran a gold border,

161

and crossed his feet, which were cased in cracked patent-leather boots. He was in frock-coat and wore yellow gloves. His collar was frayed at the edges. He had rather staring eyes, thin cheeks and a dark yellow moustache, which was clipped like a hedge. His hair was already quite grey on the temples, although according to the "May-combat" Annual he was not more than thirty years old, and under his eyes glowed patches of red which did not suggest robust health. He answered to Klaus Heinrich's congratulations: "Your Royal Highness is very kind. It was not a difficult victory. Perhaps it was hardly tactful of me to compete."

Klaus Heinrich did not understand this; but he said: "I have read your poem repeatedly with great pleasure. It seems to me a complete success, as regards both metre and rhyme. And it entirely expresses the 'Joy of Life.' "

Herr Martini bowed in his chair.

"Your skill," continued Klaus Heinrich, "must be a source of great pleasure to you—an ideal recreation. What is your calling, Herr Martini?"

Herr Martini showed that he did not understand, by describing a note of interrogation with the upper half of his body.

"I mean your main calling. Are you in the Civil Service?"

"No, Royal Highness, I have no calling; I occupy myself exclusively with poetry. . . ."

"None at all. . . . Oh, I understand. So unusual a gift deserves that a man's whole powers be devoted to it."

"I don't know about that, Royal Highness. Whether it deserves it or not, I don't know. I must own that I had no choice. I have always felt myself entirely unsuited to every other branch of human activity. It seems to me that this undoubted and unconditional unsuitability for everything else is the sole proof and touchstone of the poetical calling—indeed, that a man must not see in poetry any calling, but only the expression and refuge of that unsuitability."

It was a peculiarity with Herr Martini that when he talked

162

tears came into his eyes just like a man who comes out of the cold into a warm room and lets the heat stream through and melt his limbs.

"That's a singular idea," said Klaus Heinrich.

"Not at all, Royal Highness. I beg your pardon, no, not singular at all. It's an idea which is very generally accepted. What I say is nothing new."

"And for how long have you been living only for poetry? I suppose you were once a student?"

"Not exactly, Royal Highness; no, the unsuitability to which I alluded before began to show itself in me at an early age. I couldn't get on at school. I left it without passing my 'final.' I went up to the university with the full intention of taking it later, but I never did. And when my first volume of poems attracted a good deal of attention, it no longer suited my dignity to do so, if I may say so."

"Of course not. . . . But did your parents then agree to your choice of a career?"

"Oh no, Royal Highness! I must say to my parents' credit that they by no means agreed to it. I come of a good stock: my father was Solicitor to the Treasury. He's dead now, but he was Solicitor to the Treasury. He naturally disliked my choice of a career so much that till his death he would never give me a farthing. I lived at daggers drawn with him, although I had the greatest respect for him because of his strictness."

"Oh, so you've had a hard time of it, Herr Martini, you've had to struggle through. I can well believe that you must have knocked about a good deal!"

"Not so, Royal Highness! No, that would have been horrid, I couldn't have stood it. My health is delicate—I dare not say 'unfortunately,' for I am convinced that my talent is inseparably connected with my bodily infirmity. Neither my body nor my talent could have survived hunger and harsh winds, and they have not had to survive them. My mother was weak enough to provide me behind my father's back with

163

the means of life, modest but adequate means. I owe it to her that my talent has been able to develop under fairly favourable conditions."

"The result has shown. Herr Martini, that they were the right conditions. . . . Although it is difficult to say now what actually are good conditions. Permit me to suppose that if your mother had shown herself as strict as your father, and you had been alone in the world, and left entirely to your own resources . . . don't you think that it might have been to a certain extent a good thing for you? That you might have got a peep at things, so to speak, which have escaped you as it is?"

"People like me, Royal Highness, get peeps enough without having actually to know what hunger is; and the idea is fairly generally accepted that it is not actual hunger, but rather hunger for the actual . . . ha, ha! . . . which talent requires."

Herr Martini had been obliged to laugh a little at his play upon words. He now quickly raised one yellow-gloved hand to his mouth with the hedge-like moustache, and improved his laugh into a cough. Klaus Heinrich watched him with a look of princely expectancy.

"If your Royal Highness will allow me. . . . It is a well-known fact that the want of actuality for such as me is the seed-ground of all talent, the fountain of inspiration, indeed our suggestive genius. Enjoyment of life is forbidden to us, strictly forbidden, we have no illusions as to that—and by enjoyment of life I mean not only happiness, but also sorrow, passion, in short every serious tie with life. The representation of life claims all our forces, especially when those forces are not allotted to us in overabundant measure"—and Herr Martini coughed, drawing his shoulders repeatedly forward as he did so. "Renunciation," he added, "is our compact with the Muse, in it reposes our strength, our value; and life is our forbidden garden, our great temptation, to which we yield sometimes, but never to our profit."

164

The flow of words had again brought tears to Herr Martini's eyes. He tried to blink them away.

"Every one of us," he went on, "knows what it is to make mistakes, to run off the rails in that way, to make greedy excursions of that kind into the festival halls of life. But we return thence into our isolation humbled and sick at heart."

Herr Martini stopped. His look, from under his knotted brows, became fixed for a moment and lost in vacancy, while his mouth assumed a sour expression and his cheeks, on which the unhealthy redness glowed, seemed even thinner than before. It was only for a second; then he changed his position, and his eyes recovered their vivacity.

"But your poem," said Klaus Heinrich, with some *empressement*. "Your prize poem to the 'Joy of Life,' Herr Martini. . . . I am really grateful to you for your achievement. But will you please tell me . . . your poem—I've read it attentively. It deals on the one hand with misery and horrors, with the wickedness and cruelty of life, if I remember rightly, and on the other hand with the enjoyment of wine and fair women, does it not? . . ."

Herr Martini laughed; then rubbed the corners of his mouth with his thumb and forefinger, so as to wipe the laugh out.

"And it's all," said Klaus Heinrich, "conceived in the form of 'I,' in the first person, isn't it? And yet it is not founded on personal knowledge? You have not really experienced any of it yourself?"

"Very little, Royal Highness. Only quite trifling suggestions of it. No, the fact is the other way round—that, if I were the man to experience all that, I should not only not write such poems, but should also feel entire contempt for my present existence. I have a friend, his name is Weber; he's a rich young man; he lives, he enjoys his life. His favourite amusement consists in scorching in his motor car

165

at a mad pace over the country and picking up village girls from the roads and fields on the way, with whom he——but that's another story. In short, that young man laughs when he catches sight of me, he finds something so comic in me and my activities. But as for me, I can quite understand his amusement, and envy him it. I dare say that I too despise him a little, but not so much as I envy and admire him. . . ."

"You admire him?"

"Certainly, Royal Highness. I cannot help doing so. He spends, he squanders, he lets himself go in a most unconcerned and light-hearted way—while it is my lot to save, anxiously and greedily, to keep together, and indeed to do so on hygienic grounds. For hygiene is what I and such as I most need—it is our whole ethics. But nothing is more unhygienic than life. . . ."

"That means that you will never empty the Grand Duke's cup, then, Herr Martini?"

"Drink wine out of it? No, Royal Highness. Although it would be fine to do so. But I never touch wine. And I go to bed at ten, and generally take care of myself. If I didn't, I should never have won the cup."

"I can well believe it, Herr Martini. People who are not behind the scenes get strange ideas of what a poet's life must be like."

"Quite conceivably, Royal Highness. But it is, taken all round, by no means a very glorious life, I can assure you, especially as we aren't poets every hour of the twenty-four. In order that a poem of that sort may come into existence from time to time—who would believe how much idleness and boredom and peevish laziness is necessary? The motto on a picture postcard is often a whole day's work. We sleep a lot, we idle about with heads feeling like lead. Yes, it's too often a dog's life."

Some one knocked lightly on the white-lacquered door. It was Neumann's signal that it was high time for Klaus Heinrich to change his clothes and have himself freshened up. For there was to be a club concert that evening in the Old Schloss.

Klaus Heinrich rose. "I've been gossiping," he said; for that was the expression he used at such moments. And then he dismissed Herr Martini, wished him success in his poetical career, and accompanied the poet's respectful withdrawal with a laugh and that rather theatrical up and down movement of the hand which was not always equally effective, but which he had brought to a high pitch of perfection.

Such was the Prince's conversation with Axel Martini, the author of "Evoë!" and "The Holy Life." It gave him food for thought, it continued to occupy his mind after it had ended. He continued to think over it while Neumann was reparting his hair and helping him on with the dazzling full-dress coat with the stars, during the club concert at Court, and for several days afterwards, and he tried to reconcile the poet's state- ments with the rest of the experiences which life had vouch- safed to him.

This Herr Martini, who, while the unhealthy flush glowed under his eyes, kept crying: "How beautiful, how strong is life!" yet was careful to go to bed at ten, shut himself off from life on hygienic grounds, as he said, and avoided every serious tie with it—this poet with his frayed collar, his watery eyes, and his envy of the young Weber who scorched over the country with village girls: he left a mixed impres- sion, it was difficult to come to any certain conclusion about him. Klaus Heinrich expressed it, when he told his sister of the meeting, by saying: "Things are none too comfortable and easy for him, that's quite obvious, and that certainly entitles him to our sympathy. But somehow, I'm not sure if I'm glad to have met him, for he has something deterrent about him, Ditlinde—yes, after all, he's certainly a little repulsive."

## VII

## IMMA

FRÄULEIN VON ISENSCHNIBBE had been well informed. On the very evening of the day on which she had brought the Princess zu Reid the great news, the *Courier* published the announcement of Samuel Spoelmann's, the world-renowned Spoelmann's, impending arrival, and ten days later, at the beginning of October (it was the October of the year in which Grand Duke Albrecht had entered his thirty-second and Prince Klaus Heinrich his twenty-sixth year), thus barely giving time for public curiosity to reach a really high point, his arrival became a fact, a plain actuality on an autumn-tinged, entirely ordinary week-day, which was destined to impress itself on the future as a date to be remembered for ever.

The Spoelmanns arrived by special train—that was the only distinction about their debut to start with, for everybody knew that the "Prince's suite" in the "Spa Court" Hotel was by no means dazzlingly magnificent. A few idlers, guarded by a small detachment of policemen, had gathered behind the platform barriers; some representatives of the press were present. But whoever expected anything out of the ordinary was disappointed. Spoelmann would almost have passed unrecognized, he was so unimposing. For a long time people took his family physician for him (Doctor Watercloose, people said he was called), a tall American, who wore his hat on the back of his head and kept his mouth distended in a perpetual smile between his close-trimmed white whiskers, the while he half-closed his eyes. It was not till the last moment that people learned that it was the little clean-shaven man in the faded overcoat, he who wore his hat pulled down over his eyes, who was the actual Spoelmann, and the spectators were agreed that there was nothing striking about him. All sorts of stories had been in circulation about him; some witty fellow had spread the report that Spoelmann had front teeth of solid gold and a diamond set in the middle of each. But although the truth or untruth of this report could not be tested at once— for Spoelmann did not show his teeth, he did not laugh, but rather seemed angry and irritated by his infirmity—yet when they saw him nobody was any longer inclined to believe it.

As for Miss Spoelmann, his daughter, she had turned up the collar of her fur coat, and stuffed her hands in the pockets, so that there was hardly anything to be seen of her except a pair of disproportionately big brown-black eyes, which swept the crowd with a serious look whose meaning it was hard to interpret. By her side stood the person whom the onlookers identified as her companion, the Countess Löwenjoul, a woman of thirty-five, plainly dressed and taller than either of the Spoelmanns, who carried her little head with its thin smooth hair pensively on one side, and kept her eyes fixed in front of her with a kind of rigid meekness. What without question attracted most attention was a Scottish sheep-dog which was led on a cord by a stolid-looking servant—an exceptionally handsome, but, as it appeared, terribly excitable beast, that leaped and danced and filled the station with its frenzied barking.

People said that a few of Spoelmann's servants, male and female, had already arrived at the "Spa Court" some hours before. At any rate it was left to the servant with the dog to look after the luggage by himself; and while he was doing so his masters drove in two ordinary flies—Mr. Spoelmann with Doctor Watercloose, Miss Spoelmann with the Countess —to the Spa-Garden. There they got out, and there for six weeks they led a life the cost of which it did not need all their money to meet.

They were lucky; the weather was fine, it was a blue autumn, a long succession of sunny days from October into November.
169

and Miss Spoelmann rode daily—that was her only luxury—with her companion, on horses which she hired by the week from the livery stables. Mr. Spoelmann did not ride, although the *Courier*, with obvious reference to him, published a note by its medical colleague according to which riding had a soothing effect in cases of stone, owing to its jolting, and helped to disperse the stone. But the hotel staff knew that the famous man practised artificial riding within the four walls of his room, with the help of a machine, a stationary velocipede to whose saddle a jolting motion was imparted by the working of the pedals.

He was a zealous drinker of the healing waters, the Ditlinde Spring, by which he seemed to set great store. He appeared first thing every morning in the Füllhaus, accompanied by his daughter, who for her part was quite healthy, and only drank with him for company's sake, and then, in his faded coat and with his hat pulled over his eyes, took his exercise in the Spa-Garden and Wandelhalle, drinking the water the while through a glass tube out of a blue tumbler—watched at a distance by the two American newspaper correspondents, whose duty it was to telegraph to their papers a thousand words daily about Spoelmann's holiday resort, and who were therefore bound to try to get something to telegraph about.

Otherwise he was rarely visible. His illness—kidney colic, so people said, extremely painful attacks—seemed to confine him often to his room, if not to his bed, and while Miss Spoelmann with Countess Löwenjoul appeared two or three times at the Court Theatre (when, in a black velvet dress with an Indian silk scarf of a wonderful gold-yellow colour round her fresh young shoulders, she looked quite bewitching with her pearl-white complexion and great black pleading eyes), her father was never seen in the box with her. He took, it is true, in her company one or two drives through the capital, to do some shopping, get some idea of the town, and see a few select sights; he went for a walk with her too, through

170

the park and twice inspected there the Schloss Delphinenort—
the second time alone, when he was so much interested as to
take measurements of the walls with an ordinary yellow rule,
which he took out of his faded coat. . . . But he was never
seen in the dining-room of the "Spa Court," for whether because he was on an almost meatless diet, or for some other
reason, he took his meals exclusively with his own party in
his own rooms, and the curiosity of the public had on the
whole remarkably little to feed on.

The result was that Spoelmann's arrival at the Spa at first
did not prove so beneficial as Fräulein von Isenschnibbe and
many others beside her had expected. The export of bottles
increased, that was certain; it quickly rose to half as many
again as its previous figure, and remained at that. But the
influx of foreigners did not increase noticeably; the guests
who came to feast their eyes on so abnormal an existence soon
went away again, satisfied or disappointed, besides it was for
the most part not the most desirable elements of society that
were attracted by the millionaire's presence. Strange creatures
appeared in the streets, unkempt and wild-eyed creatures—
inventors, projectors, would-be benefactors of mankind, who
hoped to enlist Spoelmann's sympathies for their hobbies.
But the millionaire made himself absolutely inaccessible to
these people; indeed, purple with rage, he howled at one of
them who made advances towards him in the park, in such a
way that the busybody quickly skedaddled, and it was often
said that the torrent of begging letters which daily flowed in
to him—letters which often bore stamps which the officials of
the Grand Ducal post-office had never seen before—was at once
discharged into a paper-basket of quite unusual capacity.

Spoelmann seemed to have forbidden all business letters
to be sent him, seemed determined to enjoy his holiday to
the utmost, and during his travels in Europe to live exclusively
for his health—or ill-health. The *Courier*, whose reporter had
lost no time in making friends with his American colleagues,
was in a position to announce that a reliable man, a so-called
171

chief manager, was Mr. Spoelmann's representative in America. He went on to say that his yacht, a gorgeously decorated vessel, was awaiting the great man at Venice, and that as soon as he had finished his cure he intended to travel south with his party.

It told also, in answer to importunate requests from its readers—of the romantic origin of the Spoelmann millions, from their beginning in Victoria, whither his father had drifted from some German office stool or other, young, poor, and armed only with a pick, a shovel, and a tin plate. There he had begun by working as help to a gold-digger, as a day labourer, in the sweat of his brow. And then luck had come to him. A man, a claim-owner on a small scale, had fared so badly that he could no longer buy himself his tomatoes and dry bread for dinner, and in his extremity had been obliged to dispose of his claim. Spoelmann senior had bought it, had staked his one card, and, with his whole savings, amounting to £5 sterling, had bought this piece of alluvial land called "Paradise Field," not more than forty feet square. And the next day he had turned up, a foot under the surface, a nugget of pure gold, the tenth biggest nugget in the world, the "Paradise nugget," weighing 980 ounces and worth £5,000.

That, related the *Courier*, had been the beginning. Spoelmann's father had emigrated to South America with the proceeds of his find, to Bolivia, and as gold-washer, amalgam-mill-owner, and mine-owner had continued to extract the yellow metal direct from the rivers and the womb of the mountains. Then and there Spoelmann senior had married—and the *Courier* went so far as to hint in this connexion that he had done so defiantly and without regard to the prejudices generally felt in those parts. However, he had doubled his capital and succeeded in investing his money most profitably.

He had moved on northwards to Philadelphia, Pa. That was in the fifties, the time of a great boom in railway construction, and Spoelmann had begun with one investment in the Baltimore and Ohio Railway. He had also leased a coal-

172

mine in the west of the State, the profits from which had been enormous. Finally he had joined that group of fortunate young men which bought the famous Blockhead Farm for a few thousand pounds—the property which, with its petroleum wells, in a short time increased in value to a hundred times its purchase price. . . . This enterprise had made a rich man of Spoelmann senior, but he had by no means rested on his oars, but unceasingly practised the art of making money into more money, and finally into superabundant money.

He had started steel works, had floated companies for the turning of iron into steel on a large scale, and for building railway bridges. He had bought up the major part of the shares of four or five big railway companies, and had been elected in the later years of his life president, vice-president, manager, or director of the companies. When the Steel Trust was formed, so the *Courier* said, he had joined it, with a holding of shares which guaranteed him an income of $12,000,000. But at the same time he had been chief shareholder and expert adviser of the Petroleum Combine, and in virtue of his holding had dominated three or four of the other Trust Companies. And at his death his fortune, reckoned in German currency, had amounted to a round thousand million marks.

Samuel, his only son, the offspring of that early marriage, contracted in defiance of public opinion, had been his sole heir—and the *Courier*, with its usual delicacy, interpolated a remark to the effect that there was something almost sad in the idea of any one, without himself contributing, and through no fault of his own, being born to such a situation. Samuel had inherited the palace on Fifth Avenue at New York, the country mansions, and all the shares, Trust bonds, and profits of his father; he inherited also the strange position to which his father had risen, his world-fame and the hatred directed by his out-distanced competitors against the power of his gold—all the hatred to allay which he yearly distributed his huge donations to colleges, conservatories, libraries, benevo-
173

lent institutions, and that University which his father had founded and which bore his name.

Samuel Spoelmann did not deserve the hatred of the outdistanced competitors; that the *Courier* was sure of. He had gone early into the business, and had controlled the bewildering possessions of his house all by himself during his father's last years. But everybody knew that his heart had never been really in the business. His real inclinations had been, strange to say, all along much more towards music and especially organ music—and the truth of this information on the part of the *Courier* was certain, for Mr. Spoelmann actually kept a small organ in the "Spa Court," whose bellows he got a hotel servant to blow, and he could be heard from the Spa-Garden playing it for an hour every day.

He had married for love and not at all from social considerations, according to the *Courier*—a poor and pretty girl, half German, half Anglo-Saxon by descent. She had died, but she had left him a daughter, that wonderful blood-mixture of a girl, whom we now had as guest within our walls and who was at the time nineteen years old. Her name was Imma— a real German name, as the *Courier* added, nothing more than an old form of "Emma," and it might be remarked that the daily conversation in the Spoelmann household, though interlarded with scraps of English, had remained German. And how devoted father and daughter seemed to be to each other! Every morning, by going to the Spa-Garden at the right time, one could watch Fräulein Spoelmann, who usually entered the Füllhause a little later than her father, take his head between her hands and give him his morning kiss on mouth and cheeks, while he patted her tenderly on the back. Then they went arm-in-arm through the Wandelhalle and sucked their glass tubes as they went. . . .

That is how the well-informed journal gossiped and fed the public curiosity. It also reported carefully the visits which Miss Imma kindly paid with her companion to several of the charitable institutions of the town. Yesterday she had made a

174

detailed inspection of the public kitchens. To-day she had made a prolonged tour of the Trinity Almhouses for old women, and she had recently twice attended Privy Councillor Klinghammer's lectures on the theory of numbers at the university—had sat on the bench, a student among students, and scribbled away with her fountain-pen, for everybody knew that she was a learned girl and devoted to the study of algebra. Yes, all that was absorbing reading, and furnished ample food for conversation. But the topics which made themselves talked about without any help from the *Courier* were, firstly, the dog, that noble black-and-white collie which the Spoelmanns had brought with them, and secondly, in a different way, the companion, Countess Löwenjoul.

As for the dog, whose name was Percival, generally shortened to Percy, he was an animal of so excitable and emotional a disposition as beggared description. Inside the hotel he afforded no grounds for complaint, but lay in a dignified attitude on a small carpet outside the Spoelmanns' suite. But every time he went out he had an attack of light-headedness, which caused general interest and surprise, indeed more than once actual obstruction of traffic.

Followed at a distance by a swarm of native dogs, common curs which, incited by his demeanour, assailed him with censorious yaps, and which caused him no concern whatever, he flew through the streets, his nose spattered with foam and barking wildly, pirouetted madly in front of the tramcars, made the cab-horses stumble, and twice knocked Widow Klaaszen's cake stall at the Town Hall down so violently that the sugar cakes rolled half over the Market-place. But as Mr. Spoelmann or his daughter at once met such catastrophes with more than adequate compensation, as too it was discovered that Percival's attacks were really quite free from danger, that he was anything but inclined to bite and steal, but on the contrary kept to himself and would let nobody come near him, public opinion quickly turned in his favour, and to the children in particular his excursions were a constant source of pleasure.

175

Countess Löwenjoul on her side supplied food for conversation in a quieter but no less strange way. At first, when her personality and position were not yet known in the city, she had attracted the gibes of the street urchins, because, while out walking alone, she talked to herself softly and deliberately, and accompanied her words with lively and at the same time graceful and elegant gestures. But she had shown such mildness and goodness to the children who shouted after her and tugged at her dress, she had spoken to them with such affection and dignity, that her persecutors had slunk away abashed and confused, and later, when she became known, respect for her relations with the famous guests secured her from molestation. However, some unintelligible anecdotes were secretly circulated about her. One man told how the Countess had given him a gold piece with instructions that he should box the ears of a certain old woman who was understood to have made some unseemly proposal or other to her. The man had pocketed the gold piece, without, however, discharging his commission.

Further, it was declared as a fact that the Countess had accosted the sentry in front of the Fusiliers' Barracks and had told him at once to arrest the wife of the sergeant of one of the companies because of her moral shortcomings. She had written too a letter to the Colonel of the regiment to the effect that all sorts of secret and unspeakable abominations went on inside the barracks. Whether she was right in her facts, heaven only knew. But many people at once concluded that she was wrong in her head. At any rate, there was no time to investigate the matter, for six weeks were soon past, and Samuel N. Spoelmann, the millionaire, went away.

He went away after having had his portrait painted by Professor von Lindemann—an expensive portrait too, which he gave to the proprietor of the "Spa Court" as a memento; he went away with his daughter, the Countess, and Doctor Watercloose, with Percival, the chamber-velocipede, and his servants; went by special train to the South, with the view of spending

176

the winter on the Riviera, whither the two New York journalists
had hastened ahead of him, and of then crossing back home
again. It was all over. The *Courier* wished Mr. Spoelmann
a hearty farewell and expressed the hope that the cure would be
found to have done him good.

And with that the notable interlude seemed to be closed and
done with. Everyday life claimed its due, and Mr. Spoelmann
began to fade into oblivion. The winter passed. It was the
winter in which her Grand Ducal Highness the Princess zu
Ried-Hohenried was confined of a daughter. Spring came,
and his Royal Highness Grand Duke Albrecht repaired as
usual to Hollerbrunn. But then a rumour cropped up amongst
the people and in the press, which was received at first with
a shrug by the sober-minded, but became more concrete,
crystallized, took to itself quite precise details, and finally won
itself a dominant place in the solid and pithy news of the
day.

What was toward? A Grand Ducal Schloss was about
to be sold? Nonsense! Which Schloss?—Delphinenort.
Schloss Delphinenort in the North Park? Twaddle! Sold?
To whom?—To Spoelmann. Ridiculous! What could he do
with it?—Restore it, and live in it. That's all very well.
But perhaps our Parliament might have something to say to
that.—They don't care twopence. Had the State any responsibility for keeping up Schloss Delphinenort?—If they had, it's
a pity they hadn't recognized it, dear old place. No, Parliament had no say in the matter. Have the negotiations advanced
at all far?—Rather, they're completed. Goodness gracious,
then of course the exact price is known?—Naturally. Sold
for two millions, not a farthing less. Impossible! A Royal
Palace! Royal palace be blowed! We're not talking of the
Grimmburg or of the Old Schloss. We're talking of a
country house, an unused country house which is falling in
pieces for lack of funds to keep it up.

So Spoelmann intended to come back every year and spend
several weeks in Delphinenort?—No. For he intended rather
177

to come and settle among us altogether. He was sick of America, wanted to turn his back on it, and his first stay amongst us was merely to spy out the land. He was ill, he wanted to retire from business. He had always remained a German at heart. The father had emigrated, and the son wanted to come back home. He wished to take his part in the modest life and intellectual resources of our country, and to spend the rest of his days in the immediate neighbourhood of the Ditlinde Spa.

All was confusion and bustle, and discussions without end. But public opinion, with the exception of the voices of a few grumblers, trended after a short hesitation in favour of the idea of sale; indeed without this general approval the matter could never have gone very far. It was House Minister von Knobelsdorff who first ventured on a cautious announcement of Spoelmann's offer in the daily press. He had waited and allowed the popular feeling to come to a decision. And after the first confusion, solid reasons in favour of the project had made themselves felt.

The business world was enchanted at the idea of having so doughty a consumer at its doors. The æsthetes showed themselves delighted at the prospect of seeing Schloss Delphinenort restored and kept up—at seeing the noble old building restored to honour and youth in so unforeseen, indeed so romantic a way. But the economically-minded brought forward figures which were calculated to cause grave misgivings as to the financial position of the country. If Samuel N. Spoelmann settled among us, he would become a tax-payer— he would have to pay us his income-tax.

Perhaps it was worth while showing what that meant. Mr. Spoelmann would be left to declare his own income, but, from what one knew—and knew fairly accurately—his residence would mean a yearly revenue of two and a half millions, in taxes alone, not to mention what he paid in rates. Worth thinking about, wasn't it? The question was put straight to the Finance Minister, Dr. Krippenreuther. He would be wanting in his duty if he did not do all he could to recommend the sale in the highest quarters. For patriotism demanded that Spoelmann's offer should be accepted, and patriotism was paramount above all other considerations.

So Excellency von Knobelsdorff had had an interview with the Grand Duke. He had informed his master of the public opinion, had added that the price offered, two millions, considerably exceeded the real value of the Schloss in its present condition, had remarked that such a sum meant a real windfall for the Treasury, and had ended by slipping in a hint about the central heating of the Old Schloss, which, if the sale was carried through, would no longer be an impossibility. In short, the single-minded old gentleman had brought his whole influence to bear in favour of the sale, and had recommended the Grand Duke to bring the matter before a family moot. Albrecht had sucked his lower lip softly against the upper, and summoned the family moot. It had met in the Hall of the Knights over tea and biscuits. Only two feminine members, the Princess Catherine and Ditlinde, had opposed the sale, on the ground of loss of dignity.

"You will be misunderstood, Albrecht!" said Ditlinde. "They will charge you with want of respect to your high station, and that is not right, for you have on the contrary too much; you are so proud, Albrecht, that everything is all the same to you. But I say No. I do not wish to see a Crœsus living in one of your Schlosses, it is not right, and it was bad enough that he should have a family physician and take the Prince's suite in the Spa Court. The *Courier* harps on the fact that he is a tax-paying subject, but in my eyes he is simply a subject and nothing else. What do you think, Klaus Heinrich?"

But Klaus Heinrich voted for the sale. In the first place, Albrecht got his central heating; secondly, Spoelmann was not one of the common herd, he was not soap-boiler Unschlitt —he was an exception, and there was no disgrace in letting him have Delphinenort. Finally Albrecht had, with downcast
179

eyes, pronounced the whole family moot to be a farce. The people had long ago made up their minds, his Ministers urged the sale, and there was nothing left for him to do but to "wave to the engine-driver and start the train."

The family moot had taken place in spring. From that time onwards the negotiations for sale, which were carried on between Spoelmann on the one hand and the Lord Marshal von Bühl zu Bühl on the other, had proceeded apace, and the summer was not far advanced before Schloss Delphinenort with its park and out-buildings had become the lawful property of Mr. Spoelmann.

Then began a scene of bustle and confusion round and in the Schloss, which daily attracted crowds to the northern side of the park. Delphinenort was improved and partly reconstructed inside by a swarm of workmen. For quick, quick, was the order of the day, that was Spoelmann's wish, and he had only allowed five months' respite for everything to be ready for him to enter into possession. So a wooden scaffold with ladders and platforms shot up at lightning speed round the dilapidated old building, foreign workmen swarmed all over it, and an architect came with carte blanche over the seas to superintend the work. But the greater part of the work fell to our native manual workers to perform, and the stone-masons and tilers, the joiners, gilders, upholsterers, glaziers, and parquet-layers of the city, the landscape gardeners and heating and lighting experts, had plenty of remunerative work all through the summer and autumn.

When his Royal Highness Klaus Heinrich left his window in the "Hermitage" open, the noise of the work at Delphinenort penetrated right through to the Empire room, and he often drove past the Schloss amid the respectful greetings of the public, in order to satisfy himself of the progress of the restoration. The gardener's cottage was painted up, the sheds and stables, which were destined to accommodate Spoelmann's fleet of motors and carriages, were enlarged; and by October, furniture and carpets, chests and cases full of stuffs and

180

household utensils had been delivered at Schloss Delphine-nort, while it was whispered among the bystanders that inside the walls skilled hands were at work fitting Spoelmann's costly organ, which had been sent from over the sea, with electric action.

There was much excitement to know whether the park be-longing to the Schloss, which had been so splendidly cleaned up and trimmed, was to be fenced off from the public by a wall or hedge. But nothing of the sort was done. It was Spoelmann's wish that the property should continue to be accessible, that no restraint should be placed on the citizens' enjoyment of the park. The Sunday promenaders should have access right up to the Schloss, up to the clipped hedge which surrounded the big square pond—and this did not fail to make an excellent impression on the population; indeed, the *Courier* published a special article on the subject, in which it praised Mr. Spoelmann for his philanthropy.

And behold! when the leaves again began to fall, exactly one year after his first appearance, Samuel Spoelmann landed a second time at our railway station. This time the general interest in the event was much greater than in the preceding year, and it is on record that, when Mr. Spoelmann, in his well-known faded coat and with his hat over his eyes, left his saloon, loud cheers were raised by the crowd of spectators— an expression of feelings which Mr. Spoelmann seemed rather inclined to resent, and which not he but Doctor Waterclouse acknowledged with blinking eyes and a broad smile. When Miss Spoelmann too alighted, a cheer was raised, and one or two urchins even shouted when Percy, the collie, appeared springing, leaping, and altogether beside himself, on the plat-form. In addition to the doctor and Countess Löwenjoul there were two unknown persons in attendance, two clean-shaven and decided-looking men in strangely roomy coats. They were Mr. Spoelmann's secretaries, Messrs. Phlebs and Slippers, as the *Courier* announced in its report.

At that time Delphinenort was far from ready, and the

Spoelmanns at once took possession of the first floor of the chief hotel, where a big, haughty, paunch-bellied man in black, the steward or butler of the Spoelmann establishment, who had preceded them, had made preparations for them, and put the chamber-velocipede together with his own hands. Every day, while Miss Imma with her Countess and Percy went for a ride or a visit to some charitable institution, Mr. Spoelmann hung about his house, superintending the work and giving orders, and when the end of the year approached, just after the first snow had fallen, prospect became fact, and the Spoelmanns took up their abode in Schloss Delphinenort. Two motor cars (their arrival had been watched with interest —splendid cars they were) bore the six members of the party —Messrs. Phlebs and Slippers sat in the hinder one—driven by the leather-clad chauffeurs, with servants in snow-white fur coats and crossed arms beside them, in a few minutes from the hotel through the City Gardens; and as the cars dashed along the noble chestnut avenue which led to the drive, the urchins climbed up the high lamp-posts which stood at all four corners of the big spa-basin, and waved their caps and cheered. . . .

So Spoelmann and his belongings settled down among us, and we basked in the light of his presence. His white-and-gold livery was seen and known in the city, just as the brown-and-gold Grand Ducal livery was seen and known; the negro in scarlet plush who was doorkeeper at Delphinenort soon became a popular figure, and when passers-by heard the subdued rumble of Mr. Spoelmann's organ from the interior of the Schloss they lifted a finger and said: "Hark, he's playing. That means that he's not got colic for the moment."

Miss Imma was to be seen daily by the side of Countess Löwenjoul, followed by a groom and with Percy capering round, riding, or driving a smart four-in-hand through the City Gardens—while the servant who sat on the back seat stood up from time to time, drew a long silver horn from a leather sheath and wound a shrill warning of their approach;

and by getting up early one could see father and daughter every morning go in a dark-red brougham, or, in fine weather, on foot through the park of Schloss "Hermitage" to the Spa-Garden, in order to drink the waters. Imma for her part, as already mentioned, again began a course of visits to the benevolent institutions of the city, though she appeared not to give up her studies for all that; for from the beginning of the half-term she regularly attended the lectures of the Councillor Klinghammer at the University—sat daily in a black dress with white collar and cuffs among the young students in the lecture-theatre, and drove her fountain-pen—with her forefinger raised in the air, a trick of hers when writing—over the pages of her notebook.

The Spoelmanns lived in retirement, they did not mix in the life of the town, as was natural in view both of Mr. Spoelmann's ill-health and of his social loneliness. What social group could he have attached himself to? Nobody even suggested to him that he should consort with soap-boiler Unschlitt or bank-director Wolfsmilch on confidential terms. Yet he was soon approached with appeals to his generosity, and the appeals were not in vain. For Mr. Spoelmann, who, it was well known, before his departure from America had given a large sum in dollars to the Board of Education in the United States, and had also stated in so many words that he had no intention of withdrawing his yearly contributions to the Spoelmann University and his other educational foundations—he, shortly after his arrival at "Delphinenort," put his name down for a subscription of ten thousand marks to the Dorothea Children's Hospital, for which a collection was just being made; an action the nobleness of which was immediately recognized in fitting terms by the *Courier* and the rest of the press.

In fact, although the Spoelmanns lived in seclusion in a social sense, a certain amount of publicity attached to their life among us from the earliest moments, and in the local section of the daily newspapers at least their movements were
183

followed with as much particularity as those of the members of the Grand Ducal House. The public were informed when Miss Imma had played a game of lawn tennis with the Countess and Messrs. Phlebs and Slippers in the "Delphinenort" park; it was noted when she had been at the Court Theatre, and whether her father had gone with her for an act or two of the Opera; and if Mr. Spoelmann shrank from curiosity, never leaving his box during the intervals and scarcely ever showing himself on foot in the streets, yet he was obviously not insensible to the duties of a spectacular kind which were inherent in an extraordinary existence like his own, and he gave the love of gazing its due.

It has been said that the "Delphinenort" park was not divided from the Town Gardens. No walls separated the Schloss from the outer world. From the back one could walk over the turf right up to the foot of the broad covered terrace which had been built on that side, and, if bold enough, look through the big glass door straight into the high white-and-gold garden-room in which Mr. Spoelmann and his family had five-o'clock tea. Indeed, when summer came, tea was laid on the terrace outside, and Mr. and Miss Spoelmann, the Countess and Doctor Watercloose sat in basket chairs of a new-fangled shape, and took their tea as if on a public platform.

For on Sunday, at any rate, there was never wanting a public to enjoy the spectacle at a respectful distance. They called each other's attention to the silver tea-kettle, which was heated by electricity—a quite novel idea—and to the wonderful liveries of the two footmen who handed the tea and cakes, white, high-buttoned, gold-laced coats with swan's-down on the collars, cuffs, and seams. They listened to the English-German conversation and followed with open mouths every movement of the notable family on the terrace. They then went round past the front door, in order to shout a few witticisms in the local dialect to the red-plush negro, which he answered with a dental grin.

184

Klaus Heinrich saw Imma Spoelmann for the first time on a bright winter's day at noon. That does not mean that he had not already caught sight of her often at the theatre, in the street, and in the town park. But that's quite a different thing. He saw her for the first time at this midday hour in exciting circumstances.

He had been giving "free audiences" in the Old Schloss till half-past eleven, and after they were finished had not returned at once to Schloss "Hermitage," but had ordered his coachman to keep the carriage waiting in one of the courts, as he wished to smoke a cigarette with the Guards officers on duty. As he wore the uniform of that regiment, to which his personal aide-de-camp also belonged, he made an effort to maintain the semblance of some sort of camaraderie with the officers; he dined from time to time in their mess and occasionally gave them half an hour of his company on guard, although he had a dim suspicion that he was rather a nuisance as he kept them from their cards and smoking-room stories.

So there he stood, the convex silver star of the Noble Order of the Grimmburg Griffin on his breast, his left hand planted well back on his hip, with Herr von Braunbart-Schellendorf, who had given due notice of the visit in the officers' mess, which was situated on the ground floor of the Schloss near the Albrechts Gate—engaged in a trivial conversation with two or three officers in the middle of the room, while a further group of officers chatted at the deep-set window. Owing to the warmth of sun outside the window stood open, and from the barracks along the Albrechtstrasse came the strains of the drum and fife band of the approaching relief guard.

Twelve o'clock struck from the Court Chapel tower. The loud "Fall in!" of the non-commissioned officer was heard outside, and the rattle of grenadiers standing to arms. The public collected on the square. The lieutenant on duty hastily buckled on his sword belt, clapped his heels together in a salute to Klaus Heinrich and went out. Then suddenly Lieutenant von Sturmhahn, who had been looking out of the

185

window, cried with that rather poor imitation of familiarity which was proper to the relations between Klaus Heinrich and the officers: "Great heavens, here's something for you to look at, Royal Highness! There goes Miss Spoelmann, with her algebra under her arm. . . ."

Klaus Heinrich walked to the window. Miss Imma was walking by herself along the pavement. With both hands thrust into her big flat muff, which was trimmed with pendent tails, she carried her notebook pressed to her side with her elbow. She was wearing a long coat of shiny black fox, and a toque of the same fur on her dark foreign-looking hair. She was obviously coming from "Delphinenort" and hurrying towards the University. She reached the main guardhouse at the moment at which the relief guard marched up the gutter, over against the guard on duty, which standing at attention in two ranks occupied the pavement. She was absolutely compelled to go round, outside the band and the crowd of spectators—indeed, if she wished to avoid the open square with its tram-lines, to make a fairly wide detour on the footpath running round it—or to wait for the end of the military ceremony.

She showed no intention of doing either. She made as if to walk along the pavement in front of the Schloss right down between the two ranks of soldiers. The sergeant with the harsh voice stepped forward quickly. "Not this way!" he cried and held the butt of his rifle in front of her. "Not this way! Right about! Wait!"

But Miss Spoelmann fired up. "What d'you mean?" she cried. "I'm in a hurry!"

But her words were not so impressive as the expression of honest, passionate, irresistible anger with which they were uttered. How slight and lonely she was! The fair-haired soldiers round her towered head and shoulders above her. Her face was as pale as wax at this moment, her black eyebrows were knitted in a hard and expressive wrinkle, her nostrils distended, and her eyes, black with excitement and wide-opened,

186

spoke so expressive and bewitching a language that no protest seemed possible.

"What d'you mean?" she cried. "I'm in a hurry!" And as she said it she pushed the rifle-butt, and the stupefied sergeant with it, aside, and walked down between the lines, went straight on her way, turned to the left into Universitätsstrasse and vanished.

"I'm dammed!" cried Lieutenant von Sturmhahn. "That's one for us!" The officers at the window laughed. The spectators outside, too, were much amused, and not unsympathetic. Klaus Heinrich joined in the general hilarity. The changing of the guard proceeded with loud words of command and snatches of march tunes. Klaus Heinrich returned to the "Hermitage."

He lunched all alone, went for a ride in the afternoon on his brown horse Florian, and spent the evening at a big party at Dr. Krippenreuther, the Finance Minister's house. He related to several people with great animation the episode of the guard, although the story had already gone the round and become common property. Next day he had to go away, for he had been told by his brother to represent him at the inauguration of the new Town Hall in a neighbouring town. For some reason or other, he went reluctantly, he disliked leaving the capital. He had a feeling that he was missing an important, pleasant, though rather disquieting opportunity, which imperatively demanded his presence. And yet his exalted calling must be more important. But while he sat serene and gorgeously dressed on his seat of honour in the Town Hall, and read his speech to the Mayor, Klaus Heinrich's thoughts were not concentrated on the figure he presented to the eyes of the crowd, but rather were busied with this new and important topic. He also gave a passing thought to a person whose casual acquaintance he had made long years before, to Fräulein Unschlitt, the soap-boiler's daughter —a memory which had a certain connexion with the importunate topic. . . .

187

Imma Spoelmann pushed the harsh-voiced sergeant aside in her anger—walked all alone, her algebra under her arm, down the ranks of the big fair-haired grenadiers. How pearly-white her face was against her black hair under her fur toque, and how her eyes spoke! There was nobody like her. Her father was rich, surfeited with riches, and had bought one of the Grand Ducal Schlosses. What was it that the *Courier* had said about his undeserved reputation and the "romantic isolation of his life"? He was the object of the hatred of aggrieved rivals—that was the effect of the article. And her nostrils had distended with anger. There was nobody like her, nobody near or far. She was an exception. And suppose she had been at the Citizens' Ball on that occasion? He would then have had a companion, would not have made a fool of himself, and would not have ended the evening in despair. "Down, down, down with him!" Phew! Just think of how she looked as she walked, dark and pale and wonderful, down the ranks of fair-haired soldiers.

These were the thoughts which occupied Klaus Heinrich during the next few days—just these three or four mental pictures. And the strange thing is that they were amply sufficient for him, and that he did not want any more. But all things considered, it seemed to him more than desirable that he should get another glimpse of the pearly-white face soon, to-day if possible.

In the evening he went to the Court Theatre, where *The Magic Flute* was being played. And when from his box he descried Miss Spoelmann next to Countess Löwenjoul in the front of the circle, a tremor went right through him. During the opera he could watch her out of the darkness through his opera-glasses, for the light from the stage fell on her. She laid her head on her small, ringless hand, while she rested her bare arm on the velvet braid, and she did not look angry now. She wore a dress of glistening sea-green silk with a light scarf on which bright flowers were embroidered, and round her neck a long chain of sparkling diamonds. She really was not so small as she looked, Klaus Heinrich decided, when she stood up at the end of the act. No, the childish shape of her head and the narrowness of her shoulders accounted for her looking such a little thing. Her arms were well developed, and one could see that she played games and rode. But at the wrist her arm looked like a child's.

When the passage came: "He is a prince. He is more than that," Klaus Heinrich conceived the wish to have a talk with Doctor Ueberbein. Doctor Ueberbein called by chance next day at the "Hermitage" in a black frock-coat and white tie, as usual when he paid Klaus Heinrich a visit. Klaus Heinrich asked him whether he had already heard the story of the changing of the guard. Yes, answered Doctor Ueberbein, several times. But would Klaus Heinrich like to relate it to him again? . . . "No, not if you know it," said Klaus Heinrich, disappointed. Then Doctor Ueberbein jumped to quite another topic. He began to talk about opera-glasses, and remarked that opera-glasses were a wonderful invention. They brought close what was unfortunately a long way off, did they not? They formed a bridge to a longed-for goal. What did Klaus Heinrich think? Klaus Heinrich was inclined to agree to a certain extent. And it seemed that yesterday evening, so people said, he had made a free use of this grand invention, said the doctor. Klaus Heinrich could not see the point of this remark.

Then Doctor Ueberbein said: "No, look here, Klaus Heinrich, that won't do. You are stared at, and little Imma is stared at, and that's enough. If you add to it by staring at little Imma, that's too much. You must see that, surely?"

"Oh dear, Doctor Ueberbein, I never thought of that."

"But in other cases you generally do think of that sort of thing."

"I've felt so funny for the last few days," said Klaus Heinrich.

Doctor Ueberbein leaned back, pulled at his red beard near his throat, and nodded slowly with his head and neck.

189

"Really? Have you?" he asked. And then went on nodding.

Klaus Heinrich said: "You can't think how reluctant I was to go the other day to the inauguration of the Town Hall. And to-morrow I have to superintend the swearing-in of the Grenadier recruits. And then comes the Chapter of the Family Order. I don't feel a bit in the mood for that. I find no pleasure in doing my duty as the representative of my people. I've no inclination for my so-called lofty calling."

"I'm sorry to hear it!" said Doctor Ueberbein sharply.

"Yes, I might have known that you would be angry, Doctor Ueberbein. Of course you'll call it sloppiness, and will read me a sermon about 'destiny and discipline,' if I know you. But at the opera yesterday I thought of you at one point, and asked myself whether you really were so right in several particulars. . . ."

"Look here, Klaus Heinrich, once already, if I'm not mistaken, I've dragged your Royal Highness out of the mud, so to speak. . . ."

"That was quite different, Doctor Ueberbein! How I wish you could see that was absolutely different! That was at the Citizens' Ball, but it was years ago, and I don't feel a twinge in that direction. For she is . . . Look you, you have often explained to me what you understand by 'Highness,' and that it is something affecting, and something to be approached with tender sympathy. Don't you think that she of whom we are speaking, that she is affecting and that one must feel sympathy with her?"

"Perhaps," said Doctor Ueberbein. "Perhaps."

"You often said that one must not disavow exceptions, that to do so was sloppiness and slovenly and good-nature. Don't you think that she too of whom we are speaking is an exception?"

Doctor Ueberbein was silent. Then he said suddenly and

190

decidedly, "And now I, if possible, am to help to make two exceptions into a rule?"

Thereupon he went out. He said that he must get back to his work, emphasizing the word "work," and begged leave to withdraw. He took his departure in a strangely ceremonious and unfatherly way.

Klaus Heinrich did not see him for ten or twelve days. He asked him to lunch once, but Doctor Ueberbein begged to be excused, his work at the moment was too pressing. At last he came spontaneously. He was in high spirits and looked greener than ever. He blustered about this and that, and at last came to the subject of the Spoelmanns, looking at the ceiling and pulling at his throat when he did so. To be quite fair, he said, there was a striking amount of sympathy felt with Samuel Spoelmann, one could see all over the town how much beloved he was. Chiefly of course as an object of taxation, but in other respects too. There was simply a penchant for him, in every class, for his organ-playing and his faded coat and his kidney colic. Every errand boy was proud of him, and if he were not so unapproachable and morose he would already have been made to feel it.

The ten-thousand marks donation for the Dorothea Hospital had naturally made an excellent impression. His friend Sammet had told him (Ueberbein) that with the help of this donation far-reaching improvements had been undertaken in the Hospital. And for the rest, it had just occurred to him! Little Imma was going to inspect the improvements to-morrow morning, Sammet had told him. She had sent one of her swan's-down flunkeys and asked whether she would be welcome to-morrow. She and sick children were a devilish funny mixture, opined Ueberbein, but perhaps she might learn something. To-morrow morning at eleven, if his memory did not mislead him.

Then he talked about other things. On leaving he added: "The Grand Duke ought to take some interest in the Dorothea

Hospital, Klaus Heinrich, it's expected of him. It's a blessed institution. In short, somebody ought to show the way, give signs of an interest in high quarters. No wish to intrude. . . . And so good-bye."

But he came back once more, and in his green face a flush had appeared under the eyes which looked entirely out of place there. "If," he said deliberately, "I ever caught you again with a soup tureen on your head, Klaus Heinrich, I should leave it there." Then he pressed his lips together and went out.

Next morning shortly before eleven Klaus Heinrich walked with Herr von Braunbart-Schellendorf, his aide-de-camp, from Schloss "Hermitage" through the snow-covered birch avenue over rough suburban streets between humble cottages, and stopped before the neat white house over whose entrance "Dorothea Children's Hospital" was painted in broad black letters. His visit had been announced. The senior surgeon of the institution, in a frock-coat with the Albrechts Cross of the Third Class, was awaiting him with two younger surgeons and the nursing staff in the hall. The Prince and his companion were wearing helmets and fur coats. Klaus Heinrich said: "This is the renewal of an old acquaintance, my dear doctor. You were present when I came into the world. You are also a friend of my tutor Ueberbein's. I am delighted to meet you."

Doctor Sammet, who had grown grey in his life of active philanthropy, bowed to one side, with one hand on his watch-chain and his elbows close to his ribs. He presented the two junior surgeons and the sister to the Prince, and then said: "I must explain to your Royal Highness that your Royal Highness's gracious visit coincides with another visit. Yes. We are expecting Miss Spoelmann. Her father has done such a lot for our institution. . . . We could not very well upset the arrangements. The sister will take Miss Spoelmann round."

Klaus Heinrich received the news of this rencontre without

192

displeasure. He first expressed his opinion of the nurses' uniform, which he called becoming, and then his curiosity to inspect the philanthropic institution. The tour began. The sister and three nurses waited behind in the hall.

All the walls in the building were whitewashed and washable. Yes. The water taps were huge, they were meant to be worked with the elbows for reasons of cleanliness. And rinsing apparatus had been installed for washing the milk-bottles. One passed first through the reception room, which was empty save for a couple of disused beds and the surgeons' bicycles. In the adjoining preparation room there were, besides the writing-table and the stand with the students' white coats, a kind of folding table with oil-cloth cushions, an operating-table, a cupboard of provisions, and a trough-shaped perambulator. Klaus Heinrich paused at the provisions and asked for the recipes for the preparations to be explained to him. Doctor Sammet thought to himself that if the whole tour was going to be made with such attention to details, a terrible lot of time would be wasted.

Suddenly a noise was heard in the street. An automobile drove up tooting and stopped in front of the building. Cheers were heard distinctly in the preparation room, for all that it was only children that were shouting. Klaus Heinrich did not pay any particular attention to the incident. He was looking at a box of sugar of milk, which, by the way, had nothing striking about it. "A visitor apparently," he said. "Oh, of course, you said somebody was coming. Let's go on."

The party proceeded to the kitchen, the milk-kitchen, the big boiler-fitted room for the preparing of milk, the place where full milk, boiled milk, and buttermilk were kept. The daily rations were set on clean white tables in little bottles side by side. The place smelt sourish and sickly.

Klaus Heinrich gave his undivided attention to this room also. He went so far as to taste the buttermilk, and pronounced it excellent. How the children must thrive, he considered, on buttermilk like that. During this inspection the

193

door opened and Miss Spoelmann entered between the sister and Countess Löwenjoul, followed by the three nurses.

The coat, toque, and muff which she was wearing to-day were made of the costliest sable, and her muff was suspended on a golden chain set with coloured stones. Her black hair showed a tendency to fall in smooth locks over her forehead. She took in the room at a glance; her eyes were really almost unbecomingly big for her little face, they dominated it like a cat's, save that they were black as anthracite and spoke a pleading language of their own. . . . Countess Löwenjoul, with a feather hat and dressed neatly and not without distinction, as usual, smiled in a detached sort of way.

"The milk-kitchen," said the sister; "this is where the milk is cooked for the children."

"So one would have supposed," answered Miss Spoelmann. She said it quickly and lightly, with a pout of her lips and a little haughty wag of her head. Her voice was a double one; it consisted of a lower and a higher register, with a break in the middle.

The sister was quite disconcerted. "Yes," she said, "it's obvious." And a little pained look of bewilderment was visible in her face.

The position was a complicated one. Doctor Sammet looked in Klaus Heinrich's face for orders, but as Klaus Heinrich was accustomed to do what was put before him according to prescribed forms, but not to grapple with novel and complex situations, no solution of the difficulty was forthcoming. Herr von Braunbart was on the point of intervening, and Miss Spoelmann on the other side was making ready to leave the milk-kitchen, when the Prince made a gesture with his right hand which established a connexion between himself and the young girl. This was the signal for Doctor Sammet to advance towards Imma Spoelmann.

"Doctor Sammet. Yes." He desired the honour of presenting Miss Spoelmann to his Royal Highness. . . . "Miss

194

Spoelmann, Royal Highness, the daughter of Mr. Spoelmann to whom this hospital is so much indebted."

Klaus Heinrich clapped his heels together and held out his hand in its white gauntlet, and, laying her small brown-gloved hand in it, she gave him a horizontal hand-shake, English fashion, at the same time making a sort of shy curtsey, without taking her big eyes off Klaus Heinrich's face. He could think of nothing more original to say than: "So you too are paying a visit to the hospital, Miss Spoelmann?"

And she answered as quickly as before, with a pout and the little haughty wag of her head. "Nobody can deny that everything points in that direction."

Herr Braunbart involuntarily raised his hand, Doctor Sammet looked down at his watch-chain in silence, and a short snigger escaped through the nose of one of the young surgeons, which was hardly opportune. The little pained look of bewilderment now showed on Klaus Heinrich's face. He said: "Of course. . . . As you are here. . . . So I shall be able to visit the institution in your company, Miss Spoelmann. . . . Captain von Braunbart, my aide-de-camp . . ." he added quickly, recognizing that his remark laid him open to a similar answer to the last. She responded by: "Countess Löwenjoul."

The Countess made a dignified bow—with an enigmatic smile, a side glance into the unknown, which had something seductive about it. When, however, she let her strangely evasive gaze again dwell on Klaus Heinrich, who stood before her in a composed and military attitude, the laugh vanished from her face, an expression of sadness settled on her features, and for a second a look of something like hatred for Klaus Heinrich shone in her slightly swollen grey eyes. It was only a passing look. Klaus Heinrich had no time to notice it, and forgot it immediately. The two young surgeons were presented to Imma Spoelmann, and then Klaus Heinrich suggested that they should continue the tour all together.

195

They went upstairs to the first story; Klaus Heinrich and Imma Spoelmann in front, conducted by Doctor Sammet, then Countess Löwenjoul with Herr von Braunbart, and the young surgeons in the rear. Yes, the older children were here, up to fourteen years of age. An ante-room with wash-basins divided the girls' and the boys' rooms. In white bedsteads, with a name-plate at the head and a frame at the foot enclosing the temperature-and weight-charts—tended by nurses in white caps, and surrounded by cleanliness and tidiness—lay the sick children, and coughs filled the room while Klaus Heinrich and Imma Spoelmann walked down between the rows.

He walked at her left hand, out of courtesy, with the same smile as when he visited exhibitions or inspected veterans, gymnastic associations, or guards of honour. But every time he turned his head to the right he found that Imma Spoelmann was watching him—he met her great black eyes, which were directed at him in a searching, questioning way. It was so peculiar, he never remembered experiencing anything so peculiar before, her way of looking at him with her great eyes, without any respect for him or anyone else, absolutely unembarrassed and free, quite unconcerned whether anybody noticed it or not.

When Doctor Sammet stopped at a bed to describe the case—the little girl's, for instance, whose broken white-bandaged leg stuck straight out along the bed—Miss Spoelmann listened attentively to him, that was quite clear; but while she listened she did not look at the speaker, but her eyes rested in turn on Klaus Heinrich and the pinched, quiet child who, her hands folded on her breast, gazed up at them from her back-rest—rested in turn on the Prince and the little victim, the history of whose case she shared with the Prince, as if she were watching Klaus Heinrich's sympathy, or were trying to read in his face the effect of Dr. Sammet's words; or maybe for some other reason.

Yes, this was especially noticeable in the case of the boy with the bullet through his arm and the boy who had been

196

picked out of the water—two sad cases, as Dr. Sammet remarked. "A severed artery, sister," he said, and showed them
the double wound in the boy's upper arm, the entry and exit
of the revolver bullet. "The wound," said Doctor Sammet
in an undertone to his guests, turning his back to the bed,
"the wound was caused by his own father. This one was the
lucky one. The man shot his wife, three of his children, and
himself with a revolver. He made a bad shot at this boy."

Klaus Heinrich looked at the double wound. "What did
the man do it for?" he asked hesitatingly, and Doctor Sammet
answered: "In desperation, Royal Highness. It was shame
and want which brought him to it. Yes." He said no more,
just this commonplace—just as in the case of the boy, a
ten-year-old, who had been picked out of the water. "He's
wheezing," said Doctor Sammet, "he's still got some water in
his lung. He was picked out of the river early this morning
—yes. I may say that it is improbable that he *fell* into the
water. There are many indications to the contrary. He had
run away from home. Yes." He stopped.

And Klaus Heinrich again felt Miss Spoelmann looking
at him with her big, black, serious eyes—with her glance
which sought his own and seemed to challenge him insistently to ponder with her the "sad cases," to grasp the essential
meaning of Doctor Sammet's remarks, to penetrate to the
hideous truths which were incorporated and crystallized in
these two little invalid frames. . . . A little girl wept bitterly
when the steaming and hissing inhaler, together with a scrapbook full of brightly coloured pictures, was planted at her
bedside.

Miss Spoelmann bent over the little one. "It doesn't hurt,"
she said, "not a tiny bit. Don't cry." And as she straightened
herself again she added quickly, pursing up her lips, "I guess
it's not so much the apparatus as the pictures she's crying
at." Everybody laughed. One of the young assistants picked
up the scrapbook and laughed still louder when he looked at
the pictures. The party passed on into the laboratory. Klaus
197

Heinrich thought, as he went, how dry Miss Spoelmann's humour was. "I guess," she had said, and "not so much." She had seemed to find amusement not only in the pictures, but also in the neat and incisive mode of expression she had used. And that was indeed the very refinement of humour. . . .

The laboratory was the biggest room in the building. Glasses, retorts, funnels, and chemicals stood on the tables, as well as specimens in spirits which Doctor Sammet explained to his guests in few quiet words. A child had choked in a mysterious way: here was his larynx with mushroom-like growths instead of the vocal chords. Yes. This, here in the glass, was a case of pernicious enlargement of the kidney in a child, and there were dislocated joints. Klaus Heinrich and Miss Spoelmann looked at everything, they looked together into the bottles which Doctor Sammet held up to the window, and their eyes looked thoughtful while the same look of repulsion hovered round their mouths.

They took turns too at the microscope, examined, with one eye placed to the lens, a malignant secretion, a piece of blue-stained tissue stuck on a slide, with tiny spots showing near the big patch. The spots were bacilli. Klaus Heinrich wanted Miss Spoelmann to take the first turn at the microscope, but she declined, knitting her brows and pouting, as much as to say: "On no account whatever." So he took the precedence, for it seemed to him that it really did not matter who got the first look at such serious and fearful things as bacilli. And after this they were conducted up to the second story, to the infants.

They both laughed at the chorus of squalls which reached their ears while they were still on the stairs. And then they went with their party through the ward between the beds, bent side by side over the bald-headed little creatures, sleeping with closed fists or screaming with all their might and showing their naked gums—they stopped their ears and laughed again. In a kind of oven, warmed to a moderate heat lay a new-born baby.

And Doctor Sammet showed his distinguished guests a pauper baby with the grey look of a corpse and hideous big hands, the sign of a miscarriage. . . . He lifted a squealing baby out of its cot, and it at once stopped screaming. With the touch of an expert he rested the limp head in the hollow of his hand and showed the little red creature blinking and twitching spasmodically to the two—Klaus Heinrich and Miss Spoelmann, who stood side by side and looked down at the infant. Klaus Heinrich stood watching with his heels together as Doctor Sammet laid the baby back in its cot, and when he turned round he met Miss Spoelmann's searching gaze, as he had expected.

Finally they walked to one of the three windows of the ward and looked out over the squalid suburb, down into the street where, surrounded by children, the brown Court carriage and Imma's smart dark-red motor car stood one behind the other. The Spoelmanns' chauffeur, shapeless in his fur coat, was leaning back in his seat with one hand on the steering-wheel of the powerful car, and watched his companion, the footman in white, trying to start a conversation, by the carriage in front, with Klaus Heinrich's coachman.

"Our neighbours," said Doctor Sammet, holding back the white net curtain with one hand, "are the parents of our patients. Late in the evening the tipsy fathers roll shouting by. Yes."

They stood and listened, but Doctor Sammet said nothing further about the fathers and so they broke off, as they had now seen everything.

The procession, with Klaus Heinrich and Imma at the head, proceeded down the staircase and found the nurses again assembled in the front hall. Leave was taken with compliments and clapping together of heels, curtseys, and bows. Klaus Heinrich, standing stiffly in front of Doctor Sammet, who listened to him with his head on one side and his hand on his watch-chain, expressed himself, in his wonted form of words, highly satisfied with what he had seen, while he felt that Imma Spoelmann's great eyes were resting upon him. He, with Herr von Braunbart, accompanied Miss Spoelmann to her car when the leave-taking from the surgeons and nurses was over. Klaus Heinrich and Miss Spoelmann, while they crossed the pavement between children and women with children in their arms, and for a short time by the broad step of the motor car, exchanged the following remarks:

"It has been a great pleasure to meet you," he said.

She answered nothing to this, but pouted and wagged her head a little from side to side.

"It was an absorbing inspection," he went on. "A regular eye-opener."

She looked at him with her big black eyes, then said quickly and lightly in her broken voice: "Yes, to a certain extent. . . ."

He ventured on the question: "I hope you are pleased with Schloss Delphinenort?"

To which she answered with a pout: "Oh, why not? It's quite a convenient house. . . ."

"Do you like being there better than at New York?" he asked. And she answered:

"Just as much. It's much the same. Much the same everywhere."

That was all. Klaus Heinrich, and one pace behind him Herr von Braunbart, stood with their hands to their helmets as the chauffeur slipped his gear in and the motor car shivered and started.

It may be imagined that this meeting did not long remain the private property of the Dorothea Hospital; on the contrary, it was the general topic of conversation before the day was out. The *Courier* published, under a sentimental poetical heading, a detailed description of the rencontre, which, without too violent a departure from the exact truth, yet succeeded in making such a powerful impression on the public

200

mind, and evoked symptoms of such lively interest, that the vigilant newspaper was induced to keep a watchful eye for the future on any further rapprochements between the Spoelmann and Grimmburg houses. It could not report much.

It remarked a couple of times that his Royal Highness Prince Klaus Heinrich, when walking through the promenade after a performance at the Court Theatre, had stopped for a moment at the Spoelmanns' box to greet the ladies. And in its report of the fancy-dress charity bazaar, which took place in the middle of January in the Town Hall—a smart function, in which Miss Spoelmann, at the urgent request of the Committee, acted as seller—no small space was devoted to describing how Prince Klaus Heinrich, when the Court was making a round of the bazaar, had stopped before Miss Spoelmann's stall, how he had bought a piece or two of fancy glass (for Miss Spoelmann was selling porcelain and glass), and had lingered a good eight or ten minutes at her stall. It said nothing about the topic of the conversation. And yet it had not been without importance.

The Court (with the exception of Albrecht) had appeared in the Town Hall about noon. When Klaus Heinrich, with his newly bought pieces of glass in tissue paper on his knee, drove back to the "Hermitage," he had announced his intention of visiting Delphinenort and inspecting the Schloss in its renovated state, on the same occasion viewing Mr. Spoelmann's collection of glass. For three or four old pieces of glass had been included in Miss Spoelmann's stock which her father himself had given to the bazaar out of his collection, and one of them Klaus Heinrich had bought.

He saw himself again in a semicircle of people, stared at, alone, in front of Miss Spoelmann, and separated from her by the stall-counter, with its vases, jugs, its white and coloured groups of porcelain. He saw her in her red fancy dress, which, made in one piece, clung close to her neat though childish figure, while it exposed dark shoulders and arms, which were round and firm and yet like those of a child

201

just by the wrist. He saw the gold ornament, half garland
and half diadem, in the jet of her billowy hair, that showed
a tendency to fall in smooth wisps on her forehead, her big,
black, inquiring eyes in the pearly-white face, her full and
tender mouth, pouting with habitual scorn when she spoke—
and round about her in the great vaulted hall had been the
scent of firs and a babel of noise, music, the clash of gongs,
laughter, and the cries of sellers.

He had admired the piece of glass, the fine old beaker
with its ornament of silver foliage, which she proffered to
him, and she had said that it came from her father's collection. "Has your father, then, got many fine pieces like this?"
—Of course. And presumably her father had not given the
best items to the bazaar. She could guarantee that he had
much finer pieces of glass. Klaus Heinrich would very
much like to see them! Well, that might easily be managed,
Miss Spoelmann had answered in her broken voice, while she
pouted and wagged her head slightly from side to side. Her
father, she meant, would certainly have no objection to showing the fruits of his zeal as a collector to one more of a long
succession of intelligent visitors. The Spoelmanns were
always at home at tea-time.

She had gone straight to the point, taking the hint for
a definite offer, and speaking in an entirely off-hand way.
In conclusion, to Klaus Heinrich's question, what day would
suit best, she had answered: "Whichever you like, Prince, we
shall be inexpressibly delighted."

"We shall be inexpressibly delighted"—those were her
words, so mocking and pointed in the exaggeration that they
almost hurt, and were difficult to listen to without wincing.
How she had rattled and hurt the poor sister in the Hospital
the other day! But all through there was something childish
in her manner of speech; indeed, some sounds she made were
just like those children make—not only on the occasion when
she was comforting the little girl about the inhaler. And

202

how large her eyes had seemed when they told her about the children's fathers and the rest of the sad story!

Next day Klaus Heinrich went to tea at Schloss Delphinenort, the very next. Miss Spoelmann had said he might come when it suited him. But it suited him the very next day, and as the matter seemed to him urgent, he saw no point in putting it off.

Shortly before five o'clock—it was already dark—he drove over the smooth roads of the Town Garden—bare and empty, for this part of it belonged to Mr. Spoelmann. Arc-lamps lit up the park, the big square spa-basin shimmered between the trees; behind it rose the white Schloss with its pillared porch, its spacious double staircase which led by gentle degrees between the wings up to the first floor, its high leaded windows, its Roman busts in the niches—and Klaus Heinrich, as he drove along the approach avenue of mighty chestnuts, saw the red-plush negro with his staff standing on guard at the foot of the staircase.

Klaus Heinrich crossed a brightly lighted stone hall, with a floor of gilt mosaic and with white statues of gods round it, passed straight over to the broad red-carpeted marble staircase, down which the Spoelmanns' major-domo, clean shaven, with shoulders squared and arms stiff, pot-bellied and haughty, advanced to receive the guest. He escorted him up into the tapestried and marble-chimneyed ante-room, where a couple of white-and-gold swan's-down footmen took the Prince's cap and cloak, while the steward went in person to announce him to his master. . . . The footman held aside one of the tapestries for Klaus Heinrich, who descended two or three steps.

The scent of flowers met him, and he heard the soft splash of falling water; but just as the tapestry closed behind him, so wild and harsh a barking was heard that Klaus Heinrich, half deafened for a moment, stopped at the foot of the steps. Percival, the collie, had dashed at him in a fury. He pranced, he capered in uncontrollable passion, he pirouetted, beat his

203

sides with his tail, planted his forefeet on the floor, and turned wildly round and round, and seemed like to burst with noise. A voice—not Imma's—called him off, and Klaus Heinrich found himself in a winter garden, a glass conservatory with white marble columns and a floor of big square marble flags. Palms of all kinds filled it, whose trunks and tops often reached close up to the glass ceiling. A flower-bed, consisting of countless pots arranged like the stones of a mosaic, lay in the strong moonlight of the arc-lamp and filled the air with its scent. Out of a beautifully carved fountain, silver streams flowed into a marble pool, and ducks with strange and fantastic plumage swam about on the illuminated water. The background was filled by a stone walk with columns and niches.

It was Countess Löwenjoul who advanced towards the guest, and curtseyed with a smile.

"Your Royal Highness will not mind," she said, "our Percy is so uproarious. Besides, he's so unaccustomed to visitors. But he never touches anybody. Your Royal Highness must excuse Miss Spoelmann. . . . She'll be back soon. She was here just now. She was called away, her father sent for her. Mr. Spoelmann will be delighted. . . ."

And she conducted Klaus Heinrich to an arrangement of basket chairs with embroidered linen cushions which stood in front of a group of palms. She spoke in a brisk and emphatic tone, with her little head with its thin iron-grey hair bent on one side and her white teeth showing as she laughed. Her figure was distinctly graceful in the close-fitting brown dress she was wearing, and she moved as freshly and elegantly as an officer's wife. Only in her eyes, whose lids she kept blinking, there was something of mistrust or spite, something unintelligible. They sat down facing each other at the round garden-table, on which lay a few books. Percival, exhausted by his outburst, curled himself up on the narrow pearl-grey carpet on which the furniture stood. His black coat was like silk, with white paws,

204

chest, and muzzle. He had a white collar, yellow eyes, and a parting along his back. Klaus Heinrich began a conversation for conversation's sake, a formal dialogue about nothing in particular, which was all he could do.

"I hope, Countess, that I have not come at an inconvenient time. Luckily I need not feel myself an unauthorized intruder. I do not know whether Miss Spoelmann has told you. . . . She was so kind as to suggest my calling. It was about those lovely pieces of glass which Mr. Spoelmann so generously gave to yesterday's bazaar. Miss Spoelmann thought that her father would have no objection to letting me see the rest of his collection. That's why I'm here . . ."

The Countess ignored the question whether Imma had told her of the arrangement. She said: "This is tea-time, Royal Highness. Of course your visit is not inconvenient. Even if, as I hope will not be the case, Mr. Spoelmann were too unwell to appear. . . ."

"Oh, is he ill?" In reality Klaus Heinrich wished just a little that Mr. Spoelmann might be too unwell. He anticipated his meeting with him with vague anxiety.

"He was feeling ill to-day, Royal Highness. He had a touch of fever, shivering, and a little faintness. Dr. Watercloose was with him for a long time this morning. He was given an injection of morphia. There's some question of an operation being necessary."

"I am very sorry," said Klaus Heinrich quite honestly. "An operation? How dreadful!"

To which the Countess answered, letting her eyes wander: "Oh yes. But there are worse things in life—many much worse things than that."

"Undoubtedly," said Klaus Heinrich. "I can quite believe it." He felt his imagination stirred in a vague and general way by the Countess's allusion.

She looked at him with her head inclined to one side, and an expression of contempt on her face. Then her slightly distended grey eyes shifted, while she smiled the mysterious smile which Klaus Heinrich already knew and which had something seductive about it.

He felt it was necessary to resume the conversation.

"Have you lived long with the Spoelmanns, Countess?" he asked.

"A fairly long time," she answered, and appeared to calculate. "Fairly long. I have lived through so much, have had so many experiences, that I naturally cannot reckon to a day. But it was shortly after the blessing—soon after the blessing was vouchsafed to me."

"The blessing?" asked Klaus Heinrich.

"Of course," she said decidedly with some agitation. "For the blessing happened to me when the number of my experiences had become too great, and the bow had reached breaking point, to use a metaphor. You are so young," she continued, forgetting to address him by his title, "so ignorant of all that makes the world so miserable and so depraved, that you can form no conception of what I have had to suffer. I brought an action in America which involved the appearance of several generals. Things came to light which were more than my temper could stand. I had to clear out several barracks without succeeding in bringing to light every loose woman. They hid themselves in the cupboards, some even under the floors, and that's why they continue torturing me beyond measure at nights. I should at once go back to my Schloss in Burgundy if the rain did not come through the roofs. The Spoelmanns knew that, and that is why it was so obliging of them to let me live with them indefinitely, my only duty being to put the innocent Imma on her guard against the world. Only of course my health suffers from my having the women sitting at nights on my chest and forcing me to look at their disgusting faces. And that is why I ask you to call me simply Frau Meier," she said in a whisper, leaning forward and touching Klaus Heinrich's arm with her hand. "The walls have ears, and it is absolutely necessary for me to keep up the incognito I was forced to assume in order to protect myself against the persecution of the odious creatures. You will do what I ask, will you not? Look on it as a joke . . . a fad which hurts nobody. . . . Why not?"

She stopped.

Klaus Heinrich sat upright and braced up in his wicker chair opposite her and looked at her. Before leaving his rectilineal room, he had dressed himself with his valet Neumann's help with all possible care, as his life in the public eye required. His parting ran from over his left eye, straight up to the crown of his head, without a hair sticking up, and his hair was brushed up into a crest off the right side of his forehead. There he sat in his undress uniform, whose high collar and close fit helped him to maintain a composed attitude, the silver epaulettes of a major on his narrow shoulders, leaning slightly but not comfortably forward, collected, calm, with one foot slightly advanced, and with his right hand above his left on his sword-hilt. His young face looked slightly weary from the unreality, the loneliness, strictness, and difficulty of his life; he sat looking at the Countess with a friendly, clear, but composed expression in his eyes.

She stopped. Disenchantment and disgust showed themselves in her features, and, while something like hate towards Klaus Heinrich flamed up in her tired grey eyes, she blushed in the strangest of ways, for one half of her face turned red, the other white. Dropping her eyelids she answered: "I have been living with the Spoelmanns for three years, Royal Highness."

Percival darted forward. Dancing, springing, and wagging his tail he trotted towards his mistress—for Imma Spoelmann had come in—raised himself in a dignified way on his hind legs and laid his fore paws in greeting on her breast. His jaws were wide open, and his red tongue hung out between his ivory-white teeth. He looked like a heraldic supporter as he stood there before her.

She wore a wonderful dress of brick-red silk with loose hanging sleeves, and the breast covered with heavy gold em-

207

broidery. A big egg-shaped jewel on a pearl necklace lay on her bare neck, the skin of which was the colour of smoked meerschaum. Her blue-black hair was parted on one side and coiled, though a few smooth wisps tended to fall on her forehead. Holding Percival's head in her two narrow, ringless little hands, she looked into his face, saying, "Well, well, my friend. What a welcome! We are glad to see each other —we hated being parted, didn't we? Now go back and lie down." And she put his paws off the gold embroidery on her breast, and set him on his four paws again.

"Oh, Prince," she said. "Welcome to Delphinenort. You hate breaking your promise, I can see. I'm coming to sit next you. They'll tell us when tea is ready. . . . It's against all the rules, I know, for me to have kept you waiting. But my father sent for me—and besides you had somebody to entertain you." Her bright eyes passed from Klaus Heinrich to the Countess and back in a rather hesitating way.

"That's quite true," he said. And then he asked how Mr. Spoelmann was, and received a fairly reassuring answer. Mr. Spoelmann would have the pleasure of making Klaus Heinrich's acquaintance at tea-time, he begged to be excused till then. . . . What a lovely pair of horses Klaus Heinrich had in his brougham! And then they talked about their horses, about Klaus Heinrich's good-tempered brown Florian from the Hollerbrunn stud, about Miss Spoelmann's Arabian cream, the mare Fatma which had been given to Mr. Spoelmann by an oriental prince, about her fast Hungarian chestnuts, which she drove four-in-hand.

"Do you know the country round?" asked Klaus Heinrich. "Have you hunted with the Royal pack? Have you been to the 'Pheasantry'? There are lots of lovely excursions."

No, Miss Spoelmann was not at all clever in finding out new roads, and the Countess—well, her whole nature was unenterprising, so they always chose the same road, in the Town Gardens, for their ride. It was boring, perhaps, but Miss Spoelmann was not on the whole so blasé as to need constant change and adventures. Then he said that they must go together some time to a meet of the hounds or to the "Pheasantry," whereupon she pursed her lips and said that that was an idea which might be discussed some time in the future. Then the major-domo came in and gravely announced that tea was ready.

They went through the tapestry hall with the marble fireplace, conducted by the strutting butler, accompanied by the dancing Percy, and followed by Countess Löwenjoul.

"Has the Countess been letting her tongue run away with her?" asked Imma *en route*, without any particular lowering of her voice.

Klaus Heinrich started and looked at the floor. "But she can hear us!" he said softly.

"No, she doesn't hear us," answered Imma. "I can read her face. When she holds her head crooked like that and blinks her eyes it means that she is wandering and deep in her thoughts. Did she let her tongue run away with her?"

"For a minute or two," said Klaus Heinrich. "I got the impression that the Countess 'let herself go' every now and then."

"She has had a lot of trouble." And Imma looked at him with the same big searching dark eyes with which she had scanned him in the Dorothea Hospital. "I'll tell you all about it another time. It's a long story."

"Yes," he said. "Some other time. Next time. On our ride perhaps."

"On our ride?"

"Yes, on our ride to the meet, or to the 'Pheasantry.'"

"Oh, I forgot your preciseness, Prince, in the matter of appointments. Very well, on our ride. We go down here."

They found themselves at the back of the Schloss. Carpeted steps led from a gallery hung with big pictures, down into the white-and-gold garden room, behind the glass door of which lay the terrace. Everything—the big crystal lustres, which hung from the centre of the high, white-festooned
209

ceiling, the regularly arranged arm-chairs with gilt frames and fancy upholstering, the heavy white silk curtains, the elaborate clock and the vases and gilt lamps on the white marble chimneypiece in front of the tall looking-glass, the massive, lion-footed gilt candelabra which towered on either side of the entrance—everything reminded Klaus Heinrich of the Old Schloss, of the Representation Chamber, in which he had played his part from his youth up; only that the candles here were shams, with yellow electric bulbs instead of wicks, and that everything of the Spoelmanns' was new and smart in Schloss Delphinenort. A swan's-down footman was putting the last touch to the tea-table in a corner of the room; Klaus Heinrich noticed the electric kettle about which he had read in the *Courier*.

"Has Mr. Spoelmann been told?" asked the daughter of the house. . . . The butler bowed. "Then there's nothing," she said quickly and half mockingly, "to prevent us from taking our places and beginning without him. Come, Countess! I advise you, Prince, to unbuckle your sword, unless there are reasons unknown to me for your not doing so. . . ."

"Thanks," said Klaus Heinrich, "no, there is no reason why I shouldn't." And he was angry with himself for not being smart enough to think of a more adroit answer.

The footman took his sword, and carried it off. They took their seats at the tea-table with the help of the butler, who held the backs and pushed the chairs under them. Then he retired to the top of the steps, where he remained in an elegant attitude.

"I must tell you, Prince," said Miss Spoelmann, pouring the water into the pot, "that my father won't drink any tea which I have not made with my own hands. He distrusts all tea which is handed round ready-made in cups. That is barred with us. You'll have to put up with it."

"Oh, I like it much better like this," said Klaus Heinrich, "it's much more comfortable and free-and-easy at a family tea like this. . . ." He broke off, and wondered why as he

spoke these words a side-glance of hatred lighted on him from
the eyes of Countess Löwenjoul. "And your course of study?"
he asked. "May I ask about it? It's mathematics, I know.
Don't you find it too much? Isn't it terribly brain-racking?"

"Absolutely not," she said. "It's just splendid; it's like
playing in the breezes, so to speak, or rather out of the
breezes, in a dust-free atmosphere. It's as cool there as in
the Adirondacks."

"The what?"

"The Adirondacks. That's geography, Prince. Mountains
over in the States, with lovely snowfields. We have a country
cottage there, where we go in May. In summer we used to go
to the sea-side."

"At any rate," he said, "I can testify to your zeal in your
studies. You do not like being prevented from arriving punctually at your lectures. I haven't yet asked you whether
you reached that one the other day up to time."

"The other day?"

"Yes, a week or two ago. After the contretemps with the
change of guard."

"Dear, dear, Prince, now you are beginning that too.
That story seems to have reached from hut to palace. Had
I known what a bother was going to come of it, I would
rather have gone three times round the whole Schlossplatz.
It even got into the newspapers, I'm told. And now of course
the whole town thinks I am a regular fiend for temper and
rudeness. But I am the most peaceful creature in the world,
and only don't like being ordered about. Am I a fiend,
Countess? I demand a truthful answer."

"No, you're an angel," said Countess Löwenjoul.

"H'm—angel, that's too much, that's too far the other way,
Countess. . . ."

"No," said Klaus Heinrich, "no, not too far. I entirely
believe the Countess. . . ."

"I'm much honoured. But how did your Highness hear
about the adventure? Through the newspapers?"

211

"I was an eye-witness of it," said Klaus Heinrich.

"An eye-witness?"

"Yes. I happened to be standing at the window of the officers' mess, and saw the whole thing from beginning to end."

Miss Spoelmann blushed. There was no doubt about it, the pale skin of her face deepened in colour.

"Well, Prince," she said, "I assume that you had nothing better to do at the moment."

"Better?" he cried. "But it was a splendid sight. I give you my word that never in my life . . ."

Percival, who was lying with his forepaws crossed, by Miss Spoelmann, raised his head with a look of tense expectancy and beat the carpet with his tail, At the same moment the butler began to run, as fast as his ponderous frame would let him, down the steps to the lofty side-door over against the tea-table, and swiftly pulled aside the whole silk portière, sticking his double chin the while into the air with a majestic expression. Samuel Spoelmann, the millionaire, walked in.

He was a man of neat build with a strange face. He was clean shaven, with red cheeks and a prominent nose, his little eyes were of a metallic blue-black, like those of little children and animals, and had an absent and peevish look. The upper part of his head was bald, but behind and on his temples Mr. Spoelmann had a quantity of grey hair, dressed in a fashion not often seen among us. He wore it neither short nor long, but brushed up, sticking out, though cropped on the nape and round his ears. His mouth was small and finely chiselled. Dressed in a black frock-coat with a velvet waistcoat on which lay a long, thin, old-fashioned watch-chain, and soft slippers on his feet, he advanced quickly to the tea-table with a cross and pre-occupied expression on his face; but his face cleared up, it regained composure and tenderness when he caught sight of his daughter. Imma had gone to meet him.

"Greeting, most excellent father," she said, and throwing her brown little arms, in their loose brick-coloured hanging

212

sleeves, round his neck, she kissed him on the bald spot which he offered her as he inclined his head.

"Of course you knew," she continued, "that Prince Klaus Heinrich was coming to tea with us to-day?"

"No; I'm delighted, delighted," said Mr. Spoelmann no less readily and in a grating voice. "Please don't move!" he said at once. And while he shook hands (Mr. Spoelmann's hand was thin and half-covered by his unstarched white cuff) with the Prince, who was standing modestly by the table, he nodded repeatedly to one side or the other. That was his way of greeting Klaus Heinrich. He was an alien, an invalid, and a man apart as regards wealth. He was forgiven and nothing further was expected of him—Klaus Heinrich recognized the fact, and took pains to recover his self-control.

"You are at home here in a sense," added Mr. Spoelmann, cutting the conversation short, and a passing gleam of malice played round his clean-shaven mouth. Then he gave the others an example by sitting down. It was the chair between Imma and Klaus Heinrich, opposite the Countess and the veranda door, which the butler pushed under him.

As Mr. Spoelmann showed no intention of apologizing for his unpunctuality, Klaus Heinrich said: "I am sorry to hear that you are unwell this morning, Mr. Spoelmann. I hope you are better."

"Thanks, better, not but all right," answered Mr. Spoelmann crossly. "How many spoonfuls did you put in?" he asked his daughter. He was alluding to the tea.

She had filled his cup, and she handed it to him.

"Four," said she. "One for each person. Nobody shall say that I stint my grey-haired father."

"What's that?" answered Mr. Spoelmann. "I'm not grey-haired. You ought to have your tongue clipped." And he took from a silver box a kind of rusk which seemed to be his own special dainty, broke it and dipped it peevishly in the golden tea, which he, like his daughter, drank without milk or sugar.

213

Klaus Heinrich began over again: "I am much excited at the prospect of seeing your collection, Mr. Spoelmann."

"All right," answered Mr. Spoelmann. "So you want to see my glass? Are you an amateur? A collector perhaps?"

"No," said Klaus Heinrich, "my love for glass has not extended to my becoming a collector."

"No time?" asked Mr. Spoelmann. "Do your military duties take so much time?"

Klaus Heinrich answered: "I'm no longer on the active list, Mr. Spoelmann. I am à la suite of my regiment. I wear the uniform, that's all."

"I see, make believe," said Mr. Spoelmann harshly. "What do you do all day, then?"

Klaus Heinrich had stopped drinking tea, had pushed his things away in the course of the conversation which demanded his undivided attention. He sat upright and defended himself, feeling the while that Imma Spoelmann's big, black, searching eyes were resting on him.

"I have duties at Court, with the ceremonies and big occasions. I have also to represent the State in a military capacity, at the swearing-in of recruits and the presentation of colours. Then I have to hold levées as deputy for my brother, the Grand Duke. And then there are little journeys on duty to the provincial centres for unveilings and dedications and other public solemnities."

"I see," said Mr. Spoelmann. "Ceremonies, solemnities, food for spectators. No, that sort of thing's beyond me. I tell you once for all, that I wouldn't give a farthing for your calling. That's my standpoint, sir."

"I entirely understand," said Klaus Heinrich. He sat up stiffly in his uniform and smiled uneasily.

"Of course it needs practice like everything else," Mr. Spoelmann went on in a little less bitter tone of voice—"practice and training, I can see. For myself I shall never as long as I live cease feeling angry when I am obliged to play the prodigy."

214

"I only hope," said Klaus Heinrich, "that our people are not wanting in respect. . . ."

"Thanks, not so bad," answered Mr. Spoelmann. "The people are at least friendly here; one doesn't see murder written in their eyes."

"I hope, Mr. Spoelmann," and Klaus Heinrich felt more at his ease, now that the conversation had turned, and the questioning lay with him, "that, notwithstanding the unusual circumstances, you continue to enjoy your stay amongst us."

"Thanks," said Mr. Spoelmann, "I'm quite comfortable, and the water is the only thing which really does do me some good."

"You did not find it a wrench to leave America?"

Klaus Heinrich felt a look, a quick, suspicious, shy look, which he could not interpret.

"No," said Mr. Spoelmann, sharply and crossly. That was all his answer to the question whether he felt it a wrench to leave America.

A pause ensued. Countess Löwenjoul held her smooth little head inclined to one side, and smiled a distant Madonna-like smile. Miss Spoelmann watched Klaus Heinrich fixedly with her big black eyes, as if testing the effect of her father's extraordinary boorishness on the guest,—indeed, Klaus Heinrich felt that she was waiting with resignation and sympathy for him to get up and take his departure for good and all. He met her eyes, and remained. Mr. Spoelmann, for his part, drew out a gold case and took out a fat cigarette, which, when lighted, diffused a delicious fragrance.

"Smoke?" he asked. . . . And as Klaus Heinrich found that there was no objection, he helped himself, after Mr. Spoelmann, out of the proffered case.

They then discussed various topics before proceeding to an inspection of the glass—chiefly Klaus Heinrich and Miss Spoelmann, for the Countess's thoughts were wandering, and Mr. Spoelmann only interpolated a cross remark now and then: the local theatre, the huge ship in which the Spoel-

215

manns had crossed to Europe. No, they had not used their yacht for the purpose. Its primary object was to take Mr. Spoelmann to sea in the evening in the heat of summer, when he was tied to his business and Imma and the Countess were in Newport; he used to pass the night on deck. She was now lying at Venice. But they had crossed in a huge steamer, a floating hotel with concert rooms and gymnasia. "She had five storeys," said Miss Spoelmann.

"Counting from below?" asked Klaus Heinrich. And she answered at once:

"Of course. Six, counting from above."

He got muddled and lost his bearings and it was a long time before he realized that she was making fun of him. Then he tried to explain himself and to make his simple question clear, explaining that he meant to ask whether she included the under-water holds, the cellars so to speak, in the five—in short, to prove that he was not lacking in common sense, and at last he joined heartily in the merriment which was the result of his efforts. As for the Court Theatre, Miss Spoelmann gave it as her opinion, with a pout and a wag of the head, that the actress who played the *ingénue* should be strongly recommended to go through the cure at Marienbad, coupled with a course of lessons in dancing and deportment, while the hero should be warned that a voice as resonant as his should be used most sparingly, even in private life. . . . All the same, Miss Spoelmann expressed her warm admiration for the theatre in question.

Klaus Heinrich laughed and wondered, a little oppressed by so much smartness. How well she spoke, how pointed and incisive were her words! They discussed the operas also and the plays which had been produced during the winter, and Imma Spoelmann contradicted Klaus Heinrich's judgments, contradicted him in every case, just as if she thought that not to contradict would show a mean spirit; the superior wit of her tongue left him dazed, and the great black eyes in her pearl-white face glittered from sheer joy in her dia-

216

lectic skill, while Mr. Spoelmann leaned back in his chair, holding the fat cigarette between his lips and blinking through its smoke, and gazed at his daughter with fond satisfaction.

More than once Klaus Heinrich showed in his face the look of pained bewilderment which he had noticed on a previous occasion on the face of the good sister, and yet he felt convinced that it was not Imma Spoelmann's intention to wound his feelings, that she did not consider him humbled because he was not successful in standing up to her, that she rather let his poor answers pass, as if she considered that he had no need of a sharp wit to defend him—it was only she who had. But how was that, and why? He thought involuntarily of Ueberbein at many of her sallies, of the nimble-tongued blusterer Ueberbein, who was a natural misfortune, and had grown up in conditions which he described as favourable. A youth of misery, loneliness, and misfortune, shut out from the blessings of fortune—such a man knew no luxury, no comfort, he saw himself clearly and cruelly thrown on his own resources, which assuredly gave him an advantage over those who "knew not necessity."

But Imma Spoelmann sat there in her red-gold dress at the table, reclining indolently, with the mocking look of a spoiled child; there she sat in confident ease, while her tongue ran on sharply and freely, as befitted an atmosphere of refinement and lively wit. But why did she give it play? Klaus Heinrich pondered the question, the while they discussed Atlantic steamers and plays. He sat bolt upright at the table, in a dignified and uncomfortable attitude, while he concealed his left hand, and more than once he felt a sidelong glance of hatred from the eyes of Countess Löwenjoul.

A servant came in and handed Mr. Spoelmann a telegram on a silver salver. Mr. Spoelmann tore it open crossly, glanced through it, blinking and with the remains of his cigarette in the corner of his mouth, and threw it back on the salver, with the curt order: "Mr. Phlebs." Thereupon he lighted a new cigarette.

Miss Spoelmann said: "In spite of distinct medical orders, that's the fifth cigarette you've had to-day. Let me tell you that the unbridled passion with which you abandon yourself to the vice little beseems your grey hairs."

Mr. Spoelmann obviously tried to laugh, and as obviously failed; the acid tone of his daughter's words was not to his liking, and he flushed up.

"Silence!" he snarled. "You think you can say anything in fun, but please spare me your saucy jokes, chatterbox!"

Klaus Heinrich, appalled, looked at Imma, who turned her big eyes on her father's angry face, and then sadly dropped her head. Of course she had not meant any offence, she had simply amused herself with the strange, swelling words which she used to poke her fun; she had expected to raise a laugh, and had failed dismally.

"Father, darling father!" she said beseechingly, and crossed over to stroke Mr. Spoelmann's flushed cheeks.

"Surely," he grumbled on, "you've grown out of that sort of thing by now." But then he yielded to her blandishments, let her kiss the top of his head, and swallowed his anger. Klaus Heinrich, when peace was restored, alluded to the collection of glass, whereupon the party left the tea-table and went into the adjoining museum, with the exception of Countess Löwenjoul, who withdrew with a deep curtsey. Mr. Spoelmann himself switched on the electric light in the chandeliers.

Handsome cabinets in the style of the whole Schloss, with swelling curves and rounded glass doors, alternated with rich silk chairs all round the room. In these cabinets Mr. Spoelmann's collection of glass was displayed. Yes, there could be no doubt that it was the most complete collection in either hemisphere, and the glass which Klaus Heinrich had acquired was merely a most modest sample of it. It began in one corner of the room with the earliest artistic productions of the industry, with finds of heathenish designs from the culture of the earliest times; then came the products of the

218

East and West of every epoch; next, wreathed, flourished, and imposing vases and beakers from Venetian blow-pipes and costly pieces from Bohemian huts, German tankards, picturesque Guild and Electorate bowls, mixed with grotesque animals and comic figures, huge crystal cups, which reminded one of the Luck of Edenhall in the song, and in whose facets the light broke and sparkled; ruby-coloured glasses like the Holy Grail; and finally the best samples of the latest development of the art, fragile blossoms on impossibly brittle stems, and fancy glasses in the latest fashionable shape, made iridescent with the vapours of precious metals. The three, followed by Percival, who also examined the collection, walked slowly round the hall; and Mr. Spoelmann related in his harsh voice the origin of particular pieces, taking them carefully off their velvet stands with his thin, soft-cuffed hand, and holding them up to the electric light.

Klaus Heinrich had had plenty of practice in visits of inspection, in putting questions and making adroit remarks, so that he was well able at the same time to ponder over Imma Spoelmann's mode of expressing herself, that peculiar mode which worried him not a little. What amazing freedom she allowed herself! What extraordinary remarks she allowed herself to make! "Passion," "vice," where did she get the words from? where did she learn to use them so glibly? Had not Countess Löwenjoul, who herself dealt with the same topics in a confused sort of way, and had obviously seen the seamy side of life, described her as quite innocent!

And the description was undoubtedly correct, for was she not an exception by birth like himself, brought up like a girl "born to be queen," kept apart from the busy strife of men and from all the turmoil to which those sinister words corresponded in the life of reality? But she had uttered the words glibly, and had treated them as a joke. Yes, that was it, this dainty creature in her red-gold gown was merely a wielder of words; she knew no more of life than those words, she played with the most serious and most awful of them as

219

with coloured stones, and was puzzled when she made people angry by their use. Klaus Heinrich's heart, as he thought of this, filled with sympathy.

It was nearly seven o'clock when he asked for his carriage to be called—slightly uneasy about his long stay, in view of the Court and the public. His departure evoked a fresh and terrifying demonstration on the part of Percival, the collie. Every alteration or interruption in a situation seemed to throw the noble animal off his moral balance. Quivering, yelping, and deaf to all blandishments, he stormed through the rooms and the hall and up and down the steps, drowning the words of leave-taking in his hubbub. The butler did the Prince the honours as far as the floor with the statues of gods. Mr. Spoelmann did not accompany him any distance. Miss Spoelmann made the position clear: "I am convinced that your sojourn in the bosom of our family has charmed you, Prince." And he was left wondering whether the joke lay in the expression "the bosom of our family" or in the actual fact. Anyhow, Klaus Heinrich was at a loss for a reply.

Leaning back in the corner of his brougham, rather sore and battered, and yet stimulated by the unusual treatment he had experienced, he drove home, through the dark Town Gardens to the Hermitage, returned to his sober Empire room, where he dined with von Schulenburg-Tressen and Braunbart-Schellendorf. Next day he read the comments of the *Courier*. They amounted only to a statement that yesterday his Royal Highness Prince Klaus Heinrich went to Schloss Delphinenort for tea, and inspected Mr. Spoelmann's renowned collection of fancy glass.

And Klaus Heinrich continued to live his unreal life, and to carry out his exalted calling. He uttered his gracious speeches, made his gestures, represented his people at the Court and at the President of the Council's great ball, gave free audiences, lunched in the officers' mess of the Grenadier Guards, showed himself at the Court Theatre, and bestowed on this and that district of the country the privilege of his presence. With a smile, and with heels together, he carried out all due formalities and did his irksome duty with complete self-possession, albeit he had at this time so much to think of—about the peppery Mr. Spoelmann, the muddle-headed Countess Löwenjoul, the harum-scarum Percy, and especially about Imma, the daughter of the house. Many a question to which his first visit to Delphinenort had given rise he was not yet in a position to answer, but only succeeded in solving as the result of further intercourse with the Spoelmanns, which he maintained to the eager and at last feverish interest of the public, and which advanced a step further when the Prince in the early morning one day, to the astonishment of his suite, his servants, and himself—indeed, partly involuntarily, and as if carried along by destiny—appeared alone and on horseback at Delphinenort, for the purpose of taking Miss Spoelmann, whom he disturbed in her mathematical studies at the top of the Schloss, for a ride.

The grip of winter had relaxed early in this ever-to-be-remembered year. After a mild January, the middle of February had seen the coming of a preliminary spring with birds and sunshine and balmy breezes, and as Klaus Heinrich lay on the first of these mornings at the Hermitage in his roomy old mahogany bed, from one of whose posts the spherical crown was missing, he felt himself, as it were, impelled by a strange hand and irresistibly inspired to deeds of boldness.

He rang the bell-pull for Neumann (they only had draw-bells at the Hermitage), and ordered Florian to be ready saddled in an hour's time. Should a horse be got ready for the groom too? No, it was not necessary. Klaus Heinrich said that he wanted to ride alone. Then he gave himself into Neumann's skilful hands for his morning toilette, breakfasted impatiently below in the garden room, and mounted his horse at the foot of the terrace. With his spurred top-boots in the stirrups, the yellow reins in his brown-gloved

221

right hand, and the left planted on his hip under his open cloak, he rode at a walking pace through the soft morning, scanning the still bare branches for the birds whose twittering he heard. He rode through the public part of his park, through the Town Gardens and the grounds of Delphinenort. He reached it at half-past nine. Great was the general surprise.

At the main gate he gave Florian over to an English groom. The butler, who was crossing the mosaic hall busy on his household duties, stood still, taken aback at the sight of Klaus Heinrich. To the inquiry which the Prince addressed to him, in a clear and almost haughty voice, about the ladies, he did not even reply, but turned helplessly towards the marble staircase, gazing dumbly at the top step, for there stood Mr. Spoelmann.

It seemed that he had just finished breakfast, and was in the best of tempers. His hands were plunged deep in his pockets, his lounge coat drawn back from his velvet waistcoat, and the blue smoke of his cigarette was making him blink.

"Well, young Prince?" he said, and stared down at him. . . .

Klaus Heinrich saluted and hurried up the red stair-carpet. He felt that the situation could only be saved by swiftness and, so to speak, by an attack by storm.

"You will be astounded, Mr. Spoelmann," he said, "at this early hour . . ." He was out of breath, and the fact disturbed him greatly, he was so little used to it.

Mr. Spoelmann answered him by a look and a shrug of the shoulders, as much as to say that he could control himself, but desired an explanation.

"The fact is, we have an appointment . . ." said Klaus Heinrich. He was standing two steps below the millionaire and was speaking up at him. "An appointment for a ride between Miss Imma and myself. . . . I have promised to show the ladies the 'Pheasantry' and the Court Kennels. . . .

Miss Imma told me that she knew nothing about the surrounding country. It was agreed that on the first fine
day . . . It's such a lovely day to-day. . . . It is of course
subject to your approval. . . ."

Mr. Spoelmann shrugged his shoulders, and made a face
as if to say: "Approval—why so?"

"My daughter is grown up," he said. "I don't interfere.
If she rides, she rides. But I don't think she has time. You
must find that out for yourself. She's in there." And Mr.
Spoelmann pointed his chin towards the tapestry door,
through which Klaus Heinrich had already once passed.

"Thanks," said Klaus Heinrich. "I'll go and see for myself." And he ran up the remaining steps, pushed the tapestry
hanging aside with a determined gesture, and went down the
steps into the sunlit, flower-scented winter garden.

In front of the splashing fountain and the basin with
fancy-feathered ducks sat Imma Spoelmann leaning over a
table, her back turned to the incomer. Her hair was down.
It hung black and glossy on each side of her head, covered
her shoulders, and allowed nothing to be seen but a shadow
of the childlike quarter profile of her face, which showed
white as ivory against the darkness of her hair. There she
sat absorbed in her studies, working at the figures in the notebook before her, her lips pressed on the back of her left
hand, and her right grasping the pen.

The Countess too was there, also busy writing. She sat
some way off under the palms, where Klaus Heinrich had
first conversed with her, and wrote sitting upright with her
head on one side, a pile of closely scribbled note-paper lying
at her side. The clank of Klaus Heinrich's spurs made her
look up. She looked at him with half-closed eyes for two
seconds, the long pen poised in her hand, then rose and
curtseyed. "Imma," she said, "his Royal Highness Prince
Klaus Heinrich is here."

Miss Spoelmann turned quickly round in her basket chair,
shook her hair back and gazed without speaking at the intruder
223

with big, startled eyes, until Klaus Heinrich had bid the
ladies good-morning with a military salute. Then she said in
her broken voice: "Good-morning to you too, Prince. But
you are too late for breakfast. We've finished long ago."

Klaus Heinrich laughed.

"Well, it's lucky," he said, "that both parties have had breakfast, for now we can start at once for a ride."

"A ride?"

"Yes, as we agreed."

"We agreed?"

"No, don't say that you've forgotten!" he said pleadingly.
"Didn't I promise to show you the country round? Weren't
we going for a ride together when it was fine? Well, to-day
it's glorious. Just look out . . ."

"It's not a bad day," she said, "but you go too fast,
Prince. I remember that there was some suggestion of a
ride at some future time—but surely not so soon as this?
Might I not at least have expected some sort of notification,
if your Highness will allow the word? You must allow that
I can't ride like this about here."

And she stood up to show her morning dress, which consisted of a loose gown of many-coloured silk and an open
green-velvet jacket.

"No," he said, "unfortunately you cannot. But I'll wait
here while you both change. It's quite early. . . ."

"Uncommonly early. But in the second place I am rather
busy with my innocent studies, as you saw. I've got a lecture at eleven o'clock."

"No," he cried, "to-day you must not grind at algebra,
Miss Imma; you must not play in the vacuum, as you put it!
Look at the sun! . . . May I? . . ." And he went to the
table and took up the notebook.

What he saw made his head swim. A fantastic hocus-
pocus, a witches' sabbath of abbreviated symbols, written in
a childish round hand which was the obvious result of Miss
Spoelmann's peculiar way of holding her pen, covered the

pages. There were Greek and Latin letters of various heights, crossed and cancelled, arranged above and below cross lines, covered by other lines, enclosed in round brackets, formulated in square brackets. Single letters, pushed forward like sentries, kept guard above the main bodies. Cabalistic signs, quite unintelligible to the lay mind, cast their arms round letters and ciphers, while fractions stood in front of them and ciphers and letters hovered round their tops and bottoms. Strange syllables, abbreviations of mysterious words, were scattered everywhere, and between the columns were written sentences and remarks in ordinary language, whose sense was equally beyond the normal intelligence, and conveyed no more to the reader than an incantation.

Klaus Heinrich looked at the slight form, which stood by him in the shimmering frock, becurtained by her dark hair, and in whose little head all this lived and meant something. He said, "Can you really waste a lovely morning over all this God-forsaken stuff?"

A glance of anger met him from her big eyes. Then she answered with a pout:

"Your Highness seems to wish to excuse yourself for the want of intelligence you recently displayed with regard to your own exalted calling."

"No," he said, "not so! I give you my word that I respect your studies most highly. I grant that they bother me, I could never understand anything of that sort. I also grant that to-day I feel some resentment against them, as they seem likely to prevent us from going for a ride."

"Oh, I'm not the only one to interfere with your wish for exercise, Prince. There's the Countess too. She was writing—chronicling the experiences of her life, not for the world, but for private circulation, and I guarantee that the result will be a work which will teach you as well as me a good deal."

"I am quite sure of it. But I am equally sure that the Countess is incapable of refusing a request from you."

225

"And my father? There's the next stumbling-block. You know his temper. Will he consent?"

"He has consented. If you ride, you ride. Those were his words. . . ."

"You have made sure of him beforehand, then? I'm really beginning to admire your circumspection. You have assumed the rôle of a Field Marshal, although you are not really a soldier, only a make-believe one, as you told us long ago. But there's yet one more obstacle, and that is decisive. It's going to rain."

"No, that's a very weak one. The sun is shining. . . ."

"It's going to rain. The air is much too soft. I made sure of it when we were in the Spa-Gardens before breakfast. Come and look at the barometer if you don't believe me. It's hanging in the hall. . . ."

They went out into the tapestry hall, where a big weather-glass hung near the marble fireplace. The Countess went with them. Klaus Heinrich said: "It's gone up."

"Your Highness is pleased to deceive yourself," answered Miss Spoelmann. "The refraction misleads you."

"That's beyond me."

"The refraction misleads you."

"I don't know what that is, Miss Spoelmann. It's the same as with the Adirondacks. I've not had much schooling, that's a necessary result of my kind of existence. You must make allowances for me."

"Oh, I humbly beg pardon. I ought to have remembered that one must use ordinary words when talking to your Highness. You are standing crooked to the hand and that makes it look to you as if it had risen. If you would bring yourself to stand straight in front of the glass, you would see that the black has not risen above the gold hand, but has actually dropped a little below it."

"I really believe you are right," said Klaus Heinrich sadly. "The atmospheric pressure there is higher than I thought!"

"It is lower than you thought."

226

"But how about the falling quicksilver?"

"The quicksilver falls at low pressure, not at high, Royal Highness."

"Now I'm absolutely lost."

"I think, Prince, that you're exaggerating your ignorance by way of a joke, so as to hide what its extent really is. But as the atmospheric pressure is so high that the quicksilver drops, thus showing an absolute disregard for the laws of nature, let's go for a ride, Countess—shall we? I cannot assume the responsibility of sending the Prince back home again now that he has once come. He can wait in there till we're ready. . . ."

When Imma Spoelmann and the Countess came back to the winter garden they were dressed for riding, Imma in a close-fitting black habit with breast-pockets and a three-cornered felt hat, the Countess in black cloth with a man's starched shirt and high hat. They went together down the steps, through the mosaic hall, and out into the open air, where between the colonnade and the big basin two grooms were waiting with the horses. But they had not yet mounted when with a loud barking, which was the expression of his wild excitement, Percival, the collie, prancing and leaping about, tore out of the Schloss and began a frenzied dance round the horses, who tossed their heads uneasily. . . .

"I thought so," said Imma, patting her favourite Fatma's head, "there was no hiding it from him. He found it all out at the last moment. Now he intends to come with us and make a fine to-do about it too. Shall we drop the whole thing, Prince?"

But although Klaus Heinrich understood that he might just as well have allowed the groom to ride in front with the silver trumpet, so far as calling public attention to their expedition was concerned, yet he said cheerfully that Percival must come too; he was a member of the family and must learn the neighbourhood like the rest.

"Well, where shall we go?" asked Imma as they rode at a

227

walk down the chestnut avenue. She rode between Klaus Heinrich and the Countess. Percival barked in the van. The English groom, in cockaded hat and yellow boot-tops, rode at a respectful distance behind.

"The Court Kennels are fine," answered Klaus Heinrich, "but it is a bit farther to the 'Pheasantry,' and we have time before lunch. I should like to show you the Schloss. I spent three years there as a boy. It was a seminary, you know, with tutors and other boys of my age. That's where I got to know my friend Ueberbein, Doctor Ueberbein, my favourite tutor."

"You have a friend?" asked Miss Spoelmann, with some surprise, and gazed at him. "You must tell me about him some time. And you were educated at the 'Pheasantry,' were you? Then we must see it, because you're obviously set on it. Trot!" she said as they turned into a loose riding-path. "There lies your hermitage, Prince. There's plenty for the ducks to eat in your pond. Let's give a wide berth to the Spa-Gardens, if that does not take us far out of our way."

Klaus Heinrich agreed, so they left the park and trotted across country to reach the high-road which led to their goal to the north-west. In the town gardens they were greeted with surprise by a few promenaders, whose greetings Klaus Heinrich acknowledged by raising his hand to his cap, Imma Spoelmann with a grave and rather embarrassed inclination of her dark head in the three-cornered hat. By now they had reached the open country, and were no longer likely to meet people. Now and then a peasant's cart rolled along the road, or a crouching bicyclist ploughed his way along it. But they turned aside from the road when they reached the meadow-land, which provided better going for their horses. Percival danced backwards in front of them, feverish and restless as ever, turning, springing, and wagging his tail—his breath came fast, his tongue hung far out of his foaming jaws, and he vented his nervous exaltation in a succession of short, sobbing yelps. Farther on he dashed off, following some scent with

228

pricked ears and short springs, while his wild barking echoed through the air.

They discussed Fatma, which Klaus Heinrich had not yet seen close, and which he admired immensely. Fatma had a long, muscular neck and small, nodding head with fiery eyes; she had the slender legs of the Arab type, and a bushy tail. She was white as the moonlight, and saddled, girt, and bridled with white leather. Florian, a rather sleepy brown, with a short back, hogged mane, and yellow stockings, looked as homely as a donkey by the side of the distinguished foreigner, although he was carefully groomed. Countess Löwenjoul rode a big cream called Isabeau. She had an excellent seat, with her tall, straight figure, but she held her small head in its huge hat on one side, and her lids were half closed and twitched. Klaus Heinrich addressed some remarks to her behind Miss Spoelmann's back, but she did not answer, and went riding on with half-shut eyes, gazing in front of her with a Madonna-like expression, and Imma said:

"Don't let's bother the Countess, Prince, her thoughts are wandering."

"I hope," he said, "that the Countess was not annoyed at having to come with us."

And he was distinctly taken aback when Imma Spoelmann answered casually: "To tell the truth, she very likely was."

"Because of your sums?" he asked.

"Oh, the sums? They're not so urgent, only a way of passing the time—although I hope to get a good lot of useful information out of them. But I don't mind telling you, Prince, that the Countess is not enthusiastic on the subject of yourself. She has expressed herself to that effect to me. She said you were hard and stern and affected her like a cold douche."

Klaus Heinrich reddened.

"I know well," he said quietly, looking down at his reins, "that I don't act as a cordial, Miss Spoelmann, or, at any rate, only at a distance. . . . That, too, is inseparable from my kind of existence, as I said. But I am not conscious

229

of having shown myself hard and stern to the Countess."

"Probably not in words," she replied, "but you did not allow her to let herself go, you did not do her the kindness of letting her tongue run a little, that's why she's vexed with you—and I know quite well what you did, how you embarrassed the poor thing and gave her a cold douche—quite well," she repeated, and turned her head away.

Klaus Heinrich did not answer. He kept his left hand planted on his hip, and his eyes were tired. Then he said:

"You know quite well? So I act like a cold douche on you too, Miss Spoelmann, do I?"

"I warn you," she answered at once in her broken voice, and wagging her head from side to side, "on no account to overrate the effect you have upon me, Prince." And she suddenly sat Fatma off at a gallop and flew at such a pace over the fields towards the dark mass of the distant pinewoods that neither the Countess nor Klaus Heinrich could keep up with her. Not till she reached the edge of the wood through which the high-road ran did she halt and turn her horse to look mockingly at her followers.

Countess Löwenjoul on her cream was the first to come up with the runaway. Then came Florian, foaming and much exhausted by his unusual exertion. They all laughed and their breath came fast as they entered the echoing wood. The Countess had awakened and chatted merrily, making lively, graceful gestures and showing her white teeth. She poked fun at Percival, whose temper had again been excited by the gallop, and who was careering wildly among the trunks in front of the horses.

"Royal Highness," she said, "you ought to see him jump and turn somersaults. He can take a ditch six yards broad, and does it so lightly and gracefully, you'd be delighted. But only of his own accord, mind you, of his free will, for I believe he'd rather let himself be whipped to death than submit to any training or teaching of tricks. He is, one might say, his own trainer by nature, and though sometimes unruly he is never rough. He is a gentleman, an aristocrat, and full of character. He's as proud as you like, and though he seems mad he's quite able to control himself. Nobody has ever heard him cry for pain when punished and hurt. He only eats, too, when he is hungry, and at other times won't look at the most tempting dainties. In the morning he has cream . . . he must be fed. He wears himself out, he's quite thin under his glossy coat, you can feel all his ribs. For I'm afraid he'll never grow to be old, but will fall an early victim to consumption. The street curs persecute him, they go for him in every street, but he jumps clear of them, and if they succeed in joining issue with him, he distributes a few bites with his splendid teeth which the rabble don't forget in a hurry. One must love such a compound of chivalry and virtue."

Imma agreed, in words which were the most serious and grave which Klaus Heinrich had ever heard from her mouth.

"Yes," she said, "you're a good friend to me, Percy, I shall always love you. A veterinary surgeon said you were half mad and advised us to have you put away, as you were impossible and a constant danger to us. But they shan't take my Percy from me. He is impossible, I know, and often an incumbrance, but he's always appealing and noble, and I love him dearly."

The Countess continued to talk about the collie's nature, but her remarks soon became disconnected and confused, and lapsed into a monologue accompanied by lively and elegant gestures. At last, after an acid look at Klaus Heinrich, her thoughts again began to wander.

Klaus Heinrich felt happy and cheered, whether as the result of the canter—for which he had had to brace himself up, for, though a decent figure on a horse, his left hand prevented him from being a strong rider—or for some other reason. After leaving the pine-wood they rode along the quiet high-road

231

between meadows and furrowed fields, with a peasant's hut or a country inn here and there. As they drew near the next wood, he asked in a low voice:

"Won't you fulfil your promise and tell me about the Countess? What is your companion's history?"

"She is my friend," she answered, "and in a sense my governess too, although she did not come to us till I was grown up. That was three years ago, in New York, and the Countess was then in a terrible state. She was on the brink of starvation," said Miss Spoelmann, and as she said it she fastened her big black eyes with a searching, startled look on Klaus Heinrich.

"Really starvation?" he asked, and returned her look. . . . "Do please go on."

"Yes, I said that too when she came to us, and although I, of course, saw quite well that her mind was slightly affected, she made such an impression upon me that I persuaded my father to let her be my companion."

"What took her to America? Is she a countess by birth?" asked Klaus Heinrich.

"Not a countess, but of noble birth, brought up in refined and luxurious surroundings, sheltered and protected, as she expressed it to me, from every wind, because from childhood she had been impressionable and sensitive. But then she married a Count Löwenjoul, a cavalry captain—a strange specimen of the aristocracy, according to her account—not quite up to the mark, to put it mildly."

"What was wrong with him?" asked Klaus Heinrich.

"I can't exactly tell you, Prince. You must take into consideration the rather obscure way in which the Countess puts what she has to say. But, to judge from what she has told me, he must have been just about as arrant a scamp as one could well imagine—a regular blackguard."

"I see," said Klaus Heinrich, "what's called a hard case, or a tough proposition."

"Exactly; we'll say man of the world—but in the most comprehensive and unlimited sense, for, to judge by the Countess's remarks, there were no limits in his case."

"No, that's what I too gathered," said Klaus Heinrich. "I've met several people of that sort—regular devils, so to speak. I heard of one such, who used to make love in his motor car, even when it was going at full speed."

"Did your friend Ueberbein tell you of him?"

"No, somebody else. Ueberbein would not think it proper to mention anything of that sort to me."

"Then he must be a useless sort of friend, Prince."

"You'll think better of him when I tell you more about him, Miss Spoelmann. But please go on!"

"Well, I don't know whether Löwenjoul behaved like your roué. Anyhow he behaved disgracefully."

"I expect he gambled and drank."

"I guess so. And besides that of course he made love, neglected the Countess and carried on with the loose women that are always to be found everywhere—at first behind her back, and later no longer behind her back but impudently and openly without any regard for her feelings."

"But tell me, why did she ever marry him?"

"She married him against her parents' will, because, as she has told me, she was in love with him. For in the first place, he was a handsome man when she first met him—he fell off in his looks later. In the second place, his reputation as a man of the world had gone before him, and that, according to her, constituted a sort of irresistible attraction for her, for, though she had been so well sheltered and protected, nothing would shake her in her resolve to share her life with him. If one thinks it over, one can quite understand it."

"Yes," he said, "I can quite understand it. She wanted to have her fling, as it were, to get her eyes opened. And she saw the world with a vengeance."

"You may put it like that if you like: though the expression seems to me rather too flippant to describe her experiences. Her husband ill-treated her."

233

"Do you mean that he beat her?"

"Yes, he ill-treated her physically. But now comes something, Prince, which you too will not have heard about before. She gave me to understand that he ill-treated her not only in a temper, not only in anger and rage, but also without being exasperated, simply for his own satisfaction. I mean, that his caresses were so revolting as to amount to ill-treatment."

Klaus Heinrich was silent. Both looked very grave. At last he asked: "Did the Countess have any children?"

"Yes, two. They died quite young, both only a few weeks old, and that's the greatest sorrow the Countess has had to bear. It would seem from her hints that it was the fault of the loose women for whom her husband betrayed her that the children died directly after birth."

Both remained silent, and their eyes clouded over.

"Add to that," continued Imma Spoelmann, "that he dissipated his wife's dowry, at cards and with women—a respectable dowry it was too—and after her parents' death her whole fortune also. Relations of hers too helped him once, when he was near having to leave the service on account of his debts. But then came a scandal, an altogether revolting one, in which he was involved and which did for him once and for all."

"What was it?" asked Klaus Heinrich.

"I can't exactly tell you, Prince. But, according to what the Countess has let slip about it, it was a scandal of the very grossest description—we agreed just now that there are generally no limits in that direction."

"And then he went to America?"

"You're right there, Prince. I can't help admiring your 'cuteness."

"Please go on, Miss Spoelmann. I've never heard anything like the Countess's story."

"No more had I; so you can imagine what an impression it made on me when she came to us. Well, then, Count Löwenjoul bolted to America with the police at his heels, leaving pretty considerable debts behind of course. And the Countess went with him."

"She went with him? Why?"

"Because she still loved him, in spite of everything—she loves him still—and because she was determined to share his life whatever happened. He took her with him, though, because he had a better chance of getting help from her relations as long as she was with him. The relations sent him one further instalment of money from home, and then stopped—they finally buttoned·up their pockets; and when Count Löwenjoul saw that his wife was·no more use to him, he just left her—left her in absolute destitution and cleared out."

"I knew it," said Klaus Heinrich, "I expected as much. Just what does happen."

But Imma Spoelmann went on: "So there she was, destitute and helpless, and, since she had never learned to earn her own living, she was left alone to face want and hunger. And you must remember that life in the States is much harder and meaner than here in your country; also that the Countess has always been a gentle, sensitive creature, and has been cruelly treated for years. In a word, she was no fit subject for the impressions of life to which she was unceasingly exposed. And then the blessing fell to her."

"What blessing? She told me about that too. What was the blessing, Miss Spoelmann?"

"The blessing consisted in a mental disturbance. At the crisis of her troubles something in her cracked—that's the expression she used to me—so that she no longer needed to face life and to bring a clear, sober mind to bear upon it, but was permitted, so to speak, to let herself go, to relax the tension of her nerves and to drivel when she liked. In a word, the blessing was that she went wrong in her head."

"Certainly I was under the impression," said Klaus Heinrich, "that the Countess was letting herself go when she drivelled."

"That's how it is, Prince. She is quite conscious of driv-

235

elling, and often laughs as she does so, or lets her hearers understand that she doesn't mean any harm by it. Her strangeness is a beneficent disorder, which she can control to a certain extent, and which she allows herself to indulge in. It is, if you prefer it, a want of——"

"Of self-restraint," said Klaus Heinrich, and looked down at his reins.

"Right, of self-restraint," she repeated, and looked at him. "You don't seem to approve of that want, Prince."

"I consider as a general rule," he answered quietly, "that it is not right to let oneself go and to make oneself at home, but that self-restraint should always be exercised, whatever the circumstances."

"Your Highness's doctrine," she answered, "is a praiseworthy austerity." Then she pouted, and, wagging her dark head in its three-cornered hat, she added in her broken voice: "I'll tell you something, Highness, and please note it well. If your Eminence is not inclined to show a little sympathy and indulgence and mildness, I shall have to decline the pleasure of your distinguished company once and for all."

He dropped his head, and they rode a while in silence.

"Won't you go on to tell me how the Countess came to you?" he asked at last.

"No, I won't," she said, and looked straight in front of her. But he pressed her so pleadingly that she finished her story and said: "And although fifty other companions applied, my choice—for the choice rested with me—fell at once on her, I was so much taken with her at my first interview. She was odd, I could see that: but she was odd only from too rich an experience of misery and wickedness, that was clear in every word she said; and as for me, I had always been a little lonely and cut off, and absolutely without experience, except what I got at my University lectures."

"Of course, you had always been a little lonely and cut off!" repeated Klaus Heinrich, with a ring of joy in his voice.

"That's what I said. It was a dull, simple life in some

236

ways that I led, and still lead, because it has not altered much, and is all much the same. There were parties with 'lions' and balls, and often a dash in a closed motor to the Opera House, where I sat in one of the little boxes above the stalls, so as to be well observed by everybody, for show, as we say. That was a necessary part of my position."

"For show?"

"Yes, for show; I mean the duty of showing oneself off, of not raising walls against the public, but letting them come into the garden and walk on the lawn and gaze at the terrace, watching us at tea. My father, Mr. Spoelmann, disliked it intensely. But it was a necessary consequence of our position."

"What did you usually do besides, Miss Spoelmann?"

"In the spring we went to our house in the Adirondacks and in the summer to our house at Newport-on-Sea. There were garden-parties of course, and battles of flowers and lawn-tennis tournaments, and we went for rides and drove four-in-hand or motored, and the people stood and gaped, because I was Samuel Spoelmann's daughter. And many shouted rude remarks after me."

"Rude remarks?"

"Yes, and they probably had reason to. At any rate it was something of a life in the limelight that we led, and one that invited discussion."

"And between whiles," he said, "you played in the breezes, didn't you, or rather in a vacuum, where no dust came——"

"That's right. Your Highness is pleased to mock my excess of candour. But in view of all this you can guess how extraordinarily welcome the Countess was to me, when she came to see me in Fifth Avenue. She does not express herself very clearly, but rather in a mysterious sort of way, and the boundary line at which she begins to drivel is not always quite clearly apparent. But that only strikes me as right and instructive, as it gives a good idea of the boundlessness of misery and wickedness in the world. You envy me the Countess, don't you?"

237

"Envy? H'm. You seem to assume, Miss Spoelmann, that I have never had my eyes opened."

"Have you?"

"Once or twice, maybe. For instance, things have come to my ears about our lackeys, which you would scarcely dream of."

"Are your lackeys so bad?"

"Bad? Good-for-nothing, that's what they are. For one thing they play into each other's hands, and scheme, and take bribes from the tradesmen——"

"But, Prince, that's comparatively harmless."

"Yes, true, it's nothing to compare with the way the Countess has had her eyes opened."

They broke into a trot, and, leaving at the sign-post the gently rising and falling high-road, which they had followed through the pine-woods, turned into the sandy short cut, between high blackberry-covered banks, which led into the tufted meadow-land round the "Pheasantry." Klaus Heinrich was at home in these parts: he stretched out his arm (the right one) to point out everything to his companions, though there was not much worth seeing. Yonder lay the Schloss, closed and silent, with its shingle-roof and its lightning-conductors on the edge of the wood. On one side was the pheasants' enclosure, which gave the place its name, and on the other Stavenüter's tea-garden, where he had sometimes sat with Raoul Ueberbein. The spring sun shone mildly over the damp meadow-land and shed a soft haze over the distant woods.

They reined in their horses in front of the tea-garden, and Imma Spoelman took stock of the prosaic country-house which rejoiced in the name of the "Pheasantry."

"Your childhood," she said with a pout, "does not seem to have been surrounded by much giddy splendour."

"No," he laughed, "there's nothing to see in the Schloss. It's the same inside as out. No comparison with Delphinenort, even before you restored it——"

"Let's put our horses up," she said. "One must put one's

horses up on an expedition, mustn't one, Countess? Dismount, Prince. I'm thirsty, and want to see what your friend Stavenüter has got to drink."

There stood Herr Stavenüter in green apron and stockings, bowing and pressing his knitted cap to his chest with both hands, while he laughed till his gums showed.

"Royal Highness!" he said, with joy in his voice, "does your Royal Highness mean to honour me once again? And the young lady!" he added, with a tinge of deference in his voice; for he knew Samuel Spoelmann's daughter quite well, and there had been in the whole Grand Duchy no more eager reader of the newspaper articles which coupled Prince Klaus Heinrich's and Imma's names together. He helped the Countess to dismount, while Klaus Heinrich, who was the first to the ground, devoted himself to Miss Spoelmann, and he called to a lad, who, with the Spoelmanns' groom, took charge of the horses. Then followed the reception and welcome to which Klaus Heinrich was accustomed. He addressed a few formal questions in a reserved tone of voice to Herr Stavenüter, graciously asked how he was and how his business prospered, and received the answers with nods and a show of real interest. Imma Spoelmann watched his artificial, cold demeanour with serious, searching eyes, while she swung her riding-whip backwards and forwards.

"May I be so bold as to remind you that I am thirsty?" she said at last sharply and decisively, whereupon they walked into the garden and discussed whether they need go in to the coffee-room. Klaus Heinrich urged that it was still so damp under the trees; but Imma insisted on sitting outside, and herself chose one of the long narrow tables with benches on each side, which Herr Stavenüter hastened to cover with a white cloth.

"Lemonade!" he said. "That's best for a thirst, and it's sound stuff! no trash, Royal Highness, and you, ladies, but natural juice sweetened—there's no better!"

Followed the driving-in of the glass balls in the necks of

the bottles; and, while his distinguished guests tasted the drink, Herr Stavenüter dawdled a little longer at the table, meaning to serve them up a little gossip. He had long been a widower, and his three children, who in days gone by had sung here under the trees the song about common humanity, the while blowing their noses with their fingers, had now left him. The son was a soldier in the capital, one of the daughters had married a neighbouring farmer, the other, with a soul for higher things, had gone into service in the capital.

So Herr Stavenüter was in solitary control in this remote spot, in the three-fold capacity of farmer of the Schloss lands, caretaker of the Schloss, and head keeper of the "Pheasantry," and was well content with his lot. Soon, if the weather permitted, the season for bicyclists and walkers would come round, when the garden was filled on Sundays. Then business hummed. Would not his Highness and the ladies like to take a peep at the "Pheasantry"?

Yes, they would, later; so Herr Stavenüter withdrew for the present, after placing a saucer of milk for Percival by the table.

The collie had been in some muddy water on the way, and looked horrible. His legs were thin with wet, and the white parts of his ragged coat covered with dirt. His gaping mouth was black to the throat from nuzzling for field-mice, and his dark red tongue hung dripping out of his mouth. He quickly lapped up his milk, and then lay with panting sides by his mistress's feet, flat on his side, his head thrown back in an attitude of repose.

Klaus Heinrich declared it to be inexcusable for Imma to expose herself after her ride to the invidious springtime air without any wrap. "Take my cloak," he said. "I really do not want it, I'm quite warm, and my coat is padded on the chest!" She would not hear of it; but he went on asking her so insistently that she consented, and let him lay his grey military coat with a major's shoulder-straps round her shoulders. Then, resting her dark head in its three-cornered hat in

240

the hollow of her hand, she watched him as, with arm out-
stretched towards the Schloss, he described to her the life
he had once led there.

There, where the tall window opened on to the ground, had
been the mess-room, then the school-room, and up above
Klaus Heinrich's room with the plaster torso on the stove.
He told her too about Professor Kürtchen and his tactful way
of instructing his pupils, about Captain Amelung's widow,
and the aristocratic "Pheasants," who called everything "hog-
wash," and especially about Raoul Ueberbein, his friend, of
whom Imma Spoelmann more than once asked him to tell her
some more.

He told her about the doctor's obscure origin, and about
the money his parents paid to be quit of him; about the child
in the marsh or bog, and the medal for saving life; about
Ueberbein's plucky and ambitious career, pursued in circumstances calling for resolution and action, which he used to
call favourable circumstances, and about his friendship with
Doctor Sammet, whom Imma knew. He described his by no
means attractive appearance and readily owned to the attraction which he had exercised on him from the very beginning.
He described his behaviour towards himself, Klaus Heinrich
—that fatherly and jolly, blustering camaraderie which had
distinguished him so sharply from everybody else—and gave
Imma to the best of his ability an insight into his tutor's views
of life. Finally he expressed his concern that the doctor
seemed not to enjoy any sort of popularity among his fellow-
citizens.

"I can quite believe that," said Imma.

He was surprised, and asked why.

"Because I'm convinced," she said, wagging her head, "that
your Ueberbein, for all his sparkling conversation, is an un-
happy sort of creature. He may swagger about the place;
but he lacks reserve, Prince, and that means that he will come
to a bad end."

Her words startled Klaus Heinrich, and made him thought-
241

ful. Then turning to the Countess, who awoke with a smile out of a brown study, he said something complimentary about her riding, for which she thanked him gracefully. He said that anybody could see that she had learnt to ride as a child, and she confessed that riding lessons had formed a considerable part of her education. She spoke clearly and cheerfully; but gradually, almost imperceptibly, she began to wander into a strange story about a gallant ride which she had made as a lieutenant in the last manœuvres, and suddenly started talking about the dreadful wife of a sergeant in the Grenadiers, who had come into her room the previous night and scratched her breasts all over, meanwhile using language which she could not bring herself to repeat. Klaus Heinrich asked quietly whether she had not shut her door and windows.

"Of course, but anyone could break the glass!" she answered hastily, and turned pale in one cheek and red in the other. Klaus Heinrich nodded acquiescence, and, dropping his eyes, asked her quietly to let him call her "Frau Meier" now and then, a proposal which she gladly accepted, with a confidential smile and a far-away look which had something strangely attractive about it.

They got up to visit the "Pheasantry," after Klaus Heinrich had taken back his cloak; and as they left the garden, Imma Spoelmann said: "Well done, Prince. You're getting on," a commendation which made him blush, indeed gave him far more pleasure than the most fulsome newspaper report of the valuable effect of his appearance at a ceremony which Councillor Schustermann could ever show him.

Herr Stavenüter escorted his guests into the palisaded enclosure in which six or seven families of pheasants led a comfortable, petted life. They watched the greedy, red-eyed, and stiff-tailed birds, inspected the hatching house, and looked on while Herr Stavenüter fed the pheasants under a big solitary fig-tree for their benefit. Klaus Heinrich thanked him warmly for all that he had shown them, Imma Spoelmann regarding him the while with her big, searching eyes. Then they mounted at the gate of the tea-garden and rode off home-wards with Percival barking and pirouetting under the horses' noses.

But their ride home was destined to give Klaus Heinrich, in the course of his conversation with Imma Spoelmann, yet another significant indication of her real nature and charac-ter, a direct revelation of certain sides of her personality which gave him food for much thought.

For soon after they had left the bramble-hedged by-way and joined the high-road, Klaus Heinrich reverted to a subject which had been just touched on at his first visit to Delphine-nort during the conversation at tea, and had not ceased to ex-ercise him ever since.

"May I," he said, "ask you one question, Miss Spoelmann? You need not answer it if you don't want to."

"I'll see about that," she answered.

"Four weeks ago," he began, "when I first had the pleasure of a talk with your father, Mr. Spoelmann, I asked him a question which he answered so curtly and abruptly that I could not help feeling that my question had been indiscreet or a false step."

"What was it?"

"I asked him whether he had not found it hard to leave America."

"There you are, Prince, there's another question which is worthy of you, a typical Prince-question. If you had had a little more training in the use of your reasoning powers you would have known without asking that if my father had not been ready and glad to leave America, he most assuredly would not have left it."

"Very probably you are right; forgive me, I don't think enough. But if my question was nothing worse than a want of thought, I shall be quite content. Can you assure me that that is the case?"

"No, Prince, I'm afraid I cannot," she said, and looked at him suddenly with her big black eyes.

243

"Then what has want of thought to do with it? Do please explain. I ask you in the name of our friendship."

"Are we friends?"

"I hoped so," he said pleadingly.

"Well, well, patience! I didn't know it, but I'm quite ready to learn it. But to return to my father, he really did lose his temper at your question—he has a quick temper, and has plenty of occasion to practise losing it. The fact is that public opinion and sentiment were not over-friendly to us in America. There's such a lot of scheming over there—I may mention that I am not posted in the details, but there was a strong political movement towards setting the crowd, the common people, you know, against us. The result was legislation and restrictions which made my father's life over there a burden to him. You know of course, Prince, that it was not he who made us what we are, but my redoubtable grandfather with his Paradise nugget and Blockhead Farm. My father could not help it, he was born to his destiny, and it was no gratification to him, because he is naturally shy and sensitive, and would much have preferred to have lived for playing the organ and collecting glass. I really believe that the hatred which was the result of the scheming against us, so that sometimes the people hurled abuse after me when I motored past them—that the hatred quite probably brought on his stone in the kidneys; it's more than possible."

"I am cordially attached to your father," said Klaus Heinrich with emphasis.

"I should have made that, Prince, a condition of our becoming friends. But there was another point which made things worse, and made our position over there still more difficult, and that was our origin."

"Your origin?"

"Yes, Prince; we are no aristocratic pheasants, unfortunately we are not descended from Washington or from the Pilgrim Fathers."

"No, for you are German."

"Oh yes, but there's something besides to get over. Please look at me closely. Does it strike you that there is anything to be proud of in having blue-black wispy hair like mine, that's always falling where it's not wanted?"

"Goodness knows, Miss Spoelmann, you've got glorious hair!" said Klaus Heinrich. "I know that you are partly of Southern extraction, for I've read somewhere that your grandfather married in Bolivia or thereabouts."

"He did. But that's where the trouble lies, Prince. I'm a quintroon."

"A what?"

"A quintroon."

"That goes with the Adirondacks and the refraction, Miss Spoelmann. I don't know what it is. I've already told you that I don't know much."

"Well, it's a fact. My grandfather, thoughtless as he always was, married a woman of Indian blood down South."

"Indian blood!"

"Yes. She was of Indian stock at the third remove, daughter of a white and a half-Indian, and so a terceroon as it is called. She must have been wonderfully beautiful. And she was my grandmother. The grandchildren of a terceroon are called quintroons. That's how things are."

"Most interesting. But didn't you say that it had affected people's attitude towards you?"

"You don't understand, Prince. I must tell you that Indian blood over there means a heavy blot—such a blot, that friendships and affections are transformed into hatred and abuse if proof of half-blood descent comes to light. Of course things are not so serious with us, for with quadroons—why, of course, the taint is nothing like so great, and a quintroon is to all intents and purposes untainted. But in our case, exposed to gossip as we were, it was naturally different, and several times when the people shouted abuse after us I heard them say that I was a coloured girl. In short, my descent was made an excuse for insults and annoyances, and raised a barrier between us and the few who were in the same position of life as ourselves—there was always something which we had to hide or to brazen out. My grandfather had brazened it out, he was that sort of man, and knew what he was doing; besides, his blood was pure, it was only his beautiful wife who had the taint. But my father was her son, and, sensitive and quick-tempered as he is, he has always, ever since he was a boy, resented being stared at, and hated and despised at the same time; half a world's wonder and half a monument of iniquity, as he used to say. He was fed up with America. That's the whole history, Prince," said Imma Spoelmann, "and now you know why my father lost his temper over your pointed question."

Klaus Heinrich thanked her for the explanation; indeed, as he saluted and took leave (it was lunch time) of the ladies in front of the Delphinenort Gate, he repeated his thanks for what he had been told, and then rode at foot's pace home, pondering over the events of the morning.

He saw Imma Spoelmann sitting in a languid pose in her red-gold dress at the table, with a look as of a spoilt child on her face; sitting in comfortable assurance, and uttering remarks with a sting in them, such as were good coin in the United States, where clearness, hardness, and a ready wit were essentials of life. And why? Klaus Heinrich could understand now, and never a day passed that he did not try to realize it better. Stared at, hated and despised at the same time, half a world's wonder and half a monument of iniquity, that's what her life had been, and that had instilled the poison into her remarks, that acidity and mocking directness, which looked like offence but really were defence, and which evoked a look of bewilderment on the faces of those who had never had any occasion for the weapons of wit.

She had demanded of him sympathy and tenderness towards the poor Countess, when she let herself go; but she herself had a claim to sympathy and tenderness, for she was lonely and her life, like his, was a hard one. At the same time a

246

memory haunted him, a long-ago, painful memory, whose scene was the refreshment room of the "Citizen Garden," and which ended in a tureen lid——"Little sister!" he said to himself, as he quickly dismissed the scene from his thoughts. "Little sister!" But most of all his thoughts were busy with planning how soonest to enjoy Miss Spoelmann's society again.

He enjoyed it soon and often, in all sorts of circumstances. February gave place to threatening March, fickle April and soft May. And all these months Klaus Heinrich visited Schloss Delphinenort at least once a week, in the morning or in the afternoon, and always in the irresponsible mood in which he had presented himself at the Spoelmanns' that February morning, as if led by fate without any action of his own will. The proximity of the Schlosses made the visits easy, the short distance through the park from the "Hermitage" to Delphinenort was easily crossed on horseback or in a dog-cart, without exciting much attention; and when the advancing season brought more people to the neighbourhood and made it harder and harder for them to go for rides without attracting public attention, the Prince had by this time reached a state of mind which can only be described as complete indifference and blind recklessness towards the world, the Court, the capital, and the countryside. It was not till later that the public interest began to play a really important—and encouraging—part in his thoughts and actions.

He had not taken leave of the ladies after the first ride without suggesting another expedition, a suggestion to which Imma Spoelmann, pouting and wagging her head from side to side, had failed to bring any serious objection. So he came again; and they rode to the Royal Kennels, on the north side of the Town Gardens; on the third occasion they chose a third place to ride to, which also they could reach without going near the town. Then, when spring enticed the townspeople into the open air and the tea-gardens filled up, they preferred an out-of-the-way path, which really was no
247

path, but a richly wooded dyke, which stretched far away to the north along a swift-running stream.

The quietest way of reaching it was by riding out at the back of the "Hermitage" park, and past the river meadows on the edge of the northern Town Garden up to the Royal Kennels; then not crossing the river by the wooden bridge at the weir, but keeping along this side. The Kennels Farm was left behind on the right, and the ride went on through the fir-plantations. On the left lay spreading meadows, white and gaily coloured with hemlock and anemones, buttercups and bluebells, clover, daisies, and forget-me-nots; a village church tower rose in front of them beyond the plough-lands, and the busy high-road lay far away at a safe distance from the riders. Farther on, the meadows with their nut-hedges came close up to the plantations on the left, shutting out the view, and enabling them to ride in complete seclusion, generally side by side with the Countess behind, as the path was narrow. They talked or rode in silence, while Percival jumped over the stream and back again, or plunged into it for a bath or a hurried drink. They came back the same way as they went.

When, however, the quicksilver fell owing to the lowness of the atmospheric pressure, when rain followed, and Klaus Heinrich nevertheless felt another peep at Imma Spoelmann to be a necessity, he presented himself in his dogcart at Delphinenort at tea time, and they stayed indoors. Mr. Spoelmann joined them at tea not more than two or three times. His malady got worse about this time, and on several days he was obliged to stay in bed with hot poultices. When he did come, he used to say: "Hullo, young Prince," with his thin, white-cuffed hand dip a rusk in his tea, throw in a cross word here and there into the conversation, and end by offering his guest his gold cigarette-case, whereupon he left the garden room with Dr. Watercloose, who had sat silent and smiling at the table. In fine weather too they sometimes preferred not to go outside the park, but to play lawn tennis on the trim lawn below the terrace. On one occasion they went for a rapid drive in Mr. Spoelmann's motor far out beyond the "Pheasantry."

One day Klaus Heinrich asked: "Is what I have read true, Miss Spoelmann, that your father gets such a tremendous lot of letters and appeals every day?"

Then she described to him subscription lists which kept pouring in to Delphinenort, and which were dealt with as thoroughly as was practicable; of the piles of begging letters by every post from Europe and America which Messrs. Phlebs and Slippers ran through and weeded out for submission to Mr. Spoelmann. Sometimes, she said, she amused herself by glancing through the heaps, and reading the addresses; for these were often quite fantastic. For the needy or speculative senders tried to outdo each other in the deference and servility of their address on the envelopes, and every conceivable title and distinction could be found mixed up in the strangest way on the letters. But one begging-letter writer had quite recently carried off the prize by addressing his envelope to: "His Royal Highness Mr. Samuel Spoelmann." But it did not get him any more than the others.

On other occasions the Prince fell to talking mysteriously about the "Owl Chamber" in the Old Schloss, and confided to her that recently noises had again been heard in it, pointing to events of moment in his, Klaus Heinrich's, family. Then Imma Spoelmann laughed, and, pouting and wagging her head from side to side, gave him a scientific explanation of the noises, just as she had done in connexion with the secrets of the barometer. Nonsense, she said; it must be that that part of the lumber-room was ellipsoidal, and a second ellipsoidal surface with the same curvature and with a sound-source at the focus existed somewhere outside, the result being that inside the haunted room noises were audible which could not be distinguished in the immediate neighbourhood. Klaus Heinrich was rather crestfallen over this explanation, and loath to give up the common belief in the connexion between the lumber-room and the fortunes of his house.

Thus they conversed, and the Countess too took part, now sensible, now confused; Klaus Heinrich took considerable pains not to rebuff or chill her by his manner, and addressed her as "Frau Meier" whenever she appeared to think it necessary for her protection against the plots of the wicked women. He recounted to the ladies his unreal life, the gala suppers at the students' clubs, the military banquets, and his educational tour; he told them about his relations, about his once-beautiful mother, whom he visited now and then in the "Segenhaus," where she kept dismal court, and about Albrecht and Ditlinde. Imma Spoelmann in her turn related some incidents in her luxurious and singular youth, and the Countess often slipped in a few dark sayings about the horrors and secrets of life, to which the others listened with serious and thoughtful faces.

They took special delight in one kind of game—guessing existences, making estimates to the best of their knowledge of the people they happened to see in the citizen world—a strange and curious study of the passers-by from a distant standpoint, from the terrace or from horseback. What kind of young people might these be? What did they do? Where did they come from? They were certainly not apprentices, perhaps technical students or budding foresters, to judge by certain signs; maybe they belonged to the agricultural college; at any rate stout fellows enough, though rather rough, with sound careers before them. But that little untidy thing who strolled past looked like a factory hand or dressmaker's assistant. Girls like her always had a young man in their own class, who took them out to tea in the parks on Sundays. And they exchanged what they knew about people in general, discussed them like connoisseurs, and felt that this pastime brought them closer together than any amount of riding or lawn tennis.

As for the motor drive, Imma Spoelmann in the course of

it explained that she had only invited Klaus Heinrich to it
so as to let him see the chauffeur, a young American in
brown leather, who, she declared, resembled the Prince.
Klaus Heinrich objected with a smile that the back of the
driver's neck did not enable him to express an opinion on
the matter, and asked the Countess to say what she thought.
She, after long denying the likeness in polite embarrassment,
at last, on Imma's insistence, with a side glance at Klaus
Heinrich, agreed to it.

Then Miss Spoelmann said that the grave, sober, and skilful youth had originally been in her father's personal service,
driving him daily from Fifth Avenue to Broadway and back.
Mr. Spoelmann, however, had insisted on extraordinary speed,
like that of an express train, and the intense strain put upon
a driver by such speed in the crowded streets of New York
had proved at last too much for the youth. As a matter of
fact no accident had happened; the young man had stuck to it
and done his deadly duty with amazing care. But in the end
it had often happened that he had to be lifted down in a faint
from his seat at the end of a run—a proof of the inordinate
strain to which he had been daily subjected. To avoid having
to dismiss him, Mr. Spoelmann had made him his daughter's
special chauffeur, and he had continued to act in that capacity
in their new abode.

Imma had noticed the likeness between Klaus Heinrich
and him the first time she saw the Prince. It was of course
a similarity not of features, but of expression. The Countess
had agreed with her. Klaus Heinrich said that he did not
in the least object to the likeness, as the heroic young man
had all his sympathy. They then discussed further the difficult and anxious life of a chauffeur, without Countess Löwenjoul taking any further part in the conversation. She did not
prattle during this drive, though later she made a few sensible
and pointed remarks.

For the rest, Mr. Spoelmann's craze for speed seemed to
have descended in some measure to his daughter, for she never
251

lost an opportunity of repeating the wild gallop she had started on their first ride; and as Klaus Heinrich, stimulated by her gibes, urged the amazed and disapproving Florian to the top of his speed, so as not to be left behind, the gallop always degenerated into a race, which Imma Spoelmann always started at unexpected and arbitrary moments. Several of these struggles took place on the lonely river-edged causeway, and one in particular was long and bitter. It happened after a short talk about Klaus Heinrich's popularity, which was begun brusquely, and broken off as brusquely, by Imma Spoelmann. She asked suddenly: "Is it true what I hear, Prince, that you are so tremendously popular with the people? That you have won all their hearts?"

He answered: "So they say. It must be some characteristics, not necessarily good ones. What's more, I'm not sure whether I believe it, or even ought to be glad of it. I doubt whether it speaks for me. My brother, the Grand Duke, declares in so many words that popularity is hogwash."

"H'm, the Grand Duke must be a fine man: I've got a great respect for him. So we see you in an atmosphere of adulation, and everybody loves you . . . go on!" she cried suddenly, and gave Fatma a cut with her white switch. The mare started, and the race began.

It lasted a long time. Never before had they followed the stream so far. The view on the left had long become shut in. Lumps of earth and grass flew from under the horses' hoofs. The Countess had soon dropped behind. When at last they reined in their horses, Florian was trembling with exhaustion, and the riders themselves were pale and panting. They rode back in silence.

Klaus Heinrich received a visit at the "Hermitage" from Raoul Ueberbein the afternoon before his birthday this year. The Doctor came to wish him many happy returns, as he expected to be prevented by his work from doing so on the morrow. They strolled round the gravel path at the back

of the park, the tutor in his frock-coat and white tie, Klaus
Heinrich in his summer coat. The grass stood ready for
cutting under the perpendicular rays of the midday sun, and
the limes were in flower. In one corner, close by the hedge
which divided the park from the unlovely suburbs, stood a
little rustic temple.

Klaus Heinrich was telling of his visits to "Delphinenort,"
as this topic lay nearest his heart. He spoke quite clearly
about them, but did not tell the doctor any actual news,
for the latter showed that he knew all about them. How
was that? Oh, from various sources. Ueberbein had never
started the subject. So people in the town concern themselves
about it?

"Heaven forbid, Klaus Heinrich, that anybody should give
a thought to it, either to the rides, or to the teas, or to the
motor drive. You don't suppose that that sort of thing
is expected to set tongues wagging!"

"But we're so careful!"

" 'We' is rich, Klaus Heinrich, and so is the carefulness.
All the same, his Excellency von Knobelsdorff keeps himself accurately posted in all your goings-on."

"Knobelsdorff?"

"Knobelsdorff."

Klaus Heinrich was silent; then asked: "And what is
Baron Knobelsdorff's attitude towards what he learns?"

"Well, the old gentleman hasn't yet had a chance of inter-
fering in the developments."

"But the public opinion?—the people?"

"The people of course hold their breath."

"And you, you yourself, my dear Doctor Ueberbein?"

"I'm waiting for the tureen-lid," answered the doctor.

"No!" cried Klaus Heinrich joyfully. "No, there'll be no
tureen-lid this time, Doctor Ueberbein, for I am happy, oh
so happy, whatever happens—can you understand? You
taught me that happiness was no concern of mine, and you
pulled me up short when I tried to come by it; and right

253

thankful I was to you for doing so, for it was horrible, and I shall never forget it. But this is no case of high jinks at a citizens' dance, which leave one humiliated and heavy at heart; this is no breaking out and running off the rails and humiliation! For can't you see that she of whom we are speaking belongs neither to the citizens' dance, nor to the aristocratic 'Pheasants,' nor to anything in the world but to me—that she is a Princess, Doctor Ueberbein, and as good as me, and there can be no question here of a tureen-lid? You have taught me that it is silly to maintain that we're all only ordinary men, and hopeless for me to act as if we were, and that the happiness I would gain by doing so is forbidden to me and must bring me to shame in the end. But this is not that silly and forbidden happiness. It is my first taste of the happiness which is allowed me, and which I may hope for, Doctor Ueberbein, and yield myself to without misgiving, whatever comes of it. . . ."

"Good-bye, Prince Klaus Heinrich," said Doctor Ueberbein, though he did not at once leave him, but continued walking at his side with his hands clasped behind him and his red beard sunk on his breast.

"No," said Klaus Heinrich. "No, not good-bye, Doctor Ueberbein. That's just it. I mean to remain your friend, you who have had such a hard time, and have shown such pride in your duty and destiny, and have made me proud too in treating me as a companion. I have no intention of resting on my oars, now that I have found happiness, but will remain true to you and to myself and to my exalted calling. . . ."

"It cannot be," said Doctor Ueberbein in Latin, and shook his ugly head with its protruding, pointed ears.

"It can be, Doctor. I'm sure it can, they're not incompatible. And you, you ought not to show yourself so cold and distant at my side, when I am so happy, and, what's more, it's the eve of my birthday. Tell me—you've had so many experiences and seen so much of the world in all its aspects—have you never had any experiences in this direction? You know what I mean—have you never had an attack like this of mine?"

"H'm," said Doctor Ueberbein, and pressed his lips together, till his red beard rose, and the muscles knotted in his cheeks. "No doubt I may have had one once, *sub rosa.*"

"I thought so! Tell me about it, Doctor Ueberbein. You must tell me about it!"

The hour was one of quiet sunshine, and the air full of the scent of limes. So Doctor Ueberbein related an incident in his career on which he had never touched in previous accounts, though it had perhaps a decisive influence on his whole life. It had occurred in those early days when the Doctor was teacher of the young idea and at the same time working on his own account, when he used to draw in his waist-belt and give private lessons to sleek tradesmen's children, so as to get money to buy books with. With his hands still behind him and his beard sunk on his breast, the doctor related the incident in a sharp and incisive tone of voice, pressing his lips close together between each sentence.

At that date fate had forged the closest ties between him and a woman, a lovely, fair lady who was the wife of an honourable and respected man and the mother of three children. He had entered the family as tutor to the children, but had subsequently been a constant guest and visitor, and with the husband too had reached a footing of mutual confidences. The feelings of the young tutor and the fair wife for each other had been long unsuspected, and longer still unexpressed in words; but they grew stronger in the silence, and more overpowering, till one evening hour when the husband had stayed late at his office, a warm, sweet, dangerous hour, they burst into flames and were near to overwhelm them.

In that hour their longing had cried aloud for the happiness, the tremendous happiness, of their union; but, said Doctor Ueberbein, the world could sometimes show a noble action. They felt ashamed, he said, to tread the mean and ridiculous path of treachery, and to "clap horns," as the phrase goes, on the honest husband; while to spoil his life by demanding release from him as the right of passion was equally not to their taste. In short, for the children's sake and for that of the good, honest husband, whom they both respected, they denied themselves. Yes, that's what happened, but of course it needed a good deal of stern resolution. Ueberbein continued to visit the fair lady's house occasionally. He would sup there, when he had time, play a game of cards with his two friends, kiss his hostess's hand, and say good night.

But when he had told the Prince this much, he concluded in a still shorter and sharper tone than he had begun, and the balls of muscle at the corners of his mouth showed more prominently than before. For the hour which saw their act of renunciation, in that hour Ueberbein had said a final farewell to all happiness—"dalliance with happiness," as he had since called it. As he failed, or refused, to win the fair lady, he swore to himself that he would honour her, and the bonds which bound him to her, by achieving something and making himself felt in the field of hard work. To this he had dedicated his life, to this alone, and it had brought him to what he was. That was the secret, or at least a contribution of the riddle of Ueberbein's unsociability, unapproachableness, and earnest endeavour. Klaus Heinrich was quite frightened to see how unusually green his face was when he took his leave with a deep bow, saying: "My greetings to little Imma, Klaus Heinrich."

Next day the Prince received the congratulations of the staff at the Schloss, and later those of Herr von Braunbart-Schellendorf and von Schulenburg-Tressen in the Yellow Room. In the course of the morning the members of the Grand Ducal House came to the "Hermitage" to pay their respects, and at one o'clock Klaus Heinrich drove to luncheon with Prince and Princess zu Ried-Hohenried, meeting with an unusually warm reception from the public on the way. The

Grimmburgers were mustered in full force in the pretty palace in the Albrechtstrasse. The Grand Duke too came, in a frock-coat, nodded his small head to each member of the party, sucking his lower lip against his upper the while, and drank milk-and-soda during lunch. Almost immediately after lunch was finished he withdrew. Prince Lambert had come without his wife. The old habitué of the ballet was painted, hollow-cheeked, and slovenly, and his voice sounded sepulchral. He was to some extent ignored by his relations.

During luncheon the conversation turned for a while on Court matters, then on little Princess Philippine's progress, and later almost exclusively on Prince Philipp's commercial schemes. The quiet little man talked about his breweries, factories, and mills, and in particular about his peat-cuttings. He described various improvements in the machinery, quoted figures of capital invested and returns, and his cheeks glowed, while his wife's relations listened to him with looks of curiosity, approval, or mockery.

When coffee had been served in the big flower-room, the Princess, holding her gilded cup, went up to her brother and said: "You have quite deserted us lately, Klaus Heinrich."

Ditlinde's face with the Grimmburg cheek-bones was not so transparent as it had once been. It had gained more colour since the birth of her daughter, and her head seemed to be less oppressed by the weight of her fair hair.

"Have I deserted you?" he said. "Forgive me, Ditlinde, perhaps I have. But there were so many calls on my time, and I knew that there were on yours too; for you are no longer confined to flowers."

"True, the flowers have had to take a less prominent place, they don't get much thought from me now. A fairer life and flowering now occupies all my time. I believe that's where I have got my red cheeks from, like dear Philipp from his peat (he ought not to have talked about it the whole of luncheon, as he did; but it's his hobby), and it is because
257

I was so busy and rushed that I was not cross with you for never showing yourself and for going your own way, even though that way seemed to me rather a surprising one."

"Do you know what it is, Ditlinde?"

"Yes, though unfortunately not from you. But Jettchen Isenschnibble has kept me well posted—you know she is always a fund of news—and at first I was horribly shocked, I don't deny it. But after all they live in Delphinenort, he has a private physician, and Philipp thinks they are in their way of equal birth with ourselves. I believe I once spoke disparagingly about them, Klaus Heinrich; I said something about a Crœsus, if I remember rightly, and made a pun on the word 'taxpayer.' But if you consider them worthy of your friendship, I've been wrong and of course withdraw my remarks, and will try to think differently about them in future. I promise you. You always loved rummaging," she went on, after he had laughed and kissed her hand, "and I had to do it with you, and my dress (do you remember it— the red velvet?) suffered for it. Now you have to rummage alone, and God grant, Klaus Heinrich, that it won't bring you any horrible experience."

"I really believe, Ditlinde, that every experience is fine, whether it be good or bad. But my present experience is splendid."

At half-past five the Prince left the "Hermitage" again, in his dogcart, which he drove himself, with a groom at his back. It was warm, and Klaus Heinrich was wearing white trousers with a double-breasted coat. Bowing, he again drove to the town, or more precisely to the Old Schloss. He did not enter the Albrechtstor, however, but drove in through a side door, and across two courtyards till he reached that in which the rose-bush grew.

Here all was still and stony; the stair-turrets with their oblique windows, forged-iron balustrades, and fine carvings towered in the corners; the many-styled building stood there in light and shadow, partly grey and weather-worn, partly more modern-looking, with gables and box-like projections, with open porticoes and peeps through broad bow-windows into vaulted halls and narrow galleries. But in the middle, in its unfenced bed, stood the rose-bush, blooming gloriously after a favourable season.

Klaus Heinrich threw the reins to a servant, and went up and looked at the dark-red roses. They were exceptionally fine—full and velvety, grandly formed, and a real masterwork of nature. Several were already full-blown.

"Call Ezekiel, please," said Klaus Heinrich to a moustachioed door-keeper, who came forward with his hand to his hat.

Ezekiel, the custodian of the rose-bush, came. He was a greybeard of seventy years of age, in a gardener's apron, with watery eyes and a bent back.

"Have you any shears by you, Ezekiel?" said Klaus Heinrich, "I should like a rose." And Ezekiel drew some shears out of the pocket of his apron.

"That one there," said Klaus Heinrich, "that's the finest." And the old man cut the thorny branch with trembling hands.

"I'll water it, Royal Highness," he said, and shuffled off to the water-tap in a corner of the court. When he came back, glittering drops were clinging to the petals of the rose, as if to the feathers of waterfowl.

"Thanks, Ezekiel," said Klaus Heinrich, and took the rose "Still going strong? Here!" He gave the old man a gold piece, and climbing into the dogcart drove with the rose on the seat beside him through the courtyards. Everybody who saw him thought that he was driving back to the "Hermitage" from the Old Schloss, where presumably he had an interview with the Grand Duke.

But he drove through the Town Gardens to Delphinenort. The sky had clouded over, big drops were already falling on the leaves, and thunder rolled in the distance.

The ladies were at tea when Klaus Heinrich, conducted by the corpulent butler, appeared in the gallery and walked

259

down the steps into the garden room. Mr. Spoelmann, as usual recently, was not present. He was in bed with poultices on. Percival, who lay curled up like a snail close by Imma's chair, beat the carpet with his tail by way of greeting. The gilding of the furniture looked dull, as the park beyond the glass door lay in a damp mist.

Klaus Heinrich exchanged a handshake with the daughter of the house, and kissed the Countess's hand, while he gently raised her from the courtly curtsey she had begun, as usual, to make.

"You see, summer has come," he said to Imma Spoelmann, offering her the rose. It was the first time he had brought her flowers.

"How courtly of you!" she said. "Thanks, Prince. And what a beauty!" she went on in honest admiration (a thing she hardly ever showed), and held out her small, ringless hands for the glorious flower, whose dewy petals curled exquisitely at the edges. "Are there such fine roses here? Where did you get it?" And she bent her dark head eagerly over it.

Her eyes were full of horror when she looked up again.

"It doesn't smell!" she said, and a look of disgust showed round her mouth. "Wait, though—it smells of decay!" she said. "What's this you have brought me, Prince?" And her big black eyes in her pale face seemed to glow with questioning horror.

"Yes," he said, "I'm sorry; that's a way our roses have. It's from the bush in one of the courts of the Old Schloss. Have you never heard of it? There's something hangs by that. People say that one day it will begin to smell exquisite."

She seemed not to be listening to him. "It seems as if it had no soul," she said, and looked at the rose. "But it's perfectly beautiful, that one must allow. Well, that's a doubtful joke on nature's part, Prince. All the same, Prince,

260

thanks for your attention. And as it comes from your ancestral Schloss, one must regard it with due reverence."

She put the rose in a glass by her plate. A swan's-down flunkey brought the Prince a cup and plate. They discussed at tea the bewitched rose-bush, and then commonplace subjects, such as the Court Theatre, their horses, and all sorts of trivial topics. Imma Spoelmann time after time contradicted him, interposing polished quotations—to her own enjoyment, and his despair at the range of her reading—quotations which she uttered in her broken voice, with whimsical motions of her head. After a time a heavy, white-paper parcel was brought in, sent by the book-binders to Miss Spoelmann, containing a number of works which she had had bound in smart and durable bindings. She opened the parcel, and they all three examined the books to see if the binder had done his work well.

They were nearly all learned works whose contents were either as mysterious-looking as Imma Spoelmann's notebook, or dealt with scientific psychology, acute analyses of internal impulses. They were got up in the most sumptuous way, with parchment and crushed leather, gold letters, fine paper, and silk markers. Imma Spoelmann did not display much enthusiasm over the consignment, but Klaus Heinrich, who had never seen such handsome volumes, was full of admiration.

"Shall you put them all into the bookcase?" he asked. "With the others upstairs? I suppose you have quantities of books? Are they all as fine as these? Do let me see how you arrange them. I can't go yet, the weather's still bad and would ruin my white trousers. Besides, I've no idea how you live in Delphinenort, I've never seen your study. Will you show me your books?"

"That depends on the Countess," she said, busying herself with piling the volumes one on the other. "Countess, the Prince wants to see my books. Would you be so kind as to say what you think?"

Countess Löwenjoul was in a brown study. With her small head bent, she was watching Klaus Heinrich with a sharp, almost hostile look, and then let her eyes wander to Imma Spoelmann, when her expression altered and became gentle, sympathetic, and anxious. She came to herself with a smile, and drew a little watch out of her brown, close-fitting dress.

"At seven o'clock," she said brightly, "Mr. Spoelmann expects you to read to him, Imma. You have half an hour in which to do what his Royal Highness wants."

"Good; come along, Prince, and inspect my study," said Imma. "And so far as your Highness permits it, please lend a hand in carrying up these books; I'll take half."

But Klaus Heinrich took them all. He clasped them in both arms, though the left was not much use to him, and the pile reached to his chin. Then, bending backwards and going carefully, so as to drop nothing, he followed Imma over into the wing towards the drive, on the main floor of which lay Countess Löwenjoul's and Miss Spoelmann's quarters.

In the big, comfortable room which they entered through a heavy door he laid his burden down on the top of a hexagonal ebony table, which stood in front of a big gold-chintzed sofa. Imma Spoelmann's study was not furnished in the style proper to the Schloss, but in more modern taste, without any show, but with massive, masculine, serviceable luxury. It was panelled with rare woods right up to the top, and adorned with old porcelain, which glittered on the brackets all round under the ceiling. The carpets were Persian, the mantelpiece black marble, on which stood shapely vases and a gilt clock. The chairs were broad and velvet-covered, and the curtains of the same golden stuff as the sofa-cover. A capacious desk stood in front of the bow-window, which allowed a view of the big basin in front of the Schloss. One wall was covered with books, but the main library was in the adjacent room, which was smaller, and carpeted like the big one. A glass door opened into it, and

262

its walls were completely covered with bookshelves right up to the ceiling.

"Well, Prince, there's my hermitage," said Imma Spoelmann. "I hope you like it."

"Why, it's glorious," he said. But he did not look round him, but gazed unintermittently at her, as she reclined against the sofa cushions by the hexagonal table. She was wearing one of her beautiful indoor dresses, a summer one this time, made of white accordion-pleated stuff, with open sleeves and gold embroidery on the yoke. The skin of her arms and neck seemed brown as meerschaum against the white of the dress; her big, bright, earnest eyes in the strangely childlike face seemed to speak a language of their own unceasingly, and a smooth wisp of black hair hung across her forehead. She had Klaus Heinrich's rose in her hand.

"How lovely!" he said, standing before her, and not conscious of what he meant. His blue eyes, above the national cheek-bones, were heavy as with grief. "You have as many books," he added, "as my sister Ditlinde has flowers."

"Has the Princess so many flowers?"

"Yes, but of late she has not set so much store by them."

"Let's clear these away," she said and took up some books.

"No, wait," he said anxiously. "I've such a lot to say to you, and our time is so short. You must know that to-day is my birthday—that's why I came and brought you the rose."

"Oh," she said, "that is an event. Your birthday to-day? Well, I'm sure that you received all your congratulations with the dignity you always show. You may have mine as well! It was sweet of you to bring me the rose, although it has its doubtful side." And she tried the mouldy smell once more with an expression of fear on her face. "How old are you to-day, Prince?"

"Twenty-seven," he answered. "I was born twenty-seven years ago in the Grimmburg. Ever since then I've had a strenuous and lonely time of it."

She did not answer. And suddenly he saw her eyes, under

263

her slightly frowning eye-brows, move to his side. Yes, although he was standing sideways to her with his right shoulder towards her, as he had trained himself to do, he could not prevent her eyes fastening on his left arm, on the hand which he had planted right back on his hip.

"Were you born with that?" she asked softly.

He grew pale. But with a cry, which rang like a cry of redemption, he sank down before her, and clasped her wondrous form in both his arms. There he lay, in his white trousers and his blue and red coat with the major's shoulder-straps.

"Little sister," he said, "little sister——"

She answered with a pout: "Think of appearances, Prince. I consider that one should not let oneself go, but should keep up appearances on all occasions."

But he was too far gone, and raising his face to her, his eyes in a mist, he only said, "Imma—little Imma——"

Then she took his hand, the left, atrophied one, the deformity, the hindrance in his lofty calling, which he had been wont from boyhood to hide artfully and carefully—she took it and kissed it.

# VIII

## THE FULFILMENT

GRAVE reports were flying around concerning the state of health of the Finance Minister, Doctor Krippenreuther. People hinted at nervous break-down, at a progressive stomach-trouble, which indeed Herr Krippenreuther's flabby yellow complexion was calculated to suggest. . . . What is Greatness? The daily-breader, the journeyman, might envy this tortured dignitary his title, his chain, his rank at Court, his important office, to which he had climbed so pertinaciously, only to wear himself out in it: but not when these all meant the concomitant of his illness. His retirement was repeatedly announced to be impending. It was said to be due simply and solely to the Grand Duke's dislike of new faces, as well as to the consideration that matters could not be improved by a change of personnel, that his resignation had not already become a fact. Dr. Krippenreuther had spent his summer leave in a health-resort in the hills. Perhaps he might have improved somewhat up there. But anyhow after his return his recouped strength ebbed away quickly again. For at the very beginning of the Parliamentary session a rift had come between him and the Budget Commission—serious dissensions, which were certainly not from any want of industry on his part, but from the circumstances, from the incurable position of affairs.

In the middle of September Albrecht II opened the Land-tag in the Old Schloss with the traditional ceremonies. They began with an invocation to God by the Court Chaplain, Dom Wislezenus, in the Schloss Chapel. Then the Grand Duke,

accompanied by Prince Klaus Heinrich, went in solemn procession to the Throne-room. Here the members of both
Chambers, the Ministers, Court officials, and many others in
uniform and civil dress greeted the royal brothers with three
cheers, led by the President of the First Chamber, a Count
Prenzlau.

Albrecht had earnestly wished to transfer to his brother
his duties in the formal ceremony. It was only owing to the
urgent objections of Herr von Knobelsdorff that he walked
in the procession behind the pages. He was so much ashamed
of his braided hussar's coat, his gaudy trousers, and the
whole to-do, that he showed clearly in his face his anger and
his embarrassment. His shoulder-blades were twisted in his
nervousness as he mounted the steps to the throne. Then he
took his stand in front of the theatrical chair under the
faded baldachin, and sucked at his upper lip. His small,
bearded, unmilitary head rested on the white collar, which
stuck out far above the silver hussar-collar, and his blue,
lonely-looking eyes gazed vacantly in front of him. The
jangle of the spurs of the aide-de-camp who handed him the
manuscript of his Speech from the Throne rang through the
hall, in which silence now reigned. And quietly, with a slight
lisp, and more than one sudden burst of coughing, the Grand
Duke read what had been written for him.

The speech was the most palliatory that had ever been
heard, each humiliating fact from outside being counter-
balanced by some virtuous trait or other in the people. He
began by praising the industrious spirit of the whole country;
then admitted that there was no actual increase to show in
any branch of manufacture, so that the sources of revenue
failed to show under any head the fertility that could be
desired. He remarked with satisfaction how the feeling for
the public good and economical self-sacrifice were spreading
more and more through the population; and then declared
without mincing matters that "notwithstanding a general most
acceptable increase in the taxation returns as the result of the

influx of wealthy foreigners" (meaning Mr. Spoelmann) "any relaxation of the calls on the said noble self-sacrifice was not to be thought of."

Even without this, he continued, it had been impossible to budget for all the objects of the financial policy, and should it prove that sufficient reduction in the public debt had not been successfully provided for, the Government considered that the continuation of policy of moderate loans would prove the best way out of the financial complications. In any event it—the Government—felt itself supported in these most unfavourable circumstances by the confidence of the nation, that faith in the future which was so fair a heritage of our stock. . . . And the Speech from the Throne left the sinister topic of public economy as soon as possible, to apply itself to less disputatious subjects, such as ecclesiastical, educational, and legal matters. Minister of State von Knobelsdorff declared in the monarch's name the Landtag to be open. And the cheers which accompanied Albrecht when he left the hall sounded somewhat ironical and dubious.

As the weather was still summery, he went straight back to Hollerbrunn, from which necessity alone had driven him to the capital. He had done his part, and the rest was the concern of Herr Krippenreuther and the Landtag. Quarrels began, as has been said, immediately, and about several topics at once: the property tax, the meat tax, and the Civil Service estimates.

For, when the deputies proved adamant against attempts to persuade them to sanction fresh taxes, Doctor Krippenreuther's meditative mind had hit on the idea of converting the income tax which had been usual hitherto into a property tax, which on the basis of $13\frac{1}{2}$ per cent. would produce an increment of about a million. How direly needed, indeed how inadequate such an increment was, was clear from the main budget for the new financial year, which, leaving out of account the imposition of new burdens on the Treasury, concluded with an adverse balance, which was calculated to

267

damp the courage of any economical expert. But when it was realized that practically only the towns would be hit by the property tax, the combined indignation of the urban deputies turned against the assessment of 13½ per cent., and they demanded as compensation at least the abolition of the meat tax, which they called undemocratic and antediluvian. Add to this that the Commission adhered resolutely to the long promised and always postponed improvement of Civil servants' pay—for it could not be denied that the salaries of the Government officials, clergy, and teachers of the Grand Duchy were miserable.

But Doctor Krippenreuther could not make gold—he said in so many words, "I've never learnt to make gold," and he found himself equally unable to abolish the meat tax and to ameliorate the conditions in the Civil Service. His only resource was to anchor himself to his 13½ per cent., although no one knew better than he that its sanction would not really bring things any nearer their solution. For the position was serious, and despondent spirits painted it in gloomy colours.

The "Almanac of the Grand Ducal Statistical Bureau" contained alarming returns of the harvest for the last year. Agriculture had a succession of bad years to show; storms, hail, droughts, and inordinate rain had been the lot of the peasants; an exceptionally cold and snowless winter had resulted in the seed freezing; and the critics maintained, though with little proof to show for it, that the timber-cutting had already influenced the climate. At any rate figures proved that the total yield of corn had decreased in a most disquieting degree. The straw, besides being deficient in quantity, left much to be wished from the point of view of quality, in the opinion of the compilers of the report.

The figures of the potato harvest fell far below the average of the preceding decade, not to mention that no less than 10 per cent. of the potatoes were diseased. As to artificial feeding-stuffs, these showed for the last two years results both in quality and quantity which, for clover and manure, were

268

as bad as the worst of the years under review, and things were no better with the rapeseed harvest or with the first and second hay crops. The decline in agriculture was baldly shown in the increase of forced sales, whose figures in the year under review had advanced in a striking way. But the failure of crops entailed a falling off in the produce of taxation which would have been regrettable in any country, but in ours could not help having a fatal effect.

As to the forests, nothing had been made out of them. One disaster had followed another; blight and moths had attacked the woods more than once. And it will be remembered that owing to over-cutting the woods had lost seriously in capital value.

The silver-mines? They had for a long time proved barren. The work had been interrupted by convulsions of nature, and as the repairs would have cost large sums, and the results had never showed signs of coming up to expectations, it had been found necessary provisionally to suspend the workings, though this threw a number of labourers out of work and caused distress in whole districts.

Enough has been said to explain how matters stood with the ordinary State revenues in this time of trial. The slowly advancing crisis, the deficit carried forward from one year to another, had become burning owing to the straits of the people and the unfavourableness of the elements. It had begun to cry aloud for remedy, and, when one looked around despairingly for the remedy, or even for means of alleviation, the most purblind could not fail to see the whole hideousness of our financial condition. There could be no thought of voting for new expenditure, the country was naturally incapable of bearing much taxation. It was now exhausted, its tax-paying powers adversely affected, and the critics declared that the sight of insufficiently nourished human beings was becoming more and more common in the country. They attributed this firstly to the shocking taxes on provisions and secondly to the direct taxation which was known to oblige stock-owners to turn all their full-milk into cash. As to the other less respectable though enticingly easy remedy for dearth of money, of which the financial authorities were well aware, namely the raising of a loan, the time was come when an improper and inconsiderate use of this means must begin to bring its own bitter punishment.

The liquidation of the national debt had been taken in hand for a time in a clumsy and harmful way. Then under Albrecht II it had stopped altogether. The yawning rifts in the State had received an emergency stuffing of new loans and paper issues, and subsequent Finance Ministers had grown pale to find themselves faced with a floating consolidated debt redeemable at an early date, whose total was scandalously large for the total number of heads of the population.

Dr. Krippenreuther had not shrunk from the practical steps open to the State in such a predicament. He had steered clear of big capital obligations, had demanded compulsory redemption of bonds, and, while reducing the rate of interest, had converted short-dated debts over the heads of the creditors into perpetual rent-charges. But these rent-charges had to be paid; and while this incumbrance was an unbearable burden on the national economy, the lowness of the rate of exchange caused every fresh issue of bonds to bring in less capital proceeds to the Treasury. Still more: the economic crisis in the Grand Duchy had the effect of making foreign creditors demand payments at an exceptionally early date. This again lowered the rate of exchange and resulted in an increased flow of gold out of the country, and bank-smashes were daily occurrences in the business world.

In a word: our credit was shattered, our paper stood far below its nominal value; and though the Landtag might perhaps have preferred to vote a new loan to voting new taxes, the conditions which would have been imposed upon the country were such that the negotiation seemed difficult, if not impossible. For on the top of everything else came this unpleasant factor, that the people were at that moment suffering from the burden of that general economical disorder, that appreciation in the price of gold, which is still vivid in everybody's memory.

What was to be done to get safe to land? Whither turn to appease the hunger for gold which was devouring us? The disposal of the then unproductive silver-mines and the application of the proceeds to the payment of the debts at high interest was discussed at length. Yet, as matters stood, the sale could not help turning out disadvantageously. Further, not only would the State lose altogether the capital sunk in the mines, but would relinquish its prospect of a return which might perhaps sooner or later materialize. Finally, buyers did not grow on every bush. For one moment—a moment of psychical despondency—the sale of the national forests even was mooted. But it must be said that there was still sense enough in the country to prevent our woods being surrendered to private industry.

To complete the picture: still further rumours of sales were current, rumours which suggested that the financial embarrassment penetrated even to quarters which the loyal people had always hoped were far removed from all the rubs of the time. The *Courier*, which was never used to sacrifice a piece of news to its sympathetic feelings, was the first to publish the news that two of the Grand Duke's schlosses, "Pastime" and "Favourite," in the open country, had been put up for sale. Considering that neither property was of any further use as a residence for the royal family, and that both demanded yearly increasing outlay, the administrators of the Crown trust property had given notice in the proper quarter for steps to be taken to sell them: what did that imply?

It was obviously quite a different case from that of the sale of Delphinenort, which had been the result of a quite exceptional and favourable offer, as well as a smart stroke of business on behalf of the State. People who were brutal enough to give a name to things which finer feeling shrinks from specifying, declared right out that the Treasury had

271

been mercilessly set on by disquieted creditors, and that their consent to such sales showed that they were exposed to relentless pressure.

How far had matters gone? Into whose hands would the schlosses fall? The more benevolent who asked this question were inclined to find comfort in and to believe a further report, which was spread by the wiseacres; namely, that on this occasion too the buyer was no one else but Samuel Spoelmann—an entirely groundless and fantastic report, which, however, proves what a rôle in the world of popular imagination was played by the lonely, suffering little man who had settled down in such princely style in their midst.

Yonder he lived, with his physician, his electric organ, and his collection of glass, behind the pillars, the bow windows, and the chiselled festoons of the schloss which had risen from its ruins at a nod from him. He was hardly ever seen: he was always in bed with poultices. But people saw his daughter, that curious creature with the whimsical features who lived like a princess, had a countess for a companion, studied algebra, and had walked in a temper unimpeded right through the guard. People saw her, and they sometimes saw Prince Klaus Heinrich at her side.

Raoul Ueberbein had used a strong expression when he declared that the public "held their breath" at the sight. But he really was right, and it can be truly said that the population of our town as a whole never followed a social or public proceeding with such passionate, such surpassing eagerness as Klaus Heinrich's visits to Delphinenort. The Prince himself acted up to a certain point—namely up to a certain conversation with his Excellency the Minister of State, Knobelsdorff—blindly, without regard to the outside world and in obedience only to an inner impulse. But his tutor was justified in deriding in his fatherly way his idea that his proceedings could be kept hid from the world. For whether it was that the servants on both sides did not hold their tongues, or that the public had the opportunity of direct observation, at any rate Klaus Heinrich had not met Miss Spoelmann once since that first meeting in the Dorothea Hospital, without its being remarked and discussed. Remarked? No, spied on, glared at, and greedily jumped at! Discussed? Rather smothered in floods of talk.

The intercourse of the two was the topic of conversation in Court circles, salons, sitting- and bedrooms, barbers' shops, public-houses, workrooms, and servants' halls, by cabmen on the ranks and girls at the gates. It occupied the minds of men no less than women, of course with the variations which are inherent in the different ways the sexes have of looking at things. The always sympathetic interest in it had a uniting, levelling effect: it bridged over the social gaps, and one might hear the tram conductor turn to the smart passenger on the platform with the question whether he knew that yesterday afternoon the Prince had again spent an hour at Delphinenort.

But what was at once remarkable in itself and at the same time decisive for the future was that throughout there never seemed for one moment to be any feeling of scandal in the air, nor did all the tongue-wagging seem merely the vulgar pleasure in startling events in high quarters. From the very beginning, before any *arrière pensée* had had time to form, the thousand-voiced discussion of the subject, however animated, was always pitched in a key of approval and agreement. Indeed, the Prince, if it had occurred to him at an earlier stage to adapt his conduct to public opinion, would have realized at once to his delight how entirely popular that conduct was. For when he called Miss Spoelmann a "princess" to his tutor, he had, quite properly, accurately expressed his people's mind—that people which always surrounds the uncommon and visionary with a cloud of poetry.

Yes, to the people the pale, dark, precious, and strangely lovely creature of mixed blood, who had come to us from the Antipodes to live her lonely and unprecedented life amongst us—to the people she was a princess—or Fairy-child from Fableland, a princess in the world's most wonderful meaning.

273

But everything, her own behaviour as much as the attitude of the world towards her, contributed to make her appear a princess in the ordinary sense of the word also. Did she not live with her companion countess in a schloss, as was meet and right? Did she not drive in her gorgeous motor or her four-in-hand to the benevolent institutions, the homes for the blind, for orphans, and for deaconesses, the public kitchens and the milk-kitchens, to teach herself and to stimulate them by her inspection, like a complete princess?

Had she not subscribed to support the victims of flood and fire out of her "privy purse," as the *Courier* was precise enough to declare, subscriptions which nearly equalled those of the Grand Duke (did not exceed them, as was noticed with general satisfaction)? Did not the newspapers publish almost daily, immediately under the Court news, reports of Mr. Spoelmann's varying health—whether the colic kept him in bed or whether he had resumed his morning visits to the Spa-gardens? Were not the white liveries of his servants as much a part of the picture in the streets of the capital as the brown of the Grand Ducal lackeys? Did not foreigners with guide-books ask to be taken out to Delphinenort, there to gloat over the sight of Spoelmann's house—many of them before they had seen the Old Schloss?

Were not both Schlosses, the Old and Delphinenort, about equally centres and foci of the city? To what circle of society belonged that human being who had been born Samuel Spoelmann's daughter, that creature without counterpart, without analogy? To whom should she attach herself, with whom have intercourse? Nothing could be less surprising, nothing more obvious and natural than to see Klaus Heinrich at her side. And even those who had never enjoyed that sight enjoyed it in the spirit and gloated over it: the slim, solemnly familiar figure of the Prince by the side of the daughter and heiress of the prodigious little foreigner, who, ill and peevish as he was, disposed of a fortune which amounted to nearly twice as much as our national debt!

Then one day a memory, a wonderful disposition of words, took hold of the public conscience; nobody can say who first pointed to it, recalled it—that is quite uncertain. Perhaps it was a woman, perhaps a child with credulous eyes, whom somebody was sending to sleep with stories—heaven only knows. But a ghostly form began to show liveliness in the popular imagination: the shadow of an old gipsy-woman, grey and bent, with an inward squint, who drew her stick through the sand, and whose mumbling had been written down and handed down from generation to generation. . . . "The greatest happiness?" It should come to the land through a Prince "with one hand." He would give the country, the prophecy ran, more with his one hand than others could with two. . . . With one? But was everything all right with Klaus Heinrich's slim figure?

When one thought of it, was there not a weakness, a defect in his person, which one always avoided seeing when addressing him, partly from shyness, and partly because with charming skill he made it so easy not to notice it? When one saw him in his carriage, he kept his left hand on his sword-hilt covered with his right. One could see him under a baldachin, on a flag-bedecked platform, take up a position slightly turned to the left, with his left hand planted somehow on his hip. His left arm was too short, the hand was stunted, everybody knew that, and knew various explanations of the origin of the defect, although respect and distance had not allowed a clear view of it or even its recognition in so many words. But now everybody saw it. It could never be ascertained who first whispered and quoted the prophecy in this connexion—whether it was a child, or a girl, or a greybeard on the threshold of the beyond.

But what is certain is, that it was the people who started it, the people who imposed certain thoughts and hopes—and quite soon their conception of Miss Spoelmann's personality —on the cultured classes right up to the highest quarters, and exercised a powerful influence on them from below: that the impartial, unprejudiced belief of the people afforded the broad and firm foundation for all that came later. "With one hand?" people asked, and "the greatest happiness?" They saw Klaus Heinrich in the spirit by Imma Spoelmann's side with his left hand on his hip, and, still incompetent to think their thought out to its conclusion, they quivered at their half-thought.

At that time everything was still in the clouds, and nobody thought anything out to its conclusion—not even the persons most immediately concerned. For the relations between Klaus Heinrich and Imma Spoelmann were wondrous strange, and their minds—his as well—could not be brought to centre on any immediate, palpable goal. As a matter of fact, that laconic conversation on the afternoon of the Prince's birthday (when Miss Spoelmann had showed him her books) had made but the slightest, if any, alteration in their relations. Klaus Heinrich may have gone back to the "Hermitage" in that condition of heated enthusiasm proper to young people on such occasions, convinced that something decisive had happened: but he soon learned that his wooing of what he had recognized to be his only happiness was only now really beginning.

But, as has been said, this wooing could not aim at any objective result, a bourgeois promise or such-like—such an idea was almost inconceivable, and besides the Prince lived in too great seclusion from the practical world for such an end to present itself to him. In fact the object of Klaus Heinrich's pleadings with looks and words from that time onward was not that Miss Spoelmann should reciprocate the feelings he entertained towards her, but that she might feel impelled to believe in the reality and liveliness of those feelings. For that was what she did not do.

He let two weeks pass before he sent in his name at Delphinenort again, and during these he feasted spiritually on what had already occurred. He was in no hurry to supersede that happening with a new one. Besides, his time just now was occupied by several representative functions, including the annual festival of the Miniature Range Rifle Club, whose well-informed patron he was and in whose anniversary festival he annually took part. Here he was received in his green uniform, as if his sole interest in life was rifle-shooting, by the united members of the association with an enthusiastic welcome, was conducted to the butts, and, after an unappetizing luncheon with the distinguished members of the committee, fired several shots in a gracefully expert attitude in the direction of various targets.

When he proceeded—it was the middle of June—to pay another afternoon visit to the Spoelmanns, he found Imma in a very mocking mood, and her mode of expression was unusually Scriptural and solemn. Mr. Spoelmann also was present this time, and although his presence robbed Klaus Heinrich of the *tête-à-tête* he so much desired with the daughter, yet it helped him in a quite unexpected way to bear up against the wounds which Imma's sharpness gave him; for Samuel Spoelmann was friendly, and almost affectionate towards him.

They had tea on the terrace, sitting in basket-chairs of an ultra-modern shape, with the breezes from the flower-garden softly fanning them. The master of the house lay under a green-silk, fur-lined, and parrot-embroidered coverlet, stretched by the table on a cane couch fitted with silk cushions. He had left his bed for the sake of the mild air, but his cheeks to-day were not inflamed, but of a sallow paleness, and his eyes were muddy; his chin protruded sharply, his prominent nose looked longer than ever, and his tone was not cross, as usual, but sad—a bad sign. By his head sat Doctor Watercloose with his continual soft smile.

"Hullo, young Prince . . ." said Mr. Spoelmann in a tired tone, and answered the other's inquiry as to his health merely with half a grunt. Imma, in a shimmering dress with a high waist and green-velvet bolero, poured water into the pot out of the electric kettle. She congratulated the Prince

277

with a pout on his personal prowess at the rifle festival. She had, she said, as she wagged her head backwards and forwards, "read an account of it in the daily press with deep satisfaction," and had read aloud the description of his exploits as marksman to the Countess. The latter was sitting bolt upright in her tight brown dress at the table, and handling her spoon gracefully, without in any way letting herself go. It was Mr. Spoelmann who did the talking this time. He did it, as has been said, in a soft, sad way, the result of all his suffering.

He recounted an occurrence, an experience of years gone by, which was obviously still fresh to him, and which always brought him new suffering on the days when his health was bad. He recounted the short and simple story twice, with even greater self-torture the second time than the first. He had wished to make one of his endowments—not one of the first rank, but a pretty considerable one—he had given a big philanthropic institute in the United States to understand in writing that he wished to devote a million in railway bonds to the furtherance of their noble work—safe paper of the South Pacific Railway, said Mr. Spoelmann, and slapped the palm of his hand, as if to show the paper. But what had the philanthropic institute done? It had refused the gift, rejected it—adding in so many words that it preferred to go without the support of questionable and ill-gotten plunder. They had actually done that. Mr. Spoelmann's lips quivered as he recounted it, the first time no less than the second, and, longing for comfort and expressions of disapproval, he looked round the table with his little, close-set, metallic eyes.

"That was not philanthropic of the philanthropic institute," said Klaus Heinrich. "No, it certainly was not." And the shake of his head was so decided, his disgust and sympathy so obvious, that Mr. Spoelmann cheered up a little and declared that it was lovely outside to-day and the trees down yonder smelt nice. Indeed, he took the first opportunity of showing his young guest his appreciation and satisfaction in the clearest manner. For Klaus Heinrich had caught a chill with this summer's constant alternations between warm weather and cooling showers and hailstorms. His neck was swollen, his throat felt sore when he swallowed; and as his lofty calling and a certain amount of molly-coddling of his person, in request as it was for exhibition, had necessarily made him rather delicate, he could not help alluding to it and complaining of the pain in his neck.

"You must have wet compresses," said Mr. Spoelmann. "Have you any oil-silk?" Klaus Heinrich had none. Then Mr. Spoelmann threw off the parrot coverlet, stood up, and went inside the Schloss. He would not answer any questions, insisted on going, and went. When he had gone, the others asked each other what he intended to do, and Doctor Watercloose, fearing lest an attack of pain had seized his patient, hurried after him. But when Mr. Spoelmann returned he had in his hand a piece of oil-silk, whose existence in some drawer he had remembered: a rather creased piece, which he handed to the Prince with precise directions how to use it, so as to get the most good out of it. Klaus Heinrich thanked him delightedly, and Mr. Spoelmann got contentedly back on to his couch. This time he stayed there till the end of tea, when he proposed a general walk round the park, in the following order: Mr. Spoelmann in his soft slippers between Imma and Klaus Heinrich, while Countess Löwenjoul followed at a short distance with Dr. Watercloose.

When the Prince took leave for the day, Imma Spoelmann made some sharp remark about his neck and the wet compresses, adjured him half-mockingly to nurse himself and to take the utmost care of his sacred person. But although Klaus Heinrich had no adequate repartee ready for her— she did not expect or want one—yet it was in a fairly cheerful frame of mind that he mounted his dog-cart; for the piece of creased oil-silk in the back pocket of his uniform coat seemed to him, though unconsciously, a pledge of a happy future.

279

However that might be, for the present his struggle was only beginning. It was the struggle for Imma Spoelmann's faith, the struggle to make her so far trust him as to be capable of deciding to leave the clear and frosty sphere wherein she had been wont to play, to descend from the realms of algebra and conversational ridicule, and to venture with him into the untrodden zone, that warmer, more fragrant, more fruitful zone to which he showed her the way. For she was overpoweringly shy of making any such decision.

Next time he was alone with her, or as good as alone, because Countess Löwenjoul was the third, it was a cool, over-cast morning, after a break in the weather the night before. They rode along the meadow-woods, Klaus Heinrich in high boots, with the crook of his crop suspended between the buttons of his grey cloak. The sluices at the wooden bridge up stream were shut, the bed of the stream lay empty and stony. Percival, whose first outburst had died down, jumped here and there or trotted sideways, dog-fashion, in front of the horses. The Countess, on Isabeau, kept her head on one side and smiled. Klaus Heinrich was saying: "I'm always thinking, night and day, about something which must have been a dream. I lie at night and can hear Florian over in the stall snuffling, it's so quiet. And then I think, for certain it was no dream. But when I see you as I do to-day, and did the other day at tea, I cannot possibly think it anything more substantial."

She replied: "I must ask you to explain yourself, Sire."

"Did you show me your books nineteen days ago, Miss Spoelmann—or not?"

"Nineteen days ago! I must count up. No; let's see, it's eighteen and a half days, unless I'm quite out."

"You did show me your books, then?"

"That is undoubtedly correct, Prince. And I delude my-self with the hope that you liked them."

"Oh, Imma, you mustn't talk like that, not now and not to me! My heart is so heavy, and I have such lots still to say to you, which I couldn't get out nineteen days ago, when you showed me your books . . . your masses of books. How I should love to carry on where we broke off then, and to forget all that lies in between. . . ."

"For heaven's sake, Prince, rather forget the other. Why go back to it? Why remind yourself and me? I thought you had good reason to observe the strictest silence on such subjects. Fancy letting yourself go like that! Losing your self-possession to such a degree!"

"If you only knew, Imma, how unutterably pleasant it is for me to lose my self-possession!"

"No, thanks. That's insulting, do you know that? I insist on your showing the same self-possession towards me as towards the rest of the world. I'm not here to provide you with relaxation from your princely existence."

"How entirely you misunderstand me, Imma! But I am well aware that you do so deliberately and only in fun, and that shows me that you don't believe me and don't take what I say seriously. . . ."

"No, Prince, you really ask too much. Haven't you told me about your life? You went to school for show, to the University for show, you served as a soldier for show, and still wear the uniform for show, you hold audiences for show, and play at rifle-shooting and heaven knows what else for show; you came into the world for show, and am I suddenly to believe that there is anything serious about you?"

Tears came to his eyes while she said this: her words hurt him so much. He answered gently: "You are right, Imma, there is a lot of fiction in my life. But I didn't make it or choose it, you must remember, but have done my duty precisely and sternly as it was prescribed to me for the edification of the people. And it is not enough that it has been a hard one, and full of prohibitions and privations; it must now take revenge on me, by causing you not to believe me."

"You are proud," she said, "of your calling and your life,

281

Prince, I know well, and I cannot wish you to break faith with yourself."

"Oh," he cried, "leave that to me, that about being true to myself, and don't give it a thought! I have had experiences, I have been untrue to myself and have tried to get round the prohibitions, and it ended in my disgrace. But since I have known you, I know, I know for the first time, that I may for the first time, without remorse or harm to what is described as my lofty calling, let myself go like anybody else, although Doctor Ueberbein says, and says in Latin, that that must never be."

"There, you see what your friend said."

"Didn't you yourself call him a poor wretch, who would come to a sad end? He's a fine character; I esteem him greatly, and owe him many hints about myself and things in general. But I've often thought about him recently, and as you expressed so unfavourable a verdict upon him then, I have spent hours considering your verdict, and was forced to own you right. For I'll tell you, Imma, how things stand with Doctor Ueberbein. His whole life is hostile to happiness, that's what it is."

"That seems to me a very proper hostility," said Imma Spoelmann.

"Proper," he answered, "but wretched, as you yourself said, and what's more, sinful, for it is a sin against something nobler than his severe propriety, as I now see, and it's this sin in which he wished to educate me in his fatherly fashion. But I've now grown out of his education, at this point I have, I'm now independent and know better; and though I may not have convinced Ueberbein, I'll convince you, Imma, sooner or later."

"Yes, Prince, I must grant you that! You have the powers of conviction, your zeal carries one along irresistibly with it! Nineteen days, didn't you say? I maintain that eighteen and a half is right, but it comes to much the same thing.

282

In that time you have condescended to appear at Delphinenort once—four days ago."

He threw a startled look at her.

"But, Imma, you must have patience with me, and some indulgence. Consider, I'm still awkward . . . this is strange ground. I don't know how it was. . . . I believe I wanted to let us have time. And then there came several calls upon me."

"Of course, you had to fire at the targets for show. I read all about it. As usual, you had a rousing success to show for it. You stood there in your fancy dress, and let a whole meadowful of people love you."

"Halt, Imma, I beg you, don't gallop. . . . One can't get a word out. . . . Love, you say. But what sort of love is it? A meadow-love, a casual, superficial love, a love at a distance, which means nothing—a love in full dress with no familiarity about it. No, you've absolutely no reason to be angry because I express myself pleased with it, for I get no good from it; only the people do, who are elevated by it, and that's their desire. But I too have my desire, Imma, and it's to you that I turn."

"How can I help you, Prince?"

"Oh, you know well! It's confidence, Imma; couldn't you have a little confidence in me?"

She looked at him, and the scrutiny of her big eyes had never before been so dark and piercing. But for all the urgency of his dumb pleading, she turned away, and said with a look which betrayed no secrets: "No, Prince Klaus Heinrich, I cannot."

He uttered a cry of grief, and his voice shook, as he asked: "And why can't you?"

She replied: "Because you prevent me."

"How do I prevent you? Please tell me, I beg."

And, with the reserved expression still on her face, her eyes dropped on her white reins, and rocking lightly to her horse's
283

walk, she replied: "Through everything, through your conduct, through the way and manner of your being, through
your highly distinguished personality. You know well enough
how you prevented the poor Countess from letting herself
go, and forced her to be clear-brained and reasonable, although it is expressly on the ground of her excessive experiences that the blessing of craziness and oddness has been
vouchsafed to her, and that I told you that I was well aware
how you had set out to sober her. Yes, I know it well, for
you prevent me too from letting myself go, you sober me too,
continually, in every way, through your words, through your
look, through your way of sitting and standing, and it is
quite impossible to have confidence in you. I've had the opportunity of watching you in your intercourse with other
people; but whether it was Doctor Sammet in the Dorothea
Hospital or Herr Stavenüter in the 'Pheasantry' Tea-garden,
it was always the same, and it always made me shiver. You
hold yourself erect, and ask questions, but you don't do so
out of sympathy, you don't care what the questions are about
—no, you don't care about anything, and you lay nothing
to heart. I've often seen it—you speak, you express an
opinion, but you might just as well express a quite different
one, for in reality you have no opinion and no belief, and the
only thing you care about is your princely self-possession.
You say sometimes that your calling is not an easy one, but
as you have challenged me, I'll ask you to notice that it
would be easier to you if you had an opinion and a belief,
Prince, that's my opinion and belief. How could anyone
have confidence in you! No, it's not confidence that you
inspire, but coldness and embarrassment; and if I put myself out to get closer to you, that kind of embarrassment
and awkwardness would prevent me from doing so,—there's
my answer for you."

He had listened to her with painful tension, had looked
more than once at her pale face while she was speaking, and
then again, like her, dropped his eyes on the reins.

"I must indeed thank you, Imma," he answered, "for speaking so earnestly, for you know that you don't always do so, but generally speak only derisively, and in your way take things as little seriously as I in mine."

"How else but derisively can I speak to you, Prince?"

"And sometimes you are so hard and cruel, as for instance towards the head sister in the Dorothea Hospital, whom you threw into such confusion."

"Oh, I'm well aware that I too have my faults, and need somebody to help me to give them up."

"I'll be that somebody, Imma; we'll help each other."

"I don't think we can help each other, Prince."

"Yes, we can. Didn't you speak just now quite seriously and unsatirically? But as for me, you are not right when you say that I care about nothing at all and lay nothing to heart, for I care about you, Imma—about you, I have laid you to heart; and as this matter is one of such inexpressible seriousness to me, I cannot fail finally to win your confidence. Were you aware of my joy when I heard you talk of putting yourself out and coming nearer to me? Yes, put yourself out a little, and do not let yourself ever again be confused with that sort of awkwardness, or whatever it is, which you are so liable to feel in my presence. Ah, I know it, I know only too well, how much to blame I am for that! But laugh at yourself and at me when I make you feel like that, and attach yourself to me. Will you promise me to put yourself out a little?"

But Imma Spoelmann promised nothing, but insisted now on her gallop; and many a subsequent conversation remained, like this, without result.

Sometimes, when Klaus Heinrich had come to tea, the Prince, Miss Spoelmann, the Countess, and Percival went into the park. The splendid collie kept decorously at Imma's side, and Countess Löwenjoul walked two or three yards behind the young people; for soon after they had started she had stopped for a second, to twine her bent and bony fingers round a blossom, and she had never made good the distance she had then lost. So Klaus Heinrich and Imma walked in front of her, and talked. But when they had covered a certain distance, they turned round, thus getting the Countess two or three yards in front of them. Then Klaus Heinrich followed up his conversational efforts, and, carefully and without looking up, took Imma Spoelmann's small, ringless hand from her side and clasped it in both his, the while he imploringly asked whether she was taking pains, and had made any progress in her confidence in him.

It displeased him to hear that she had been working, poring over algebra and playing in the lofty spheres since they had last met. He would beg her to lay her books aside now, as they might distract her and divert her from the matter to which all her thinking powers must now be devoted. He talked also about himself, about that sobering effect and awkwardness which, according to her, his existence inspired; he tried to explain it, and in doing so to weaken it. He spoke about the cold, stern, and barren existence which had been his hitherto, he described to her how everybody had always flocked to gaze at him, while it had been his lofty calling to show himself and to be gazed at, a much more difficult task. He did his best to make her recognize that the remedy for that which caused him to prevent the poor Countess from drivelling and to estrange her to his own sorrow, that this remedy could be found in her, only in her, and was given over absolutely into her hands.

She looked at him, her big eyes sparkled in dark scrutiny, and it was clear that she, she too, was struggling. But then she would shake her head or break off the conversation, introducing with a pout some topic over which she made merry, incapable of bringing herself to take the responsibility of the "Yes" for which he begged her, that undefined and, as matters stood, absolutely non-committal surrender.

She did not prevent him from coming once or twice a week; she did not prevent him from speaking, from assailing her

286

with prayers and asseverations and from taking her hand now and then between his own. But she was only patient, she remained unmoved, her dread of taking the decisive step, that aversion from leaving her cool and derisive kingdom and confessing herself his, seemed unconquerable; and she could not help, in her anguish and exhaustion, breaking out with the words: "Oh, Prince, we ought never to have met—it would have been best if we hadn't. Then you would have pursued your lofty calling as calmly as ever, and I should have preserved my peace of mind, and neither would have harassed the other!"

The Prince had much difficulty in inducing her to recant, and in extorting from her the confession that she did not entirely regret having made his acquaintance. But all this took time. The summer came to an end, early night-frosts loosened the still-green leaves from the trees, Fatma's, Florian's, and Isabeau's hoofs rustled in the red-and-gold leafage when they went for a ride. Autumn came with its mists and sharp smells—and nobody could have prophesied an end, or indeed any decisive turn in the course of the strangely fluctuating affair.

The credit of having placed things on the foundation of actuality, of having given events the lead in the direction of a happy issue, must for ever be ascribed to the distinguished gentleman who had up till now wisely kept in the background, but at the right moment intervened carefully but firmly. I refer to Excellency von Knobelsdorff, Minister of the Interior, Foreign Affairs, and the Grand Ducal Household.

Dr. Ueberbein had been correct in his assertion that the President of the Council had kept himself posted in the stages of Klaus Heinrich's love affair. What is more, well served by intelligent and sagacious assistants, he had kept himself well in touch with the state of public opinion, with the rôle which Samuel Spoelmann and his daughter played in the imaginative powers of the people, with the royal rank with

287

which the popular idea invested them, with the great and superstitious tension with which the population followed the intercourse between the Schlosses "Hermitage" and Delphine-nort, with the popularity of that intercourse: in a word, he was well aware how the Spoelmanns, for everyone who did not deliberately shut his eyes, were the general topic of conversation and rumour, not only in the capital, but in the whole country. A characteristic incident was enough to make Herr Knobelsdorff sure of his ground.

At the beginning of October—the Landtag had been opened a fortnight before, and the disputes with the Budget Commission were in full swing—Imma Spoelmann fell ill, very seriously ill, so it was said at first. It seemed that the imprudent girl, for some whim or mood, while out with her countess, had ventured on a gallop of nearly half an hour's duration on her white Fatma in the teeth of a strong northeast wind, and had come home with an attack of congestion of the lungs, which threatened to end her altogether.

The news soon got about. People said the girl was hovering between life and death, which, as luckily soon emerged, was a great exaggeration. But the consternation, the general sympathy, could not have been greater if a serious accident had happened to a member of the House of Grimmburg, even to the Grand Duke himself. It was the sole topic of conversation. In the humbler parts of the city, near the Dorothea Hospital for instance, the women stood in the evening outside their front doors, pressed the palms of their hands against their breasts, and coughed, as if to show each other what it meant to be short of breath. The evening papers published searching and expert news of the condition of Miss Spoelmann, which passed from hand to hand, were read at family gatherings and cafés, and were discussed in the tram-cars. The *Courier's* reporter had been seen to drive in a cab to Delphinenort, where, in the hall with the mosaic floor, he had been snubbed by the Spoelmanns' butler, and had talked English to him—though he found that no easy task.

The press, moreover, could not escape the reproach of having magnified the whole business, and made a quite unnecessary fuss about it. There was absolutely no question of any danger. Six days in bed under the care of the Spoelmanns' private physician sufficed to relieve the congestion, and to make Miss Spoelmann's lungs quite well again. But these six days sufficed also to make clear the importance which the Spoelmanns, and Miss Imma's personality in particular, had achieved in our public opinion. Every morning found the envoys of the newspapers, commissioners of the general curiosity, gathered in the mosaic hall at Delphinenort to hear the butler's curt bulletins, which they then reproduced in their papers at the inordinate length which the public desired.

One read of greetings and wishes for recovery sent to Delphinenort by various benevolent institutions which Imma Spoelmann had visited and richly subscribed to (and the wits remarked that the Grand Ducal Treasury might have taken the opportunity of offering their homage in a similar way). The public read also and dropped the paper to exchange a significant look—of a "beautiful floral tribute," which Prince Klaus Heinrich had sent with his card (the truth being that the Prince, so long as Miss Spoelmann kept to her bed, sent flowers not once, but daily, to Delphinenort, a fact which was not mentioned by those in the know, so as not to make too great a sensation).

The public read further that the popular young patient had left her bed for the first time, and finally the news came that she was soon to go out for the first time. But this going out, which took place on a sunny autumn morning, eight days after the patient had been taken ill, was calculated to give rise to such an expression of feeling on the part of the population as people of stern self-possession labelled immoderate. For round the Spoelmanns' huge olive-varnished, red-cushioned motor, which, with a pale young chauffeur of an Anglo-Saxon type on the box, waited in front of the main door at Delphinenort, a big crowd had gathered; and when

Miss Spoelmann and Countess Löwenjoul, followed by a lackey with a rug, came out, cheers broke out, hats and handkerchiefs were waved, until the motor had forced a way through the crowd and had left the demonstrators behind in a cloud of vapour. It must be confessed that these consisted of those rather doubtful elements who usually collect on such occasions: half-grown youths, a few women with market-baskets, one or two schoolboys, gapers, loafers, and out-of-works of various descriptions.

·But what is the public and what should its composition be to make it an average public? One further assertion must not be passed over entirely in silence which was later disseminated by the cynics. It was to the effect that among the crowd round the motor there was an agent in Herr von Knobelsdorff's pay, a member of the secret police, who had started the cheers and vigorously kept them going. We can leave that in doubt, and not grudge the belittlers of important events their satisfaction.

At least, in the case of this particular crowd, it only amounts to saying that the agent's task was the mechanical release of feelings which must have been there and must have been vivid. At any rate this scene, which of course was described at length in the daily press, did not fail to impress everybody, and persons with any acumen for the connexion of things felt no doubt that a further piece of news, which busied men's minds a few days later, stood in hidden relation to all these phenomena and symptoms.

The news ran that his Royal Highness Prince Klaus Heinrich had received his Excellency the Minister of State von Knobelsdorff in audience at the Schloss "Hermitage," and had been closeted with him from three o'clock in the afternoon till seven o'clock in the evening. A whole four hours! What had they discussed? Surely not the next Court Ball? As a matter of fact, the Court Ball had been one among several topics of conversation.

Herr von Knobelsdorff had preferred his request for a confidential talk with the Prince in connexion with the Court Hunt, which had taken place on October 10th in the woods to the west near Schloss "Jägerpreis," and in which Klaus Heinrich and his red-haired cousins, dressed in green uniforms, soft felt hats, and top-boots, and hung with field-glasses, hangers, hunting-knives, bandoliers, and pistol cases, had taken part. Herr von Braunbart-Schellendorf had been consulted, and three o'clock on October 12th decided on. Klaus Heinrich himself had offered to visit the old gentleman at his official residence, but Herr von Knobelsdorff had preferred coming to the "Hermitage." He came punctually, and was received with all the affection and warmth which Klaus Heinrich thought that propriety demanded in the case of the aged counsellor of his father and his brother. The sober little room, in which stood the three fine mahogany Empire armchairs, with the blue lyre-embroidery on the yellow ground, was the scene of the interview.

Though close on seventy, Excellency von Knobelsdorff was vigorous both in body and mind. His frock-coat showed not one senile wrinkle, but was tightly and well filled with the compact and comfortable form of a man of happy disposition. His well-preserved hair was pure white, like his short moustache, and parted smoothly in the middle; his chin had a sympathetic pit in it, which might pass for a dimple. The fan-shaped wrinkles at the corners of his eyes played as livelily as ever—indeed, they had gained with the years some little branches and additional lines, so that the whole complication of ever-shifting wrinkles imparted to his blue eyes an expression of humorous subtlety.

Klaus Heinrich was attached to Herr von Knobelsdorff, though no closer relations had been established between them. The Minister of State had actually superintended and organized the Prince's life. He had begun by fixing on Dröge to be his first tutor; had then called the "Pheasantry" into life for him; had sent him later to the University with Dr. Ueberbein; had also arranged his military service for show, and

291

had put Schloss "Hermitage" at his disposal to live in. But all this he had done at second-hand, and had rarely interviewed him in person. Indeed, when Herr von Knobelsdorff had met Klaus Heinrich during those years of education, he had inquired most respectfully as to the Prince's resolves and plans for the future, as if he were in complete ignorance of them; and perhaps it was just this fiction, which was firmly bolstered up on both sides, which had kept their intercourse throughout within the bounds of formality.

Herr von Knobelsdorff began the conversation in an easy though respectful tone, while Klaus Heinrich tried to discover the objects of his visit. The former then chatted about the hunt of the day before yesterday, made some pleasant reference to the amount of ground they had covered, and then mentioned casually his admirable colleague at the Treasury, Dr. Krippenreuther, who had also taken part in the hunt, and whose invalid appearance he regretted. Herr Krippenreuther had really not hit a thing.

"Yes, worry makes the hand unsteady," remarked Herr von Knobelsdorff, and so gave the Prince the cue for a direct reference to this worry. He spoke about the "by no means trifling" shortage in the estimates, about the Minister's discussions with the Budget Commission, the new property-tax, the rate of 13½ per cent., and the bitter opposition of the urban deputies, of the antediluvian meat tax, and the Civil Service's cries of hunger; and Klaus Heinrich, who had been surprised at first by so many dry facts, listened to him intently and nodded his head repeatedly.

The two men, the old and young, sat side by side on a slender, hardish sofa with yellow upholstery and wreath-like brass mountings, which stood behind the round table opposite the narrow glass door. The latter opened on to the terrace, and through it one could see the half-bare park and the duck pond floating in the autumn mist. The low, white, smooth stove, in which a fire was crackling, diffused a gentle warmth through the severely and scantily furnished room. Klaus

Heinrich, though not quite able to follow the political proceedings, yet proud and happy at being so seriously talked
to by the experienced dignitary, felt his mood growing more
and more grateful and confidential. Herr von Knobelsdorff
spoke pleasantly about the most unpleasant subjects. His
voice was comforting, his remarks ably strung together and
insinuating—and suddenly Klaus Heinrich became aware that
he had dropped the subject of the State finances, and had
passed on from Doctor Krippenreuther's worries to his, Klaus
Heinrich's, own condition. Was Herr von Knobelsdorff
mistaken? His eyes were beginning occasionally to play
him tricks. But he wished he could think that his Royal
Highness looked a little better, fresher, brighter—a look of
tiredness, of worry, was unmistakable. . . . Herr von Knobelsdorff feared to seem importunate; but he must hope that
these symptoms did not arise from any malady, bodily or
mental?

Klaus Heinrich looked out at the mist. His look was still
sealed: but though he sat on the hard sofa in his usual stiff,
upright attitude, his feet crossed, his right hand over his
left, and the upper part of his body turned towards Herr
von Knobelsdorff, yet inwardly his stiffness relaxed at this
juncture, and, worn out as he was by his strangely ineffectual
struggle, it did not want much more to make his eyes fill
with tears. He was so lonely, so destitute of counsellors.
Dr. Ueberbein had recently kept far away from the "Hermitage." . . . Klaus Heinrich merely said: "Ah, Excellency,
that would take us too far."

But Herr von Knobelsdorff answered: "Too far? No,
your Royal Highness need not be afraid of being too prolix.
I confess that my knowledge of your Royal Highness's experiences is greater than I allowed to appear just now. Your
Royal Highness can scarcely have anything new to tell me,
apart from those refinements and details which rumour can
never collect. But if it might comfort your Royal Highness
to open his heart to an old servant, who carried you in his

293

arms . . . perhaps I might not be quite incapable of standing by your Royal Highness in word and deed."

And then it happened that something gave way in Klaus Heinrich's bosom, and poured out in a stream of confession: he told Herr von Knobelsdorff the whole story. He told it as one tells when the heart is full and everything comes tumbling out all at once through the lips; according to no plan, no chronological order, and with undue emphasis on unessentials, but with a burst of passion, and with that concreteness which is the product of passionate observation. He began in the middle, jumped unexpectedly to the beginning, hurried on to the conclusion (which did not exist), tumbled over himself, and more than once hesitated and stuck fast.

But Herr von Knobelsdorff's fore-knowledge made the review easier for him, enabled him by slipping in suggestive questions to float the ship again. And at last the picture of Klaus Heinrich's experiences with all their characters and leading actors, with the figures of Samuel Spoelmann, of the crazy Countess Löwenjoul, even of the collie, Percival, and especially that of Imma Spoelmann, with all its contrariness, lay there complete and full, ready to be discussed. The piece of oil-silk was referred to in full detail, for Herr von Knobelsdorff seemed to attach importance to it. Nothing was omitted, from the impressive incident at the changing of the guard to the last intimate and distressing struggles on horseback and on foot.

Klaus Heinrich was much wrought up when he finished, and his steel-blue eyes in the national cheek-bones were full of tears. He had left the sofa, thereby forcing Herr von Knobelsdorff also to get up, and wished on account of the heat to open the glass door into the little veranda, but Herr von Knobelsdorff stopped this by calling attention to the risk of a chill. He begged the Prince humbly to sit down again, as his Royal Highness could not conceal from himself the need for a calm discussion of the state of affairs. And both sat down again on the thinly cushioned sofa.

Herr von Knobelsdorff meditated awhile, and his face was as serious as it ever could be with his dimpled chin and the play of his eye-wrinkles. Then, breaking silence, he thanked the Prince with emotion for the great honour he had shown him by confiding in him. And in direct connexion with this Herr von Knobelsdorff, emphasizing each word, announced that whatever attitude the Prince had expected him, Herr von Knobelsdorff, to assume at this juncture, he, Herr von Knobelsdorff, was certainly not the man to oppose the wishes and hopes of the Prince, but much rather to show his Royal Highness the way to the longed-for goal to the best of his power.

Long silence ensued. Klaus Heinrich looked rapturously at Herr von Knobelsdorff's eyes with the fan-like wrinkles. Had he these wishes and hopes? Was there a goal? He was not sure of his ears. He said: "Your Excellency is kind enough . . ."

Then Herr von Knobelsdorff added to his declaration a condition, and said: Frankly, on one condition only did he, as first official of the State, dare to exercise his modest influence on behalf of his Royal Highness.

"On one condition?"

"On condition that your Royal Highness does not take account only of your own happiness in a selfish and frivolous way, but, as your lofty calling demands, regards your personal destiny from the point of view of the Mass, the Whole."

Klaus Heinrich was silent, and his eyes were heavy in thought.

"Perhaps your Royal Highness," continued Herr von Knobelsdorff after a pause, "will allow me to leave this delicate and yet quite unavoidable topic for a while, and to turn to more general matters! This is the hour of confidence and mutual understanding . . . I respectfully beg to be allowed to take advantage of it. Your Royal Highness is through your exalted position cut off from rude actuality, severed from it by delicate precautions. I shall not forget

295

that this actuality is not—or only at second-hand—a matter for your Royal Highness. And yet the moment seems to me to have come for bringing at least a certain portion of this rude world to the immediate notice of your Royal Highness, entirely for your own sake. I plead beforehand for forgiveness, if I chance to stir up your Royal H_ ' ness's emotions too harshly by what I tell you."

"Please speak on, Excellency," said Klaus Heinrich hastily. Involuntarily he sat upright, just as one sits up straight in a dentist's chair and collects one's natural powers to withstand an attack of pain.

"I must ask for your undivided attention," said Herr von Knobelsdorff almost sternly. And then, as a corollary to the discussions with the Budget Commission, followed the statement, the clear, exhaustive, unembroidered lesson, well primed with figures and explanations of the fundamental facts and technical expressions, which showed the economical position of the country, the State, and brought our whole miserable plight with relentless clearness before the Prince's eyes.

Naturally these things were not entirely new and strange to him. Indeed, ever since he had assumed his representative rôle, they had served as a motive and subject for those formal questions which he used to address to burgomasters, agriculturists, and high officials, and to which he received answers which were merely answers and nothing more, and which were often accompanied by the smile which he had known all his life and which reminded him that he was born to be king. But all this had not yet forced itself upon him in its naked actuality, nor made serious claims on his thinking powers.

Herr von Knobelsdorff was by no means satisfied to get a few of Klaus Heinrich's usual encouraging words; he pressed the matter home, he cross-examined the young man, made him repeat whole sentences; he kept him relentlessly to the point, and reminded the Prince of a dry and skinny index-finger which stopped at each separate place and would not go on until convinced that the pupil really understood the lesson.

Herr von Knobelsdorff began at the rudiments, and talked about the country and its lack of development from a commercial and industrial point of view: he talked about the people, Klaus Heinrich's people, that shrewd and honest, sound and reliable stock. He spoke about the deficiency in the State reserves, the poor dividends paid by the railways, the insufficient coal supply. He touched on the administration of the forests, game preserves and stock-raising; he talked about the woods, the excessive felling, the immoderate stripping of litter, the crippling of the industry, the falling revenues from the forests. Then he went more closely into our stock of gold, discussed the natural inability of the people to pay heavy taxes, described the reckless finance of earlier periods. Thereupon he added up the figures of the State debt, which Herr von Knobelsdorff forced the Prince to repeat several times. They reached six hundred millions.

The lesson extended further to the debentures, conditions for interest and repayment. It came back to Doctor Krippenreuther's present anxiety, and described the seriousness of the situation. Suddenly pulling the "Annual of the Statistical Bureau" out of his pocket, Herr von Knobelsdorff instructed his pupil in the harvest returns for the previous years, summed up the untoward events which had caused their decline, pointed to the deficiencies in the taxes, the figures of which he had brought with him, and referred to the underfed adults and children whom one might see throughout the country-side. Then he turned to the general condition of the gold market, discoursed on the rise in the value of gold and the general economic unsoundness. Klaus Heinrich learned also about the lowness of the Exchange, the restlessness of the creditors, the leakage of gold, and the bank smashes; he saw our credit shaken, our paper valueless, and grasped to the full that the raising of a new loan was almost impossible.

297

The night was closing in, it was long past five, when Herr von Knobelsdorff ended his statement of the national economics. At this time Klaus Heinrich usually had his tea, but this time he only gave a passing thought to it, and nobody outside dared to disturb a conversation whose importance was shown by its duration. Klaus Heinrich listened and listened. He scarcely realized how much affected he was. But how could the other bring himself to say all that to him? He had not called him "Royal Highness" one single time during the interview, he had to some extent forced him, and grossly ignored the fact that he was "born to be king." And yet it was good and stimulating to hear all that and to have to bury oneself in it for reality's sake. He forgot to have the lights brought, his attention was so much occupied.

"It was these circumstances," concluded Herr von Knobelsdorff, "which I had in mind when I begged your Royal Highness to regard your personal wishes and plans continually in the light of the general good. I have no doubt that your Royal Highness will profit by this talk and by the facts I have been bold enough to put before you. And in this connexion I beg your Royal Highness to allow me to revert to your more personal case."

Herr von Knobelsdorff waited till Klaus Heinrich had made a sign of consent with his hand, and then went on: "If this affair is to have any future, it is desirable that it should now advance a step in its development. It is stagnating, it remains as formless and prospectless as the mist outside. That's intolerable. We must give it form, must thicken it out, must mark its outlines more clearly before the eyes of the world."

"Quite so! quite so! Give it form . . . thicken it out. . . . That's it. That's absolutely necessary," agreed Klaus Heinrich, so much excited that he left the sofa and began to walk up and down the room. "But how? For heaven's sake, Excellency, tell me how?"

"The next external step," said Herr von Knobelsdorff, and

remained sitting—so unusual was the occasion—"must be this, that the Spoelmanns be seen at Court."

Klaus Heinrich stopped still.

"No," he said, "never, if I know Mr. Spoelmann, will he let himself be persuaded to go to Court."

"Which," answered Herr von Knobelsdorff, "doesn't prevent his daughter from doing us this pleasure. The Court Ball's not so very far off; it rests with you, Royal Highness, to induce Miss Spoelmann to take part in it. Her companion is a countess . . . a peculiar one, perhaps, but a countess, and that helps things. When I assure your Royal Highness that the Court will not fail to make things easy, I am speaking with the approbation of the Chief Master of the Ceremonies, Herr von Bühl zu Bühl."

The conversation now turned for three-quarters of an hour on questions of precedence, and the ceremonial conditions under which the presentation must be carried out. The distribution of cards was always left to Princess Catherine's Mistress of the Robes, a widowed Countess Trummerhauff, who led the ladies' world at the festivities in the Old Castle.

But as to the act of presentation itself, Herr von Knobelsdorff had managed to secure some concessions of a deliberate, in fact definite character. There was no American Consul in the place—no reason on that account, explained Herr von Knobelsdorff, for letting the ladies be presented by any casual chamberlain; no, the Master of the Ceremonies himself requested the honour of presenting them to the Grand Duke. When? At what point of the prescribed procession? Why, undoubtedly, unusual circumstances demand exceptions. In the first place, then, in front of all the débutantes of the various ranks—Klaus Heinrich might assure Miss Spoelmann that this would be arranged. It would give rise to talk and sensation at Court and in the city. But never mind, so much the better. Sensation was by no means undesirable, sensation was useful, even necessary. . . .

Herr von Knobelsdorff went. It had become so dark when
299

he took his leave that the Prince and he could scarcely see each other. Klaus Heinrich, who now first became aware of it, excused himself in some confusion, but Herr von Knobelsdorff declared it to be a matter of no importance in what sort of light a conversation like that was carried on. He took the hand which Klaus Heinrich offered him, and grasped it in both his.

"Never," he said warmly, and these were his last words before he went, "never was the happiness of a prince more inseparable from that of his people. No, whatever your Royal Highness ponders and does, you will bear in mind that the happiness of your Royal Highness by the disposition of destiny has become a condition of the public weal, but that your Royal Highness on your side must recognize in the weal of your country the indispensable condition and justification of your own happiness."

Much moved, and not yet in a condition to arrange the thoughts which poured in on him in thousands, Klaus Heinrich remained behind in his homely Empire room.

He passed a restless night, and went next morning, despite misty and damp weather, for a long and lonely ride. Herr von Knobelsdorff had talked clearly and voluminously, had given and accepted facts; but for the fusion, modelling, and working up of these multifarious raw products he had given only curt, aphoristic instructions, and Klaus Heinrich found himself doomed to some heavy thinking while he lay awake at night, and later when he went for a ride on Florian.

When he got back to the "Hermitage" he did a remarkable thing. He wrote with a pencil on a piece of paper an order, a certain commission, and sent Neumann, the valet, with it to the Academy Bookshop in the University Strasse: Neumann came back with a package of books, which Klaus Heinrich had set out in his room, and which he began at once to read.

They were works of a sober and school-bookish appearance, with glazed paper backs, ugly leather sides, and coarse paper,

300

and the contents were divided up minutely into sections, main divisions, sub-divisions, and paragraphs. Their titles were not stimulating. They were manuals and hand-books of economy, abstracts and outlines of State finance, systematic treatises on political economy. The Prince shut himself up in his study with these books, and gave instructions that he wished on no account to be disturbed.

The autumn was damp, and Klaus Heinrich felt little tempted to leave the "Hermitage." On Saturday he drove to the Old Schloss to give free audiences: otherwise his time was his own all this week, and he knew how to make use of it. Wrapped in his dressing-gown, he sat in the warmth of the low stove at his small, old-fashioned, little-used desk, and pored over his books on finance, with his temples resting in his hands. He read about the State expenditure and what it always consisted of, about the receipts and whence they flowed in when things were going well; he ploughed through the whole subject of taxation in all its branches; he buried himself in the doctrine of the budget, of the balance, of the surplus, and particularly of the deficit; he lingered longest over, and went deepest into, the public debt and its varieties, into loans, and relation between interest and capital and liquidation, and from time to time he raised his head from the book and dreamed with a smile about what he had read, as if it had been the gayest poetry.

For the rest, he found that it was not hard to grasp it all, when one set one's mind to it. No, this really serious actuality, in which he now played a part, this simple and rude texture of interests, this system of down-right logical needs and necessities, which countless young men of ordinary birth had to stuff into their heads, to be able to pass examinations in it, it was by no means so difficult to get hold of as he in his Highness had thought. The rôle of representation, in his opinion, was harder. And much, much more ticklish and difficult were his gentle struggles with Imma Spoelmann on horseback and on foot. His studies made him warm and

331

happy, he felt that his zeal was making his cheeks hot, like those of his brother-in-law zu Ried-Hohenried over his peat.

After thus giving the facts which he had learnt from Herr von Knobelsdorff a general academic basis, and also accomplishing a feat of hard thinking in bringing together inward connexions and weighing possibilities, he again presented himself at Delphinenort at tea-time. The lights in the candelabra with the lions' feet and the big crystal lustres were burning in the garden room. The ladies were alone.

Klaus Heinrich first asked after Mr. Spoelmann's health and Imma's indisposition. He upbraided her freely for her strange impetuosity, to which she answered with a pout that as far as she knew she was her own mistress, and could do as she liked with her health. The conversation then turned to the autumn, to the damp weather which forbade rides, to the advanced time of year, and the proximity of winter, and Klaus Heinrich suddenly mentioned the Court Ball in connexion with which it occurred to him to ask whether the ladies —if unfortunately Mr. Spoelmann were prevented by the state of his health—would not care to take part in one this time. But when Imma answered, "No, really, she had no wish to be rude, but she had absolutely not the faintest desire to go to a Court Ball," he did not press the point, but postponed the question for the time.

What had he done these last few days?—Oh, he'd been very busy, he might say that he'd been chock-a-block with work.—Work? Doubtless he meant the Court Hunt at "Jägerpreis."—The Court Hunt? No. He had gone in for real study which he had by no means got to the bottom of yet; on the contrary he was sticking deep in the literature on the subject. . . . And Klaus Heinrich began to talk about his ugly books, his peeps into financial science, and he spoke with such pleasure and respect of this discipline that Imma Spoelmann looked at him with her big eyes. But when— almost timidly—she questioned him as to the motive and impulse for this activity, he answered that it was living, only

302

too burning, questions of the day which had brought him to it: circumstances and conditions which were certainly not well suited for a cheerful talk at tea. This remark obviously offended Imma Spoelmann.

"On what observations," she asked sharply, wagging her head from side to side, "did he base his conviction that she was approachable only or preferably by way of cheerful conversation?" And she commanded him rather than asked him to be kind enough to explain about the burning questions of the day.

Then Klaus Heinrich explained what he had learnt from Herr von Knobelsdorff, and talked about the land and its state. He was well posted on every point at which the skinny index-finger had paused: he talked about the natural and the indebted, the general and the particular, the inherited and the intensifying misfortunes; he emphasized particularly the figures of the State debt, and the burden they laid on our national economy—they were six hundred millions—and he did not forget to mention the underfed peasants in the country-side.

He did not speak connectedly; Imma Spoelmann interrupted him with questions and helped him on with questions. She listened carefully, and asked for explanations of what she did not at once understand. Dressed in her loose-sleeved, red-silk dress with the broad embroidery on the yoke, an old-Spanish chain round her child-like neck, she sat leaning on one elbow over the table, her chin buried in her ringless hand, and listened with her whole soul, while her big, dark eyes scrutinized the Prince's face.

But while he spoke, in answer to Imma's verbal and ocular questions, worked at his subject, grew excited and entirely absorbed in it, Countess Löwenjoul no longer felt herself restricted to sober clarity by his presence, but let herself go and indulged in the luxury of drivelling. All the misery, she explained with dignified gestures, even the bad harvest, the burden of debt and the rise in the price of gold, were

303

due to the shameless women who swarmed everywhere, and unfortunately had discovered the way through the floor, as last night the wife of a sergeant from the Grenadiers' Barracks had scratched her breasts and pommelled her in a horrible way. Then she alluded to her Schlosses in Burgundy, through the roofs of which the rain came, and went so far as to relate that she had gone as lieutenant in an expedition against the Turks, on which she had been the only one who "had not lost her head." Imma Spoelmann and Klaus Heinrich threw her a kind word now and then, readily promised to call her Frau Meier in future, and for the rest took no notice of her.

The cheeks of both were burning when Klaus Heinrich had said all he knew—even on Miss Spoelmann's usually pearl-white cheeks there was a shade of red to be seen. They then stopped, the Countess too kept quiet, with her little head inclined on her shoulder, and staring into vacancy. Klaus Heinrich played on the white and sharply folded table-cloth with the stem of an orchid, which had stood in a glass by his plate; but as soon as he raised his head he met Imma Spoelmann's large, flaming eyes, which spoke a message of secret entreaty across the table, a darkly eloquent language.

"It has been nice to-day," she said in her broken voice, when she said good-bye this time, and he felt her small, soft hands clasp his with a firm squeeze. "Next time your Highness honours our unworthy house, do bring me one or two of those excellent books you have bought." She could not entirely resist mocking him, but she asked him for his finance books, and he brought them to her.

He brought her two of them, which he considered the most informative and comprehensive; he brought them some days later in his carriage through the damp Town Garden, and she thanked him for doing so. As soon as tea was over, they retired to a corner of the room, and there, while the Countess absently continued sitting at the tea-table, they began their common studies in throne-like chairs at a gilt table, bending

304

over the first page of a manual called "The Science of Finance." They even read the headings to the sections, each reading a sentence softly in turn; for Imma Spoelmann insisted on going methodically to work and beginning at the beginning.

Klaus Heinrich, well prepared as he was, acted as guide through the paragraphs, and nobody could have followed more smartly or clear-headedly than Imma.

"It's quite easy!" she said and looked up with a laugh. "I'm surprised that it is at bottom so simple. Algebra is much harder, Prince."

But as they went so deeply into things, they did not get far in one afternoon, so made a mark in the book at which to start next time.

And so they went on, and the Prince's visits to Delphinenort were devoted to dull realities. Whenever Mr. Spoelmann did not come to tea, or, with Dr. Watercloose, left them, after eating his rusk, Imma and Klaus Heinrich sat down at the gilt table with their books, and plunged heads together into the Science of Economics. But as they progressed, they compared what they learned with the reality, applied what they read to the circumstances of the country, as Klaus Heinrich conceived them to be, and made their studies profitable, though it happened not seldom that their investigations were interrupted by considerations of a personal kind.

"It seems, then," said Imma, "that the issue may be effected either directly or indirectly—yes, that's obvious. Either the State turns directly to the capitalists and opens a subscription list . . . Your hand is twice as broad as mine," she said; "look, Prince."

And they looked laughingly at their hands, his right and her left, as they lay next each other on the gilt table.

"Or," went on Imma, "the loan is procured by negotiation, and it is some big bank, or group of banks, to which the State . . ."

"Wait!" he said softly. "Wait, Imma, and answer me one

305

question. Aren't you missing the main point? Are you making progress? What about the disenchantment and embarrassment, dear little Imma? Have you now just one spark of confidence in me?" His lips asked the question close to her hair, from which a delicate fragrance arose, and she held her dark head still and bent over the book, though she did not answer his question frankly.

"But must it be a bank or group of banks?" she pondered. "There's nothing about it there; I can't think it would be necessary in practice."

She spoke gravely and deliberately on these occasions, for she too for her part had to grapple with the mental exercises which Klaus Heinrich had successfully managed after the conversation with Herr von Knobelsdorff. And when some weeks later he repeated his question, whether she would not like to go to the Court Ball, and told her of the ceremonial conditions which had been sanctioned for this occasion, behold, she replied that she would like to, and would go next day with Countess Löwenjoul and leave cards on the widowed Countess Trümmerhauff.

This year the Court Ball took place earlier than usual; at the end of November—an arrangement which was said to be due to the wishes of the Grand Ducal Party. Herr von Bühl zu Bühl bitterly bewailed this precipitation, which obliged him and his subordinates to cancel the arrangements for the most important Court function, especially the improvements which the Gala Rooms in the Old Schloss so much needed. But the wish of the particular member of the Grand Ducal family had had the support of Herr von Knobelsdorff, and the Court Marshal had to give way. But it happened thus that people's minds scarcely had time to prepare themselves sufficiently for what really was the event of the evening, in comparison with which the unusual date seemed as nothing. Indeed, when the *Courier* published in leaded type the news of the leaving of cards and the invitation—not without expressing in rather smaller type and in glowing words its

306

satisfaction thereat, and welcoming Spoelmann's daughter to the Court—the important evening was already close at hand, and before tongues could get fairly wagging the whole thing was a completed reality.

Never had more envy attached to the five hundred favoured ones whose names stood on the Court Ball list, never had the bourgeois more eagerly devoured the account in the *Courier*—those dazzling columns which were written every year by a nobleman who had degenerated through drink, and which were such glorious reading that one felt they gave one a peep into Fairyland, while as a matter of fact the ball in the Old Schloss went off quite modestly and soberly. But the report only extended to the supper, including the French menu, and everything that came later, especially all the delicate significance of the great occasion, were necessarily left to be reported by word of mouth.

The ladies, in a huge olive-coloured motor, had pulled up in front of the Albrechtstor at the Old Schloss fairly punctually, though not so punctually that Herr von Bühl zu Bühl had not had time to get anxious. From a quarter-past seven onwards he had waited in full uniform, covered with orders down to his waist, with a bright brown toupée and his gold pince-nez on his nose, in the middle of the armour-hung Knights' Hall where the Grand Ducal family and the chief officials were collected; standing now on one foot, then on the other, and every now and then dispatching a footman to the ballroom to find out whether Miss Spoelmann had not yet come. He thought of all sorts of unheard-of possibilities. If this Queen of Sheba came too late—and what might one not expect of a girl who had walked right through the guard?—the entry of the Grand Ducal cortège would have to be delayed, and the Court would have to wait for her, for she simply must be introduced first, and it was out of the question that she should enter the ballroom after the Grand Duke.

But thank heaven! a bare minute before half-past seven she arrived with her Countess; and it made a great sensation when
307

the Chamberlains who received them arranged them next the diplomats, and so in front of the nobility, the Court ladies, the Ministers, the Generals, the Presidents of Chambers, and all the Court world. Aide-de-camp von Platow had fetched the Grand Duke from his rooms. Albrecht, in hussar uniform, had greeted the members of his House with down-cast eyes in the Knights' Hall, had offered his arm to Aunt Catherine, and then, after Herr von Bühl had tapped three times with his staff on the parquet in the open doors, the procession of the Court into the ballroom had begun.

Eye-witnesses asserted later that the general inattention had verged on the scandalous during the perambulation of the Grand Duke. As Albrecht reached successive spots with his dignified aunt, a hasty bowing and billowing without the fitting composure ensued, but otherwise all faces were turned to one point only in the ball, all eyes directed with burning curiosity on this point alone. . . . She who stood yonder had had enemies in the hall, at least among the women, the female Trümmerhauffs, Prenzlaus, Wehrzahns, and Platows, who were plying their fans here, and sharp and cold female glances had scrutinized her. But whether her position was now too well established for criticism to venture to assail her, or her personality itself had conquered the secret opposition—all had declared with one voice that Imma Spoelmann was as fine as the daughter of the King of the Mountains.

The whole town, the clerk in the Government office, the messenger at the street corner, knew her toilette by heart next morning. It had been a gown of pale-green crêpe de chine, with silver embroidery and priceless old silver lace on the bodice. A tiara of diamonds had glittered in her dark hair, which showed a tendency to fall in smooth wisps across her forehead, and a long hanging chain of the same stones was wound two or three times round her brown throat. Small and child-like, yet strangely earnest and sensible-looking, with her pale face and big, strangely speaking eyes, she had stood in her place of honour by the side of Countess Löwenjoul, who had been dressed in brown as usual, though this time in satin. When the cortège reached her, she had, with a kind of coy pertness, made a suggestion of a curtsey, without completing it; but when Prince Klaus Heinrich, with the yellow ribbon and the flat chain of the Family Order "For Constancy" over his tunic, the silver star of the Grimmburg Griffin on his chest, and his anæmic cousin on his arm whose conversation was limited to "Yes," passed by her directly after the Grand Duke, she had smiled with closed lips and nodded to him like a comrade—which sent something like a quiver through the company.

Then, after the diplomats had been received by the Grand Ducal party, the presentations had begun—begun with Imma Spoelmann, although there had been two Countess Hundskeels and one Baroness von Schulenburg-Tressen among the débutantes. With an ingratiating smile, which showed his false teeth, Herr von Bühl had presented Spoelmann's daughter to his master. And Albrecht, sucking his lower lip against his upper, had looked down on her coy semi-curtsey, from which she had raised herself to scrutinize with her speaking eyes the suffering Hussar Colonel in his silent pride. The Grand Duke had addressed several questions to her, an exception to an otherwise strict rule; he had asked her how her father was, what effect the Ditlinde Spa had, and how she liked on the whole being with us  questions which she had answered in her broken voice with a pout and a wag of her dark head. Then, after a pause, a pause perhaps of internal struggle, Albrecht had expressed his pleasure at seeing her at Court; whereupon Countess Löwenjoul had executed her curtsey, with an evasive glance from her eyes.

This scene, Imma Spoelmann in the presence of Albrecht, long remained the favourite topic of conversation, and although it had passed, as it was bound to pass, without anything unusual happening, yet its charm and importance must not be overlooked. It was not indeed the climax of the evening. That, in the eyes of many, was the Quadrille d'honneur;

in the eyes of others, the supper,—in reality, however, it was a secret duologue between the two chief actors in the piece, a short, unnoticed exchange of words, whose contents and actual result the public could only guess—the settlement of certain tender struggles on horseback and on foot.

As to the Quadrille d'honneur, there were people who declared next day that Miss Spoelmann had danced in it, with Prince Klaus Heinrich as her partner. Only the first part of this story was correct. Miss Spoelmann had taken part in the solemn dance, but as the British Consul's partner and Prince Klaus Heinrich's *vis-à-vis*. This was fairly strong, but what was still stronger was that the majority of the guests did not consider it an unheard-of thing, but on the contrary almost a matter of course.

Yes, Imma Spoelmann's position was established; the popular conception of her personality—as the public learned next day—had prevailed in the Court ballroom, and, what is more, Herr von Knobelsdorff had taken care that this conception should be expressed with all the publicity he thought desirable. Not with distinctive or aggressive respect; no, Imma Spoelmann had been treated ceremoniously, and at the same time with systematic, intentional emphasis. The two Masters of the Ceremonies on duty—Chamberlains in rank—had introduced selected dancers to her; and when she had left her place, close by the low red platform where the Grand Ducal family sat on damask chairs, to dance with her partners, they had busied themselves, just as when the princesses danced, in clearing her a space under the chandelier in the middle and protecting her from collisions—an easy task in any case, for a protective circle of curiosity had formed round her when she danced.

It was reported that when Prince Klaus Heinrich asked Miss Spoelmann for the first time, a deep drawing of breath, a formal "Sh" of excitement had been heard in the ballroom, and the Masters of the Ceremonies had found it difficult to keep the ball going and to prevent the whole company standing round the dancers in gaping curiosity. The women especially had watched the pair with an excited delight, which, had Miss Spoelmann's position been only a little weaker, would undoubtedly have taken on the form of rage and malice. But the pressure and influence of public feeling, that powerful inspiration from below, had worked too powerfully on every one of the five hundred guests for them to be able to regard this spectacle through any eyes other than those of the people. It did not seem to have occurred to the Prince to impose any restraint upon himself. His name—shortened to "K. H."—appeared twice on Miss Spoelmann's programme, and besides he had sat out several other dances with her. They had danced yonder. Her brown arm had rested on the yellow-silk ribbon that crossed his shoulder, and his right arm had encircled her light and child-like figure, while, as usual when he danced, he had placed the left on his hip and guided his partner with one hand only. With one hand! . . .

When supper-time came, a further article in the ceremonial conditions which Herr von Knobelsdorff had contrived for Imma Spoelmann's visit to Court came into staggering force. It was the article which dealt with the order of seating at the table. For while the majority of the guests supped at long tables in the picture gallery and in the Hall of the Twelve Months, supper was laid in the Silver Hall for the Grand Ducal family, diplomats, and leading Court officials In solemn procession, as when they entered the ballroom, Albrecht and his party entered the supper-room punctually at eleven o'clock. And Imma Spoelmann passed by the lackeys, who kept the doors and repelled the uninvited, on the arm of the British Consul, and entered the Silver Hall to take her place at the Grand Ducal table.

That was unheard of—and at the same time, after all that had gone before, so logically consequential, that any surprise or disgust would have been idiotic. The motto for the day was to be prepared for anything in the way of omens and phenomena. But after supper, when the Grand Duke

311

had withdrawn and Princes Griseldis had opened the cotillon with a Chamberlain, expectation was again raised to fever point, for the general question was, had the Prince been allowed to present Miss Spoelmann with a bouquet? His instructions had obviously been not to give her the first. He had first given one each to his Aunt Catherine and a red-haired cousin; but he had then advanced towards Imma Spoelmann with a bouquet of lilac from the Court gardens. As she was about to raise the lovely bunch to her nose, she had hesitated for some unknown reason with a look of apprehension, and it was not till he had encouraged her with a laugh and a nod that she decided to test the fragrance of the bouquet. Then they had danced and chatted quietly together for a long time.

And yet it was during this dance that that unnoticed duologue, that conversation of a palpably bourgeois tenor and practical result, had taken place—and this is what it was.

"Are you satisfied this time, Imma, with the flowers I bring you?"

"Of course, Prince, your lilac is lovely and smells quite as it should. I love it."

"Really, Imma? But I'm sorry for the poor rose-bush down in the court, because its roses disgust you with their mouldy smell."

"I won't say that they disgust me, Prince."

"But they disenchant and chill you, don't they?"

"Yes, perhaps."

"But have I ever told you of the popular belief that the rose-bush will one day be redeemed, on a day of general happiness, and will bear roses which will add to their great beauty the gift of a lovely natural scent?"

"Well, Prince, we'll have to wait for that."

"No, Imma, we must help and act! We must decide, and have done with all hesitation, little Imma! Tell me—tell me to-day—have you confidence in me?"

"Yes, Prince. I have gained confidence in you latterly."

312

"There you are! Thank heaven! Didn't I say that I must succeed in the long run? And so you think now that I am in earnest, real, serious earnest about you and about us?"

"Yes, Prince; latterly I have thought that I can think so."

"At last, at last, irresolute little Imma! Oh, how I thank you, I thank you! But in that case you're not afraid, and will let the whole world know that you belong to me?"

"Let them know that you belong to me, Royal Highness, if it's all the same to you."

"That I will, Imma, loudly and surely. But only on one condition, namely, that we don't only think of our own happiness in a selfish and frivolous way, but regard it all from the point of view of the Mass, the Whole. For the public weal and our happiness, you see, are interdependent."

"Well said, Prince. For without our studies of the public weal I should have found it difficult to decide to have confidence in you."

"And without you, Imma, to warm my heart, I should have found it difficult to tackle such practical problems."

"Right; then we'll see what we can do, each in our own place. You with your folk and I—with my father."

"Little sister," he answered quietly, and pressed her more closely to him in the dance. "Little bride."

Undoubtedly a peculiar plighting of troth.

To be frank, everything was not yet settled, or nearly settled. Looking back, one must say that, if one factor in the whole had been altered or removed, the whole would have been in imminent danger of coming to nothing. What a blessing, the chronicler feels tempted to cry, what a blessing that there was a man at the head of affairs who faced the music firmly and undaunted, indeed not without a dash of rashness, and did not judge a thing to be impossible just because it had never happened before.

The conversation which Excellency von Knobelsdorff had about eight days after the memorable Court Ball with Grand Duke Albrecht II in the Old Schloss belongs to the history

313

of the times. The day before, the President of Council had presided over a session of the Cabinet, about which the *Courier* had been in the position to report that questions of finance and the private affairs of the Grand Ducal family had been discussed, and further—added the newspaper in spaced type— that complete unanimity of opinion had been reached among the Ministers. So Herr von Knobelsdorff found himself in a strong position towards his young Monarch at the audience; for he had not only the swarming mass of the people, but also the unanimous will of the Government at his back.

The conversation in Albrecht's draughty study took scarcely less time than that in the little yellow room at Schloss "Hermitage." A pause was made while the Grand Duke had a lemonade and Herr von Knobelsdorff a glass of port and biscuits. The long duration of the conversation was due only to the importance of the material to be discussed, not to the Monarch's opposition; for Albrecht raised none. In his close frock-coat, with his thin, sensitive hands crossed on his lap, his proud, refined head with its pointed beard and narrow temples raised and his eyelids sunk, he sucked gently with his lower lip against his upper, and accompanied Herr von Knobelsdorff's remarks with an occasional slight nod, which expressed agreement and disagreement at the same time, an uninterested formal agreement without prejudice to his unassailable personal dignity.

Herr von Knobelsdorff plunged straight into the middle of things, and spoke about Prince Klaus Heinrich's visits to Schloss Delphinenort. Albrecht knew of them. A subdued echo of the events which kept the city and the country on tip-toe had penetrated even into his loneliness; he knew, too, his brother Klaus Heinrich, who had "rummaged" and gossiped with the lackeys, and, then he knocked his forehead against the big table, had wept for sympathy with his forehead—and in effect he needed no coaching. Lisping and reddening slightly, he gave Herr von Knobelsdorff to understand this, and added that, seeing that the other had not intervened, but had caused

314

the millionaire's daughter to be introduced to him, he concluded that Herr von Knobelsdorff approved of the Prince's
behaviour, although he, the Grand Duke, could not clearly see
what it would lead to.

"The Government," answered Herr von Knobelsdorff, "would
set itself in prejudicial and estranging opposition to the will
of the people if it thwarted the Prince's projects."

"Has my brother, then, definite projects?"

"For a long time," corrected Herr von Knobelsdorff, "he
acted without any plan and merely as his heart dictated; but
since he has found himself with the people on terms of
reality, his wishes have taken a practical form."

"All of which means that the public approves the steps
taken by the Prince?"

"That it acclaims them, Royal Highness—that its dearest
hopes are fixed on them."

And now Herr von Knobelsdorff unrolled once more the
dark picture of the state of the country, of its distress, of
the serious embarrassment. Where was a remedy to be
found? Yonder, only yonder, in the Town Park, in the
second centre of the city, in the house of the invalid Money-
Prince, our guest and resident, round whose person the people
wove their dreams, and for whom it would be a small matter
to put an end to all our difficulties. It he could be induced
to take upon himself our national finances, their recovery
would be assured. Would he be induced? But fate had
ordained an exchange of sympathy between the mighty man's
only daughter and Prince Klaus Heinrich. And was this
wise and gracious ordinance to be flouted? Ought one for
the sake of mulish, out-of-date traditions to prevent a union
which embraced so immeasurable a blessing for the country
and its people? For that it did was a necessary hypothesis,
from which the union must draw its justification and validity.
But if this condition were fulfilled, if Samuel Spoelmann were
ready, not to mince words, to finance the State, then this union
was not only admissible, it was necessary, it was salvation,
315

the welfare of the State demanded it, and prayers rose to heaven for it, far beyond the frontiers, wherever any interest was felt in the restoration of our finances and the avoidance of an economic panic.

At this point the Grand Duke asked a question quietly, with a mocking smile and without looking up.

"And the succession to the throne?" he asked.

"The law," answered Herr von Knobelsdorff, unshaken, "places it in your Royal Highness's hand to put aside dynastic scruples. With us the grant of an advance in rank and even of equal birth belongs to the prerogatives of the monarch, and when could history show a more potent motive for the exercise of these privileges? This union bears the mark of its own genuineness, preparations have been long in making for its reception in the heart of the people, and your entire princely and State approval would signify to the people nothing more than an outward satisfaction of their inmost convictions."

And Herr von Knobelsdorff went on to speak of Imma Spoelmann's popularity, of the significant demonstration in connexion with her recovery from a slight indisposition, of the position of equal birth which this exceptional person assumed in popular fancy—and the wrinkles played round his eyes as he reminded Albrecht of the old prophecy current among the people, which told of a prince who would give the country more with one hand than others had given it with two, and eloquently demonstrated how the union between Klaus Heinrich and Spoelmann's daughter must seem to the people the fulfilment of the oracle, and thus God's will and right and proper.

Herr von Knobelsdorff said a great deal more which was clever, honest, and good. He alluded to the fourfold mixture of blood in Imma Spoelmann—for besides the Anglo-Saxon, Portuguese and German, some drops of ancient Indian blood were said to flow in her veins—and emphasized the fact that he expected the dynasty to benefit greatly by the quicken-

ing effect of the mixture of races on ancient stocks. But the
artless old gentleman made his greatest effect when he talked
about the huge and beneficial alterations which would be
caused in the economical state of the Court itself, our debt-
laden and sore-pressed Court, through the heir to the throne's
bold marriage.

It was at this point that Albrecht sucked most proudly at
his upper lip. The value of gold was falling, the out-goings
were increasing—increasing in pursuance of an economic law
which held for the Court finances just as much as for every
private household; and there was no possibility of increasing
the revenues. But it was not right that the monarch's means
should be inferior to those of many of his subjects; it was
from the monarch's point of view intolerable that soap-boiler
Unschlitt's house should have had central heating a long time
ago, but that the Old Schloss should not have got it yet. A
remedy was necessary, in more than one way, and lucky was
the princely house to which so grand a remedy as this offered
itself.

It was noteworthy in our times that all the old-time modesty
as to busying oneself in the financial concerns of the Court
had vanished. That self-renunciation with which princely
families used formerly to make the heaviest sacrifices, so as to
keep the public from disenchanting glimpses into their
financial affairs, was no longer to be found, and law-suits and
questionable sales were the order of the day. But was not
an alliance with sovereign riches preferable to this petty and
bourgeois kind of device—a union which would exalt the
monarch for ever high above all economic worries and place
him in a position to reveal himself to the people with all those
outward signs for which they longed?

So ran Herr von Knobelsdorff's questions, which he himself answered with an unqualified Yes! In short, his speech
was so clever and so irresistible that he did not leave the
Old Schloss without taking with him consents and authoriza-
tions, delivered to him with a proud lisp, which were quite

comprehensive enough to warrant unprecedented conclusions, if only Miss Spoelmann had done her share.

And so things ran their memorable course to a happy conclusion. Even before the end of December names were mentioned of people who had seen (not only heard tell of) Lord Marshal von Bühl zu Bühl in a fur coat, a top-hat on his brown head, and his gold pince-nez on his nose, get out of a Court carriage at Delphinenort, at 11 o'clock on a snow-dark morning, and disappear waddling into the Schloss. At the beginning of January there were individuals going about the town who swore that the man who, this time also in the morning and in fur coat and top-hat, had passed by the grinning negro in plush, through the door of Delphinenort, and, with feverish haste, had flung himself into a cab which was waiting for him, was undoubtedly our Finance Minister, Dr. Krippenreuther. And at the same time there appeared in the semi-official *Courier* the first preparatory notices of rumours touching an impending betrothal in the Grand Ducal House—tentative notifications which, becoming carefully clearer and clearer, at last exhibited the two names, Klaus Heinrich and Imma Spoelmann, in clear print next each other. . . . It was no new collocation, but to see it in black on white had the same effect as strong wine.

It was most absorbing to notice what attitude, in the journalistic discussions which ensued, our enlightened and open-minded press took up towards the popular aspect of the affair, namely, the prophecy, which had won too great political significance not to demand education and intelligence to deal satisfactorily with it. Sooth-saying, chiromancy, and similar magic, explained the *Courier*, were, so far as the destiny of individuals was concerned, to be relegated to the murky regions of superstition. They belonged to the grey middle ages, and no ridicule was too severe for the idiots who (very rarely in the cities nowadays) let experienced pick-pockets empty their purses in return for reading, from their hands, the cards, or coffee-grounds, their insignificant fortunes, or for invoking

318

sound health, for a homœopathic cure, or for freeing their sick cattle from invading demons—as if the Apostle had not already asked: "Doth God take care for oxen?"

But, surveyed as a whole and restricted to decisive turns in the destiny of whole nations or dynasties, the proposition did not necessarily repel a well-trained and scientific mind, that, as time is only an illusion and, truly viewed, all happenings are stationary in eternity, such revolutions while still in the lap of the future might give the human brain a premonitory shock and reveal themselves palpably to it. And in proof of this the zealous newspaper published an exhaustive composition, kindly put at its disposal by one of our high-school professors, which gave a conspectus of all the cases in the history of mankind in which oracle and horoscope, somnambulism, clairvoyance, dreams, sleep-walking, second-sight, and inspiration had played a rôle, a most meritorious production, which produced the due effect in cultured circles.

So press, Government, Court, and public closed their ranks in complete understanding, and assuredly the *Courier* would have held its tongue had its philosophical contributions been premature and politically dangerous at that time—in a word, had not the negotiations at Delphinenort already advanced far in a favourable direction. It is pretty accurately known by now how these negotiations developed, and what a difficult, indeed painful, task our Counsel had in them: the Counsel, to whom as proxy of the Court the delicate mission had fallen of preparing the way for Prince Klaus Heinrich's courtship, as well as the Chief Financial Assessor, who, notwithstanding his infirm state of health, insisted on nursing his country's interests by a personal interview with Samuel Spoelmann.

In this connexion account must be taken firstly of Mr. Spoelmann's fiery and excitable disposition, and secondly of the fact that to the prodigious little man a favourable termination to the business from our point of view seemed far less important than it did to us. Apart from Mr. Spoelmann's love for his daughter, who had opened her heart to him and

319

told him of her pretty wish to make herself useful in her love, our proxies had not one trump to play against him, and he was the last man to whom Dr. Krippenreuther could dictate conditions in virtue of what Herr von Bühl had to offer. Mr. Spoelmann always spoke of Prince Klaus Heinrich as "the young man," and expressed so little pleasure at the prospect of giving his daughter to a Royal Highness to wife, that Dr. Krippenreuther, as well as Herr von Bühl, were more than once plunged into deadly embarrassment.

"If he'd only learnt something, had some respectable business," he snarled peevishly. "But a young man who only knows how to get cheered . . ." He was really furious, the first time a remark was dropped about morganatic marriage. His daughter, he declared once for all, was no concubine, and would be no left-handed wife. Who marries her, marries her. . . . But the interests of the dynasty and the country coincided at this point with his own. The obtaining of issue entitled to succeed was a necessity, and Herr von Bühl was equipped with all the powers which Herr von Knobelsdorff had succeeded in extracting from the Grand Duke. As for Dr. Krippenreuther's mission, however, it owed its success not to the envoy's eloquence, but simply to Mr. Spoelmann's paternal affection, the complaisance of a suffering, weary father, whose abnormal existence had long ago made him a paradox, towards his only daughter and heiress, whom he allowed to choose for herself the public funds in which she wished to invest her fortune.

And so came into existence the agreements, which were at first shrouded in deep secrecy and only came to light bit by bit, as events developed themselves, though here they can be summarized in a few plain words.

The betrothal of Klaus Heinrich with Imma Spoelmann was approved and recognized by Samuel Spoelmann and by the House of Grimmburg. Simultaneously with the publication of the betrothal in the *Gazette* appeared the announcement of the elevation of the bride to the rank of countess—

under a fancy name of romantic sound, like that which Klaus Heinrich had borne during his educational tour in the fair southern lands; and on the day of their wedding the wife of the heir-presumptive was to be given the dignity of a princess. The two rises in rank, which might have cost four thousand eight hundred marks, were to be free of duty.

The wedding was to be only preliminarily a left-handed one, till the world had got used to it: for on the day on which it appeared that the bride was to be blessed with off-spring, Albrecht II, in view of the unparalleled circumstances, would declare his brother's morganatic wife to be of equal birth, and would give her the rank of a princess of the Grand Ducal House with the title of Royal Highness. The new member of the ruling House would waive all claim to an appanage. As for the Court ceremony, only a semi-Court was appointed for the celebration of the left-handed marriage, but a Processional Court, that highest and completest form of showing allegiance, was fixed for the celebration of the declaration of equal birth. Samuel Spoelmann, for his part, granted the State a loan of three hundred and fifty million marks, and on such fatherly conditions that the loan showed all the symptoms of being a gift.

It was the Grand Duke Albrecht who acquainted the Heir Presumptive with these conclusions. Once more Klaus Heinrich stood in the great, draughty study under the battered ceiling-paintings, in front of his brother, as once before when Albrecht had delegated to him his representative duties, and standing in an official attitude received the great news. He had put on the tunic of a major in the Fusiliers of the Guard for this audience, while the Grand Duke had lately added to his black frock-coat a pair of dark-red wool mittens, which his aunt had made him to protect him from the draught through the high windows of the Old Schloss.

When Albrecht had finished, Klaus Heinrich stepped one pace sideways, closed his heels with a fresh salute, and said: "I beg, dear Albrecht, to offer my heart-felt and respectful

321

thanks, in my own name and that of the whole country. For it is you in the long run who make all these blessings possible, and the redoubled love of the people will be your reward for your magnanimous resolutions."

He pressed his brother's thin, sensitive hand, which he kept close to his chest, and extended to him only to the extent of moving his forearm. The Grand Duke had thrust forward his short, round underlip, and his eyelids were half-closed. He answered softly with a lisp:

"I am the less inclined to entertain illusions about the people's love, as I can, as you know, dispense with such questionable love without a pang. So question whether I deserve it is scarcely worth notice. When it's time to start, I go to the station and give the signal to the engine-driver, which is silly rather than dutiful, but it's my duty. But you're in a different position. You're a Sunday child. Everything turns out trumps for you. . . . I wish you luck," he said, raising the lids from his lonely-looking, blue eyes. And it was clear at this moment that he loved Klaus Heinrich. "I wish you happiness, Klaus Heinrich—but not too much, and that you may not repose too comfortably in the love of the people. I have already said that everything turns out trumps for you. The girl of your choice is very strange, very undomesticated, and, most important of all, very original. She has a mixture of blood, I've been told that Indian blood flows in her veins. That's perhaps a good thing. With a wife like that, there's less danger, perhaps, of your having too easy a time."

"Neither happiness," said Klaus Heinrich, "nor the people's love will have the effect of making me cease to be your brother."

He left to face a difficult interview, a *tête-à-tête* with Mr. Spoelmann, his personal proposal for Imma's hand. He found he had to swallow what his negotiators had swallowed, for Samuel Spoelmann showed not the smallest pleasure and snarled several refreshing truths at him. But it was over at last, and the morning came when the betrothal appeared in the *Gazette.* The long tensions resolved into endless jubilation. Dignified men waved pocket-handkerchiefs at one another, and embraced in the open square: bunting flew from every flag-staff.

But the same day the news reached Schloss "Hermitage," that Raoul Ueberbein had committed suicide.

The story was a vile as well as stupid one, and would not be worth relating had not its end been so horrible. No attempt will be made here to apportion the blame. The Doctor's death gave rise to two opposing factions. One affirmed that he had been driven to take his life owing to the misgivings which his desperate act had evoked: the others declared with a shrug that his conduct was impossible and crazy, and that he had shown all his life a total lack of self-control. The point need not be decided. At any rate nothing justified so tragic an end; indeed, a man with the gifts of Raoul Ueberbein deserved something better than ruin. . . . Here is the story.

At Easter the year before the professor in charge of the top class but one at our Grammar School, who suffered from heart-weakness, had been temporarily retired on the ground of his illness, and Doctor Ueberbein, notwithstanding his comparative youth, had been given the first vacant chair simply in view of his professional zeal and his undeniably remarkable success in a lower class. It was a happy experiment, as events proved; the class had never done so well as this year. The professor on leave, a popular man with his colleagues, had become a peevish as well as careless and indolent man as the result of his infirmity, with which was combined a sociable but immoderate inclination for beer. He had shut his eyes to details and had sent up every year an extremely badly prepared batch of pupils into the Select. A new spirit had come into the class with the temporary professor, and nobody was surprised at it. People knew his uncomfortable professional zeal, his single-minded and never-resting energy.

323

They foresaw that he would not miss such an opportunity for self-advancement, round which he had doubtless built ambitious hopes.

So an end had soon been put to laziness and boredom in the second class. Dr. Ueberbein had pitched his expectations high, and his skill in inspiring even the most recalcitrant had proved irresistible. The boys worshipped him. His superior, fatherly, and jolly, swaggering way kept them on the alert, shook them up, and made them feel it a point of honour to follow their teacher through thick and thin. He won their hearts by going for Sunday excursions with them, when they were allowed to smoke, while he bewitched their imaginations by boyishly conceived rodomontades about the greatness and severity of public life. And on Monday the members of yesterday's expedition would meet for work in a cheerful and eager frame of mind.

Three-quarters of the school year had thus passed, when the news went round, before Christmas, that the professor on leave, now fairly strong again, would resume his duties after the holidays, and would again act as professor of the second class. And now it came out what sort of man Doctor Ueberbein was, with his green complexion and superior manner. He objected and remonstrated; he lodged a vigorous and, in form, not incontestable protest against the class with which he had spent three-quarters of the year, and whose work and recreation he had shared up to the very mouth of the goal, being taken from its professor for the last quarter and restored to the official who had spent three-quarters of the year on leave. His action was intelligible and comprehensible, and one must sympathize with it. He had undoubtedly hoped to send up a model class to the head master, who taught the Select, a class whose forwardness would put his skill in the best light and would hasten his promotion; and it must grieve him to look forward to another's reaping the fruits of his devotion. But though his disgust might be excusable, his frenzy was not: and it is an unfortunate fact

324

that, when the head master proved deaf to his representations, he became simply frenzied. He lost his head, he lost all balance, he set heaven and hell to work to prevent this loafer, this alcohol-heart, this blankety-blank, as he did not hesitate to describe the professor on leave, from taking his class from him. And when he found no support among his colleagues, as was natural in the case of so unsociable a man, the poor wretch had so far forgotten himself as to incite the pupils entrusted to him to rebel.

He had put the question to them from his desk—Whom do you want for your master for the last quarter, me or that other fellow? And, wound up by his stirring appeal, they had shouted that they wanted him. Then, he said, they must take matters into their own hands, show their colours, and act as one boy—though goodness knows what in his excitement he meant by that. But when after the holidays the returned professor entered the class-room, they screamed Doctor Ueberbein's name at him for minutes on end—and there was a fine scandal.

It was kept as quiet as possible. The revolutionaries got off almost unpunished, as Doctor Ueberbein himself put on record, at the inquiry which was at once initiated, his appeal to them. As to the Doctor himself, too, the authorities seemed generally inclined to close their eyes to what had happened. His zeal and skill were highly valued, certain learned works, the fruits of his mighty industry, had made his name known, he was popular in high quarters—quarters, be it noticed, with which he personally did not come into contact, and which therefore he could not incense by his patronizing bearing. Further, his record as tutor of Prince Klaus Heinrich weighed in the scales. In short, he was not simply dismissed, as one might have expected him to be. The President of the Grand Ducal Council of Education, before whom the matter came, administered a grave reprimand to him, and Doctor Ueberbein, who had stopped teaching directly after the scandal, was provisionally retired. But people who knew declared later that

325

nothing was intended beyond the professor's transfer to another grammar school; that in high quarters the only wish was to hush up the whole business, and that the promise of a brilliant future had been actually extended to the Doctor. Everything would have turned out all right.

But the milder the authorities showed themselves towards the Doctor, the more hostile was the attitude of his colleagues towards him. The "Teachers' Union" at once established a court of honour, whose object was to secure satisfaction for their beloved member, the alcohol-hearted professor rejected of his pupils. The written statement laid before Ueberbein in his retirement in his lodgings ran as follows: Whereas Ueberbein had resisted the return of the colleague for whom he acted to the professorship of the second class; whereas further he had agitated against him and in the end had actually incited the pupils to insubordination against him, he had been guilty of disloyal conduct to his colleague of such a kind as must be considered dishonourable not only in a professional, but also in a general sense. That was the verdict. The expected result was that Doctor Ueberbein, who had only been a nominal member of the "Teachers' Union," withdrew his membership—and there, so many thought, he might well have let the matter rest.

But whether it was that in his seclusion he did not know the goodwill he inspired in higher quarters; that he thought his prospects more hopeless than they were; that he could not stand idleness, unreconciled as he was to the premature loss of his beloved class; that the expression "dishonourable" poisoned his blood, or that his mind was not strong enough to stand all the shocks it received at this time: five weeks after the New Year his landlady found him on the threadbare carpet of his room, no greener than usual, but with a bullet through his heart.

Such was the end of Raoul Ueberbein, such his false step, such the cause of his fall. "I told you so," was the burden of all the discussions of his pitiful break-down. The quarrel-

326

some and uncongenial man, who had never been a man amongst men at his club, who had haughtily resisted familiarity, and had ordered his life cold-bloodedly with a view to results alone, and had supposed that that gave him the right to patronize the whole world—there he lay now: the first hitch, the first obstacle in the field of accomplishment, had brought him to a miserable end. Few of the bourgeois regretted, none of them mourned him—with one single exception, the chief surgeon at the Dorothea Hospital, Ueberbein's congenial friend, and perhaps a fair lady with whom he used once to play Casino. But Klaus Heinrich always cherished an honourable and cordial memory of his ill-fated tutor.

## IX

## THE ROSE-BUSH

AND Spoelmann financed the state. The outlines of the transaction were bold and clear; a child could have understood them—and as a fact beaming fathers explained it to their children, as they dangled them on their knees.

Samuel Spoelmann nodded, Messrs. Phlebs and Slippers got to work, and his mighty orders flashed under the waves of the Atlantic to the Continent of the Western Hemisphere. He withdrew a third of his share from the Sugar trust, a quarter from the Petroleum trust, and half from the Steel trust; he had his floating capital paid in to accounts in his name in several banks over here; and he bought from Herr Krippenreuther at par 350,000,000 new $3\frac{1}{2}$ per cent. consols at one stroke. That is what Spoelmann did.

He who knows by experience the influence of the state of mind on the human organs will believe that Dr. Krippenreuther cheered up and in a short time was unrecognizable. He carried himself upright and free, his walk was springy, the yellow look faded from his face, which became red and white, his eyes flashed, and his stomach regained its powers in a few months to such an extent that his friends were delighted to observe that the Minister could give himself up to the enjoyment of blue cabbage and gherkin salad with impunity. That was one pleasant though purely personal result of Spoelmann's interference in our finances, which was of but slight account in comparison with the effects which that interference had on our public and economic life.

A part of the loan was devoted to the sinking fund, and

328

troublesome public debts were paid off. But this was scarcely needed to secure us breathing space and credit on every side; for no sooner was it known, for all the secrecy with which the matter was treated officially, that Samuel Spoelmann had become the State banker, in fact if not in name, than the skies cleared up above us and all our need was changed into joy and rapture. There was an end to the scare-selling of active debts, the customary rate of interest dropped, our written promises were eagerly sought after as investments, and each twenty-four hours saw a rise in the quotation of our high-interest loan from a deplorably low figure up to above par. The pressure, the nightmare which for decades had weighed down our national finances, was removed; Doctor Krippenreuther puffed out his chest and spoke in the Landtag in favour of all-round reduction in taxation. This was adopted unanimously, and the antediluvian meat tax was finally buried amid the rejoicings of all those who cared for their fellowmen.

A distinct improvement in the pay of the Civil Service, and in the salaries of teachers, clergymen, and all State functionaries was readily voted. Means were now available for restarting the closed-down silver-mines; several hundred workmen were given work, and productive veins were unexpectedly struck. Money, money was forthcoming, the standard of economic morality rose, the forests were replanted, the litter was left in the woods, the stock-owners no longer were compelled to sell their milk, they drank it themselves, and the critics would have sought in vain for ill-nourished peasants in the fields. The nation showed gratitude towards their rulers, who had brought so boundless a blessing to land and people.

Herr von Knobelsdorff needed but few words to induce Parliament to increase the Crown subsidy. The orders for the putting up for sale of the Schlosses "Pastime" and "Favourite" were cancelled. Skilled workmen invaded the Old Schloss, to instal central heating from top to bottom.

329

Our agents in the negotiations with Spoelmann, von Bühl and
Dr. Krippenreuther, received the Grand Cross of the Albrechts
Order in brilliants; the Finance Minister was also ennobled,
and Herr von Knobelsdorff was made happy with a life-size
portrait of the exalted couple—painted by the skilful hand of
old Professor von Lindemann and exquisitely framed.

After the betrothal the people gave rein to their fancy in
calculating the dowry which Imma Spoelmann was to receive
from her father. It made them giddy; they were possessed
by a mad desire to scatter figures of truly astronomical dimen-
sions about. But the dowry did not exceed an earthly figure,
comfortably big though it was. It amounted to a hundred
million.

"Gracious!" said Ditlinde zu Ried-Hohenried, when she first
heard it. "And my dear Philipp with his peat." Many another had the same thought; but Spoelmann's daughter
allayed the nervous anger which might arise in simple hearts
in face of such monstrous wealth, for she did not forget to do
good and share her good fortune, and on the very day of the
public betrothal she gave a sum of 500,000 marks, the yearly
interest on which was to be divided among the four county
councils for charitable and generally useful purposes.

Klaus Heinrich and Imma drove in one of Spoelmann's
olive-coloured, red-cushioned motors on a round of visits to
the members of the House of Grimmburg. A young chauffeur
drove the sumptuous car—the one in which Imma had found
a likeness to Klaus Heinrich. But his nervous tension was
but small on this trip, for he had to restrain the motor's giant
strength so far as possible and go slowly—so closely were
they surrounded by admiring crowds; for as the more remote
authors of our happiness, Grand Duke Albrecht and Samuel
Spoelmann, each in his own fashion, concealed themselves
from the crowd, the latter heaped all its love and gratitude
on the heads of the exalted couple. Boys could be seen
through the plate glass of the motor throwing their caps in
the air, the shouts of men and women came surging in, clear

and shrill, and Klaus Heinrich, his hand to his helmet, said admonishingly: "You must respond too, Imma, to your side, otherwise they'll think you cold."

They drove to Princess Katharine's, and were received with dignity. In the time of Grand Duke Johann Albrecht, her brother, said the aunt to her nephew, it would never have been allowed. But the times moved fast, and she prayed Heaven that his betrothed would accustom herself to the Court. They proceeded to Princess zu Ried-Hohenried's, and there it was love she met with. Ditlinde's Grimmburg pride found comfort in the assurance that Leviathan's daughter might become Princess of the Grand Ducal House and Royal Highness, but could never be Grand Ducal Princess like herself; for the rest, she was overjoyed that Klaus Heinrich had rummaged out for himself anything so sweet and precious. As the wife of Philipp with his peat, she had the best reasons for knowing how to value the advantages of the match, and cordially welcomed her sister-in-law to her arms.

They drove too to Prince Lambert's villa, and while the Countess-bride struggled to keep up a conversation with the dazzling but very uneducated Baroness von Rohrdorf, the old petticoat-hunter congratulated his nephew in his sepulchral voice on the unprejudiced choice he had made, and on so boldly snapping his fingers at Court and Highness. "I am not snapping my fingers at my Highness, uncle; not only have I had an eye to my own happiness in no inconsiderable measure, but I have acted throughout with the Mass, the Whole, in view," said Klaus Heinrich rather rudely; whereupon they broke off, and drove to Schloss "Segenhaus," where Dorothea, the poor Dowager, held her dreary Court. She cried as she kissed the young bride on the forehead, without knowing why she did so.

Meanwhile Samuel Spoelmann sat at Delphinenort surrounded with plans and sketches of furniture and silk carpet-patterns, and drawings of gold plate. He left his organ untouched, and forgot the stone in his kidney, and got quite red

331

cheeks from merely having so much to do; for however small the opinion he had formed of "the young man," or the hope he held out of his ever being seen at Court, yet his daughter was going to be married, and he wanted the arrangements to be worthy of his means. The plans had to do with the new Schloss "Hermitage," for Klaus Heinrich's bachelor quarters were to be razed to the ground, and a new Schloss built on its site, roomy and bright and decorated, by Klaus Heinrich's wish, in a mixture of Empire and modern styles, combining cool severity with homely comfort. Mr. Spoelmann appeared one morning in person, after drinking the waters in the spa-garden, in his faded great-coat at the "Hermitage," in order to find out whether this or that piece of furniture could be used for the new Schloss. "Let's see, young Prince, what you've got," he snarled, and Klaus Heinrich showed him everything in his sober room—the thin sofas, the stiff-legged tables, the white-enamelled tables in the corners.

"Gimcrack," said Mr. Spoelmann, "no use for anything." Three arm-chairs only in the little yellow room, of heavy mahogany, with snail-shaped convolute arms and the yellow covers embroidered with blue lyres, found favour in his eyes.

"We can put those in an ante-room," he said, and Klaus Heinrich was relieved that these arm-chairs should be contributed to the furnishing by the Grimmburg side; for of course it would have been rather painful to him if Mr. Spoelmann had had to find every single thing.

But the ragged park and flower-garden at the "Hermitage" had to be cleared and restocked; the flower-garden in particular was honoured with a special ornament which Klaus Heinrich had asked his brother to give him as a wedding-present. For it was arranged that the rose-bush from the Old Schloss should be transplanted to the big middle bed in front of the approach; and then, no longer surrounded by mouldy walls, but in the air and sunshine and the stiffest clay obtainable, it should be seen what sort of roses it could bear in future—and give the lie to the popular report, if it were obstinate and arrogant enough.

And when March and April had passed, May came, bringing the great event of Klaus Heinrich's and Imma's marriage. It was a glorious day, with golden clouds in the sky, and its dawn was greeted by a choir from the town-hall tower. The people streamed in on foot and in carts, that fair, thick-set, healthy, reliable stock with blue, meditative eyes and broad, high cheek-bones, dressed in the handsome national dress— the men in red jackets, top-boots, and broad-brimmed black-velvet hats, the women in brightly embroidered bodices, thick, wide skirts, and big black veils as a head-dress. They joined the throng of town-folk in the streets between the Spa-Garden and the Old Schloss, which had been transformed into a processional route with garlands and wreathed stands and white-enamelled poles covered with flowers.

Banners of the Trades Unions, rifle-corps, and gymnastic associations began early in the morning to be carried through the streets. The fire brigade turned out in gleaming helmets. The officers of the Corps of Students drove round in open landaus in full state with banners flying. Maids of Honour in white, with rose-twined staves, stood about in groups. The offices and factories were deserted, the schools closed, festival services were held in the churches. And the morning editions of the *Courier* and *Gazette* contained, in addition to cordial leading articles, the announcement of a comprehensive amnesty, in pursuance of which cancellation or remission of sentence was granted to several prisoners by the grace of the Grand Duke. Even the murderer Gudebus, who had been condemned to death, and then to penal servitude for life, was released on ticket of leave. But he soon had to be put back into prison again.

Two o'clock was the hour fixed for the City Council's luncheon in the hall of the Museum, with an orchestra and telegrams of respectful congratulations. But the public made
333

merry outside the gates, with fried chips and currant-loaf, a fair, lucky-booths and shooting galleries, sack-races, and men's climbing competitions for treacle cakes. And then came the moment when Imma Spoelmann drove from Delphinenort to the Old Schloss. She did so in processional pomp.

The banners fluttered in the spring breeze, the thick garlands, interwoven with red roses, stretched from one pole to another, the crowd was packed in a black mass on the balconies, roofs, and steps; and between the fences of rifle-corps and firemen, guilds, unions, students, and school-children, the bridal procession advanced slowly amid tumultuous uproar along the sand-strewn road. Two out-riders in laced hats and shoulder-knots, preceded by a moustachioed equerry in a three-cornered hat, came first. Then came a four-horsed carriage, in which the Grand Ducal Commissary, an official of the Board of Green Cloth, who had been deputed to fetch the bride, rode with a chamberlain. Next a second four-horsed carriage, in which sat the Countess Löwenjoul, looking askance at the two maids of honour in the carriage with her, whose morals she mistrusted. Then came ten postilions on horseback, in yellow breeches and blue coats, who played: "We wind for thee the maiden's wreath." Then twelve girls in white, who strewed roses and sprigs of arbor vitæ on the road.

And lastly, followed by fifty master-mechanics on powerful horses, the six-horsed transparent bridal coach. The red-faced coachman in the laced hat proudly extended his gaitered legs on the high white-velvet box, holding the reins with arms similarly extended; grooms in top-boots walked at the head of each pair of horses, and two lackeys stood behind the creaking carriage in great state, showing in their impenetrable faces no signs that plotting and underhand dealing were part of their daily life. Behind the glass and gilded window-frames sat Imma Spoelmann in veil and wreath, with an old Court lady as lady of honour at her side. Her dress of

shimmering silk glittered like snow in the sunshine, and on her lap she held the white bouquet which Prince Klaus Heinrich had sent her an hour before. Her strangely childlike face was as pale as an ocean-pearl, and a smooth wisp of dark hair fell across her forehead under the veil, while her big black eyes threw glances of pleading eloquence over the close-packed throng. And what was that din, that barking close by the coach-door? It was Percival, the collie, more beside himself than anyone had ever seen him. The confusion and the slow pace at which the procession went excited him beyond measure, robbed him of all self-restraint, and convulsed him almost beyond bearance. He raged, he danced, he leaped, he circled blindly round and round in the intoxication of his nerves, and the shouts redoubled in the balconies and street and on the roofs on both sides as the people recognized him.

That is how Imma Spoelmann drove to the Old Schloss, and the boom and buzz of the bells mingled with the cheers of the people and Percival's mad bark. The procession crossed the Albrechtsplatz at a walk and went through the Albrechtstor. In the Courtyard of the Schloss the mounted corps of the guilds rode to one side, and took up their position as a guard of honour, and in the corridor, in front of the weather-beaten front door, Grand Duke Albrecht, dressed as a Colonel of Hussars, received the bride with his brother and the rest of his House, offered her his arm and conducted her up the grey stone steps into the state-rooms, at whose doors guards of honour were posted and in which the Court was assembled. The princesses of the House stayed in the Hall of the Knights, and it was there that Herr von Knobelsdorff, surrounded by the Grand Ducal family, executed the civil marriage. Never, it was said later, had the wrinkles played round his eyes more lively than whilst he joined Klaus Heinrich and Imma Spoelmann in civil wedlock. When this was over, Albrecht II commanded that the church festivities should begin.

335

Herr von Bühl zu Bühl had done his best to get together an imposing procession—the bridal procession, which passed up Heinrich the Luxurious's staircase and along a covered way into the Court Chapel. Stooping under the weight of years, yet in a brown toupée and with a youthful waddle, he marched, covered with orders down to his waist and planting his long staff in front of him, in front of the chamberlains, who walked along in silk stockings with their feather hats under their arms and a key embroidered on their coat-tails. The young pair drew near; the foreign-looking bride in a shimmer of white and Klaus Heinrich, the Heir Presumptive, in a Grenadier uniform with the yellow ribbon across his chest and back. Four maidens belonging to the nobility of the land, with demure looks, carried Imma Spoelmann's train, accompanied by Countess Löwenjoul, who looked suspiciously out of the corners of her eyes. Behind the bridegroom walked Herr von Schulenburg-Tressen and Herr von Braunbart-Schellendorf. The Master of the Royal Hunt, von Stieglitz, and the ballet-loving Grand Duke walked in front of the young monarch, who sucked quietly at his upper lip. At his side came Aunt Catherine, followed by the Minister of the Household, von Knobelsdorff, the Adjutant, the princely zu Ried-Hohenried couple, and the remaining members of the House. The rear of the procession was brought up by more chamberlains.

Inside the Court Chapel, which was decorated with plants and draperies, the invited guests had awaited the procession. There were diplomats with their wives, the Court and county nobility, the corps of officers in the capital, the Ministers, amongst them the beaming face of Herr von Krippenreuther, the Knights of the Grand Order of the Grimmburg Griffin, the Presidents of the Landtag, and all sorts of dignitaries. And as the Lord Marshal had ordered invitations to be sent to every class of society, the seats were filled with tradesmen, countrymen, and simple artisans with hearts attuned to the event. In front of the altar the relations of the bridegroom took their places in a semicircle in red-velvet arm-chairs. The voices of the choir rang pure and sweet under the vaulted ceiling, and then the whole congregation sang a hymn of thanksgiving with full organ accompaniment. When it died away, the musical voice of the President of the High Consistory, Dom Wislezenus, was heard, as with his silver hair, and a convex star on his silk gown, he stood before the exalted pair and preached an eloquent sermon. He built it on a theme, to borrow a musical expression. And the theme was the passage from the Psalms which runs: "He shall live, and unto him shall be given of the gold of Arabia." There was not a dry eye left in the chapel.

Then Dom Wislezenus completed the marriage, and at the moment when the bridal pair exchanged rings, fanfares of trumpets blared forth, and a salvo of three times twelve guns began to roll over city and country-side, fired by the soldiers on the wall of the "Citadel." Directly afterwards the fire brigade let off the town guns by way of salute; but long pauses occurred between each detonation, giving rise to inexhaustible laughter among the people.

After the blessing had been pronounced, the procession re-formed and returned to the Hall of the Knights, where the House of Grimmburg congratulated the newly married pair. Then came the Court, and Klaus Heinrich and Imma Spoelmann walked arm-in-arm through the Gala Rooms, where the Court was drawn up, and spoke to various members of the company, smiling across an interval of shining parquet; and Imma pouted and wagged her head as she spoke to anyone who curtsied low and answered deferentially. After the Court there was a State supper in the Marble Hall, and a Marshal's supper in that of the Twelve Months, and everything was of the best that money could buy, out of regard to what Klaus Heinrich's wife had been accustomed to. Even Percival, now restored to his senses, was among the guests, and was given some roast meat. After supper the students and the populace had arranged in honour of the young

337

couple a demonstration with serenades and a torchlight procession on the Albrechtsplatz. The square outside was a blaze of light, and resounded with shouts.

Lackeys drew aside the curtains from one of the windows in the Silver Hall, and Klaus Heinrich and Imma advanced to the open window. They threw it open, and stood in the opening just as they were, for outside it was a warm spring night. Next them, in a dignified attitude and looking most imposing, sat Percival, the collie, and looked down like his mistress.

Several of the town bands played in the illuminated square, which was packed tight with human beings, and the upturned faces of the people were lighted to a smoky dark red by the students' torches as they marched past the Schloss. Cheers broke forth when the newly married couple appeared at the window. They bowed their thanks, and then stayed there awhile, looking and letting themselves be looked at. The people, looking up, could see their lips moving in conversation. This is what they said:

"Listen, Imma, how thankful they are that we have not forgotten their need and affliction. What crowds there are, standing there and shouting up to us! Of course many of them are scoundrels, and take each other in, and sadly need to be elevated above the work-day and its reality. But they are really grateful when one shows oneself conscious of their need and affliction."

"But we are so stupid and so lonely, Prince—on the peaks of humanity, as Doctor Ueberbein used always to say—and we know absolutely nothing of life."

"Nothing, little Imma? What was it, then, which at last gave you confidence in me, and brought us to study so practically the public weal? Knows he nothing of life who knows of love? That shall be our business in future: Highness and Love—an austere happiness."